by LOVE & GRACE

A Novel

Anita Stansfield

Covenant Comunications, Inc.

Covenant.

Published by Covenant Communications, Inc.
American Fork, Utah

Printed in the USA
First Printing: July 1996

11 10 09 08 07 06   12 11 10 9 8

ISBN 1-55503-981-2

Library of Congress Catalog-in-Publication Data

Stansfield, Anita, 1961.
    By Love and Grace: a novel/Anita Stansfield.
        p. cm.
ISBN 1-55503-981-2
    I. Title.
PS3569.T33354B9 1996
813' .54-dc20   96-20847
                              CIP

To Vince, with all my love . . . forever.

And a special thank-you to Crystal Bloodworth,
for your example and your experience.

Just when you think you can't take it
Dreams disappear into space
Trust in your heart, you can make it
When you're living in a state of grace.

In the hour of need you stood ready
Looked danger right in the face
Your heart is moved by the spirit
When you're living in a state of grace.

Steve Winwood, Jim Capaldi

PROLOGUE

Sean O'Hara detested religion. At the least he could say he'd been raised on it. But he felt it was more accurate to say that it had been shoved down his throat as long as he could remember. If anyone had ever told him he would sacrifice everything for the sake of religion, he would have laughed in their face.

But as Sean sat on the edge of the bed and stared at his hands, he wondered if it had come to that. Religion was the reason he had rebelled in the first place, but the events that had led up to this change in his life were complicated. How could he ever make his father understand that what he wanted now meant more than anything to him—even more than his family?

Sean's parents were both born in Ireland, and had a great respect for their Irish background. Sean didn't have a problem with that; Ireland was nice. If only his parents could have been content to just be Irish. But no, they had to be Irish-*Catholic*. The latter having similarities to being forced to swallow cod-liver oil.

It wasn't until many years later that Sean realized not all Catholics were that way. There were, in fact, many good Catholic people. But the closed-minded rigidity in his home was difficult for a teenager to cope with.

Sean was almost nineteen when he moved in with a woman, determined to live a life of free agency. But a day came when his own choices slapped him in the face. That was a day he tried to forget. He attempted to drink it away, and when that didn't work he turned to drugs, trying just about anything he could get his hands on. But instead of forgetting, he ended up in intensive care. He recalled very little about the accident, but they told him he'd gone face first through the windshield of the car—though his hands had saved his face from the full impact. He didn't even know the woman he'd been in the car with, but they told him she'd been killed.

Intermixed with the vague images of his mother and sisters crying and praying by his bedside, Sean learned that if he ever walked out of that hospital it would be a miracle. He had so many broken bones, and so many surgeries, that he lost track. There were times when he just wished he had died, but after he heard the phrase "It's a miracle he's alive" for about the hundredth time, he began to wonder why.

Humbled as he was, Sean asked his parents' forgiveness for the difficulties he had caused by his rebellion. His mother forgave him readily; his father didn't even acknowledge his son's penitence. Sean developed a new love for his mother, as she was rarely far away. But his father hardly showed his face.

It was through the unbelievable commitment of some Mormon missionaries that Sean found the answers he was seeking. By the time he was released from the hospital, he had read the Book of Mormon, managing to keep it from his family. And by the time he was declared sound and healthy, beyond the reconstruction on his hands, he had a testimony that burned through him with such undeniable verity, he could do nothing but embrace Mormonism.

The hard part was breaking the news to his parents that he intended to be baptized. His mother had nurtured him back to health, and his father had covered every penny that the insurance hadn't. They had helped him through the recuperation every step of the way. He was living under their roof, dependent on them for survival. He didn't even have the use of his hands. How could he tell them he was turning his back on Catholicism to join another religion?

The missionaries fasted with him, and they all agreed that it just had to be done. It wasn't something he could do secretly. If he knew the Church was true, he had to believe that God would help him through this. But the news affected his parents far worse than he ever could have expected. His mother numbly stared at him, crossing herself and kissing her rosary, while his father ranted about all they had done for him. Sean was called rebellious, disrespectful, ungrateful, and a hellion. He pleaded and cried. He tried every avenue he could think of to convince them that Mormonism was Christianity and it was right. But his father was Irish, stubborn and proud, Catholic bred for generations. And his mother would never go against his father, even if she didn't agree. But Sean knew that although it broke her heart, deep inside she agreed with her husband.

When the arguing finally ran down, his father summed it up with a final statement. "If ye join that church, Sean O'Hara, ye will never step through m' door again. Ye can consider yerself disowned. I'll have nothing t' do with ye, and anyone in th' family who goes against m' wishes will receive th' same fate."

Sean was so stunned he couldn't speak. He saw panic and dread in his mother's face. She knew his convictions ran deep, and she likely believed it would happen.

"And don't forget," his father added, "that includes th' insurance benefits that'll pay for yer hands t' be repaired. Once ye walk out that door, I'll not help ye. Ye'll be crippled. There is no way on heaven or earth ye could possibly afford what it would take t' make those hands useful again."

Later that night, as Sean stared at his mangled hands and cried, he wondered if he could possibly do it. He had learned to manage eating, if he concentrated very carefully. He could write, but it resembled his third-grade penmanship at best. How could he ever get a degree and make a living without hands? Beyond their uselessness, they were atrocious. He didn't go into public without gloves. Could he live the rest of his life that way for the sake of religion?

Again the missionaries fasted with him. Sean made the decision to wait to be baptized until his hands were mended. He could still live the gospel privately, and he would be able to make it on his own by then.

With his decision made, Sean expected to feel better, more at ease. But instead he felt the opposite. He was confused and uptight. The missionaries consulted with him on the concepts of decision-making found in the Doctrine and Covenants. Again he fasted and prayed. When the confusion remained, he asked for a priesthood blessing. In it he was told that as he made the sacrifices to become a part of the gospel, and committed himself to it fully, he would be led to opportunities that would more than compensate for the sacrifices he made now. Sean was told that the Lord was mindful of his pain; that it would temper him for the good he could bring into the lives of others. He was told that he was a choice spirit with a purpose to fulfill that could not be met without embracing the Church fully. He was promised that if he put the past behind him, he would be blessed with a bright future.

Struggling for faith and courage, Sean stepped into the waters of baptism, knowing with every fiber of his being that he was doing the right thing. He was confirmed the next day and ordained a priest. Then he told his new ward members good-bye, having barely gotten to know them. That same day, Sean loaded everything of value to him into the back of his truck. He left his mother sobbing hysterically, and his father as cold as ice.

Sean drove toward Utah, praying the truck would make it, thinking often of Nephi, who went forward not knowing beforehand what he was to do. He cried through the miles, but in his heart he felt peace.

Almost five years later, Sean couldn't deny the miracles in his life. He had been led to a job that he could do by punching phone buttons and a computer keyboard. He inherited a trust fund from his maternal grandfather that was paying for his education. He was eventually led to friends who had given him a home away from home, as well as the funding to have his hands repaired. They had also supported him on his mission. But the Hamiltons had now returned to their homeland of Australia. And though Sean admitted he had much to be grateful for, still, he was lonely.

CHAPTER ONE

Provo, Utah

Becoming a Mormon was the most difficult thing Sean O'Hara had ever done. Falling in love with Tara was the easiest. The nice thing was that one would not have happened without the other. The irony was in the timing. Sean knew beyond any doubt that God had led him to Tara—just in the nick of time. Another week, and the tragedy that struck her life could have come irreparably between them.

BYU was an obvious choice for a disowned convert. But Sean had been there nearly five years before he met Tara, and the rightness of everything finally fell into place.

Barely into the fall semester, Sean sat quietly in the library studying. His mind began to wander and he stopped to ask himself why. While searching for the answer, he tipped his head just slightly to get a different angle on that neck. The girl sitting at the next table had the most beautiful neck. He realized then that he'd seen her here many times, and if he'd just now noticed her consciously, he had obviously been aware of her before.

Her reddish-golden hair was long and she usually wore it down. He had watched her lift it over the back of the chair many times, and he calculated that it hung to the top of her shoulder blades. But today her hair was pulled off her neck into a carefully wound bun.

Now, Sean had certainly found women attractive before. He thought about Melissa. She was the only woman he'd felt anything romantic for since he became a Mormon. He'd wanted to marry her, and he'd believed they could be happy together. Thoughts of her often crowded into his mind. But she had chosen a life without him, and there was nothing to be done about it. Sean missed her, yes. But in his heart he knew that he and Melissa were not meant to be together. He'd begun to wonder if he was meant to be with *anyone.* But everything changed when he noticed that woman's neck. He wanted to take the pins out of her hair and watch all those thick curls fall down over her shoulders.

When Sean realized she was gathering her things to leave, he quickly did the same. While he was scrambling to make certain he had everything, she stood and walked past him. He hurried to hold the door for her, wondering why she stirred something totally foreign in him. Something that made his relationship with Melissa seem almost trite.

Apparently surprised by his gesture, she looked up at him and smiled with a warm, "Thank you." Sean just smiled back and watched her walk the opposite direction he needed to go.

A few days later, Sean realized that he and this girl attended the same psychology class. She sat on the other side of the room and back a few rows. How could he have noticed her there when it was impossible to look her way without being conspicuous? And she always managed to get away before he could ever cross her path.

Four weeks into the semester, Sean had managed to end up at the library the same time as this girl on several occasions. She always sat at the same table, and he had the back of her memorized. He figured her hair was naturally curly rather than permed. She had two pair of earrings that she wore in delicate, pierced lobes: tiny gold loops, and imitation pearls. She didn't seem to have many different clothes, but she had good taste. She chose simple colors and non-faddish, modest styles. Her favorite color was pink, he assumed, from two pink sweaters and a pink notebook. She didn't paint her nails. She did wear perfume and very little makeup.

Sean really wanted to talk to her, but everything he could think to say sounded so pathetically banal. Choosing to remain silent for the present, he made a game out of being there to hold the door for her, and he hoped an opportunity would come to get to know her without looking like a fool.

On a warm Friday evening in October, Sean went with a couple of his buddies to their typical pizza hangout. Buzz and Joe lived in the apartment next door. Even though Sean kept much to himself, they were fun to be around, and occasionally they coerced him into going out for pizza. The running joke was that this elect group couldn't find girls worth going out with. Sean had to admit there was some truth to that. He had a pretty clear image of the woman he wanted to marry, and he only knew one girl who fit that image. But he didn't even know her name.

Sean was barely seated in the usual booth when he looked up and his heart began to pound. There she was, coming in with her hand over some guy's arm as if they'd known each other forever. They were probably engaged, he thought with consternation. And if that wasn't bad enough, they were seated in the next booth where he could look between Buzz and Joe and get a perfect view of the back of her head.

Sean was barely aware of the talk at his own table. His concentration was one booth over. He was so preoccupied with her that he began to wonder if he was going crazy. Had he been so lonely that he would have these feelings for a woman he didn't even know? Sean couldn't see this guy she was with at all, but halfway through the meal he started to get the impression they were arguing. As his buddies began to notice as well, Sean motioned for Buzz to trade him places.

With his ear closer, Sean tried to listen. Though he only caught disjointed words, it was evident the guy was trying to bully her into doing something she wasn't comfortable with. And the arrogant jerk wouldn't listen to anything she had to say.

The man in question huffed off to the rest room just as Sean's group was heading toward the cashier. Sean acted on the opportunity without even thinking about it. He noticed his buddies nudging each other and chuckling as they moved away.

Casually he sat down across from her, and she looked up in surprise. "Do I know you?" she asked tersely.

"No," he said, "I'm just the doorman at the library."

He felt some relief when she smiled. "Oh, of course. I thought you looked familiar."

"Listen," he leaned forward and whispered, "I know it's none of my business, but what is a girl like you doing with this guy? I don't have to be a rocket scientist to diagnose the man as a jerk."

"Well," irritation rose in her voice, "aren't you being just a wee bit presumptuous?"

"Yes," he agreed, "I suppose I am. But if you were out with me, I'd treat you like a queen."

Her eyes widened, but he stood and walked away before she had a chance to respond.

Sean spent the weekend speculating and stewing. He liked this girl, and he didn't even know her. He hated to think of her being on serious terms with this guy who had said things to her like, "You're a thoughtless, insensitive woman." And, "You have no idea what you're talking about." The tone of his voice was clear in Sean's memory, and it made him angry.

By Monday, he had to remind himself that he had no right to involve himself in her life. And perhaps she wasn't so wonderful as she had become in his imagination. Maybe she *was* a thoughtless, insensitive woman.

While he sat in the library, wondering if she would come, he made up his mind to just let it be and forget about her. If he talked to himself about it long enough, there was a remote possibility that he could do it.

* * * * *

Tara Parr walked slowly into the campus library, toward her usual study spot. She carried no books, because she had not come to study. She had attempted to study at home, perhaps hoping to avoid the library for some reason. But she found little success as the image of a man she didn't even know kept popping into her mind. Finally convincing herself that a brisk walk would solve the problem, Tara left her books open on her bed and wandered outside. She wandered herself right to the library doors and wondered what she was doing there. Of course, she couldn't help being curious. What woman wouldn't be after that little speech he'd given her Friday evening? It wasn't until she'd lain awake half the night thinking about it, that she realized he'd held the door for her at the library several times. Could it possibly be a coincidence?

Curiosity kept her feet moving until something she'd never felt before turned her to stone. For what seemed like several minutes, Tara just stood behind him, pretending to browse through a book, wondering what on earth had gotten into her. She didn't know his name. She knew absolutely nothing about him. But just the sight of him sent her heart racing. It was a sensation she'd never felt before—except in cases of extreme exercise, which she figured didn't count. Taking advantage of the opportunity to just watch him, Tara absorbed every detail. He wore a forest-green colored T-shirt, and faded jeans that bunched up over his high-topped hiking shoes. A tasteful tweed jacket hung over the back of his chair. His dark hair was combed back over his ears and hung in loose curls over the top of his collar. She remembered from seeing him face to face last Friday, that a few stray curls fell over his forehead, as if they'd just tumbled down accidentally, yet were meant to be there. She wished she could remember the color of his eyes, but she could hardly forget the two scars on the left side of his face—one a thin white line that ran diagonally from high on his temple, almost to his eyebrow, the other more reddish, and deeper, moving the opposite direction across his cheekbone. His features were fair but strong, and even from here she could see a dark, five o'clock shadow when he turned just so. She was almost startled when he raised both hands to stretch, then he rubbed the back of his neck with long fingers and shifted in his seat. He was certainly handsome, and from what he'd said to her, obviously arrogant. The combination made her wary.

Pondering her options now that she was here, Tara had to admit she wouldn't have come without good reason. She had always followed her instincts, and she'd never had to search too deeply to feel them. She simply took for granted that if something felt okay, she did it. If it wasn't right, the negative vibes were blatant and she steered clear without any difficulty. But there was certainly nothing negative about this. Everything inside her felt challenged. Her senses were aroused.

Just talk to him and get it over with, she told herself, but she still had trouble gathering the courage. Thinking back to his confidence with her, she steeled herself to have the same self-assurance. If she could keep her guard up just long enough to find out if he was really sincere, she could at least quench her curiosity. When he began to gather his books, she realized it was now or never.

Sean had almost talked himself into forgetting about the girl who was supposed to be sitting at the next table, when he saw two hands come down flat on the table in front of him. He looked up and found her staring at him, close enough that he could see the color of her eyes. Though he couldn't figure if they were green or blue. Either way, she really *was* beautiful.

"Okay," she said as if he should know what she was talking about, "I'll take you on."

"I'm sorry?" He leaned forward, disoriented. He hoped she couldn't see his pulse pounding in his neck.

"You told me if I went out with you, you'd treat me like a queen." Tara took a deep breath and reminded herself not to get lost in his eyes—blue eyes, she noticed—and forget what she was saying. "I want to know what a queen feels like, so put your money where your mouth is."

She was relieved when he smiled. "All right, I will. What time should I pick you up?"

"I'm busy tonight," she stated without apology. "Actually, the week is pretty booked up. How about Friday or Saturday?"

"How about both?"

Tara couldn't help giving a sly grin that countered his. "We'll start with Friday and see how you do."

"In that case," he came to his feet and picked up his books, starting toward the door, "we'll plan on Sunday as well."

"I don't know your name, but you're awfully arrogant."

"My name is Sean."

"Is that the Irish spelling?" she asked, intrigued.

"Actually, yes. It goes with my Irish blood. And you're awfully spunky."

Tara found it tempting to just linger with him and talk on and on. But the feelings he stirred in her were unnerving at the very least, and she felt the need to get away, if only to come to terms with them.

Hoping to keep an air of mystery for the time being, as if it might protect these feelings, she only smiled. "This could be interesting," she said and moved on.

Sean held the door for her as if it were expected, but she walked away before he could even get her name.

The remainder of the week dragged for Sean. Somehow she always managed to evade him when there was any opportunity to speak. It was only an occasional meeting of their eyes that made him feel the anticipation of Friday as a reality.

When Friday's class ended, Sean practically ran to stop her from leaving. "If you want me to pick you up," he stated, "you had better give me your address."

Tara looked up into his face, then quickly down, for fear of losing her composure. She estimated him to be about six foot two by the way she had a perfect view of his shoulder. She had spent the last few days trying to avoid him, as if it might keep this intrigue she felt from getting out of hand. She'd always felt in control before now, had always taken the steps of her life carefully and with much thought. She simply didn't know how to handle these feelings, and she'd almost hoped he would renege on the date. But here he was, looking at her in a way that could almost make her believe he had become a victim to the same feelings. Either that or he was just another handsome, stuck-on-himself male who believed that flowers and flattery could somehow make her feel cared for.

Tara hoped he didn't notice that she was shaking as she opened a notebook and started scribbling in it.

"Your name wouldn't hurt either," he added.

Sean wondered what he had gotten himself into as she tore out the page and handed it to him with a patronizing smile, as if she were doing him a big favor.

"I'll see you at seven," Sean said before he took it, then she walked away.

He looked down to read simply *Tara*, with an address written below it in elegant script.

At seven sharp he rang the bell and realized he was nervous. He was let in by a plain-looking girl who greeted him kindly and went to get Tara. Standing in the front room, it was evident that several girls lived here. He could hear giggling from the other room. Tara finally came down the hall at 7:05, wearing nice jeans, sandals, and a pink blouse he'd never seen before. She carried a white sweater. Her hair was pulled back on the sides with pink combs, revealing the pearl earrings.

"Hi." Tara glanced over him quickly. Same shoes, jeans, and jacket, but the striped, button-up shirt looked good. In fact, he looked so good she suddenly felt more nervous than she had while anticipating this evening. She'd had just enough negative experiences with dating that her priority at the moment was to make certain he knew she wasn't gullible.

"You look nice," she blurted, "but where are the flowers?"

"Flowers?" he questioned.

"I just assumed that a man who claimed to treat a woman like a queen would bring flowers."

Sean almost felt angry, but he kept it in check. "If that's what it takes to impress you, I'll go out alone. I'm quite accustomed to it."

He expected her to become indignant or defensive, but she simply smiled. In fact, her face nearly glowed. "I think I like you, Sean." She held out her hand. "Shall we go?"

Sean wasn't sure what to think as they walked to the Blazer in silence. He held the door for her, and she slid in and buckled her seat belt.

They drove in silence toward Provo Canyon. Tara took advantage of it to try and figure where she stood. She had come to BYU expecting to find decent men she could enjoy dating until she was ready to get married. She felt sure there were decent men out there, but for some reason she'd had rotten luck finding them. Instinctively, she was a kind and honest person. But she realized, by observing her behavior with Sean, that she was pretending to be something that she wasn't, for the sake of . . . what? Self-protection?

She could feel the tension thickening and suspected it was her fault. Fearing this date would end in disaster if she didn't change its course, she prompted herself to honesty. If she couldn't be completely up front about her feelings, she would never be able to cope with the intrigue he inspired in her. And if he couldn't accept her for who and what she was, he would not be worth it anyway.

"That wasn't very nice of me, was it."

"No," he stated.

Tara swallowed hard, realizing his opinion mattered to her. *Honesty,* she reminded herself. "I didn't take you for the kind of man who would clam up at the first hint of aggravation."

He looked over at her. "Now who's being presumptuous?"

"I am," she admitted. "But now that we've gotten past the formalities a little, I would like to be completely honest with you."

"I didn't take you as the kind of woman who would be anything less."

A slight nod complimented him on his wit, if not his perception. "Forgive me for being obnoxious, Sean. But I have been at BYU for over two years now, and I've yet to go out with a man who will not make me feel either cheap or patronized. The truth is, I love flowers, but I hate it when a man believes they can somehow make up for treating me like a dispensable commodity."

Sean kept looking back and forth between the road and this Tara, wondering whether to love her or hate her.

"I wouldn't be telling you all of this, but your proposal last weekend impressed me."

Sean lifted one eyebrow.

"I was beginning to think there wasn't a man on this campus, or perhaps in the world, who had enough respect for a woman to risk embarrassment to make a point on her behalf. The truth is, I like Danny. We have fun together and he can make me laugh. But there are times when I don't appreciate the way he treats me. It was nice to find someone else who didn't appreciate it, either."

Sean chuckled and shook his head slightly, amazed by this woman.

"So," she added firmly, "I should thank you. Thank you for having the guts to say what you did, for taking me out in spite of myself. And for not bringing me flowers. I'm impressed."

Sean looked over at her and had to admit, "So am I."

Tara sighed audibly and relaxed some. Perhaps the evening would not be a disaster after all.

As they turned up the mountain toward Sundance, Sean asked, "So, where is this Danny now?"

"He went home for the weekend."

"Ah," Sean said with curt enlightenment, "while the cat's away—"

"Don't jump to any conclusions, Sean." Tara thought quickly. They weren't over the disaster hump yet. "Danny and I have gone out a great deal over the last few months, but I could never get serious with him. I've not gone out with anyone else for weeks, but it's not because of any commitment to Danny. It's because I haven't been asked by anyone worth going out with. And Danny knows it."

"I'll try to take that as a compliment."

"I was hoping you would."

Sean smiled. "Tara what?"

"Parr," she stated. "And I'm from Colorado. You?"

"I'm from Chicago," he said. Her eyes sparkled with interest, but he found no motivation to go on. Even after five years, he still couldn't bring it up without getting emotional.

After a brief silence she said, "The Blazer is nice. It looks practically new."

"Yes, it's nice," he admitted. "But don't get the idea I have enough money to pay for something like this. I was driving a beat-up old thing until some friends gave this to me."

"Gave it to you?" She chuckled. "What kind of friends do you have?"

Sean smiled, warmed by thoughts of Michael and Emily Hamilton. "Actually," he said, "it's kind of a long story. In a nutshell, I had been out here about a year when this family kind of took me in. I was in their home many times over the course of several weeks before I realized they were independently wealthy. He was from Australia, and he met his wife at BYU. They were here so she could get her degree. They supported me on my mission and helped me through some tough times. When they returned to Australia, they gave me the Blazer. It's one of many miracles in my life."

Tara seemed intrigued. "Where did you go on your mission?"

Sean smiled. "Ireland."

"How quaint. You *did* say you were Irish."

"My parents are both Irish," he stated flatly, then his voice lightened. "I celebrate St. Patrick's Day religiously."

Tara smiled again. "Were your parents born in Ireland, then?"

"Yes, they came here as newlyweds, and they have stuck strongly to their heritage."

Tara wondered if it was her imagination that he found it uncomfortable to talk about his parents. She recalled her mother saying that a lot could be said about a man by his relationship with his parents. Was this a red flag of warning?

"They must have been thrilled with your opportunity to go to Ireland and . . ." Tara stopped when his discomfort became too obvious to ignore. The muscles in his jaw went tight and his scars became more visible when he glanced toward her. "I sense something . . . disagreeable about that."

Sean told himself he had to learn to keep his emotions from showing so blatantly. He tried to think of an answer that would avoid the sorest points. "I'm proud of my heritage, and after spending two years in Ireland, I am grateful for my father's desire to hang on to it amidst this American melting pot. But in my younger days, we had many differences. Some of the memories are not good."

Tara's uneasiness increased. Did she want to pursue a relationship with a man who had such contemptuous feelings toward his father? "And where are your parents now?" she asked cautiously. "Still in Chicago?"

Sean took a deep breath. He knew it was a common question, and he had learned not to take offense. But it was still difficult to answer honestly. "I assume they are still in Chicago. But I have not seen or heard from them in five years."

Tara's eyes widened. "I don't understand," she admitted, hoping there was an explanation that would take away this nagging doubt. But she wasn't prepared for a quick lesson in judgment.

Sean cleared his throat unintentionally. "My family is not only Irish, they are staunch Catholic. When I joined the Church five years ago, my father disowned me and made it clear that anyone in the family associating with me would receive the same fate."

Tara reminded herself to breathe. Sean turned and met her eyes briefly; she could have sworn there was a glisten of tears in them.

"It hasn't been easy," he finished and turned to look at the road. Sean had told a hundred different people that, but he'd rarely seen the genuine compassion that rose in Tara's eyes. She said nothing, but he could feel emotion emanating from her that told him she cared.

Tara looked out the window, attempting to blink back her emotion before it became visible. She had known many converts to the Church, and she had heard many stories of sacrifice and hardship. But she'd never personally seen such commitment. Perhaps being born into a good Mormon family was something she had taken for granted. And here was this man. She had barely met him, and yet knew without it being spoken that the gospel was the most important thing to him. And the family that meant almost as much, was the very thing he'd sacrificed to become a part of it. She was relieved to be in a moving vehicle when she was overcome with the urge to just give him a big hug. And a minute earlier, she had been ready to denounce him as a man unable to get along with his parents.

"So," Sean broke another tense silence, "how did you get a name like Tara?"

"Why don't you guess?"

"How would I know?" he chuckled.

"Just try," she challenged.

He thought for a minute. "The only Tara I know is in *Gone With the Wind.*"

"Now that wasn't too hard." She laughed softly and leaned back.

"You were named after a plantation?" he asked lightly, pulling the Blazer into a parking space.

"Yes, I was," she said proudly. "An Irish plantation, actually." He lifted an eyebrow curiously. "In the sequel, *Scarlett,* she goes to Ireland, to the original Tara, where her father had come from."

Sean smiled. "What a charming coincidence."

"Charming," Tara repeated, trying to ignore the delightful little shiver that skittered over her shoulders and down her back.

Sean turned off the ignition and looked at her. As their eyes met, he felt something spark to life in him that was almost frightening. He didn't realize he'd been staring until she turned away and cleared her throat, straightening her hair with a delicate hand.

Sean helped Tara out of the Blazer and continued to hold her hand as they walked into the Tree Room. Once they had ordered he said, "So, tell me more about your name."

"My mother saw the movie while she was pregnant with me, and she cried through the whole thing. She decided that if I was a girl I would be Tara. Actually, it's Taralee, which she thought was better than Scarlett. She loves *Gone With the Wind,* but she didn't want to sound too eccentric."

Sean grinned at her as he realized he was truly enjoying himself. "And what about you? Do you share your mother's sentiments for the movie?"

"Oh, I love it," she said with a certain passion. "I have books, and posters, and . . ." She stopped herself. "Well, I love it. What about you?"

"I saw it once or twice," Sean stated, then changed the subject. "Might I ask what drove you to take a psychology class?"

"My sister suggested it," she informed him. "She's much older than me and has four children. She told me her college psychology helped her more with child-rearing than any other class she'd ever taken."

Sean nodded slightly. He was impressed.

"What about you?" she asked.

"Well, I must confess, I took it before and—"

"You failed?" She nearly laughed.

"Not exactly," he explained. "I didn't do very well, but I did pass. I just wanted to take it again for a personal challenge—to see if I've got it mastered, so to speak." Her expectant expression made it clear she wanted to hear more. "I have a bachelor's degree in psychology, but I'm working on my master's."

"Oooh." Her exaggerated tone told him she was impressed. "What do you plan to do with this psychology?"

"I'm going to be a counselor," he stated. "Right now I'm working at the state hospital. I do all kinds of odd jobs, but it's giving me a lot of exposure to emotional illnesses."

"Oooooh," she said again, more dramatically. But he knew she wasn't mocking him. She really seemed impressed. "You must be a good listener."

"I try to be," he said humbly. "I'm still attempting to hone my skills."

"You sound as if you enjoy it."

"I do," he admitted. "I can't tell you why. I just do."

"You must have a gift." She smiled sweetly, and he found it an intriguing contrast to see her now and compare her manner to the guarded way she had behaved toward him previously.

"I don't know about that," he laughed, "but I enjoy it."

Sean felt her eyes on him and couldn't resist meeting them. His pulse rushed and he wanted to ask her what made him react so intensely to just being with her. He saw her glance timidly away, and sensing she was not a timid woman, his intrigue only increased.

"I don't even know your last name." Tara laughed tensely, hoping to somehow avoid these feelings until she figured out what to do with them. Why did he have to look at her that way—as if he could see right through her and read her deepest thoughts?

"O'Hara," he stated.

She pointed a finger at him, appreciating the comic relief. "Oh, that's funny, Sean."

"It is?" He didn't grasp the implication.

"Don't play dumb with me. After that discussion we just had about my favorite movie, you expect me to believe your name is really O'Hara?"

Sean laughed and put his elbows on the table. "I've never made the connection," he said, "but I swear to you, my name is Sean O'Hara."

"I don't believe you," she said and he laughed again. Sean pulled his wallet out of his pocket and showed her his driver's license. Tara wanted to melt into her chair with embarrassment. "I can't believe it."

"I did tell you I was Irish," he stated, putting his wallet back.

"So you did." She smiled sweetly. "What a charming coincidence."

"Charming," he repeated.

In an attempt to counter her embarrassment, Tara held her hand across the table. "It's a pleasure to meet you, Mr. O'Hara."

Sean slowly took her dainty fingers into his and squeezed them. "And you, Miss Parr." She smiled and attempted to draw her hand away, but before he let it go, Sean urged it to his lips, watching her eyes as he kissed her soft skin that smelled like roses. She always smelled like roses.

"Did you grow up on a farm?" he asked in the middle of their meal.

"Yes, I did," she answered. "How did you know?"

"Just a guess," he admitted. "You remind me of someone I once knew, who grew up on a farm."

"Is this a woman from your past?" she asked like a mischievous child.

Sean chuckled. "I must admit there are a couple of women *from my past* if you want to put it that way. But actually, I was thinking of Emily Hamilton. She's the woman who took me in. She's married to Michael Hamilton. They gave me the Blazer."

"Ah," she smiled, "your wealthy friends."

"When you meet them, don't let on to that. They don't like to be known as wealthy."

"I'll have to remember that," she said, feeling a warmth inside at the thought of being in his life long enough to meet Michael and Emily Hamilton.

While they slowly indulged in an exquisite meal, they shared their backgrounds and goals and found they had very little in common—except a mutual desire to be together, which became evident when she asked, "Are we still on for tomorrow?"

Sean smiled. "I've got tickets for the game."

"Is that an announcement that you're busy, or—"

"Will you go with me?" he interrupted.

"I think I'd like that," she smiled.

Sean held Tara's hand most of the way home, and he sat on her porch and talked to her for nearly an hour before she pleaded exhaustion. As they stood to say good-night, Sean wanted to kiss her so badly he had to force himself to take a step back to avoid it. He would not mar his respect for her by attempting a kiss on the first date.

While he was lying awake far into the night, wondering how someone could come into a life and change it so completely in so little time, he had no idea that Tara was doing exactly the same thing.

That Saturday was the best Sean had spent since Michael and Emily had gone back to Australia. He hadn't realized how lonely he really was until now. He'd never enjoyed a game so much, and never wanted so badly for a day to last forever. BYU even won. After the game and a Sensuous Sandwich, Sean said casually, "I have something for you back at my apartment. Can we go get it?"

"Sure," Tara agreed easily. After such an incredible day, she had no desire for it to end.

"You don't have to come in if you don't want to," he said when they pulled up in front of the renovated house that had been divided into apartments. "I live alone, but—"

"But you'll be a perfect gentleman," she finished for him and he smiled.

"Yeah, I will. Do you believe me?"

"Yes," she said without hesitation, and he led her inside.

Tara stood by the door and quickly absorbed her surroundings. To the right was a small front room. It was basic, tidy, and comfortable. She liked it. Especially the clever arrangement on one wall of an Irish flag, a piece of Irish plaid, and what appeared to be a family crest; O'Hara, no doubt.

To the left was a tiny kitchen/dining area. It too was tidy, except for a few dirty dishes. At least he wasn't trying to impress her. He obviously studied at the table, which barely had enough room around it for the two chairs that were there. *Cozy,* she thought.

Straight ahead of her was a hall, with two doors opposite each other. A bedroom and bathroom, she concluded.

"Have a seat." Sean motioned toward the kitchen table, then he turned to open the fridge. He came out with his hands behind his back and she grinned expectantly. "Close your eyes," he said, and she did. Carefully Sean held the pink rosebud just beneath her nose until she caught the fragrance, and her eyes flew open.

Tara looked deeply at the flower, then at Sean. "It's beautiful." She took the single rose as if it were made of porcelain.

"Pink is your favorite color, isn't it?"

"How did you know?" she asked, inhaling its fragrance.

"Lucky guess," he said, and Tara wondered whether to laugh or cry. She met his eyes and wondered why she would recall the moment she had known the Book of Mormon was true. She had always been a romantic, and always expected to fall in love with a wonderful man. But no romantic fantasy could have ever prepared her for what she felt now.

Sean watched her closely, wondering what she was thinking. He impulsively leaned over and kissed her on the cheek. The moment felt so perfect that it was tempting to propose. Still, he was surprised when she came to her feet and put her arms around his shoulders with a big hug.

"Thank you," she said close to his ear. "I mean that."

"It was nothing," he admitted, unable to resist hugging her back. Everything about her was so soft, so sweet. He held her a moment longer than he knew was appropriate, but she didn't seem to mind. She drew back and cleared her throat. Sean chuckled tensely. Then, as if they had both heard thunder rumble somewhere in the distance, their expressions sobered and their eyes met. Sean wondered again what she might be thinking, then he unconsciously put a hand to her face.

Tara was beginning to think her heart could tolerate being this close to him, when he touched her and her breath caught in her throat. She began to wish he'd kiss her. She could count on her fingers the times she'd been kissed. Already Sean O'Hara had stirred her senses more than all those kisses combined. What made her think she could bear it if he *did* kiss her? His arm tightened subtly around her waist, and she couldn't recall ever being this close to a man before. She reminded herself of the values that had kept her pure and innocent, and at the same time, she had no desire to back away from this situation.

Sean rubbed a thumb over Tara's cheek, marveling at its softness. He wondered what made him think he could do such a thing without appearing forward and presumptuous. But Tara showed no sign of dismay. In fact, her eyes softened, while they seemed to bore right through him.

He thought about kissing her. He thought about it long and hard, trying to talk himself out of it. This was only their second date, for crying out loud! He didn't want her to feel "cheap or patronized," as she had put it. He told himself to back away, to stop caressing her face as if he had a right to do so. But almost by their own will, his shoulders bent toward her. Tara turned her face, and for a moment he thought she was trying to ease away without embarrassing him. But she closed her eyes and he felt her lips move subtly across the palm of his hand then back again. As she opened her eyes to look at him, her lips parted. She closed her eyes again, and Sean needed no more permission than that.

His mouth came over hers as if it was meant to be there. He almost expected her to be guarded or withdrawn. She certainly had a right to be. But Tara's response was immediate, even torrid. While he should have been thinking about minding his manners, Sean was more preoccupied with the feel of her hand in his hair. And the way she melded to him, in body and spirit, as if they had spent eternity waiting for this moment. Their kiss was slow and sweet, only mildly passionate. The respect they had established for each other was delicately integrated, making it easy for him to hold back. While it only lasted a long moment, it felt like a slice of forever before she stepped back so abruptly that Sean nearly stumbled. Her eyes were wide with . . . what? Fear?

"I'm sorry," he muttered, reaching for her hand. But she took another step back. "I said I would be a gentleman, and I shouldn't have done that. I . . ." Sean quit stammering when he saw huge tears well in her eyes. She glanced down quickly as if she wanted to hide them, but her gaze returned to his, apparently unashamed of the tears spilling over her face.

Tara couldn't begin to find the words to explain her actions, when she hardly understood them herself. She touched her lips as if to assure herself it had really happened.

"My intention was not to hurt you," he said quietly, lifting a finger to wipe at her tears, relieved that she didn't recoil.

"I know," she answered with no hint of the anger he expected, or felt he deserved, for kissing her like that, so soon.

Their eyes seemed locked in some invisible hold while Sean wondered what he could possibly say to rationalize it away. How could he put into perspective the intensity of what they had just shared without hurting her further?

"I should take you home," he finally managed.

Tara nodded, her eyes glowing with a shameless innocence that stirred him. He could have stared at her all night, but he forced himself to take her hand and lead her out to the Blazer. They were almost to the street where she lived before she said, "Thank you for the rose, Sean. It's beautiful."

"You're welcome," he replied and squeezed her hand. He parked the Blazer in front of her apartment, but felt hesitant to take her inside. He couldn't let her go with this tension, wondering if she would ever want to see him again.

"Tara," he said, and she glanced toward him. He wished he could see her eyes through the darkness. "Would you go to church with me tomorrow?"

He heard her chuckle softly. "I'd love to, but . . ." His heart began to pound. "But I have to conduct in Relief Society tomorrow." She paused, and he could almost hear her telling him that the day had been nice but she wasn't interested. "Why don't you come to my ward with me?" she asked and he let out a long, slow breath. "It starts at eleven."

"I'll be here at 10:40," he answered and walked her to the door. "Good night," he said and squeezed her hand.

"Good night," she replied and he walked away. "And thank you," she called. He turned and waved before he got into the Blazer and drove away.

On Sunday, Sean wasn't certain what to expect from Tara after what had happened last night. But she positively beamed when she saw him, and she was relaxed and friendly through the church meetings. She introduced him warmly to others as a good friend, while she held his hand almost possessively. And occasionally she would look at him with something in her eyes that made him hopeful he was not alone in these feelings.

"So, what now?" he asked as he was driving her home. He wanted to tell her that Sundays were long and lonely for a man who had no family to call, and the only true friends he'd ever had were halfway around the world.

"Oh," she drawled, wondering how to tell him she dreaded Sundays, cooped up with three other women she had nothing in common with, "I'll scrape up something to eat then go hide in my bedroom and read the *Ensign* or something. My mother will probably call this evening."

Sean was just wondering how to tell her they had the same problem without sounding coercive, when she turned to him and said, "I'd cook dinner for you if I had a kitchen that wasn't overrunning with three other women, always cackling like a bunch of old hens."

Sean chuckled at the analogy. "You could use mine," he offered, trying not to sound *too* eager. "I've got food on hand. And I'm not such a bad cook myself. We could work together." She smiled, but he sensed that she was somehow . . . hesitant? "And believe it or not, I *will* be a perfect gentleman."

"I know," she said, her eyes filling with that warmth again. "I'd love to."

Sean glanced over his shoulder then quickly made a U-turn. They laughed and talked together as they cooked, ate, and cleaned up the kitchen. Sean asked her if she would go to a fireside with him. She was worried about missing her mother's call, but he insisted she call her mother from his place. He stayed in the other room to give her privacy, then they left together and spent the evening holding hands while an excellent speaker discussed the fine points of recognizing the Spirit working in one's life. Sean glanced at Tara often. He hoped he was not being presumptuous to believe it was the Spirit evoking these feelings for her.

When they were standing on her doorstep to say good night, Sean somehow knew this was meant to be forever. "What are you doing with the rest of your life?" he asked, not wanting to leave her here and go home alone.

He expected her to laugh, but she only looked up at him, as serious as he felt. "Nothing definite . . . yet," she said softly.

"What are you doing tomorrow?" He got more specific.

"I have family home evening with a group," she said, "and a lot of studying to catch up on."

"How about Tuesday?" he pressed, and Tara suddenly got a sick knot in her stomach.

"What?" Sean demanded when her eyes flew open as if she'd remembered something horrible.

"I have a date with Danny."

"Break it," he insisted.

"I can't," she explained. "He has tickets for a play that I'm supposed to see for my humanities class. We've had this planned for weeks. But don't worry." She pressed her fingers over the lapel of his jacket. "I doubt I'll have much need for Danny after Tuesday."

Tara reached up to kiss him quickly on the mouth, then she turned and walked inside. Sean touched his lips to verify the reality and pushed thoughts of Danny away. He drove home with a prayer of gratitude in his heart for being led to a religion that had filled his life with peace, and to a woman who simply filled him.

CHAPTER TWO

On Monday, Sean only saw Tara during the class they shared, where he managed to trade seats with someone who usually sat directly behind her. They discreetly passed notes like a couple of children and hardly paid attention to the lecture. He assured her that he could help her catch up.

Later, while Sean sat with his own home evening group, he began to get an awful feeling about this Danny. He wondered if it was simply jealousy. But reasoning it out in his mind, Sean felt a strong impression that Tara should not go out with him. By nine o'clock, the dread was so strong he had to call her.

"Don't go," he said as soon as she picked up the phone.

"I have to. I already told you that."

"Figure out some other way. But don't go out with him."

"Sean, you're being silly," she said as if she'd known him for years. "Or perhaps jealous?" she teased.

"Yes, I *am* jealous, if you must know. But that's not what this is about. I just have this feeling that you shouldn't go."

"I appreciate your concern," she said. "If you must know, I'm not too thrilled about it myself, but I need it for my credit. I do know how to stick up for myself, and I assure you this will be our last date."

What else could Sean say? When the silence grew uncomfortable, he finally said, "So, I guess I should let you get some sleep."

"Oh, I'm too wound up to sleep right now. I was thinking I might take a walk or something to clear my head."

"Not alone, I hope." Sean suddenly felt like an overprotective parent.

"Actually, I often walk with one of my roommates for exercise, but she left town this morning. I guess I'll have to stay in, unless you know someone who might want to go with me," she said lightly.

"I'll be there in five minutes," he said eagerly and hung up the phone.

Tara was waiting just outside her front door, wearing a heavy sweater, when Sean got out of the Blazer.

"What took you so long?" she laughed, slipping her hand into his.

"I missed you," he admitted.

"I didn't mean to take you away from your studies, or—"

"There's nothing I would rather be doing than this," he said as they started slowly down the sidewalk.

Tara glanced around at the starlit sky, then she turned to see Sean watching her. She marveled at the warmth that seemed to surround her in his presence. At moments, her feelings were so strong they almost scared her. She cleared her throat, attempting to distract herself. "Last night after the fireside, I got thinking about what happened with your family . . . when you joined the Church." Tara sensed a rising tension in Sean and wondered if the subject was better avoided. "I'm sorry," she said. "You don't have to talk about it if you don't want to. It's just that . . . I suppose I can't help being curious. Maybe growing up in the Church has made me take it for granted. I don't know. I was just wondering how a Catholic boy from Chicago ends up becoming a Mormon. But if you don't want to talk about it, then—"

"I don't mind talking about it, really," he said. "I just have trouble remaining unemotional. It's still a bit . . . touchy."

"That's understandable." Tara said nothing more, wondering if he would tell her about it or just let it drop. Her mind wandered to the feel of her hand in his, and the subtle, masculine aroma that hovered around him.

As they continued to walk down the tree-lined street, Sean's mind wandered into the paths he generally avoided. He quickly tried to think what he could say to answer her question, without treading into territory that was better left alone for the time being.

"Well," he finally said, "I suppose there were a lot of things that contributed to my conversion. I went through some rough times. But when it comes right down to it, I owe it all to some committed missionaries. I was about nineteen when these two guys in suits approached me at the car wash where I worked. I told them I didn't want anything to do with *any* religion. I *hated* religion. My parents had been so pious and rigid, especially my father. I guess the very idea of religion just left a bad taste in my mouth."

Sean chuckled, recalling the conversation. "But these guys were so smooth," he said. "Before I knew it, they had coerced me into playing basketball with them once a week. They did it for exercise on their day off, and had a little group of inner-city guys they played with. It seems like a couple of them were baptized eventually, but I wasn't paying much attention at the time. Then I . . ." Sean hesitated, trying to steer past the sensitive details. "Well, like I said, I went through some rough times. God has a way of humbling people like me. And there's no question that God let those elders know they needed to stick with me. Eventually I came around."

"And I take it your family wasn't happy about that."

"My *father* wasn't happy about it," he corrected, unable to avoid the cynical tone. "My mother didn't like it, but she would have accepted me no matter what. My father is a proud, stubborn man. But still, he warned me. I made my choice."

"I don't understand."

"He told me if I joined the Church, he would turn me out. I fasted and prayed. I had a priesthood blessing. I knew I had to do it."

"You can't imagine how that touches me," Tara admitted, wishing she could find the words to explain it.

"Really?" Sean was surprised. He would describe his situation in many ways, but "touching" wasn't one of them.

"Do you ever wonder if you did the right thing?" she asked.

"No," he answered immediately. "I've never been more sure of anything in my life. I only wonder if my father ever thinks of me. I wonder if he's ever questioned whether or not he did the right thing."

Sean felt the inevitable emotion rise into his throat and figured it was a good time to change the subject. He asked Tara questions about her family as they came around the block and back to her apartment. As they stood facing each other to say good night, Sean wanted to bring up the date with Danny again. But not wanting to spoil the mood between them, he said nothing, convincing himself that maybe he *was* jealous.

But Sean hardly slept that night. His heart was filled with an unexplained dread. Trying to distract himself from things that were beyond his control, his mind wandered back to his conversation with Tara earlier in the evening. As he'd told her, he couldn't help wondering what his father might be thinking now. And he wondered, as he often did, why it had to be this way. He could acknowledge that his parents were good people in many ways, but he just didn't understand. No matter how many times he took his mind through the memories, he simply couldn't come up with a reasonable explanation. Why couldn't he be a Mormon and still have a family who accepted him for who and what he was?

Sean's parents were both born in Ireland and married there before they came to Chicago, where his father had risen up the ladder of American life with his knack for woodworking. The name O'Hara had come to mean something in quality wood products, and their lifestyle had been good. Sean, his three brothers, and two sisters had never wanted for anything—except the space to breathe.

Sean believed in God. He truly did. There were many things about the world he didn't understand. But even in his youth, something deep inside told him that God had not intended for children to grow up unable to speak their minds in the event that it might interfere with pious rituals.

Sean was barely fifteen when he decided he'd had enough. His home felt like a monastery, where religion was the code for everything. He truly believed that his father feared laughter would somehow bring the condemnation of God upon their household. Sean's mother began to cross herself every time Sean opened his mouth. He couldn't seem to express himself without disrupting the severity that dominated their home. But Sean believed in the ten commandments, and he tried to honor his parents. Keeping his opinions to himself and staying out of their way seemed the best way to do it.

When he turned eighteen, Sean did a lot of thinking about God, and he decided there was a definite difference between spirituality and religion. It was possible to be devoted to God and live according to the laws of the universe, without kissing a rosary or attending mass with rigid regulations. But when he tried to have a mature discussion about it with his parents, he felt as if he'd ignited a nuclear bomb. He threatened to move out—and he would have done it if he'd had the money.

Then Liza drove into his life in a red Thunderbird. She was two years older than he, barely twenty-one, working as a waitress in a bar where the tips were great. As she shared her theories on free agency and exploring the endless possibilities of becoming one with the universe, Sean felt something inside of him come to life.

Free agency. It could have been a four-letter word in his home. When Sean expressed his theories on free agency to his family, his mother crossed herself into a fainting spell. His father flew through the roof. And his siblings stared at him as if he were Oliver Twist asking for more to eat. He moved in with Liza the next day.

The first five or six months of living his life of freedom, Sean believed he was happy. He did what he wanted, said what he wanted, gratified every desire. Liza taught him things about life he'd never thought possible. She was vibrant and fun, and he liked their arrangement. But in his heart he knew he didn't love her, and in rare moments of self-honesty, he knew it couldn't last.

Around that time the missionaries approached him. Sean enjoyed their regular meetings at a church basketball court. They talked and laughed and got a good workout, and they had an agreement to not discuss religion. He couldn't imagine someone his age committing their life to such restrictions for any church. But he couldn't help having a healthy respect for them—something he couldn't feel for his parents.

And then everything in his life had fallen apart. To this day, the memories of all that had led up to that accident still made Sean feel sick inside. It was after he'd finally come out of intensive care that the missionaries began visiting him. They came regularly, talking about funny or trivial things, but they never brought up religion. They were there the first time he sat up in bed, and they were there when the physical therapists helped him take his first steps. Eventually they walked with him down the hall and back again to his room, encouraging him when he felt exhausted and defeated.

The missionaries became friendly with Sean's mother and sisters, but he warned the elders not to bring up religion with them, either. It wasn't until Sean went on his own mission that he realized these elders must have been divinely inspired. Only God could have known how much Sean needed them to persist in spite of the apparently hopeless situation.

One afternoon when Sean had made it to the lobby without any assistance, he asked, "Why do you do this? Why do you guys keep coming to see someone like me?"

"I can't answer that and keep my promise, Sean."

"Why not?"

"You asked me not to talk about religion."

"What has religion got to do with it?"

"We're with you because we know that God wants us to be."

Sean took a moment to absorb this statement. "How do you know that?" he asked.

"That's a little difficult to explain," the other elder said. "We just know."

Sean turned away and blinked several times.

"So," one of them asked in a lighter tone, "what's the verdict on the hands?"

Sean looked down at his bandaged hands. He tried to be grateful that they had saved his face from the full impact. His face had escaped with only a couple of significant scars, but his hands were described by one doctor as looking like hamburger when they'd first brought him in. The delicate structures of bones, tendons, and ligaments had been crushed and mutilated. They had gone through many surgeries already, but the reconstruction necessary to make them fully usable had not yet begun.

"My father's insurance will cover most of the cost necessary to do the reconstruction, but it will take time," Sean reported. Then he turned back to look the elders in the eye. "Why do you do it?" he repeated.

"I don't know how to talk about it without—"

"I can't believe that your reason for being here has anything to do with religion—at least not the religion I know. What I know of worship has nothing to do with what the two of you have done for me."

The senior companion said pointedly, "Perhaps there's a difference, in some respects, between religion and spirituality."

Sean didn't understand why warm goose bumps rushed over his shoulders. He only knew he wanted to hear more. "You said that God wanted you to help me. If you know that, maybe you could figure out why God made me survive this."

"I'm only guessing, but I would think that God knows your life has a greater purpose." After a brief silence he added, "Why were you drunk and in that car to begin with?"

Sean shot him a harsh glare, but he had to admit that it was a question he'd asked himself many times. "It's a long story, but I think it had something to do with free agency."

"Now, there's something we can talk about," the other elder chuckled.

Sean's eyes widened. "What about it?"

"That's what this life is all about, Sean. Free agency."

It *all* boiled down to free agency. Sean had made the choice to reject his father's beliefs, and he'd made choices that had brought bitter and painful consequences. He'd made the choice to accept what the missionaries taught him, but it was still difficult to believe that he'd had to choose between his beliefs and his family.

As Sean's thoughts only discouraged him, he forced himself to think of all that was good in his life. He had much to be grateful for, and just as he'd told Tara, he'd never once wondered if he'd made the right choice. As lonely as he was, he couldn't imagine not having the gospel in his life. And now there was Tara. He finally drifted to sleep, thinking only of her.

Sean awoke with that uneasiness still nagging at him. In class he told Tara again he had this feeling she shouldn't go out with Danny, but she passed it off and teased him about being a jealous man.

Through the evening Sean tried to study, but his mind was with Tara. Knowing he had to get something done or he'd be missing credits, he finally convinced himself it *was* jealousy and forced himself to study.

* * * * *

It took only a few minutes in Danny's presence for Tara to realize why she liked Sean O'Hara so much. And so far, Danny was on his best behavior.

Through the play she tried to be attentive, knowing she had to absorb it for a decent grade. But part of her was with Sean. She smiled to think of his outward display of jealousy, and the way it made her feel so feminine, so appreciated.

Tara's mind wandered as she tried to comprehend the impact Sean O'Hara had had on her life—already. Absently she touched her lips, recalling so clearly the way he had kissed her in his kitchen on Saturday evening. The intensity of her feelings could almost be frightening. But there was an underlying peace she couldn't deny. And oh, how she longed to have him kiss her like that again! For the first time in her life, everything seemed to fit perfectly. Tara could look at the paths she had followed and be grateful for the choices she'd made. It was gratifying to be at this point in her life, with the possibility of sharing her future with a man like Sean.

During intermission, Danny surprised her with an unusually perceptive question. "What's on your mind? You seem . . . lost."

Tara considered Danny nothing more than a friend, and she felt certain he would take no offense when she admitted outright, "Oh, I went out this last weekend with a guy I really like. I think it might come to something; or at least I hope it will."

Danny looked astonished at first, then he clammed up through the rest of the play. He remained silent as they walked to the parking lot and he drove toward her apartment.

"Thanks for taking me to the play, Danny," Tara said sweetly as they approached her building. She was determined not to give in to what she believed was a childish attempt at manipulating her attention. "You've been a good friend."

Tara wondered what she had said when he turned piercingly angry eyes toward her and drove past her apartment with purpose. A formless fear pounded into her throat as she began to wonder if

Danny felt something more for her than she'd realized. She could honestly say he had given no indication of romantic feelings. He had always seemed matter-of-fact about everything, and his only allusion to anything beyond friendship had been an occasional joke about marrying her for her money.

It was no secret that she had a semi-wealthy grandmother who was helping her through college. But Danny knew she was conservative and frugal and money meant little to her. And it wasn't as if she, personally, had enough to make any man rich. Danny knew that. Didn't he? "Danny," she said, "I really need to get home." He made no response. "If something I've said has upset you, let's talk about it." Still nothing. "Danny," she insisted, "please take me home." He ignored her. A state of fear unlike anything she'd ever experienced took hold, as if evil hands were literally holding her captive.

Danny drove the car toward Rock Canyon, recklessly taking the turns at a speed that put Tara's fingerprints into the upholstery. Frantically she wondered what to say to make him stop this madness and take her home. But as she watched him, apparently consumed with some unreachable fury, an eerie resignation overcame her.

"Take me home, now!" she demanded, wishing she could believe it would make a difference. He only stopped the vehicle abruptly. As she wondered what his motives could be, the possibilities that filed through her mind were too outrageous to even consider. She had no intention of ending up on the ten o'clock news, or as a statistic on some police record. She realized she was shaking, but attempted a calm voice. "What are we doing here? I really should be studying, or—"

Tara's next realization was an assault upon her lips that by no means resembled a kiss. She tasted blood, and her fear dropped like a lead weight to the deepest part of her. While she was trying to push his face away, she found her legs pinned to the seat with the weight of his body. She screamed and protested, threatening to put him behind bars, insisting that he take her home, and she had no intention of letting him take advantage of her. But Tara's fear became a solid reality as her words only seemed to make him more angry, as if he were somehow determined to vent some warped anger toward her by proving his physical supremacy. She tried to disconnect her mind from the reality of what he was doing to her as he ranted like a madman, telling her she was deceitful and misleading. He called her a witch, and a snob, and worse.

Tara resorted to pleading as he only held her tighter and became more aggressive. Impulsively she bit his lip and lifted a knee into his stomach. He groaned and cursed. She used the distraction to open her door and run. She tried to pray inwardly for help, while she couldn't help recalling Sean's repeated warnings. Her heart pounded into her ears as she wondered where she could go to escape him. How could she possibly get away? She wished she had listened. She wished she had prayed about it and tried to be more in tune with the Spirit. Tara wished she were *anywhere* but here as Danny caught her from behind and she fell to the ground.

She was keenly aware of the gravel embedding in her legs and arms as they struggled. She screamed but knew no one would hear her. Just when she nearly broke free again, Danny backhanded her across the cheekbone and she fell to the ground, barely coherent, stars swimming above her. With his hand firmly around her wrists, Danny pinned her hands above her head and pressed his other hand around her throat. While she struggled to breathe, he hissed close to her face, "If you move, I will *kill* you!"

Tara felt the rocks grinding into her back. She heard more than felt fabric tearing. As her coherency came back to her fully, she almost wished he *would* kill her. The rest was a nightmare.

Before it was over, Tara became somehow detached from herself, as if she were watching all of this from a distance. Danny hauled her to her feet and practically dragged her to the car. The shock was so intense that she felt somehow incapable of connecting her mind to her body enough to react. She was vaguely aware of Danny's attitude of triumph in the midst of the smoldering sickness agitating in the pit of her stomach. A persistent, unfamiliar throbbing left little doubt of the reality of what had just happened. It was as if she'd been torn in half.

She managed the will to look over at him as he drove down the canyon, as casual as if they'd just been out to dinner. Words rumbled around in her mind but never made it through the numbness to her lips. He glanced at her and almost smiled, as if he could read the rage and hatred bristling through her every nerve. Then Danny laughed. And somewhere in the back of her head, Tara could almost hear the devil laughing right along with him. How could she have been so stupid?

"Whatever you're thinking is pointless, Tara. It's your word against mine," he snarled. "Imagine how humiliating it would be to sit in a courtroom in front of all those people and tell them all the details, then listen while I tell them how you led me on and teased me, and then expected me to stop."

Tara thought of a thousand retorts, but even if she had been physically capable of expressing them, she could not question the despairing reality of his words. The humiliation would not be worth the small chance that she might win. She didn't have the strength to think about living through the next hour; how could she even consider finding the strength to press charges? He'd taken *everything* from her, against her will, and he was going to get away with it because facing it publicly was simply unbearable.

At least he had the decency to take her home, she thought as he pulled up in front of her apartment. He looked over at her like the cat that swallowed the canary. She wanted to get out and run, but she couldn't move. He reached across her and opened the door, then tersely grabbed her chin, looking her in the eye. "You'd best clean yourself up, Tara. You wouldn't want anyone to see you like that." For a moment she caught something in his eyes that went against this cruel confidence, but she was too numb to grasp it. "No man would want you now," he spat, and practically pushed her out.

Tara was grateful for the lawn between the road and the sidewalk, cold as it was. She didn't know how long she stayed there after she heard the car pull away. She wanted to just lie there and die, but a fresh fear seized her as she imagined someone discovering her in this condition. The thought of *anyone* finding out about this finally gave her the fortitude to scramble to her feet and shuffle toward the door. She'd never been so grateful to be on the ground floor of the apartment building as she fought with the pain to simply stand. Her hands shook violently as she fumbled for the key and turned it in the lock, grateful that her roommates were likely in bed. Locking the door behind her, Tara groped through the darkness into the bathroom.

With great determination she looked into the mirror. The numbness shattered as if a rock had been thrown at the glass reflecting her image. The reality of what had happened seized her like an iron vise. She collapsed in a heap of stifled sobs on the floor.

While Tara fought to remain silent and not arouse anyone's attention, she wondered what she had ever done to deserve this. She was a good girl from a good family, and she had always tried to do what she knew was right. But now she had to wonder. Had she done something wrong somewhere—something that made her deserving of such an act?

The memories became vivid and assaulting. Unwillingly she crawled to the toilet and threw up, as if it might rid her of the filth she had been exposed to. When it didn't seem to help, she shed her clothes and took a long, vigorous shower, cleaning herself almost raw, wanting to be free of Danny's revolting touch. She brushed her teeth three times, then threw up again and brushed them twice more. She sat in the tub again with the shower running over her until the water turned cold. When she realized there was nothing more she could do, she leaned against the wall and looked in the mirror again.

Her eye was slightly discolored and swollen. Her neck and wrists showed vague bruises with the outlines of fingertips. Her arms and legs were scraped from the rocky dirt, and her eyes were hollow. Her spirit felt dead.

Unable to look at herself any longer, Tara gathered her torn clothing into her arms and lumbered to her room, grateful that the girl she shared with had gone home for a funeral and wouldn't be returning for several days. With her door locked, she stuffed her clothes into the waste basket and put on a nightgown. She crawled into bed, where she cried herself into a restless slumber, interrupted frequently by horrid dreams.

She was awakened by a pounding on her door. "Hey, Tara," Vicky called. "You're going to be late. You overslept."

Tara's mind raced frantically. She couldn't go out looking like this. "I think I have the flu," she called back. "I'm staying in bed today."

"Is there anything I can get you?" Vicky called back.

"No, thanks. I'll be fine. I just need to rest."

"Oh," Vicky added, "some guy called for you about six times last night. Said his name was Sean O'Hara."

Tara winced. "All right. Thank you."

Tara listened carefully and waited until she was sure the others had left before she even got out of bed. She groaned when every muscle protested. She made it to the bathroom where the mirror convinced her she hadn't dreamt it, if the pain hadn't already.

The day wore on with a sinking depression unlike anything she had ever experienced. Never had she known such darkness. She didn't eat. She couldn't sleep. She soaked in a hot tub with Epsom salts, hoping to ease some of this pain. She sobbed hysterically at moments, and cried silent tears of despair at others. She ignored the phone when it rang, and made sure she was finished in the bathroom for a while before her roommates were expected back from classes.

Lying on her bed, staring at the ceiling, Tara tried to compare her life yesterday to what she felt today. How could everything change so quickly? An unbearable pain pounded into her head and constricted her chest. And the worst of it was thinking of Sean. If he knew, she felt certain he'd want nothing more to do with her. And she couldn't blame him. The phone rang again and she almost knew it was him, but she couldn't bring herself to answer it. Twenty minutes later, Vicky and Heather came home and inquired how she was doing through the closed door.

"It's not horrible," she called back calmly, "but I can't seem to find any strength. I'll just sleep it out. Thanks."

The phone rang and she heard Heather call, "Tara, it's your mother."

"Oh, no," Tara whispered, then she called, "Tell her I'll call her back tomorrow, unless it's an emergency. My head is just pounding."

Apparently the message got through, as Heather said nothing more. Ten minutes later the phone rang again, but Tara's head was under the pillow.

* * * * *

When Tara didn't show up for psychology, Sean felt an undeniable panic that kept his heart at a jogging pace through the entire class. Once class was dismissed, he found a phone and dialed her number. No answer. He continued to call between every class, and called again the minute he got home late in the afternoon.

He nearly gasped when someone actually answered. "Who is this?" he asked, knowing it sounded rude.

"This is Vicky. Who is this?"

"Is Tara there?" he asked. "I've been trying to call her all day, and she wasn't in class. Oh, this is Sean O'Hara. Have you seen her?"

"No," she said and he wanted to die, "but I've heard her. She's on the other side of her bedroom door with the flu. She's alive, if that's what you're wondering."

"Actually, I was," he admitted breathily.

Vicky chuckled. "She'll be flattered to know someone missed her."

"Can I talk to her?"

"I don't know, but I'll ask."

Tara heard the knock at her door and wanted to disappear. She knew what it was before Vicky called, "Sean O'Hara is on the phone. Do you want to talk to him?"

"Tell him I'm sick."

"I already did."

In truth, Tara *did* want to talk to him. In spite of fearing what might happen if he knew the truth, she needed him. But facts be faced, if she opened the door to get the phone, Vicky would see the bruises and suspicion would run rampant.

"Tell him I'll talk to him tomorrow. I really ache." At least that was true.

"Sorry," Vicky said into the phone. "But don't feel too bad. She wouldn't talk to her mother, either. She says she'll talk to you tomorrow."

"Thanks," Sean said and hung up, wishing he could get rid of this uneasiness. His feelings about her going out last night, combined with this sudden illness, just didn't feel right to him. Telling himself he was letting his imagination run away with him, he forced himself to study. But he was determined to see her tomorrow, flu or not.

Again Sean found it difficult to sleep. This relentless uneasiness reminded him all too much of a period in his life that he'd rather not think about at all. But if he forced his mind away from his concern for Tara, it was inevitably drawn to a time when he'd hit rock bottom. Here in the dark of his room, the memories seemed almost dream-like. He couldn't be sure if that was because he'd changed so much that it was difficult to comprehend himself in such circumstances, or because he'd rarely been sober at the time.

"Rock bottom," Sean muttered to the glass of golden liquid in his hand. He took a hearty swallow then wondered why he could still make out his surroundings. The noisy bar looked hazy, but he figured that was because of the smoke. He could still hear the music, and he knew he was in a less desirable neighborhood in his hometown of Chicago.

"Not good enough," he murmured, actually liking the slur he could hear in his own voice. Oblivion was getting closer. He couldn't remember what pills he'd taken, but he felt sure they would begin to take effect soon, and he could forget. . . . Or better yet, maybe he would never wake up.

Sean pressed his head into his hands and heard himself groan, as if from a distance. He tried to will the memories away, but as the noise of the crowded bar room became more distant, his father's heated words burst through his mind in perfect clarity. That was what started it all, he concluded. If his parents weren't so pathetically stubborn, it never would have come to this.

Sean tried just about anything he could get his hands on, hoping that something would take away the reality. But the memories always came back with the hangovers, and there were moments when Sean believed that only ending his life would end his misery.

"Hey," a feminine voice said from somewhere on the edge of his coherency, "are you okay?"

Sean lifted his head slowly, feeling as if it weighed half a ton. The face swimming above him was pretty—as far as he could tell. He tried to smile, and assumed he'd managed when she smiled back.

"Maybe I should give you a ride home," she said, then she giggled. Even through the haze, Sean noticed her teeter a little and wondered if she was any more sober than he was. But that word, "home," was suddenly enticing. He had to admit he didn't like the combined effect of whatever he'd taken along with the alcohol. He'd have to find out what it was and remember to avoid this one next time.

Sean heard himself laugh as he tried to stand up, then realized this woman's arm was the only thing that had kept him from falling on his face.

"You okay?" she asked.

"Oh, yeah," he replied and allowed her to guide him toward the door.

Sean didn't remember getting in the car, but he liked the feel of the seat beneath him, and was vaguely aware of someone getting in beside him and starting the engine. He could hear this woman talking as they drove, and realized she was trying to get him to tell her his address. For the life of him he couldn't remember. He felt the car swerve, and wondered if it was his foggy head or her driving.

Sean was trying to dig out his wallet when he heard her scream. For an instant he felt completely sober. He had no trouble absorbing the glare of oncoming headlights, the screech of tires beneath him, and the shrieking of a distant horn. It sounded like a semi—a big one.

Sean sat up with a start, feeling sweat bead over his face and chest. Had he been dreaming? Or were the memories so vivid that they frightened him still?

Forcing his mind to the present, he thought of Tara. But the uneasiness only increased. As the darkness of his thoughts seemed to close around him, Sean turned on the light and read from the scriptures until he finally drifted off from pure exhaustion, praying in his mind that everything would be all right—for himself as well as for Tara.

CHAPTER THREE

The next morning, Tara tried to resign herself to living. She was afraid to even walk past the door, but at least she was managing to walk without looking as if she'd just had a baby or something. Her tuition was wasting away while she lay there wallowing. And she convinced herself she was not the kind of woman to let something do her in—not even this. She almost talked herself into it, then the reality struck freshly and she fell apart in helpless tears.

While Vicky and Heather were out, she tried twice to call Sean but got no answer. Of course he would be in class. She kept hoping he would call, but the only time the phone rang it was her mother.

"How are you?" Mary Parr asked with concern. "Vicky said you have the flu."

"Oh, I'm all right," Tara lied, proud of herself for her steady tone.

"I've just been thinking about you more than usual," Mary added. "That's why I called yesterday. I must have known you were sick."

Tara swallowed hard and prayed her mother wouldn't suspect something was *really* wrong. With the way her parents worried, if they knew it would kill them. "That must have been it," she said lightly. "It's nice to know my mother is so in tune."

They chatted for a few minutes and hung up, then Tara managed to choke down some lunch. She was washing dishes when a knock came at the door. Tara pretended not to be there, but it persisted. She was startled to hear Sean call, "I know you're in there, Tara Parr. Open up this door and let me in."

Tara hesitated. Instinctively she needed him, but she couldn't let him see her like this—at least not yet. Before she could face the world, she had to come to terms with these emotions and come up with some reasonable explanation for her appearance.

"Tara!" he called again. "I know you're in there. You can't possibly be asleep. Now get over here and open this door."

"Or what?" she called, and Sean sighed with a degree of relief. "You'll huff and puff and blow the door down?"

"Maybe," he called back.

"Well, start huffing, Mr. O'Hara. I'm not opening this door."

"Why not?"

"I'm sick, and I don't want you to get it," she lied with a perfectly light voice.

"I'm tough. I can take it. Now, open this door."

"Tough or not, I'm not letting you see me like this."

"Like what?" He sounded amused.

"I haven't showered in two days. My hair's a sight. And I'm in my nightgown."

"Ah, come on," he chuckled, feeling some comfort in the normality of her voice. "I want to see."

"Go away, Sean."

"Only if you promise that I can see you tomorrow."

"And what if I don't?"

"I will sit here until your roommates come home, and I will come in there and find you."

"You're so blasted arrogant, you'd probably do it."

"You'd better believe it."

"Okay. I'll see you tomorrow. I'll probably be in class. I can't afford to miss any more."

Sean hesitated, wishing he could just see her, just to know she was really all right. But how could he explain, through this door, the feelings that had kept him awake at night with worry?

"Tara," he said gently, "are you all right?"

The depth of concern in his voice brought tears rushing into Tara's eyes. He had told her not to go out with Danny. Did he sense something was wrong, the same way her mother had? With great effort, she swallowed the emotion and pressed her hands to the door as if she could touch him. "Yes, I'm fine," she said with a little chuckle. "Just one of those tacky flu bugs. And I look awful." She cleared her throat. "I'll see you tomorrow."

"If you're not in class, I'm coming to see you," he insisted.

"Bring flowers," she teased.

"I just might do that," he retorted too seriously.

When she was sure he'd gone, Tara went into the bathroom to examine her appearance. There was no mistaking the purplish shine near her eye, however vague. The marks on her neck were fading a little, but the scrapes on her arms and legs had scabbed and looked atrocious.

Still, she either had to go to classes or face Sean. And she really needed to get back to school, or she'd never keep up her grades. Trying to be resourceful, Tara decided that with some makeup she could disguise the eye. If it was noticed, she could probably get away with saying she'd run into a door in the dark or something. She didn't have a turtleneck sweater, and didn't want to get close enough to Vicky to ask to borrow one. But she figured if she wore her hair down, it would cover what little evidence was left of the bruises. Slacks and a long-sleeved sweater would cover the bruised wrists and scrapes, except for one on her hand, and that could have happened anywhere.

The following morning, Tara waited until the others left before she hurried to shower and get ready. She was a few minutes late for her first class, then found her mind wandering. Occasionally she had to use great self-control to stifle her tears. She wondered if she was getting an occasional skeptical glance, or if she was simply paranoid. She didn't care what people thought about her, just as long as no one knew the truth. She could almost imagine the speculative stares she would get if they knew, as if she were some kind of freak in a circus, with people whispering and theorizing about the specifics. No, she would rather take this ugly secret with her to the grave than have anyone know.

Tara found she was visibly nervous as she approached her psychology class. She purposely waited to go in until the professor had begun, then she slithered into her seat. She immediately felt Sean's hand on her shoulder. Her heart quickened as she realized how afraid she was of what might happen if he found out. In the brief time she had known him, he had touched her in a way no man ever had. The thought of losing that was terrifying. She didn't turn around, but somehow found comfort in his touch. She put a hand over his and squeezed with more strength than she believed she possessed.

Sean watched Tara carefully through the class. His initial joy at seeing her quickly faded. The knots in his stomach tightened until they threatened to explode. This woman, whom he had become accustomed to watching as she'd studied at the library, always sat straight with poise and confidence. She'd had an aura of vibrancy and self-assurance. But this . . . this was someone else. The Tara Parr sitting in front of him now hunched down in her chair as if she could somehow make herself invisible. She kept her head down, and fidgeted with her hair as if she could somehow hide behind it. Her movements were slow, almost labored, as if she were in some kind of pain. While Sean had spent the last few days trying to convince himself he was letting his imagination run away with him, he realized now that his feelings had been valid. Something had changed her. Something horrible had happened. And he wasn't letting her out of his sight until he got to the bottom of it.

While Tara dreaded having the lecture end, the time flew and she had no choice but to stand and face Sean. His eyes were expectant and she could do nothing but walk out, knowing he would follow.

"Where you going?" he asked. Panic hit him like a brick. Added up, the last few days were all too strange to pass off as coincidence any longer.

"I have to get to my next class," she insisted and hurried along.

"Tara," he grabbed her arm, forcing her to stop and face him. He didn't miss the subtle grimace that passed over her face. "If you don't want to talk to me, just say so, but don't walk away and leave me standing."

Tara heard pulse beats in her ears, and the endless supply of tears threatened behind her eyes. She wanted to glare at him, but instead she turned her face quickly to the side, hoping he wouldn't notice the fading bruise.

"What in heaven's name is this?" He turned her chin to bring her face into full view. Tara leaned back against the wall and glanced in both directions, wanting to look anywhere but at him.

"Tara," he insisted, "I'm waiting." Still she said nothing, and wouldn't even look at him. "You didn't have the flu, did you." It was not a question. Still she made no comment, but her breathing became sharp. She was trembling. "Where did you get the shiner, Tara?"

She chuckled tensely, as if she'd just now figured out what he was talking about. "I ran into a door in the dark," she said flippantly, but Sean wasn't even remotely convinced.

"And you stayed home for two days to nurse a black eye?" he asked skeptically. "That doesn't sound like you."

"How could you possibly know me well enough to know one way or the other?" she snapped.

"Let's stick to the real issue here, Tara," he said gently.

Tara felt herself faltering from the inside out. She wished she had stayed home. She met his eyes for only a second, and his genuine concern made her want to die inside. Why hadn't she listened to him? What could she possibly say to him now?

"I really should get to class," she insisted with a shaky voice.

"I'm not sure you should go." He put a hand on the wall to prevent her from moving. "You're as white as a sheet."

"My sheets are pink." She attempted some comic relief, but he didn't even crack a smile.

"You're not a good liar, Tara. What happened to your eye?"

"I told you," she snarled.

"And I don't believe you."

She turned to the side and folded her arms. "That's your problem. Now, please, let me go."

"Not until you tell me the truth," he said harshly, then his voice softened. "If something is wrong, Tara, I want to help you."

Tara choked back the sob hovering in her throat. "I told you," she insisted. "I ran into a door."

Sean sensed her rising emotion and reached up to push her hair back so he could see her face. If not for the perfect angle of the light, he might not have noticed the fading bruises on her neck; her beautiful neck. He looked closer while she was unaware, and he could almost swear they had the outline of fingertips.

Tara turned to investigate his silence, and panic struck her freshly. She tried to run, but he caught her arm and held her between the wall and his hard chest. Unwillingly she groaned and tried not to move as her scraped back went against the wall and every muscle in her body screamed in agony, some more than others. She had little choice but to allow him to lift her hair further and examine her neck. Her only relief was that the hall was practically empty.

"And did you get these from running into the refrigerator?" he asked. Tara didn't answer. She only looked away until he took her arms and gave her a gentle shake that forced her to look at him. She moaned and he realized he had hurt her. He wondered where else she was bruised.

"I want the truth, Tara, and I am not leaving you until I get it." She said nothing. His eyes narrowed and he got to the real point of his fears. "What happened Tuesday night?"

With that, Tara lost all reason. Her breathing became so sharp she was afraid she'd hyperventilate. She would have collapsed if not for the way he held her, and she was grateful when he shifted his weight to keep her steady.

"Tell me," he whispered vehemently, unable to fight this fear any longer.

Realizing that her attempt to evade the issue was futile, Tara finally looked into his eyes directly. His kindness and concern made her realize he was the closest thing she had to a real friend in this town. And though she was afraid of him discovering the truth, at the moment she was more afraid to be alone.

"Can we go someplace else?" she asked through a quiet sob. "I don't feel well at all."

Sean nodded and put his arm around her for support as they walked. Tara felt the tears coming and found no will to hold them back any longer.

Sean knew Tara was crying as she buried her face in the folds of his shirt and walked blindly within his embrace until he opened the door of the Blazer. Was it his imagination that she sat down a little too carefully?

Sean helped her in and hurried to the other side, where he just sat and watched her, silent tears spilling over her face. He tried to take her hand, but she rejected his effort and folded her arms tightly. There was so much he wanted to say, to know. But all he could do was ask, "Where do you want to go?"

"Your place, if it's all right," she murmured quietly.

Sean nodded and put the key in the ignition.

Tara looked over at him as he drove and wished she could just tell him everything. How much better she would feel to be free of the burden. But she feared what he might do. If it became public, she knew the humiliation would be unbearable. And how would Sean feel about her? Could they have any future together when she had been so completely defiled? She didn't doubt that he would be kind to her, but she felt certain it would end at that.

"Why are you being so sweet to me?" she asked.

He looked surprised. "It's easy. If you must know, I've been worried sick. I've hardly slept for days."

Tara turned toward the window and swallowed hard. "You shouldn't be missing classes on my account," she said distantly.

"I'll manage. I've hardly heard anything that's been said the last few days anyway."

Tara looked at him again. "Have you really been so worried?"

"Yes," he gave a humorless chuckle, "I have."

"Why?" she asked, both fearing and hoping what his answer might be. She partly expected some admission that he cared for her, and it wouldn't have been surprising. But she simply was not prepared for his response.

The words came into Sean's mind so easily that he couldn't find any will or reason to hold them back. "Because I love you," he said with such strength that it surprised even him.

Tara looked at him in disbelief, but the sincerity in his eyes was evident. The irony made her insides churn. She pressed a hand over her mouth to hold back the emotion, but it only continued to build.

Sean knew something was *terribly* wrong long before he helped her into his apartment and sat beside her on the couch. But he didn't know how to ask. What could possibly have happened to upset her so completely? The possibilities that flashed through his mind made him seethe.

"Something happened Tuesday night," Sean said in a calm voice that belied what he felt inside. "And I can tell you don't want to talk about it, but I think maybe you'd better."

His perception was more than Tara could take, and the emotion burst forth. Helplessly she cried in heaving sobs. Sean tried to put his arms around her, but she pushed him away and buried her face in her hands. He tried not to take it personally. He knew it was good for her to vent her emotions, and he wanted to allow her the time and space to do it. But his ignorance frustrated him to impatience. He paced back and forth in the little front room while she curled up on the couch and continued to cry.

Tara didn't know how long she cried before she settled once again into the numb despair that was becoming familiar. She became so caught up in the pain that she was almost startled when she realized Sean was sitting at the other end of the couch, his hand over his mouth, his eyes betraying some kind of shock.

With an embarrassed chuckle she sat up straight, saying lightly, "I doubt you expected something like this less than a week after our first date."

It took him a moment to respond. "It's a good thing we didn't wait another week to go out."

"Or maybe we should have," she muttered.

Sean tried to read between the words. "Is there a reason you would prefer to not have me in your life right now?"

Sean didn't like the way she contemplated it, until she firmly shook her head. "I'm glad you're here, Sean. I really am, but . . ." She squeezed her eyes shut and said nothing more.

"I know you don't want to, Tara, but you've got to tell me what happened."

"No, I do not!" She sat up straight and began to fidget with her hands. Again he noticed that every movement was subtly tinged with pain. Her attempts to conceal it were admirable, but futile.

"You've got to tell someone," he insisted. "Do you talk to your roommates?"

"No," she admitted. "They're very sweet, and they care about me, but I . . . I can't talk to them. We're just not close."

"Is there anyone else you talk to?" he asked, knowing she'd not mentioned any friends.

"No one but my mother," she reported, "and I . . ." Her voice cracked. "I . . . can't tell her. She already worries so, and . . ."

"Tell me," he whispered.

Feeling suddenly unable to face this, Tara came to her feet. "Can I use your bathroom?" she asked and hurried away without waiting for permission.

Once alone, Tara leaned her head against the basin and tried to think straight. No matter how she looked at it, she just couldn't tell Sean the whole truth of it. She quickly splashed cold water on her face, then she blotted it with a fluffy, gray towel. Taking a deep breath, she fixed a partial story in her mind and went stoically to face him.

"I don't know why I'm so upset," she said lightly, sitting on the couch again.

Sean leaned toward her. "I dare say there's a valid reason."

"Actually, it's not as horrible as I've probably made it seem." She sighed. "I don't know what started it. I suppose you've already figured out this has to do with Danny. I told him I'd met someone, and suddenly he became Mr. Hyde."

Tara was aware of Sean going tense. She exercised great willpower to remain calm and get this over with. "He just got aggressive. That's all. I fought. We struggled. I finally talked some sense into him and he took me home."

Sean pondered her explanation for a minute and wondered what she was leaving out. "How aggressive?" he asked at the risk of offending her.

Unconsciously Tara pulled up the sleeves of her sweater as she contemplated a suitable answer. How could Sean not notice the scabs and scrapes? Before she could pull back, he took her arm and lifted it to his view. An urge to retch rose inside him when he saw the bruises on her wrist. A quick glance verified that both wrists were the same. His anger deepened as a sickening reality dawned.

Tara tried to squirm away but quickly realized it was futile, especially when every movement hurt. He looked closer at her arm then gave her a silent glare. "And how do you explain these perfect little fingerprints on your wrists?" he asked almost cynically.

"I don't know," she insisted. "I don't remember. It all happened so fast."

"There's something you're not telling me." His voice picked up an edge that didn't begin to express what was smoldering inside him.

"Oh, really, Sean." She stood and moved to the window, folding her arms tightly around her middle. "He knocked me around a little and I am understandably shaky. Don't go reading something serious into it just because I'm a wreck at the moment. It was upsetting. That's all."

Sean wanted to believe her. But he couldn't shake the feeling that she wasn't giving him the whole story. She had every textbook symptom of a rape victim, one of the most obvious being the bruised wrists. But he would never have expected to find such a thing on the woman he was falling in love with. He felt a rage building inside him that he wasn't certain he could control. He thought back to his training. He wasn't supposed to get emotionally involved. But she wasn't some client, for heaven's sake. He *loved* her. Still, he knew his rage would only provoke her to put more guilt onto herself. Praying inwardly, he took a deep breath and forced himself to be calm. Trying to be logical, he knew that if she suppressed the reality it would only eat at her. He had seen victims of rape and abuse, months, even years beyond the fact, still struggling with every aspect of their lives because they were unable to face the trauma. On the other hand, if he pushed her too hard and she wasn't ready to let it out, he would only be encouraging denial. Still, he had to try.

"Tara," he said gently, "are you trying to tell me that a guy who would give a woman a black eye, was content to just knock you around a little?"

Tara had an urge to just turn around and tell him to mind his own business. But she reminded herself that he was just concerned, and perhaps he sensed she was lying. She would certainly look a lot more guilty if she got defensive and tried to deny it.

"Yes," she said straightly without looking at him, "that is exactly what I am telling you."

Sean stood beside her and felt prompted to make a point. Silently he took her hands into his and looked down at them as he carefully maneuvered both her wrists into his left hand, placing his fingers over the outline of the bruises. When Tara realized what he was doing she groaned and tried to squirm away, but he held her tightly.

"It's okay," he said gently, meeting her eyes with an expression of perfect concern. "I'm not going to hurt you, Tara."

She swallowed hard and tried to relax, but she found it difficult to keep from screaming when he gently put his right hand to her throat, again placing his fingers over the bruises.

"If he was just out to beat you up a little," Sean said, close to her face, "if he was just trying to scare you, why was he holding you like this?"

Their eyes met for only a second. Tara wondered if this indescribable fear was a result of his coming so close to the truth, or a sudden vulnerability at the realization that he was strong enough to hurt her if he wanted to. Either way, she was scared and she didn't like it.

"I don't know!" she shouted and pushed him away. She began to pace the room like a caged animal, and he knew he'd hit a nerve. "Why are you doing this to me?" she screamed.

"I'm sorry," he admitted humbly. "I'm just trying to find out what happened, Tara. My intention was not to upset you. If you're not ready to talk about it, then—" He stopped when she slumped onto the couch, grimacing as she sat down. She wrapped both arms around her middle and let out a guttural moan. Sean told himself to remain calm, for her sake. But as he tried to comprehend the pain she was in, he felt more like throwing something, breaking something—killing someone; a particular someone. Desperation rose in him, but he managed a steady voice as he said, "Maybe you should see a doctor."

It took a minute for Sean's words to register. But Tara knew it was out of the question. Any doctor in his right mind would know immediately what had happened. She simply couldn't face it. In truth, there were places that hurt so bad, she wondered if she *should* see a doctor. But she couldn't. She just *couldn't*.

"Tara," Sean said with an impatience that made his voice sharp. Her head snapped up, fear showing blatantly in her eyes. He took a deep breath and repeated it calmly. "Maybe you should see a doctor."

"What on earth for?" She attempted a flippant little laugh, but it came out sounding more like a moan. "I've got some scrapes and bruises. My wounds will heal."

"All of them?" he questioned firmly. She met his eyes and he felt sure she knew what he meant. Still, he clarified, "Tara, every morning when I go to work, I am surrounded by people who cannot cope with the real world. In most cases, it boils down to fear. They're afraid of something, somewhere deep inside. And most of that fear stems from abuse." He wondered if she was even listening as she stared at the wall, hugging herself and rubbing her hands up and down over her arms. "Tara, do you hear what I'm telling you? Someone has hurt you. You're a victim. It's not your fault. But if you don't talk about it and deal with it, the pain will only get worse. You have a right to be afraid, Tara. But I don't believe you want to spend the rest of your life in fear."

Tara turned to look at him, and for a moment he hoped she would consider opening up. Instead she snapped, "Take me home." She got carefully to her feet and headed for the door. He could see her attempts to mask and guard the hurt, but every movement caused her pain and he knew it.

"No, wait!" He grabbed her as she reached for the door knob and she cried out in apparent anguish. He let go but blocked her way. He hardly dared touch her. Their eyes met as she seemed to realize what should have been obvious. He knew more than she wanted him to. Willing himself to stay calm and somehow overcome this frustration, he said gently, "Please . . . don't go. Not yet. Not like this."

She looked both skeptical and afraid.

"You're hurting. Let me help you, Tara. Please."

She pushed both hands through her hair then rubbed them over her face, as if she were trying to wipe something away.

"Tara," he took a step toward her and reached out a hand, "I think you need to see a doctor, and—"

"No!" She stepped back and made an attempt to soften her defensiveness. "I'm fine," she chuckled tensely. "Really, I'll be all right."

Sean felt himself almost seething. With the scrapes and bruises that were visible, what kind of injuries did she have where he couldn't see? And if she *had* been raped . . . The thought made bile rise into his throat. He felt a growing desperation to get her to a doctor, to get her to face it, to make the animal *pay* for this. But it was increasingly evident she was not going to let him help any more than he already had. And in truth, why should she? What had he done in the week since they'd first gone out to earn enough trust to share such personal anguish?

Taking a deep breath, Sean resigned himself to giving this some time. He felt sure that pressing her any further for the truth right now would only cause more harm. Trying to look at it rationally, he opted for a different approach. "Okay," he said, "if you don't want to go to a doctor, okay. But you're hurting. Is there anything I can do, anything I can get for you?"

"No," her voice was gentler now, more calm, "thank you." She took a deep breath and sat down. "I appreciate your concern, Sean. I really do . . . but I just need to . . . try and forget about it."

Sean nodded reluctantly in agreement. But there was another issue he felt he had to press. "Just where do I find this Danny?"

"Oh, yes." Tara sat up straighter as the issue apparently became less tender. "That's it, Sean. Hunt him down and beat him up or something. That ought to make things better."

"It would make *me* feel better."

"Well, it's immature and it's . . . not Christian. So just *forget* about it!"

"I just want to have a little talk with him," Sean insisted.

"Forget it, Sean," she said through clenched teeth. "It's his word against mine, and I'm not going to allow you to humiliate me any further by pushing this."

Sean pressed his fingers to his temples and squeezed his eyes shut, trying to convince himself to let this go. He tried to see it from her point of view. While he was praying for the strength to handle this, Tara's voice softened with a plea. "You're right about one thing. I have no one else to talk to right now. You're the only real friend I've got, so don't go and blow it by acting like a little boy. I need someone to lean on." Her voice faltered. "I need you."

What could Sean say? He had no choice but to resign himself to honoring her wishes, at least for the time being. The whole thing made him so angry he wanted to scream and throw things. But he found a certain peace in her admission that she needed him. It was easier to let the anger go, knowing he could accomplish more by simply being there for her and accepting the circumstances—for now.

Instinctively he went to his knees in front of her. She pulled back slightly as he took her hands into his, but as he attempted to make it clear that she could trust him, she seemed to relax. "Tara." He looked into her eyes and tried to choose his words carefully. "Whatever happened, it makes no difference to you and me—to us." She shook her head as if she didn't believe him. "Are you listening to me?" he asked. She squeezed her eyes shut. "Tara." He touched her chin and rubbed a gentle thumb over her bruised cheek as if he could somehow take the pain away. "No matter what he did to you, Tara, it doesn't change the way I feel about you. You must believe me."

Tara took hold of his arms and pressed her face to his shoulder in order to avoid looking at him. If only she *could* believe him. A part of her wanted to, but the very thought of admitting it was too terrifying to even think about. Instead she just held to him, wanting to forget everything but Sean O'Hara.

Sean held her and stroked her hair. Carefully he blinked back his own emotion and attempted a distraction. Perhaps with time it would be easier to face.

"Are you hungry?" he asked lightly.

"Not really, but . . ."

"Why don't you get some rest, and I'll go get us a pizza or something." He touched his nose to hers and she almost smiled.

"That sounds nice," she admitted. "I've hardly eaten for days."

"Make yourself at home," he said, "and I'll hurry."

"Thanks," she said and he walked out the door, leaving her to wonder where all of this would lead.

Once alone in the Blazer, Sean's emotion erupted and he had to pull over and just let it out before he could go on. He sobbed and cursed and asked himself over and over why something like this had to happen to *her.* It made no sense, and he *hated* this feeling. He'd felt it before, but he didn't like it any more now than he had when he'd been lying in a hospital, wondering why he was alive.

Sean finally managed to calm down and forced himself through the motions of picking up something to eat. He convinced himself he had to be strong—for her. But deep inside, he wondered if he had what it would take to carry her through this. He could only pray that he did.

CHAPTER FOUR

Once alone, Tara attempted to vent some of her overwhelming emotion. Normally she might have wanted to snoop a little and see what she could discover about this man and his habits, but she felt hard-pressed just to cry enough to relieve the pressure in her head. She attempted to repair herself as much as possible in the bathroom mirror, then she sat down to try and gather her wits. She wondered if Sean sensed she wasn't telling him everything. Just her luck that he was practically a psychologist. The man could probably read minds. Still, she had no intention of telling *anyone*—especially Sean. Let him think what he wanted. She was not about to tell him she had been so thoroughly used as a result of ignoring his warning. And she would not allow him to bully the truth out of her. In that moment she had no comprehension or concern for the long-term effects of keeping it to herself. She could only think about making it one day at a time. And today, she could no more bring herself to admit aloud what had happened to her, than she could fly to Venus.

Tara had barely decided she was prepared to face Sean again when she heard the door and looked up to see his face blocked by a pizza box with a sack balanced on top of it. He set it on the table and grinned at her, as if the previous episode had not transpired.

"I got pizza, salads, and that really great root beer that tastes homemade."

"Sounds wonderful." She smiled, appreciating his attitude. What she needed right now was distraction.

"I left something in the car. Would you mind getting the dressings out of the fridge and some glasses and stuff?" He pointed.

"They're in that cupboard."

Tara nodded and opened the fridge as he walked out, leaving the door open. She found ranch, blue cheese, and Catalina. He liked salads. That was a good sign. She set them on the table and took the salads out of the sack, then she turned to find glasses and forks. She gasped when she turned back to find Sean sitting at the table with his arms folded. She didn't have to ask herself why she was so jumpy, but she wondered why there were a dozen pink roses in a vase in the center of the table. Frozen where she stood, her eyes went to Sean in question.

"They must be for you," he said. "I don't see anyone else here who's beautiful enough to put a dozen roses to shame."

Tara set down the glasses and forks and looked at him again. But she couldn't find any words to express all she felt. She almost expected his words to sound flattering and phony. But coming from Sean, they had an air of genuine giving that touched her heart and made it pound a little faster. If only life could be as it had been a week ago. If only . . .

As if Sean had read her mind, he said softly, "Forget about him. Whatever you shared with him is over. Whatever he did to you is in the past. Your life begins anew from this moment, Tara. With any luck, you will let me be a part of it."

"Your luck or mine?" she asked, wishing she could speak without her voice cracking.

He grinned. "The luck of the Irish."

Tara knew it was supposed to be funny, and she did laugh. But the reality of his being in her life at this time seemed incredibly lucky for her. And despite all that had happened, she suddenly felt grateful to be alive and to know that God was looking out for her. She momentarily wondered how she would feel now without him, and for the first time in her life she could almost understand how one might feel suicidal.

Their eyes met, and Tara could feel that mind-reading gaze penetrating her again. The shame returned and she looked away, wishing she could find the will to just sit down and begin eating.

Sensing her discomfort, Sean came to his feet and stood beside her. He reached an arm toward her and she recoiled. Had she changed so much that she would be repulsed by *any* man's touch?

"It's all right," he whispered and pulled her carefully into his arms, holding her as if she were made of glass. It was evident that he knew she was hurting. For a moment she just closed her eyes and absorbed the comfort, reminded of the times her father had held her when she was discouraged or upset. She looked up at him and he smiled. Gingerly he touched the bruise near her eye as if he could heal it, then he pressed his lips there in a gesture of acceptance to the pain that had marred her life. Tara closed her eyes again, relishing his simple offering and the peace it gave her.

Sean wanted to kiss her, but while he was contemplating it, he noticed from this angle that the inside of her lower lip was cut and slightly swollen. He was about to question her, but the possibilities of how it might have happened flashed through his mind and he forced the thought away. Instead he pressed his lips to her brow, wondering why this madness had to happen to a woman so good and pure.

Tara opened her eyes and looked up at Sean. His face was so close she could feel the warmth of his breath. "I meant what I said," he whispered and drew away. Tara wasn't sure what exactly he was referring to, but she took it as a declaration of his sincerity, and found no reason to disagree.

"Let's eat," he smiled and she nodded. He helped her with her chair, then said a simple blessing over the food. They ate in silence until he went into the other room to put on an *Enya* CD that eased the tension a little. Tara kept looking at him, then at the roses. She'd been given flowers many times in the past, but she decided they had never meant more to her than now. She wondered again if he suspected the truth. But whether or not he did, she felt certain he was making it clear that it didn't matter. When they had finished a slow, silent meal, Tara helped clean up the mess. She wrapped the leftover pizza in aluminum foil and put it in the fridge. Sean filled the sink with sudsy water and washed what few dishes he'd left dirty. Tara watched him a moment, then picked up a clean towel and started to dry.

"You okay?" he asked quietly without looking at her.

"Yeah," she said lightly, "why?"

"Last weekend we couldn't find enough time to talk about

everything we wanted to say. Now we can't find anything to say."

"So talk," she said, wishing she could avoid the memory of what had changed her during the week.

Sean looked at her then, and Tara felt herself pale, certain he could read her memories. Nonchalantly she opened a cupboard door to find the proper resting place for a couple of bowls, while inside she wished she could just melt into the floor and disappear.

"Maybe I should go home," she said. "I'm certain you have studies or . . ."

"Tomorrow is Saturday, and I was all caught up last night." He dried his hands and hung up the towel. "Of course, if you want to go home . . ."

Tara wanted to beg him to never leave her alone, but she only folded her arms and leaned against the counter.

"Why don't you tell me what you're thinking?" he asked gently.

"You know," she said tersely, "you really would make a great counselor. Is it a habit of yours to pry into people's minds?"

"Am I prying?" he asked so calmly it almost infuriated her.

"I told you what happened, Sean."

"But you didn't tell me how it made you feel, and why you're falling apart inside."

"What makes you think I'm falling apart inside?" she snapped.

"What makes you so defensive?"

"Because I don't want to talk about it!" she shouted.

"Okay," he said, "I'll make you a deal."

"What kind of deal?"

"You give me one—just one—genuine sentence beginning with: I feel. And then we'll let it drop. But I'm not going to sit here and pretend to have a good time when I know you're hurting inside and you're not willing to tell anyone about it."

"I guess you're implying I could use some counseling."

"I'm not implying anything. But I know that you'll feel better if you tell somebody how you feel."

Tara chuckled cynically. "If you were my counselor, you would infuriate me to no end." He shrugged his shoulders and waited. She took a deep breath. "All right. I feel . . ." She hesitated, wondering if she could be honest with this and keep him from knowing the entire truth. The silence went on too long, but he waited patiently. "Vulnerable," she finally said.

"That's understandable. So how does feeling vulnerable affect your being with me right now?"

Tara narrowed her eyes and looked at him hard. At least he was bringing himself into this now, and she didn't have to feel like a client. "I feel safe when I'm with you," she admitted, playing with the bottom of her sweater.

"I'm glad," he said, "but did you feel safe with Danny until Tuesday night?"

"I thought you said we could drop it!"

"As soon as I understand whether or not you want to be with me, and why, I would be happy to drop it. Forget your feelings. Let's talk about *mine!*"

Tara was taken off guard by the realization that he was not only concerned, this was hard on him. She swallowed and glanced at the floor, willing herself to remain calm. "Okay. If you must know, I give myself some credit for discernment. I don't think I ever completely trusted Danny, but I always figured . . ." That wretched crack came into her voice. "I always thought I could put a man in his place if it became necessary." She cleared her throat. "It would seem I was wrong."

Sean reached over and touched her face. "I can promise you, Taralee Parr, you will never have to put me in my place."

She looked up at him and smiled. "Thank you for being here for me, Sean. I don't know what I'd have done without you."

"It's my pleasure." He smiled back.

"Is it okay if I stay a while longer? My roommates tend to get a little rowdy in the evenings."

"You're welcome to stay as long as you like," he said, "and I'll do my best to not be infuriating."

Tara chuckled and he pointed at her. "See, you can laugh."

"You seem to have that effect on me."

"How about a movie? I have a few select possibilities, or we could rent one."

"That sounds nice."

"You go pick one out," he suggested. "I'll start some popcorn."

Tara went to find the video tapes. She opened a drawer beneath the T.V. and began to read labels. "You like Cary Grant," she called.

"Just a little."

"Where did you get all of these?"

"I mostly record them when they come on T.V. I've bought very few prerecorded movies." He came behind her as he spoke, and she could hear corn popping in the distance.

Tara continued down the row of tapes, coming across a title that made her stop and look up at him in question. *"Gone With the Wind?"*

"Frankly, my dear, it's one of my favorites."

Tara smiled, then she laughed. With a huge bowl of buttered popcorn and more of that wonderful root beer, they sat on the floor and leaned against the couch to watch four hours of classic film, pausing for two intermissions: once for a bathroom break, and again to heat up the leftover pizza.

Sean found himself watching Tara more than the screen. As the movie progressed, he began to see her true self emerge. He found it endearing to see her unconsciously mouthing the lines with the characters. He held her hand and watched her cry at the end, then he got up to turn off the T.V. The reality fell back over her face immediately. Something unspeakable had happened to her, and he knew it with every fiber of his being. But the best thing he could do for her now was just to be there, which would certainly be no sacrifice for him. He could think of nothing he would rather do than just be with Tara Parr.

"I suppose I should go home now," she said, glancing at the clock. "I can't exactly move in with you, now can I?"

"Not yet," he said, and he meant it.

While Sean went to get his keys, Tara stood by the door, feeling a tangible fear at the prospect of being alone. He was almost to the door when the phone rang. He looked at it skeptically and she asked, "What's wrong?"

"I don't get many phone calls. It's probably someone wanting to clean my carpet."

Tara smirked and grabbed the phone. "Hello."

After a long pause, an accented voice said, "Hello, is Sean at home?"

"Just a minute," she said and handed him the phone.

"Hello?" Sean said.

"A woman answered your phone. What are you up to, boy?"

Sean laughed. "Michael! Are you sure you can afford these long-distance calls?"

"I can handle it. I've been thinking about you. Maybe it's because we sent Allison off on her mission. I believe you had a lot to do with that."

"I don't think so," Sean chuckled humbly, "but I'm sure she'll make a fine missionary."

"So," Michael drawled, "I assume from your answering service that you won't be waiting for Allie."

"Did you think I would?" Sean asked soberly.

"Not really," Michael admitted with a laugh. "If it's not there, it's not there. But I like to give you a hard time. You still haven't told me about this woman."

Sean took Tara's hand into his and smiled at her as he continued his conversation. "Well, her name is Taralee Parr. She reminds me a little of Emily; well, not really. But she *did* grow up on a farm."

"Good . . . I guess."

Tara smiled timidly and pretended not to listen as Sean went on. "I found her in the library. She's the most incredible woman I've ever met."

"Oh, it sounds serious." Michael's voice was full of pleasure. "I bet she's pretty."

"Prettier than you can possibly believe," Sean said as he stroked a finger over her face. "And whether she knows it or not, I intend to marry her."

Tara looked up, her eyes wide with astonishment. Sean only smiled.

"You *are* serious," Michael said. "How long have you known her?"

"A week," Sean said, then he laughed. "If it's there, it's there. How long did it take you to fall in love with Emily?"

"About forty-five seconds."

"By the way, I got the package. Thank you. Tell Emily I loved the cookies. No one makes them like her."

"She's a clever woman," Michael said, then he laughed as if he'd told himself a joke.

"I miss you," Sean said earnestly. "All of you."

"We miss you, too, kid," Michael admitted. "Let us know when the wedding will be. Maybe we can scrape together the money to fly over."

"Start scrimping," Sean said and they both laughed.

While Sean wrapped up his conversation, Tara realized she was getting sleepy and leaned her head on his shoulder. He put his arm around her and kissed the top of her head. She pondered what he had just said about her and wondered if it was as sincere as it seemed. Were his feelings for her so strong? Could she possibly deny what she felt for him? If only she could erase the disaster in her life and enjoy the reality that she truly believed she'd found a man she could spend eternity with and be happy.

When Sean hung up the phone he said, "That was Michael, calling from Australia."

"I gathered that."

"He told me he'd save his money so they could fly up for the wedding."

Tara looked at him in disbelief then started to chuckle. "I thought you said he was rich."

"He is. But Emily keeps him on a budget."

"I see." She paused. "What wedding?"

"Ours, of course."

"Sean O'Hara, I have barely known your name for a week. Are you trying to propose to me?"

"No," he said quietly, "I'll wait another day or two for that."

All humor fled once they were in the Blazer. Sean reached a hand over to take hers. "Will you be all right?"

"Of course," she said lightly, trying not to think about the reality.

"Do you have any plans for tomorrow?" he persisted.

"Not yet."

"Good. I don't either. What do you want to do?"

"Whatever you want to do would be fine with me."

"What time should I pick you up?" he asked.

"As soon as you can get there," she said too intently.

"I'll see you at nine." He squeezed her hand and she smiled, however weakly.

"Why don't you come in for a minute?" She wished her voice hadn't betrayed her fear of being without him. "You might as well meet the gang. Just don't take them too seriously."

Sean could hear boisterous laughter before Tara opened the door. Three girls and a guy were sitting around a Monopoly board in the middle of the front room floor. There were signs of junk food strewn about and the kitchen was a mess, as if they'd fixed a big dinner, then eaten and let it be. All eyes turned toward them as they entered.

"Tara," Vicky said. "What did you do to your eye?"

Sean sensed her panic and said quickly, "She ran into a door in the dark." He felt appreciation in the way she squeezed his hand.

"And who is this fine gentleman?" Heather asked.

"This is Sean O'Hara," she informed them. "He's in my psychology class."

"Ah," Vicky said, "we've talked on the phone a few times."

Sean nodded toward her.

"Sean," Tara said, "this is Heather and Vicky, my roommates. And that's Jill. She lives upstairs. And that's Quinn. I don't know where he lives, but he's always here on the weekends."

"Hello," Sean nodded again.

"Want to play?" Vicky asked. "We're not too far into it, and—"

"Thanks," Tara said quickly, "but I'm not sure I'm up to a late night of Monopoly. Perhaps another time."

"Oh, yeah," Heather said, "you had the flu. How are you feeling now?"

"Better," she said, "but tired."

Tara urged Sean to the kitchen, and the others returned noisily to their game.

"Thank you," she said quietly.

"For what?"

"For saying what you did, and . . . and for being there. It felt good to get out."

"It was my pleasure, Tara, I can assure you."

"I suppose I should get some sleep," she said, but Sean sensed she was uptight. If propriety didn't make it impossible, he'd be tempted to stay with her longer. But it was late and they both needed some sleep.

"How can you?" he asked, glancing toward the other room.

"I have some good ear plugs," she smiled.

Sean chuckled, then he remembered, "You forgot your roses." She looked slightly panicked and he added, "I'll bring them in the morning."

"I'll be ready at nine," she said and he reluctantly slipped away.

Tara stood a moment by the door, wishing she didn't have to feel this way. She just wanted her life to go back the way it was before . . . But she couldn't think about that. She just *couldn't*.

Heather's voice startled her. "How do you rate, Tara? He's adorable."

"The luck of the Irish," she replied.

"But you're not Irish."

"No, but he is." She smiled and moved down the hall. "Good night."

Tara prepared for bed and set her alarm clock. She put in her ear plugs and crawled between the covers. Staring toward the ceiling, she prayed and cried silent tears until exhaustion brought a peaceful rest without an amen being spoken.

CHAPTER FIVE

Heather and Vicky slept soundly while Tara showered and ate some toast and orange juice. She straightened her room and washed some dishes, even though she hadn't dirtied any of them. At eight-thirty she put on a little makeup, concentrating on an attempt to smooth over the bruises. Not sure what she and Sean would be doing, she packed a purse for several options, and found she was ready at ten minutes to nine. She released more nervous energy by picking up the Monopoly game and the wrappers and pop cans. It was beyond her how anyone could live like this. She was startled by the knock at the door, but went eagerly to answer it.

"Good morning," Sean said brightly and handed over the vase of roses.

"Thank you," she smiled. "I'll just set these in my room and we can go."

Sean noticed the peacefulness of the apartment in contrast to the night before. He also noted the improvement of its appearance. It was just a guess, but he doubted that Vicky and Heather had cleaned it up before they went to bed. He was relieved to see Tara, and even more so to see a glimmer of the vibrant woman he knew she was.

"Where are we going?" she asked as he helped her into a jacket.

"You'll see," was all he said before they stepped out into the brisk October sun.

"You know," he said when he had barely begun to drive, "it isn't necessary for you to pretend you're not in pain." She looked alarmed and he quickly added, "I mean, it's obvious that it hurts you to move, and I understand why. I don't want you to feel like you have to put on an act for my sake." She gave a barely detectable nod and looked out the window. He took her hand and asked gently, "Is it getting any better?"

"A little," was all she said.

Determined to not let the day pass in silence, Sean started asking her questions about her childhood as they drove the freeway to Salt Lake City. She soon became caught up in telling him stories of growing up on a sheep ranch in Colorado. She told him about herding and feeding, shearing and lambing. Sean listened with growing intrigue, and concluded firmly, "It looks like I've found an honest-to-goodness shepherd girl."

She smiled serenely and wondered again what she would do without him.

"So," Tara said after a brief lull in the conversation, "tell me about Chicago."

"It's a city," he said blandly, but there was no mistaking the rigid line that developed in his jaw. She felt sure he would say no more.

Tara contemplated his reaction. "Is it so difficult to talk about?"

Sean looked over at her, surprised by her perception. "In some ways, yes," he admitted. "It's hard for me to think about any aspect of growing up there without being reminded that I can never go home again."

"I cannot even comprehend." She squeezed his hand gently.

Sean returned the gesture eagerly and managed a little chuckle. "So, you told me you work at a bookstore. That sounds fun."

Tara was tempted to maneuver past his attempt to change the subject, but recalling her own determination to not discuss painful issues, she decided against it. She talked a little about her work and how she enjoyed it, then she asked, "What made you decide to go into psychology?"

Sean seemed to relax. "When I first came to Utah, I got a job making calls for a credit bureau. I was surprised to find that I was rather good at it. It just seemed to come naturally for me to calm down angry people and help them find solutions to their problems. It didn't pay very well, but I kept at it until my mission."

Sean talked for a while of experiences from his mission, some tender, some funny. Tara became so lost in the present that she almost forgot about the pain in her life. She was startled when he asked a question that somehow tied everything together. "Last Saturday evening," he began, looking at her carefully, "why did you cry when I kissed you?"

Tara looked at him to be certain he was serious, then she glanced down and felt warmth rise in her face. "You certainly are gifted at being straightforward," she said.

"Forgive me if I . . . I mean, I didn't mean to make you feel uncomfortable, or . . ."

"No, it's all right, I just . . ." While Tara contemplated an answer, the memory of those moments in his arms came back to her with clarity. A pleasant warmth filled her and soothed her troubled heart. How could she deny what had spurred those tears? The feelings Sean brought out in her made it tempting to be shy. But something about him vanquished such temptations. She looked directly at him, and for a moment she completely forgot about the things Danny had done to her. It was easy to say, "I was just so overcome with emotion, it nearly frightened me." He looked alarmed and she quickly clarified, "No, I don't mean that you . . . scared me or anything. I mean . . ." She chuckled tensely, unable to recall ever having such a candid discussion with anyone, let alone a man. "I don't know how to explain it." He glanced back and forth between her face and the road. His eyes silently asked her to try. "This might sound funny," she admitted, "but the thing that keeps coming to mind is . . . well, it was almost like one of those moments when I would be reading the scriptures, or sitting in a church meeting, and I would just know that it was all true." She hesitantly added, "Only more so."

Tara only wondered for a moment why there was moisture in his eyes. As she realized what she'd said, the feeling she had just described rushed over her.

They drove into the city in silence, as neither of them felt prone to break the spell. Sean parked the Blazer in the Crossroads Mall multi-level garage, then he turned in his seat to face her. "What are you thinking?" he asked, pressing his hand to her face.

Tara looked at him and marveled at these feelings, as intensely positive as the pain she wanted to bury was negative. "Is it really possible . . . to feel this way . . . so soon?"

"If you feel it, Tara, it's possible."

As much as she wanted to just admit her feelings for him openly and bring him into her life fully, she had to admit, "With everything that's happened this last week, it's difficult to know what I feel, Sean." She absently pushed a hand through her hair. "I need time."

Sean smiled and leaned forward to press a kiss to her cheek. "That's something we have plenty of."

Hand in hand, they walked into the mall and browsed until lunch time, when they went to the lowest level to eat in the atmosphere of an indoor street cafe. The walking seemed to relieve Tara's stiffness. She felt completely at ease some moments, and at others she found herself feeling unclean and somehow unworthy of Sean O'Hara's company. There were times when she could almost forget about the horror; but occasionally when he looked at her, she felt sure he was seeing only the signs of abuse on her face. And perhaps he suspected the truth about how she had been defiled. Still, she had to admit that she would far rather be in his company, distracted by the things surrounding them, than to be alone at home, wallowing in her misery.

Tara felt vaguely uneasy when they went outside and crossed the street to Temple Square. It had been a long time since she'd come here, and there was no denying its beauty and magnificence. But part of her ached for something inside that no longer felt worthy of the dreams she'd always had for herself. From her childhood she had been taught to always choose the right, to keep herself morally clean, with the promise that she would be rewarded with joy and blessings. Tara's mother had often told her there was nothing so sweet as being able to give yourself to a man in marriage, knowing that you were pure and innocent. How ironic, she thought, not only that she would be denied such peace, but that she would be robbed of her purity the same week she met the man she wanted to share her life with. Tara reminded herself that this was not her fault, and God would not hold her accountable. But she still had to wonder if she'd made a bad choice somewhere that had led to this catastrophe. It was difficult to distinguish such fine lines of spiritual laws when she felt so unclean from the inside out.

Tara began to feel better as they explored the North Visitors'

Center and watched a couple of short films. Sean held her hand tightly as they ambled up the circular walkway leading to the Christus statue. Tara lost track of the time as they stood before it, staring up at the huge stone likeness of Christ, his arms open and outstretched, the nail prints evident in his hands. And she was even less aware of how long she let the tears fall before Sean's arm came around her, startling her back to reality.

"It's okay," he said, "I feel it, too."

After some contemplative time, they walked outside, lingering over the beautiful foliage of the temple grounds and admiring forty years of pioneer craftsmanship in the temple spires rising above the square. While Tara felt physically exhausted, she wished she could somehow linger there forever.

It was getting dusky when they left the square and returned to the mall for dinner. While they were waiting for the food to arrive, Sean took Tara's hand across the table. Not knowing what to say, Tara concentrated on his hand encircling hers. As she did so, she noticed in greater detail something that she had only been subtly aware of before. Figuring now was as good a time as any to ask, she followed his example of being straightforward. "Is it my imagination that your hands seem . . . different?"

"Do they?" He held them up and looked at them as if he'd never seen them before, but he didn't seem uncomfortable. "I suppose they are a little strange." Tara caught a sparkle of humor in his eyes just before he smiled. "Actually, it's nice to have known you this long and not have you notice the problem before now."

"Problem? I don't understand."

"Five years ago, my hands were absolutely useless. I could barely manage to feed myself. That job I told you about, with a credit bureau . . . the only thing I could do to support myself was work a telephone and a computer keyboard, and I was slow at that. Since then I've had several surgeries on my hands. But, as you can see, the results aren't bad. If you look closely, you can see some scars."

He pointed them out, and she turned each of his hands over in hers to examine details. "It's amazing," she admitted. "No one would ever detect anything wrong without looking closely."

"Then you must have been looking closely." Something akin to mischief glowed in his eyes.

"Let's just say I've found it enjoyable to observe everything about you."

He gave a smile that warmed her.

"So," she continued curiously, "were you born with the problem, or—"

"Not hardly," he chuckled, albeit tensely. Sean watched the question in her eyes and suddenly felt like a hypocrite. While he sat here feeling frustrated because she wouldn't talk about her pain and fears, he had to admit there were things inside him that he was equally reluctant to talk about; things that were long in the past, but still continued to haunt him. While he contemplated giving her an answer that was truthful without identifying the real problem, he wondered if this was how she had felt yesterday when he'd questioned her about the incident with Danny.

Sean cleared his throat and said carefully, "I was in a car accident. I went face first through the windshield." He noticed her sharp intake of breath, but he continued. "Apparently I put my hands over my face before the impact. They saved my face, and more importantly, my eyes. But they paid a dear price."

"That must have been horrible for you," Tara said, taking his hand across the table. She actually found it comforting to feel compassion for him, to realize he'd been through something difficult, to simply turn her thoughts from herself.

Sean shrugged off her comment, but she persisted, "Was it serious—besides your hands, I mean?"

Sean pressed his fingers to his temples and took a deep breath. "Well, I was in intensive care for weeks, so they tell me. They told me many times it was a miracle I hadn't died instantly. There were moments when I wished I had."

"I'm glad you didn't," she said gently.

When Sean looked into Tara's eyes, he had to admit with more fervency than he'd felt since it happened, "So am I."

Somewhere in the middle of the meal, Tara asked, "So how did it happen?" He looked confused and she clarified, "The accident. Were you driving, or—"

"No, I was not driving," he almost snapped, and Tara wondered what she had said wrong. She saw him take a deep breath and offer an apologetic smile. "I'm sorry. You'd think after all these years it wouldn't get to me, but . . . well, there are aspects of it that are difficult to admit to."

"Why?" she asked with such genuine concern that he almost wanted to cry.

"Perhaps because it was a troubling time in my life, or maybe I don't want to admit to things that would make you think less of me."

"What? That you're human and you've made mistakes? I cannot comprehend thinking less of you for anything."

She said it with such sincerity that Sean almost became angry. She was so sweet and innocent; he doubted that she had any comprehension of the kind of man he had once been. Impulsively deciding that he'd rather have her know than fear her finding out, he leaned toward her and said severely, "You don't understand, Tara. I was drunk when that accident happened. And I was not *only* drunk, I was stoned. Do you understand the difference?" She barely nodded before he went on. "I left a bar with a woman I had never met before. I would not have ever known her name, if not for her obituary. You see, she died in that accident. Her parents came to the hospital to talk to me, but I was semi-comatose. My sister told me later they were angry that I had lived and their daughter was dead. Until they saw me. She said they went away crying, grateful that she was dead. At least she was out of her misery.

"I don't remember *anything* about that accident except the actual impact, and sometimes I wonder if it's a memory or a nightmare I've conjured up from what they told me. The only thing I know for certain is that the entire thing was a nightmare, and when I think about the reasons that I was out drinking and getting stoned to begin with, I want to just—"

Sean stopped when he saw the emotion in Tara's eyes. "I'm sorry," he said gently. "I didn't intend to get so . . . well, it's been hard to deal with. But when it all comes down to the bottom line, if I had to do it over again, I would."

Tara's eyes widened. She'd been trying to compare how he must have felt then, to how she was feeling now. And she certainly couldn't comprehend choosing to live through something like that again.

"Why?" she finally asked.

"Well, it's a long story that should probably wait, but the simple truth is that I would not have joined the Church if not for that accident." His voice softened, and that natural sparkle returned to his eyes. "And I would not have met you if I hadn't joined the Church. For those two things, I would do it all again and more."

Tara glanced down timidly. "I don't understand how you can say such things about me, when you know me so little."

"I know how I feel *about* you, and I've had too many miracles in my life to doubt such feelings." Sean took a deep breath and felt compelled to add, "My only concern is wondering if a man with my kind of past is worthy to—"

"Don't even say it," she said with a laugh so labored he wondered if it was an attempt to keep from crying.

They finished their meal mostly in silence, while Tara contemplated all she had just learned about him. She was surprised by the intense relief she felt to know there were aspects of his life that might somehow balance out the changes in hers. But she was almost disturbed by the question that captured her mind. Would she have felt the same if this horrid incident had not occurred? Would she have had compassion for his mistakes and suffering if she had not fallen into such a vile trap? It was impossible to answer such a question objectively, but there was a tiny glimmer of appreciation for being opened to this understanding.

The drive home was quiet, but without the tension they had felt the previous evening. Tara was actually surprised to realize how far she had come in twenty-four hours. In spite of the pain, both physical and emotional, reminding her frequently of what had happened, there was an underlying peace beginning to grow in her. If Sean could accept this situation and still care for her, then she had reason to go on and find hope in her future. And even if a time came when he learned the whole truth and *couldn't* accept it fully, she knew that her Savior would always love her. And if no one else understood, he did.

"Would you go to church with me tomorrow?" Sean asked as they took the first Provo exit. "I went to your ward last week."

Tara smiled. "That would be nice. Do you think anyone will

notice that I ran into a door?" She touched the bruise near her eye and they both chuckled.

"I doubt anyone will notice," he said. "They'll be too entranced by this beautiful woman, wondering why she has nothing better to do than hang around with Sean O'Hara."

"In my opinion," she laughed softly, "there is *nothing* better to do than hang around with Sean O'Hara."

"Keep it up, and you'll never get rid of me."

"Keep it up, and I won't want to."

Back at Tara's apartment, they found Heather watching T.V. with Jill, and Vicky studying at the kitchen table with headphones on. Tara didn't want Sean to go, but the apartment felt so crowded. Impulsively she motioned for him to follow her to her room.

Sean's eyes went first to the *Gone With the Wind* poster and he chuckled. He absorbed the remainder of the room, and it was easy to tell which side was Tara's.

"Who else sleeps here?" he asked, sitting on the edge of her bed.

"Carla. But she went to Virginia for a funeral. She should be back soon."

Sean nodded, and to avoid any tension, Tara planted a large book on his lap about the making of *Gone With the Wind.* Together they perused it, talking and laughing until they realized it was getting late. The other girls wandered in and out occasionally and Sean found them mostly agreeable, though he could understand why Tara had said she couldn't get close to them.

Finally he had to say, "I should be going, but I'll pick you up for church."

Tara walked him outside. "Thank you for a wonderful day." She squeezed his hand. "And I mean that. I think it was exactly what I needed."

"Good." He reached up a hand to touch her face and she briefly flinched. "It's okay," he whispered.

"I know," she said with embarrassment. "I don't know why I'm so jumpy."

"I think it's understandable." He rubbed a thumb over her cheek and their eyes met. He wanted to kiss her so badly he ached. But he reminded himself that it would take time to build trust with her after what she'd been through. Instead he kissed her brow, holding his lips there for a long moment.

"Will you be all right?" he asked.

"I think so," she said with a seriousness that made him realize he was not the only one who felt reluctant to say good night.

"Call me, Tara," he insisted. "Even if it's the middle of the night. If you need to talk, or cry, or you just don't want to feel alone. Call me. I mean it."

"Thank you." She smiled up at him, unable to deny the relief he instilled in her.

He kissed her brow once more quickly, then walked slowly to the Blazer, making certain she'd gone back inside before he drove away.

Once alone, Tara began to feel the oppression return. But the peace she'd felt earlier in the day prompted her to open her scriptures and seek a positive distraction. She read until she was exhausted and drifted into a dreamless sleep.

* * * * *

Sean found it difficult to sleep as images of Tara's ordeal flashed through his mind. He began to seethe inside as he wondered exactly what had happened to her. And where was this Danny now? Out laughing it up somewhere, as if nothing had happened?

Attempting to honor Tara's wish to let it go, Sean tried not to think about it. He concentrated on keeping Tara's spirits up, and was pleased to see her doing better. But a week after her date with Danny, Sean knew if he didn't do something about it, he could never live with himself. He could only pray that Tara would forgive him.

Thinking it through carefully, Sean first went to the professor of Tara's humanities class. With some simple acting and careful maneuvering, Sean discovered Danny's last name. It wasn't too difficult to find out where he lived. Sean called his number, wondering what on earth he'd say if he actually got through to him. He was kindly told that Danny had left town unexpectedly about a week ago. Sean tried to accept this explanation, but for all he knew it had been Danny lying to him from the other end of the phone. Since he knew what Danny looked like, Sean casually dropped by the apartment. It took three tries before he found somebody home. Danny's only roommate, Kevin, was kind and more helpful than Sean had expected. He explained that Danny was prone to just leave town occasionally; that he kept to himself and pretty much minded his own business.

"Well, do you have any idea where I could get hold of him?" Sean pressed. "I've got some information for him, and I believe he's anxious to get it, if you could—"

"He's not in trouble again, is he?"

"Trouble?" Sean was proud of himself for the natural surprise in his voice. "What makes you think he'd be in trouble?"

"Nothing really," Kevin replied, leaving Sean disappointed. "It's just hard to say what Danny's up to most of the time. But I can give you his mother's number, if you like. She'd probably know where to find him. He might even be there. I know he visits her frequently."

"That would be great," Sean said, trying to disguise his enthusiasm.

Sean leaned in the door while Kevin jotted down a number from a list by the phone. "She lives in Canada," he said as he handed over the little piece of paper, "though I'm not sure where."

"Thank you," Sean said.

"No problem," Kevin replied. "Good luck. Hey," he added as Sean moved away, "if I hear from him, do you want me to give him a message, or—"

"No, thank you anyway," Sean smiled. "I'm sure I'll catch up with him sooner or later."

Sean's hope that he would find Danny through his mother was quickly dashed. She told him that she hadn't seen or heard from him in quite some time. She suggested he might be with his father, but they had been divorced for many years and she had no idea how to contact him. As she began pressing Sean with questions, it occurred to him that he didn't want Danny alerted by his mother that someone was looking for him; otherwise he might never come back to Provo. Sean summed up the conversation with an easy, "Oh, it's nothing that can't wait. I was simply calling to see if he would be making a pledge for KBYU television again this year. I appreciate your time."

Sean hung up the phone feeling helpless and frustrated. The more he thought about it, the angrier he became. Then he convinced himself that these feelings would not do anyone any good. If Tara wasn't willing to press charges, finding Danny would make little difference. But at least he knew he'd tried.

Praying for peace and guidance, Sean resigned himself to letting it go—at least for now. He turned his thoughts and efforts toward Tara, hoping that it would all work itself out.

As the days wore on, they quickly established a habit of being together whenever possible. Sean usually worked early mornings, and while his class schedule was light, his studies were intense. He began picking Tara up after classes and giving her a ride back and forth to work when he realized she had either been walking or taking the bus. The little car she had bought just out of high school had something wrong with it that she couldn't afford to have fixed, and it was sitting in the parking lot outside her apartment. Sean got under it one Saturday afternoon and had it running a week later, though she rarely got a chance to drive it since he was often there to take her where she needed to go. Through all the work and studying, the back-and-forth time was appreciated and helped keep her spirits up. Tara forced herself through classes and studies while the pain gradually eased. As the physical signs of the incident gradually healed and disappeared, the oppression also fell away.

Being together came so naturally that Tara spent less and less time at her apartment. It was rare that she didn't share a meal with Sean, and she found his apartment the perfect place to do the cooking and baking she enjoyed, but could rarely do in a kitchen where she had to work around three other girls' food preferences and eating habits. Sean gave her a key to his apartment and often found her there with dinner waiting when he came home from late classes.

Together they attended church meetings and home evening groups, alternating between wards, then leaning more toward Sean's as they seemed to somehow fit in better there. As they worked mutually in doing all they knew was right, the bond between them deepened. Sean watched Tara gradually lose the pain and fear of her experience with Danny, and each day she became more vibrant and full of life. Occasionally he contemplated trying again to find Danny, but a part of him feared opening up something with no evidence to back him up. Prayerfully trying to deal with his feelings, Sean felt certain it was best to let it go. While he knew that one day Tara would have to face it and deal with it, he felt it was best to allow time to give her some strength. And in the same light, he knew there were things of his own to deal with. His hope was that they could face the struggles of their lives together. Tara had a way of compensating for the family he'd left behind, and he was more certain every day that they were meant to be together.

The relationship developed so quickly into something comfortable and easy, that Sean hesitated to bring up marriage any more than he already had. He still saw signs of sensitivity in Tara that he believed were more a result of Danny's indiscretions, than indications of her real character. He didn't want to push her too fast. But he often wished they could be together completely, and it didn't take much inner searching to know undeniably that marrying her was the most excellent thing he could do with his life.

Sean's thoughts were filled with Tara as he left his last class and walked through a heavy snow to the Blazer. The storm was a surprise, as thus far November had been unusually warm and dry. He drove carefully home, anticipating a scene that gave him peace. It felt so right to walk through the door and find her there, that he wondered why he was holding back.

"Hello," she called from inside the refrigerator. Sean set his books down and put his arms around her from behind as she backed up with a salad in her hands. She laughed, and he only allowed her time to set it down before he hugged her tightly. Just as every time he got this close, he wanted to kiss her. He had kissed her many times these past weeks, but it was little more than a peck here and there. Only once had he really kissed her, and it had been unforgettable. Each time since, when the opportunity had come, he'd always found a reason to talk himself out of it. But at the moment, he couldn't think of any excuse not to. He'd just made up his mind to do it when the timer rang on the stove and startled them both.

"Sorry," she said as she escaped his grasp to turn it off and pull freshly baked rolls from the oven. "I think we can eat now."

"It smells wonderful." He helped her with her chair and sat across from her. "You're really too good to me."

Tara only smiled and offered the blessing at his request.

"It never ceases to amaze me what you can do with food," he insisted.

"You're just flattering me. I can cook, but I'm not that good."

Sean chuckled. "That all depends." He pointed his fork at her. "You know, I never realized this before, but I think my mother was a lousy cook."

"Well," she smiled, "it's apparent you grew up healthy. It couldn't have been too bad."

"No," he agreed, "I guess not."

Tara met his eyes and felt what had become common lately. It was as if she could somehow see a part of herself that she didn't know or understand, but was compelled to discover; as if learning to love Sean O'Hara was teaching her to love herself, and to learn who she really was. He filled her life in a way that complemented all she had been taught and believed in, but she had never felt it working so keenly. Premortality and life beyond this somehow came together for her in Sean's eyes. More and more it seemed their eyes would meet with no shame or uneasiness, and she was intrigued with the time they could spend just watching each other, silently sharing an unspoken dream.

The meal passed in small talk, then Sean rose to start clearing the table. "Let me help you," she said.

"That's not the deal. When you cook, I do the dishes. When I bring home pizza, you do the dishes."

"But I'd rather help you do the dishes than study," she admitted. They were almost finished before Tara found the courage to say something she'd wanted to say for a long time, but had never found what seemed to be the right moment.

"Sean." She put a hand over his and he leaned toward her, sensing the solemnity in her tone. "Do you remember the day I came to class with my black eye, and you brought me here?"

"I remember." He touched the now perfect skin with the back of his hand.

"You told me something that day, and I know at the time I didn't acknowledge it as I should have. I suppose I was caught up in the . . . well, you know."

He nodded and she knew he understood.

"I want you to know that I've thought a great deal about what you said, and it's brought me a lot of peace to know that it's true. I know you wouldn't have said it if you didn't mean it, and you've proven to me that you do."

"I must say I'm glad, but I said a lot of things that day, Tara. You'll have to tell me what exactly we are discussing."

Tara smiled and touched his face the way he had touched hers a moment ago. She leaned forward and meekly pressed her lips to his, then she drew back only slightly to say, "I love you, too, Sean O'Hara."

She felt more than heard him laugh. He pulled her to him in a warm hug and said close to her ear, "Those are the most beautiful words I've ever heard; or at least since I was baptized."

"Then I take it your sentiments haven't changed?" she tested.

"Never," he said vehemently. Their eyes locked in a way that made his pulse quicken. He didn't even have to think about kissing her. He just did it. It was as if every aspect of Sean's life fell into place at her response. She yielded to him, even clung to him as he held her closer, kissed her harder. Sean finally forced himself to draw away when he knew he could take no more without pressing boundaries that couldn't be pressed. Not only for the sake of their moral beliefs, but he had to consider the sensitive emotional state she had been in not so long ago.

Tara seemed hesitant to let him go and Sean eagerly held her, relishing her closeness, her display of trust and acceptance. He rummaged his hand through her hair, then his lips, marveling at its softness and beauty, so much like her in every way. "I love you, Tara," he muttered close to her ear. "I love you more than life."

She looked up at him with tears glistening in her eyes. "I love you, too," she replied, then buried her face against his throat as if she found great comfort there.

Trying to distract himself from these desires, Sean cleared his throat and said, "There is something I would like to ask you, as long as we're establishing that we're madly in love with each other." Tara smiled timidly and kept her arms around him. "What would you say if I asked you to marry me?"

Sean felt more nervous than he ever had in his life when her expression fell like hail from the sky. "Is this a proposal?"

He shrugged his shoulders and took a step back to put some distance between them. He hoped she couldn't sense the way his heart was pounding. "At this point, let's just say it's a speculation."

Tara looked down and folded her arms. "I . . . I just don't know, Sean, I . . ."

"But you just said you love me, and . . ."

"I do love you, but . . ."

"And you know that I love you, Tara, and I would . . ."

"It's not that, Sean." She wouldn't look at him, and he wondered if this had anything to do with Danny.

"I hope you know I would always respect you, and I'd do my best to treat you good, and take care of you, and . . ."

"I know that, Sean. Really I do."

"Then what?" He threw his hands up in exasperation. "Do you think I'm moving too fast? Is it because of my family—"

"No, Sean," she said soberly.

"Is it because of my past? I mean, I know I made some lousy mistakes, but—"

"It has nothing to with your past, Sean." Still she wouldn't look at him. "I dare say that things like that have a way of balancing out. I've got my own past."

While Sean wanted to question her further on that, he was more concerned with the issue at hand. "Then what?" he nearly whispered, hating the desperation in his voice.

Tara looked up at him with a sour frown, but looking closer he caught a sparkle in her eyes. Was she teasing him? As soon as he thought it her face broke into a beaming smile. "I don't know how you could possibly expect me to spend the rest of my life with a name like Tara O'Hara."

She started to laugh, and Sean was so relieved he nearly collapsed, pressing his brow against her shoulder with a groan of laughter.

"I had you going there, didn't I?" she giggled.

"Yes," he said breathily, "you did."

"Now, do you want the truth?"

He lifted his head to look at her. "Yes, I do."

"Since we're just speculating, I have to say that I can't think of anything I would rather do than spend the rest of forever with you." Sean grinned. "Of course, we've only known each other a short time and . . ."

"Oh, of course. We can talk about it, and pray about it, and . . ."

"And when the time is right, we'll know, and . . ."

"And it will be perfect," Sean declared.

"Perfect," she repeated and their eyes locked in that timeless grip again.

"Maybe we should finish the dishes," she said. "I need to study for that English test tomorrow, and you've got to work on that essay."

"True," he had to admit, but he chose to kiss her again instead.

As Tara lost herself in his kiss, she felt certain life could be no better than this. The nightmarish incident with Danny was the furthest thing from her mind.

CHAPTER SIX

The week before Thanksgiving, Tara awoke on a cold day with an uncomfortable churning in her stomach. She ran to the bathroom to throw up and heaved her empty stomach for several minutes; then she went back to bed, convinced she had the flu. She called Sean and told him she wasn't going to classes, and he said he'd stop by later.

By the time he got there she felt pretty good, and figured it must have been one of those brief flu bugs. But the next morning it happened again. Tara didn't have to worry about missing classes since it was Saturday, but when she climbed back into bed, the reality struck her like a stab in the heart.

"No!" she muttered aloud. "Please, no."

Frantically she scrambled to her dresser in search of her calendar book. But rather than offering any assurance, it only deepened the evidence. She'd not had a period since she'd met Sean.

For more than an hour Tara cried, then she stared numbly at her ceiling, wondering what she had done to deserve this. The pain of the initial incident came back to her freshly, every bit as harsh, every bit as devastating. She thought of Sean and wanted to die. Deep inside she'd wanted to tell him. But she had believed a day would come when it would be easy to talk to him about it, knowing it was in the past. But there was no keeping her ugly secret now. The truth would soon be known, and she had to tell him before he figured it out for himself. She couldn't comprehend what this would do to her life. She couldn't expect Sean to marry her now. And what about her education? Her family? Her religion?

Tara poured her heart out in prayer until the supposed "study session" in the other room got way out of hand and she couldn't bear listening to the laughter any longer. Impulsively she grabbed her purse and threw a few extra things into it, then she picked up a jacket and headed outside, not realizing it was raining hard until she was already wet. She got in her car but it wouldn't start, so she just started to walk, feeling an aimless despair.

After she'd walked a block, Tara could only manage one conscious thought. *Call Sean.* Even if he didn't want to marry her now, she needed him. He was the only real friend she had, and she couldn't face this alone. With shaky hands she put a quarter into the phone and dialed his number.

"Sean?" was all she said before he knew she was upset.

"What's wrong?" he insisted.

"Something's happened," she said with chattering teeth. "I . . . I left the apartment. My car wouldn't start. I can't go back right now. Will you come and get me?"

"Where are you?" he asked without hesitation.

"The phone booth two blocks west of my apartment."

"I'll be there in less than five minutes," he said and grabbed a blanket on his way out the door when he realized it was pouring.

The rain was turning to sleet when Sean pulled up to the curb and reached over to open the passenger door. She slid in and found a blanket beneath her. Sean eased it around her shoulders and headed for his apartment.

"Thank you," she said, but Sean didn't miss the look in her eyes that reminded him of the day she'd told him she'd been beaten up.

"What happened?" he asked.

She looked at him as if she wanted to speak, but her teeth were chattering and she was shaking.

"That's not much of a coat for a day like this. What possessed you to venture out dressed like that?"

Tara only looked out the window until Sean stopped and helped her out of the Blazer. She had a bad sense of deja-vu as they went inside and she felt the concerned expectancy in Sean. He pulled the blanket away. "You are soaked to the skin. Get in that bathroom and into a warm shower. I'll find you something to wear until your clothes dry."

Tara dutifully obeyed and lingered beneath the warm spray, wishing it could wash away the reality. She cried again, grateful for the running water that muffled the noise. While she was drying herself, Sean knocked at the door and called, "Here's something that might work. I'll set it by the door."

"Thank you," she called and heard him go into the kitchen. She reached out to pull in a bundle of clothes which proved to be a navy blue sweatshirt and matching pants with a drawstring waist. And heavy socks. She managed to make them work and opened the bathroom door as soon as she was dressed.

Sean came in while she was hanging her clothes over the shower rod to dry. He plugged in the hair dryer then urged her within its reach. Their eyes met repeatedly in the mirror while he stood behind her and dried her hair, allowing his fingers to toy in the long curls as he did.

"There," he announced when he turned it off, "that's better." He took a brush out of the drawer and began gingerly pulling it through her hair until she took over and he just watched her, leaning against the vanity, his arms folded over his chest.

"Now," he said firmly, "you can tell me what's wrong." Tara met his eyes, then looked away. While she groped for words to begin, he persisted. "You told me on the phone that something happened."

Tara set the brush down and wrapped her arms over her head as a sob erupted without warning. Feeling suddenly lightheaded, she realized she'd not eaten anything. Impulsively she shuffled past him. "I need to sit down."

Tara only made it to the hall before she pressed her head to the wall, trying to gain some equilibrium. Sean's arms came around her from behind as she slumped to her knees. She pressed her head into her hands and cried over and over, "Why me? I don't understand why this had to happen to me."

Sean knelt to hold her. "What, Tara? Tell me what."

She only shook her head and cried harder, clinging to him with desperation.

"Does this have something to do with Danny?" he asked.

She nodded but was crying too hard to speak.

"Did you see him somewhere? Did he call you?"

She shook her head and pressed her face to his shoulder. Sean let her cry when it became evident he'd get nothing out of her until she did. He was tempted to cry himself as he tried to speculate what could be wrong. For the life of him, he had no idea what would bring on something like this. Knowing she'd been in denial to some degree regarding her incident with Danny, he felt sure that whatever had happened was forcing the reality back to the surface. It was as if she had experienced the initial shock all over again. When she finally calmed down, he helped her to a chair at the kitchen table and sat to face her.

"Are you going to be all right?" he asked.

She only planted her elbows on the table and buried her face in her hands.

"Out with it, Tara," he pressed at the risk of being rude. "I thought we'd gotten past this sort of thing. Surely we've come far enough to be able to talk through our problems, whatever they may be. We're two mature adults, Tara. If you can't tell me, who can you tell?"

"No one," she admitted. "That's why I'm here, Sean. I have nowhere else to turn. You're all I have."

"I'm not sure if that was an insult or a compliment."

Tara sighed, wishing she could avoid hurting him. "This has nothing to do with you, Sean."

"You're the woman I love. It certainly does have something to do with me." Still, she said nothing. "Tara, whatever it is, we can work it out. I promise you that."

She turned to him defiantly, almost angry. "Don't make me promises you can't keep, Sean. How can you possibly know whether or not we can work it out, when you have no idea what I'm dealing with?"

"How can I when you won't tell me?" His exasperation was evident.

"I don't know how to tell you," she muttered, her voice cracking again.

"Just say it and get it over with."

She nodded in agreement and took a deep breath. "You know how I was sick yesterday morning, and then I felt better?"

"Yes."

"Well, it happened again this morning."

Sean furrowed his brow, certain it was supposed to mean something, but he couldn't quite put it together in his mind. She looked directly at him then, and he saw courage gather in her eyes. But he didn't realize just how much courage she needed until she said, "And I'm late, Sean. *Very* late."

Tara kept her eyes focused on his, waiting for him to perceive the stark reality, wondering if he would. She didn't want to say any more. Her heart began to pound the same moment his eyes widened with understanding. "You're pregnant," he muttered, his voice dry.

Hearing the word, Tara winced and turned away, unable to face him any longer.

Sean tried to catch his breath, but he couldn't find the strength to fill his lungs. Questions pounded into his mind. Who? Where? *Why?*

Tara felt humiliated by his silence and turned further away, wishing she had the strength to get up and walk into the other room. The realization that his attitude could determine a great deal of her future was unnerving at the very least. Facing anything beyond Sean's reaction at this moment was incomprehensible.

It only took Sean a moment to figure it out, and his heart fell to the pit of his stomach. There was no other possibility. Suddenly all the pieces fit together, and part of him just wanted to break something.

"Tara," he said hoarsely, but she gave no response. "Tara," he repeated, taking her arm with one hand and lifting her chin with the other. He wanted to see her eyes when he asked her this. Still, it was not a question. "He raped you, didn't he."

That word struck her with unbearable harshness. Hearing it vocalized in reference to her was like a noose around her throat. Tara would have turned away had he not been holding firmly to her chin. Instead she just squeezed her eyes shut and tears trickled out.

"Well?" he nearly shouted, and she gave a barely perceptible nod. Sean's hand fell numbly from her face and she hung her head in despair. When the reality hit, Sean came to his feet so quickly the chair toppled over. Tara heard him groan and looked up to see him push a hand sharply into his hair. He kicked the fallen chair and it slid across the floor. Tara winced and put a hand over her mouth to suppress a whimper.

"I'm sorry," she cried softly. "I never meant to hurt you this way. Please forgive me, Sean. I'm so sorry for—"

"What in heaven's name are you talking about?" he demanded angrily, and she looked up in surprise. She shook her head to indicate she didn't understand and he added firmly, "What have you got to be apologizing for?"

"You . . . you told me not to go out with him. I should have listened to you. I should have been more in tune with the Spirit. I shouldn't have let it happen. I—"

"Tara!" He was appalled. "You are a victim here. Don't you *dare* even think of blaming yourself for this." Sean stuffed his hands into his pockets and kicked the chair again. He heard Tara whimper and fought to gain control of himself. Losing his temper would not solve anything. He drew a calming breath and asked more softly, "Why didn't you tell me before?"

"Oh, really, Sean." She turned away from him. "We had barely known each other a week. I couldn't bring myself to admit it to anyone. And somehow I made myself believe that it would just go away . . . that pregnancy wasn't a possibility. Oh," she cried, "I've been such a fool."

Sean went to his knees beside her and took her hands into his. "Tara," his voice broke. "I . . . I don't know what to do . . . to say."

"There's nothing anyone can do."

"Something like this shouldn't have happened to someone like you. Oh, dear God above," he cried, "why? Why!?" He took hold of her and buried his face into the folds of her shirt. Tara pressed her face into his hair and cried.

"Oh," she muttered when her stomach lurched, "I've got to get something to eat." Sean looked up in alarm just as she clamped a hand over her mouth. He started listing what he had in the fridge that he could feed her, but she ran into the bathroom and slammed the door.

Sean sat on the chair she had occupied. He felt angry and scared and sick, all at the same time. He pushed his hands into his hair and realized they were shaking. While she was obviously very ill on the other side of the bathroom door, he prayed inwardly and tried to think this through with some logic. He was practically a psychologist, for crying out loud. He ought to know how to deal with something like this. Then why was he falling apart inside? Because he *loved* her! That's why. But surely he could think clearly enough to handle this. Someone had to. She had no one else to turn to, and in truth, he wouldn't want her to. He couldn't expect her to think rationally. *He* had to. He just *had* to.

Then, somewhere in the back of Sean's mind, a memory started to trickle in. It caught him off guard and enhanced the sickness smoldering inside him. It was the reason he'd starting drinking and doing drugs. It was the source of the anger that had led to the accident. Was it possible that he might have a chance to redeem himself through this opportunity to help Tara? Whether it was or not, the thought gave him a glimmer of hope that helped him think more clearly.

When Tara emerged from the bathroom, she looked pale and drawn. "I think I need to lie down," she said and moved past him into the front room.

"Are you all right?" he asked. She glanced at him dubiously and he added, "Stupid question. You said you need something to eat. What can I get you?"

"Toast," she stated. "Make it dry."

"You're joking."

"No, I want dry toast, and some of that herb tea you have hiding in the back of the cupboard."

While Sean prepared what she'd asked for, he had to stop three times to will himself to quit shaking. He took the toast and tea to the front room and set them on the end table.

Tara sat up and took the steaming cup into her hands. "Thank you." She closed her eyes and put her face into the rising steam. "You're really very good to me, Sean. I don't know what I would do without you."

"It's the other way around," he said quietly, but she didn't acknowledge it.

After she ate a piece of toast and seemed to relax, Sean put a gentle hand to her shoulder. "Everything will be okay, Tara."

She shook her head skeptically. "How can you possibly say that?

This is not something we can just rationalize away, Sean. I've got a very real problem that could affect my entire life." She pressed her fingers to her forehead and squeezed her eyes shut. "I can't even imagine how I'm going to face my family, or go to church, or even walk the streets. And what about my education? Oh, I can't even begin to think what to do, where to start. I can't imagine what I ever did to deserve this."

"Now, hold on." Sean sat forward to face her. "Let's get one thing straight right now. You're a *victim,* Tara. This is not some punishment from God. It's just one of those awful things that happen in this world."

Tara closed her eyes and sighed. "You can't know how I've needed to hear someone say that."

He put his arms around her and held her close. If nothing else, she was not recoiling from him as she had when this had happened initially. In spite of the enormity of the problem, there were no secrets between them now, and he felt a deepening of the bond they shared.

"Just so you don't have to wonder," he said quietly, "I'm with you in this. You're not alone, and don't forget it for a minute."

Tara held to him tighter and silently thanked God for sending Sean O'Hara into her life. Even if they never married, he was the right friend at the right time, and she needed him. "Thank you, Sean," she whispered. "You can't know what that means to me."

"All right," he cleared his throat, "we need to talk this through. There are decisions to be made that can't be avoided."

Tara nodded stoutly and sniffled.

"But first of all, I think you should have a pregnancy test, just to be sure. I can pick one up when I get groceries."

Tara wanted to protest, but she nodded in agreement. In her present state of mind, she needed him to think this through.

"And once we know for certain, you need to see a doctor and—"

"Now, wait a minute." She held up her hands. "Slow down. I'm too exhausted to think at all right now, and—"

"You're right." He touched her face, her hair. "I'm sorry. Why don't you rest a bit, and I'll hurry and get my errands done. That will give us a while to absorb this a little, then we can talk it through."

Tara nodded gratefully and he left a few minutes later. She hoped Sean wouldn't mind if she used his bed. She lay there for nearly an hour, wishing she could feel anything but despair. Then she slipped into an exhausted oblivion.

Sean returned and momentarily panicked, wondering where she had gone. Then he found her sleeping soundly in his bed. He couldn't resist just watching her. He couldn't believe how much he loved her. And he could hardly bear the heartache that crept in when he thought of what she had been through, and what she would still have to endure as a result.

Not wanting to disturb her, he quietly closed the door and went to the kitchen, fighting the anguish inside as he put away the groceries and threw together a casserole and a salad so she could have something decent to eat when she woke up.

Tara slept until late afternoon, and while Sean knew she needed her rest, he felt anxious, wanting to be with her, to talk this through. The phone's ringing startled him. He picked it up with an unintentionally terse, "Hello."

"I'm looking for Tara Parr," a woman's voice said. "One of her roommates gave me this number. Is she there, by chance?"

Sean was about to lie, not wanting to admit she was asleep here when he didn't know who he was talking to. But he looked up to see Tara standing in the hall.

"Yes, she's here," he said quickly. "May I ask who's calling?"

"This is her mother."

Sean was really glad he hadn't said she was asleep. Or better yet, he could have told her Tara's clothes were hanging in his bathroom. He quickly tried to cover his nerves by saying, "Well, hello Mrs. Parr. We meet at last."

"You must be Sean," she said cheerfully.

"Yes, I am."

"Tara's told us so much about you. All good, of course."

"I can say the same about you," he replied. "Just a minute, I'll get her."

He handed the phone to Tara. After a moment she said, "Yes, Mother, we're minding our manners." Sean smiled at her, but her expression told him she was wondering how she could ever tell her parents that she was pregnant. He went to the other room to give her some privacy, and had dinner ready to serve when she hung up the phone.

"You okay?" he asked.

"As good as could be expected, I suppose. At least I got some rest."

"You looked beautiful asleep," he said, and a timid smile managed to peek through her disheartened countenance.

"At least I don't have to wonder why I've been so tired lately." She yawned and absently straightened her hair. "I thought it was because I stay up late too often, talking to you."

"That could be part of it. Because I'm always tired, too."

Tara sat at the table and lowered her head into her hands.

"What did your mother want?" he asked, pouring her a glass of milk.

"She just felt like . . ." her voice trembled, ". . . she should call and see if everything was all right."

"She obviously cares for you very much."

"Yes," Tara admitted, "my parents are good people, and . . ." She startled him when she pushed her plate away and pressed her hands over her eyes. "How can I ever face my family?" she cried. "How am I even going to function without feeling like some kind of spectacle wherever I go and—"

"Tara, have you ever considered that it might be better to just make it known publicly and—"

"No," she snapped, "absolutely not! Obviously there are some people who will *have* to know, but I will not be known publicly as 'the rape victim.' I won't do it. I can just imagine people staring at me and speculating about the whole thing—wondering where it happened, and who did it to me." Her voice rose steadily in a heated rage as she mimicked the gossip. "What kind of things did he say to her while she was pinned on the ground? What did she do to lead him on? What kind of person is she to bring this kind of tragedy upon herself? Where did he touch her, and what did he . . . Oh!" She almost howled toward the ceiling, then she wrapped her arms over her head and sobbed.

Sean wanted to just take her in his arms and soothe the hurt away. But he felt stunned and unable to react. While he convinced himself it was likely better to just let her get it all out without his interference, he was beginning to feel a little nauseated himself.

"I can't face it publicly, Sean," she cried. "I can't even face it privately."

"Okay," was all he said.

"You know," she went on, instinctively wanting to rid herself of the thoughts she'd been nursing in solitude all these weeks, "I always tried to do the right thing. I've never seen an R-rated movie, Sean, because I didn't want my mind polluted with words and images that might plague me. I double-dated until college, and I always tried to make the right choices, because I wanted to come into a marriage and be able to give myself as a pure, undefiled woman."

Tara couldn't help looking at Sean then, but the anguish in his eyes only deepened the poignancy of what she'd just said.

"And here I sit." She threw her hands up, then pushed them almost brutally through her hair. "Just when I think I can get it out of my mind, I close my eyes at night and hear the vile, filthy things he said to me. I've awakened in a cold sweat so many times, feeling as if his hands were all over me again. And now—now—I'm pregnant with a child conceived in an act of violence." She finished in a tone of despair, "I don't know how to deal with this, Sean. I don't know where to start."

Sean was surprised at how quickly he knew what to say. "Do you believe this is your fault?"

Tara thought about it. "No. I mean . . . there are moments when I wonder what I could have done differently. And I should have listened to you when you told me not to go out with him. But it's done, and it can't be changed. And no matter what mistake I might have made, it didn't warrant such a consequence. He had no *right* to do that to me."

"I agree with you, Tara," he said, relieved to see that her attitude was emotionally healthy for the most part. "And what about Danny? Do you think he should get away with doing this to you?"

"He obviously has."

"Why?"

"Because he told me in no uncertain terms that he would testify that I had led him on, and teased him, and then expected him to stop."

"You were bruised and battered, Tara. You could hardly sit down for a week. There was evidence enough to—"

"Well, the evidence is gone now, Sean!"

"Not all rape victims are battered, Tara. Some have no physical evidence at all, but they still have a case. Maybe you should—"

"I'm *not* pressing charges, Sean. I can only cope with so much. I'm pregnant. But what evidence is that? It could have happened any time, with anyone."

"They can prove the baby is his, and—"

"I'm not pressing charges, Sean. It's easy now to look back and think I should have handled things differently. But I was in shock. I'm *still* in shock. I'm not going to sit around stewing over what I might have done differently, because it's going to take everything I've got just to make it through this."

After a long silence, Sean spoke again. "Tara, there's something that's been bothering me. I don't want to ask this, but . . . well, you told me a long time ago that he turned into Mr. Hyde when you told him about me. What happened, Tara? Obviously I have something to do with this, and I need to know what happened."

Tara expected to feel upset, but she was relatively calm as she began to repeat the story to Sean. Perhaps she was becoming accustomed to despair. Feeling somehow detached and numb, she told him everything—things she would have never contemplated saying aloud to a man. But he listened with compassion. She finished by telling him her fears of anyone finding out, and how hard she had tried to keep it a secret.

"But you knew," she stated, "didn't you."

"Like you, a part of me didn't want to accept it, but deep inside I knew. You had all the signs."

"So what now, counselor?" she asked. "What do I do now?"

"First of all, I think you should eat something. You're going to need your strength. And then I think you should find out for certain. I bought a pregnancy test. It's in the bathroom."

Tara swallowed hard. "Okay," she stated, rising to her feet with fortitude, "I think I'll take care of that right now."

"I'll heat up your lunch." He glanced at the clock. "Well, I guess it's your dinner now."

The meal passed in tense silence. Sean knew there was much they needed to talk through, but he was afraid if he brought it up now, she wouldn't eat.

"So, now what?" she asked again while they were washing dishes together. "I need some direction here, Sean."

"Well, before we consider the effects of this on the long-term aspects of our lives, we have to decide where we stand on what to do initially."

"What do you mean?" she asked, liking the way he used *we*.

"I mean . . . what to do with . . . the baby."

Tara said with conviction, "Well, abortion is out of the question."

Sean had been hoping with all his heart and soul that she would say that. He had strong personal feelings on the issue, but he was not about to impose them on her. In truth, he felt he needed to give her all options, and support her in whatever she chose.

"I understand where you're coming from, Tara, and I agree. But I think we have to consider the fact that in some cases of rape or incest, the Church is not necessarily against it."

Tara had to think about that, but it only took a moment before she unconsciously put a hand to her belly. "This child is already alive and growing inside me. It has no control or knowledge concerning its conception. Perhaps such a thing would be right for others, but not for me."

Sean nodded, feeling his love for her deepen. He wished he could tell her what that meant to him. But now was not the time. He couldn't help but admire her for such conviction, knowing what the other options would mean to her life.

"That leaves two choices," he said.

"Which are?" Though she already knew, she needed to hear them.

"Either you keep the baby, or you put it up for adoption."

This answer was not so easy. "I have to think about that," she said, "and pray. I suppose I can't fast under the circumstances."

"No, but I can. And I will. Now, in the meantime, I think you should talk all of this through. We need to explore how you feel about each issue you have to face. Start by telling me what makes you the most afraid."

"I think the worst is facing my parents," she admitted. "They'll be heartbroken."

"I don't know them well," Sean said gently, "but I know what kind of daughter they raised. It won't be easy, but I believe if you tell them the truth they will support you in your decision."

"I'm sure you're right. I certainly can't go on keeping it from them. And at least I'm living here in Provo. I don't have to face my parents every day like I have to face my friends and associates here. How can I go to church and—"

Sean interrupted. "In my opinion, if you discuss this with your bishop, what anyone else thinks doesn't matter. They have no right to judge, and if they do, it will be for them to deal with."

"Yes, that's easy to say. But the thought of dealing with it a week at a time is not pleasant."

"I know," he agreed.

"And then there's my education. I can't imagine what I'll do about that."

"Right off, I'd say you finish through April, then you'll just have to take some time off. You can start up again when this is over." He paused and asked, "When do you figure it's due?"

"Early July, I believe." It sounded so far away that she felt suddenly overwhelmed with emotion all over again. "Oh, Sean," she put her head to his shoulder, "what am I going to do? How am I going to face this?"

"We'll face it together," he whispered and brushed his lips over her brow.

"You're so sweet," she said softly, "but honestly, Sean, I can't expect you to—" Tara stopped when he looked at her sharply.

"To what?" he insisted.

"Well, I mean . . . this changes everything. I certainly don't expect you to see this relationship through under the circumstances."

"Tara!" Sean was appalled. "I can't believe you're saying this. It changes nothing as far as you and I are concerned. This is only a temporary setback. If you think I'm going to give up the prospect of sharing my life with you because some jackass has no scruples, you can just reprogram your brain right now. We are going to get through this together, Tara, and I can promise you that somehow, everything will be all right. Whatever your decision, I will support you in it. And that's all there is to it."

Looking into his eyes, Tara could find no words to express her gratitude. She surprised herself by laughing. After all these weeks of fearing what he might do if he found out, the relief was immense. If not for the pregnancy, she could almost believe it was possible to put it behind her.

The pregnancy test was positive. Seeing the evidence brought on a fresh bout of tears, but Tara couldn't deny an underlying peace that she hadn't felt since this had begun. She was terrified by the reality, but Sean reminded her that the Lord was with her, and He understood. Tara knew he was right.

CHAPTER SEVEN

Tara cried herself to sleep in Sean's arms and woke up in the dark, disoriented and afraid. The vague scent of Sean's aftershave made her realize she was in his bed. But how did she get here? And where was Sean? She groped her way to the hall and searched for the light switch. By the time she found it, Sean was there.

"Are you all right?" he whispered.

"I think so." She squinted against the light. "It just took me a minute to figure out where I was. How did I . . ."

"You fell asleep, and I carried you to the bed."

"That's a romantic thought," she said, leaning her head against his shoulder.

"Well," he added facetiously, "I slept on the couch."

"What time is it?"

"It's nearly three."

"Whoa. It's a good thing my roommates don't pay much attention to when I come in."

"Actually, I called and talked to Vicky. I told her you weren't feeling well and fell asleep. I assured her I would mind my manners and take care of you."

"You think of everything."

"I try. But right now, why don't you think about getting a little more sleep?"

Tara nodded and went into the bathroom. When she came out, Sean was back on the couch. She turned off the hall light and crawled back into the bed.

It seemed that Sean had barely drifted back to sleep when an unfamiliar noise startled him awake. He waited with his heart pounding, wondering what it was.

"Tara!" he murmured under his breath and scrambled toward the bedroom, following the sound of her muffled cries. The hall light illuminated a path to the bed and he hurried to her side. It only took a moment to realize she was asleep. He shuddered at the way she thrashed about, moaning and muttering indiscernible sounds of protest.

"Tara, wake up." He nudged her carefully but nothing changed. "Tara," he said more loudly. When she didn't respond, he took her arms into his hands and shook her gently. She came awake abruptly, and immediately tried to hit him. He grabbed her arm to block it, and she erupted.

"No!" she cried and pushed him away.

"Tara." He reached for her, but she scrambled out of his arms and rolled onto the floor. "Tara, it's me," he insisted, but she was apparently so consumed with fear she paid no attention. Her breathing was sharp and frantic as she tried to get to her feet, and she stumbled into his arms. But rather than finding comfort there, the contact made her almost hysterical.

"Tara!" He spoke directly into her face and wrestled her to the bed, fearing she'd either hurt him or herself. "Tara, it's Sean. You're with me, and I'm not going to let anybody hurt you." She stopped struggling but her breathing was still strained. "Tara," he soothed close to her ear, "it's all right. It was a dream. You were sleeping in my bed, and I was on the couch. Do you remember?"

She moved suddenly, and he feared she would try to hit him again. Instead she took hold of him as if he could save her from drowning. She pressed her face to his chest and groaned.

"It's all right," he whispered, rocking her back and forth. "You were only dreaming, Tara. Everything's going to be all right."

Tara held to him tightly and cried, piecing together what had just happened now that she was coherent. She wanted to feel embarrassed, but she was too caught up in nightmarish memories to care. Trying to be free of them, she concentrated instead on Sean. Everything about him represented comfort and security in the midst of all this madness. He relaxed his head onto the pillow and eased hers to his shoulder.

"Are you going to be all right?" he asked.

"Eventually," she answered, trembling.

"Are you cold?" he asked and eased her subtly closer.

"A little," she admitted and he pulled the covers over them.

Tara tried to relax, but her attempt to distract herself was suddenly overcompensating. She moved her hand from his shoulder, slowly over his chest, allowing it to linger at the neckline of his T-shirt. Idly she toyed with the dark hair she had often noticed at the base of his throat. Her mind began to wander into areas it never had before. She wondered what it would be like to have him hold her and touch her. She was a woman with child, and yet she knew nothing of lovemaking and the pleasure meant to be shared between a man and a woman. As if Sean had read her mind, he shifted just enough to press his lips briefly to hers. She longed for it to go on and on, if only to keep her from feeling the despair of reality. But his kiss ended quickly and he eased away.

"Maybe I should go back to the couch, eh?" He said it lightly, but there was an unfamiliar husky quality to his voice. "You'll be all right now, won't you?"

"Yes," she admitted, "but . . ."

Tara tilted her face toward Sean's and he noticed how the angle of the light accentuated an innocent quality in her expression. He wanted more than anything to just love her here and now, to prove to her that intimacy between a man and a woman was meant to be beautiful. But if he did that now, he would betray the trust he was working so hard to earn. He would be turning his back on beliefs that he had sacrificed too much to be a part of. And worst of all, he would be offending God, who had brought so many miracles and blessings into his life. He just *couldn't*.

"Tara," he whispered, "I can't stay here with you like this and expect myself to . . ." He faltered when she held to him tighter, as if she were somehow afraid to let him go. "It's all right," he said gently and kissed her, wanting to offer comfort and assurance. But her response was so intense he knew immediately he shouldn't have done it.

"Tara." He drew away slightly but she nuzzled her face against his throat. "If we're not careful," he tried to say it lightly, hanging on to a single thread of rationality, "you're going to find yourself compromised."

"I don't care," she muttered. "I need you."

She pressed her lips to his again, and Sean didn't bother to analyze where her motives were coming from. He just kissed her like he never had before. A little voice at the back of his mind told him he'd had more than his fair share of loneliness. He needed her, needed to feel her close to him and share his life completely. How could he not recall that he'd had an active sex life at nineteen? And he'd not been in a situation since where it was necessary to draw the line and stop himself. Temptation ushered his body through a crack of weak thoughts. He drew her against him as if there was nothing beyond this moment. He kissed her face and throat almost wildly, keeping his hands pressed firmly to her back for fear of them wandering elsewhere by their own will. Somewhere in the middle of his internal battle between body and spirit, his mind uttered a silent plea for help. He could feel himself drowning, dragging Tara under the current with him, and he had no desire to come up for air. Then, at the same instant he felt the last grain of reason dissipate, Tara became abruptly stiff in his arms. A tiny whimper of protest escaped her lips, but it was all he needed to give himself a lucid slap in the face.

Tara didn't stop to analyze why she suddenly stopped enjoying herself. She only knew the pleasure had turned to fear instantaneously. There was no logical reason why being with Sean should remind her of the incident with Danny. But it did. It was so subtle she couldn't pinpoint it. In truth, she didn't want to. She only knew there was something in the way Sean had moved against her that brought all the memories rushing back. Sean seemed so caught up that she feared trying to stop him, but she barely reacted when he rolled away from her and sat on the edge of the bed as if he'd been struck by lightning. She turned the other way and tried to keep the tears silent.

"Heaven help me," he muttered under his breath. "What on earth am I doing?"

"It's not your fault, Sean," she tried to say calmly, but it came out in a squeak of emotion. "I shouldn't have—"

"Don't you dare try putting this on yourself." He sounded angry, and she just wanted to disappear. "After what you have been through, you shouldn't be expected to think clearly. I should be man enough to help you through this, not make it worse."

Sean shot to his feet and paced back and forth to release some of his nervous energy before he turned around and started all over again. Even now, he'd never wanted anything so badly in his entire life.

"I'm the one who wouldn't let you leave," she cried. "I'm the one who said I didn't care. I—"

"You *should* care," he countered just loud enough that he was glad this old house had thick walls. Eavesdropping neighbors had never been a problem.

"You're right," she admitted. "I should be thinking about you instead of myself. I shouldn't be so selfish and draw you into this just because—"

"You should care about *you!*" He sounded angry again, and she wanted to put her head under the pillow. "Do you have any idea what we are dealing with here, Tara? Your virtue is worth far more than a passionate moment in some—"

"I lost my virtue a long time ago," she retorted with the same anger. "But that doesn't give me the right to pull you into this and—"

In one agile movement, Sean's knees hit the floor beside the bed and he pulled her arms into his hands. "Stop it!" he demanded. "Do you hear me? Stop doing that to yourself." Tara held her breath as he almost touched her face with his, speaking in heated spurts. "You are a virtuous woman, Tara Parr. You are whole and pure. Do you under- stand me? You need to heal, Tara, not repent. You have committed no sin. You have done nothing wrong."

Tara finally caught her breath with a wispy sob. She crumbled into tears and he urged her face to his shoulder.

"I'm so sorry," she finally managed.

"You shouldn't be apologizing," he insisted. "I mean, it's not like you purposely planned for a nightmare."

She made a noise that almost resembled a chuckle.

"Do you have dreams like that often?" he asked.

"All the time," she answered, wiping at her face. "But this is the first time I dreamt I was struggling with a man and woke up to find one holding me. I guess I didn't react very well."

"It's okay." He handed her a tissue from the bedside table. "If I had taken you home when I should have, I wouldn't have been intruding and none of this would have happened."

Sean hugged her tightly, feeling suddenly emotional as he contemplated how grateful he was that it had stopped when it did. He wondered if she had any idea how close he had come to crossing irrevocable boundaries.

"I love you, Tara," he said close to her ear. "I love you more than life. That's why I'm never letting you stay here past your bedtime again. We have plenty to keep us busy, and we'd do well to stay that way." She gave a resigned nod and he kissed her quickly. "Now, try to get a little more sleep before morning. I'm going back to the couch."

Sean hurried out of the room before he changed his mind, but he didn't go back to sleep. Instead he stared into the darkness until it turned to light, consumed with the helplessness of Tara's situation. There were many things he could do to support her through this, but he couldn't stop her from having nightmares, and he couldn't make this pregnancy go away. He could be there for her to lean on and talk to, but he couldn't heal her wounded spirit. A little past eight o'clock, he finally came to the obvious conclusion. He couldn't help her, but the Lord could. Sean just had to figure out what the Lord wanted him to do.

Tara finally drifted into a fitful sleep. Her next awareness was daylight and Sean nudging her gently.

"Hey, beautiful," he said close to her face, "church starts in an hour."

Tara groaned and tried to sit up.

"Do you want me to go get some of your things, or—"

"I think I'm sick," she interrupted and hurried to the bathroom for the morning ritual of dry heaves, made worse by a headache that she knew was a result of all the tears she'd shed yesterday. She came out and announced, "Maybe you'd better go without me. I'm not sure I'm up to it just yet. I promise I won't make a habit of it. If it's all right, I'll just rest here."

Sean was obviously disappointed, but he made certain she got something to eat and promised they would talk when he got back. Tara locked the door behind him and finished her breakfast. She watched the morning broadcast of the Tabernacle Choir, then took a long shower. Wearing her own clothes again, she straightened up and made the bed, then went back to the kitchen when she became nauseated again. She was quickly learning that if she kept something in her stomach, she could avoid the queasiness.

In the quiet, Tara began to wish she had gone to church with Sean. She felt the oppression descend on her freshly, and the tears came with it. In the best of times, a week never seemed right without going to church and taking the sacrament. But right now she needed spiritual sustenance more than ever before in her life. Attempting to seek it elsewhere, she knelt by Sean's bed and prayed longer than she ever had in her life. Her knees were stiff when she finally stood up, and she went to find the latest *Ensign*. It was the conference issue, and she enjoyed rereading her favorite talks until she got sleepy and laid down on the couch to rest for just a few minutes.

Hearing a key in the lock startled her awake. She looked up to see Sean close the door and realized she had been dreaming.

"You okay?" he asked.

"Just a little sleepy." She laid her head back down and closed her eyes, trying to recall her dream. When it came to her she took a sharp breath and her eyes flew open, as if to test the reality. Would it still hold up in the light of day?

"Is something wrong?" Sean asked. She sat up and realized he was still standing there.

"I was just . . . dreaming."

Sean removed his jacket and tie and tossed them over the back of a chair. She thought how handsome he looked in suspenders, and held out a hand toward him. He took it and sat beside her, pulling her close to him and brushing his lips over her brow.

"I've been thinking," he said quietly, "that maybe you should have a priesthood blessing."

She pulled back, alarmed. "I don't want anyone to know that—"

"Hey," he touched her face softly, "hear me out, okay?" She nodded and he went on. "What you are up against is understandably difficult. I think it would be good for you to get some specific comfort and guidance from the Lord."

"I won't question that, but . . ." She looked at him searchingly. "Would you do it?"

Sean glanced down and took a deep breath. "I would be honored to give you a blessing, Tara. And I *could* do it, but under the circumstances, I think it would be more appropriate if you called your home teachers and . . ." He saw the protest in her eyes and lifted a hand to stop it. "Except in extreme cases, you should go through the proper channels. And I don't think you should be concerned about anyone finding out. The blessing comes from the Lord, Tara. He knows the situation, and I'm certain He can handle getting the message through without embarrassing you."

Tara thought about it for a minute and couldn't come up with a protest. She knew he was right and couldn't deny the wisdom in his suggestion. "Okay," she said, if only to be agreeable, "I'll call them."

He smiled and kissed her brow.

"How was church?" she asked.

He started telling her bits and pieces from the talks and lessons, but Tara's mind drifted back to her dream.

"Hey," he startled her, "where are you?"

"I'm sorry, I just . . ."

"What?" he persisted.

"It's just . . . this dream I had."

"Another nightmare?" he asked with concern.

"No," she drawled, then asked gingerly, "Is it . . . possible for prayers to be answered in dreams?"

"Of course. As long as the Spirit verifies to you that it's true."

Tara looked up at him with tears in her eyes. As soon as he said it, it happened. In her heart she knew what she was supposed to do. And the underlying peace she had begun to feel since she had been able to talk it all out with Sean filtered through her with verity. She knew the months ahead would be hard, but she could do it. Because she knew *why*.

In response to the silent question in Sean's eyes, Tara spoke in hushed reverence. "I dreamt that you and I were sitting together, much like we are now. We were holding each other and crying because of the heartache of what's happening."

"That's not too difficult to imagine," he said almost lightly.

Tara smiled and went on. "And then we became somebody else." Sean lifted an eyebrow. "It was vague, but I saw another couple, holding each other and crying, just the same way. I couldn't see their faces. I only knew why they were crying. And that was all."

"Why were they crying?" Sean asked, caught up in the spell.

"They wanted a baby." Her voice trembled. "They had everything in life they could ever want, except what they wanted most. They couldn't have a baby."

Sean was stunned.

"Don't you see, Sean?" Tara nearly beamed as she pressed his hand to her belly. "I don't know who they are, but this is their baby."

She leaned back and sighed, overwhelmed by the very idea. "It could take months to get used to the idea and deal with it. But I know it's right. I can't explain how I know, I just know. Somebody, somewhere, is praying for a baby they can't have themselves."

Overcome with emotion, Sean pulled her into his arms and just held her. He couldn't believe how his love and respect for her grew each day.

"It scares me," she said close to his ear, then she pulled back to look at him. "Part of me wants to be free of this child and the memories associated with it, while a part of me fears having to let go of something that is my own flesh and blood. But I believe it will be better this way. I will have the opportunity for more children. This child is not mine, Sean. I'm only being blessed with the privilege of giving it life." Tara looked at him deeply, wishing he'd say something. "Well, what do you think?" she pressed.

Sean swallowed and blinked several times. "I think you've made a wise and inspired decision. And I admire you for it. I'll do everything in my power to help you through it, Tara. Which brings up another point. I've made a decision of my own."

Tara felt some of the reality return as she wondered if he might tell her he didn't want to be seen in public with her once she started to show. She could hardly blame him. But it made her wonder how she would ever make it through the next several months.

"I want to marry you, Tara."

She absently put a hand to her heart. "I was hoping that when this was all over, you would still want—"

"No, Tara," he interrupted, "I want to marry you *now.*"

For a moment she was too stunned to speak. "Sean, you can't possibly mean that you—"

"Listen." He took her upper arms into his hands. "I love you. You love me. I think we both know we're supposed to be together. I've felt right about you since the moment I laid eyes on you. But I see no reason to wait. If I marry you now, we can stop the gossip and speculation before it starts."

Tara had to catch her breath. "I can't believe this. I don't understand why you would want to—"

"Tara," he interrupted again, "hear me out. You and I have been seen together for weeks. You've spent late hours with me and there are people who know it. Now, you have valid reasons to keep the truth from becoming public. So, if people are not aware that your pregnancy is a result of rape, they will assume that I am the father, and—"

"Good heavens!" she gasped. "It never occurred to me what the implications would be concerning you." She eased away and began to fidget with her hands. "Perhaps we shouldn't be seen together, or—"

"Don't you dare even say it! I am not staying away from you for the sake of a few gossipmongers. If people are going to think it's my baby, let them think it. I don't care. But I'm not going to let them wonder why I'm not marrying you to make it right."

"I'm so sorry, Sean," she muttered. "You shouldn't have to face this kind of thing and—"

"You're missing the point, Tara. I don't care about the implications. All I care about is having you as my wife. So, what if it's sooner than later? That's all the better as far as I'm concerned. I love you and I want to be with you. If I can marry you now and help ease some of the struggles, then we're just making a good thing better."

Sean waited expectantly for a response, but she just wrung her hands, obviously deep in thought. "Tara," his voice was gentle, "there are many things to consider. How do you think Vicky, and Heather, and Carla will feel about having a pregnant roommate?"

She squeezed her eyes shut. Just one more thing that had never occurred to her. A moment ago she had felt so sure that she could handle this, but the reality was far from easy.

When Tara remained silent, a nervous twitch crept up the back of Sean's neck. As unbearable as it seemed, he felt he had to offer her every option. "Of course, if you don't feel right about marrying me, all you have to do is say so." Tara opened her mouth to protest, but he held up a hand to stop her. "Just let me say this. Neither of us wants to wonder in later years if this marriage came about simply because of the pressure of these circumstances. I want your decision of whether or not to marry me to be completely separated from this dilemma. Do you understand what I'm saying?"

Tara nodded. But her head was spinning so fast she could hardly think. "I need some time," she said. "This is all so much . . . so fast."

"I understand." He pulled her close again. "Take all the time you need."

Sean was fasting, but Tara heated up some leftovers for herself and he helped her wash up the dishes. She called one of her home teachers and made arrangements to meet them both at five-thirty.

"Will you go with me?" she asked Sean as she hung up the phone.

"Of course," he smiled. "I wouldn't want to miss it."

Sean kept her distracted through the afternoon by reading some *Ensign* articles with her, then they read the Sunday School scripture assignment and discussed the lesson. All things considered, the day was relatively pleasant. Though Sean dreaded bringing it up, he knew what had happened between them the night before couldn't be ignored. They discussed it carefully and set some specific ground rules to avoid further temptations. Then they prayed together for much-needed help in remaining morally clean.

Tara dreaded the appointment with her home teachers, but she came away filled with immense gratitude—to Sean for having the insight to think of it, and to these good men for being worthy priesthood holders, willing to help her in a time of need. And mostly, to her Father in Heaven, for his compassion and mercy.

Tara did well at controlling her emotion until she was sitting in the Blazer. Then the full impact of the blessing came home to her and she cried cleansing tears, recalling again the words that had given her peace and strength.

In the blessing Tara was told that the Lord understood the circumstances she was in, and he was there to help her carry the burden. Many lives would be blessed as a result of her sacrifice and her obedience. She was told that her sins were wiped clean, and she was a pure and virtuous woman in the eyes of the Lord, just as she always had been. Tara was promised the guidance and comfort she needed to help her through her trials, and that hearts would be softened to understanding.

"You okay?" Sean asked, startling her from her reverie.

"Yes," she smiled serenely, "I believe I am. Thank you—for thinking of it, and for making sure I followed through. It was just what I needed."

"I'm glad it helped." He touched her face for a moment, then turned his attention back to the road. Tara looked ahead and realized they were turning into the main gate of the Provo Temple. The parking lot was empty, and Sean pulled into a space marked *General Authority.* He smiled at her then walked around and opened her door.

The day was cold in spite of blue skies, but the snow had been cleared off the walks. They strolled hand in hand around to the east side of the temple, where they sat close together on a bench and marveled at the beautiful edifice before them and all it represented. Following several minutes of contemplative silence, Sean abruptly took both her hands into his and went down on one knee.

"What are you doing?" she laughed.

"I'm proposing." He tried to be serious, but humor sparkled in his eyes.

"You already did that once today."

"Well, I don't want you to think I'm not sincere." His expression sobered so quickly that it took Tara's breath away. "I love you, Tara, and I'm asking you to marry me. I want to spend the rest of forever holding your hand."

Tara touched one side of his face and kissed the other. "I just need a little time . . . to be sure," she answered.

"Take all the time you need," he replied and came to his feet.

They went to a fireside together, and Tara couldn't deny that she felt much better. But she dreaded going back to her apartment. Being alone always made it harder.

That night as she lay staring at her ceiling, she wondered why it had been so easy to fall asleep at Sean's apartment, when she couldn't sleep at all here. She kept her mind in constant prayer, expressing gratitude for the answer to one dilemma, and requesting the answer to another. Everything logical told her she should marry Sean as soon as possible. But there was just a tiny nagging doubt inside.

At three she got up to read from the Book of Mormon and eat a sandwich. It seemed she was always hungry. Reading about the brother of Jared asking the Lord to light the stones for his barges, Tara realized that she needed to make a decision on her own. Then she could ask the Lord if it was right, instead of expecting him to make the decision for her. Just because she had been given an answer concerning this baby in such a miraculous way, by no means indicated she could expect such an answer for everything in her life.

Tara went back to bed and continued to pray silently. She told the Lord she wanted to marry Sean as soon as possible, and that she felt it was the right thing to do. She wanted to be with him forever, but if she could be with him through the coming months, it would make the whole thing so much easier.

Tara finally drifted into a peaceful sleep, but woke up nauseated and exhausted. She hurried to get to her first class, with crackers hidden in her purse. The morning was horrible, but Sean was waiting in the usual place to take her to lunch, just as he did every Monday.

As Tara walked toward him, he caught her eyes and smiled. She stopped for a moment and just watched him. She knew. It was as simple as that. There was no lightning strike. No thunderous feeling swelling inside her. She just felt peace, and knew it was because of him.

Sean's heart skipped a beat when he saw Tara approaching, then she stopped and he felt suddenly apprehensive. Was that any indication of how she was feeling about his proposal? In his heart, he knew he and Tara would be married eventually, no matter what. But he felt so strongly about doing it soon. Was he just impatient, tired of being alone? Or were his feelings warranted?

When Tara stood as she was, Sean walked toward her, fearing she had made the decision to wait. Or maybe she hadn't made a decision yet at all. Either way, he felt on edge as he reached out to take her hand. "Is something wrong?" he asked, pressing a quick kiss to her lips.

"Nothing unusual," she replied. Their eyes met and he felt a little better. She did love him. That was evident.

"How about skipping the cafeteria and getting some *real* lunch?"

"Okay," she replied eagerly.

Sean took her to J.B.'s and watched in amazement at how much she was eating.

"What?" she asked with her mouth full.

"Your appetite has certainly improved."

"Yes." She scowled, feeling a little torn concerning the reason. "Sean, there's something I need to tell you."

"Okay," he said calmly, defying the way his pulse was racing.

She leaned over the table and lowered her voice. "When this happened to me, one of my worst fears was the thought of losing you as a result. I suppose that's the biggest reason I didn't want to tell you. I . . ." Her voice softened with emotion. "I wouldn't have blamed or criticized you for not wanting to continue our relationship."

Sean's eyes widened; he was distressed that she would think such a thing. He tried to tell her but she spoke before he could.

"But, Sean," she took his hand across the table and squeezed it, "I'm so grateful that you love me enough to stay in spite of it. Ever since it happened, I've asked myself over and over what I did to deserve something so horrible. But in the last two days I've come to see it differently. Perhaps the Lord knew this would happen, and he knew it would be hard. But it was no coincidence that you came into my life when you did. Now I have to wonder what I did to deserve having such a wonderful man here to help me through the hardest thing I've ever had to face."

Sean gave an embarrassed chuckle. "There are still things you don't know about me, Tara."

"What?" she laughed. "Something worse than drugs, and drinking, and being disowned by your family?"

"Maybe," he said too seriously.

"I was kind of hoping you'd tell me there had been a woman in your life who had . . ." Tara stopped when his lips tightened and he looked away. The scar in his cheek turned white.

"There *was* a woman, Tara," he said soberly and turned to look at her. "I've wanted to tell you, but it never felt right. When I was baptized, the bishop told me it was not necessary for me to tell the woman I married about it. It was in the past and I had been forgiven. But I *have* to tell you. I can't live with something like that between us. I don't want to omit certain segments of my past when we talk. I can't."

"I'm listening," she said in a soothing voice that calmed him slightly.

"I was a troubled young man, Tara. Instinctively I knew that the pious beliefs in my home weren't right. But instead of searching for something higher and better, I went looking for my free agency. I was nineteen when I moved in with Liza. It lasted seven or eight months. She was the only one."

Sean held his breath, waiting for a reaction.

"Now we're even," she said straightly.

"Even?" he almost hissed. "Oh, no, Tara. Don't you dare try to compare. I made a choice. I had an immoral relationship with a woman because I *wanted* to. There is no comparison."

"It was before the accident. Before you were baptized."

"Yes."

"Then it's in the past. It's forgotten. The problems in my life are in the present. *We* have to live with them. I don't want to compare, Sean. I just want you to understand that until this happened to me, I somehow believed that people brought problems upon themselves with bad choices. If nothing else, I'm grateful to have the empathy to not only understand and accept your past, but to consider it a blessing. It would be far more difficult to give myself in marriage in this condition to a man who had lived a perfectly exemplary life."

Sean shook his head in disbelief. He loved her more every day. Being absorbed in what an incredible woman she was, it took him a moment to realize what she'd said. "In what condition?" he asked carefully.

"Pregnant with another man's baby," she whispered. "Or had you forgotten?"

"Are you trying to tell me that . . ." He couldn't find the words.

"I'm trying to tell you that I've made my decision. I want to marry you as soon as possible. I need you, Sean. Not just now, but forever. And when this is all over, we'll have our own family."

Sean squeezed his eyes shut for a moment, absorbing the news, then he leaned over the table and kissed her as if no one else were around. He laughed in the midst of it, then he kissed her again. "I love you, Tara."

"I love you, too," she smiled. "Now, eat your lunch before it gets cold. We've got classes to get to."

When they were back in the Blazer, Tara said, "There's something else I need to tell you."

"Okay."

"I have to tell my family the truth. They need to know. Friends and acquaintances change over the years, but family will always be there."

Sean swallowed the irony he felt concerning his own family. "If you feel you should tell them, then you should."

"I guess what I'm getting at is . . . I'm supposed to go home for Thanksgiving, Sean. I've been trying to think of a good excuse not to go. I didn't think I could face it. But now I know that I have to go home, and I have to tell them."

Sean's eyes showed so much compassion that she had to glance down to avoid crying. "It's not going to be easy. My parents will be hurt."

Sean reached over and touched her face. "You should be grateful to have parents who care so much."

"Yes, I know." She managed a smile. "But I'm terrified to tell them." After a long pause and a warm glance, she added, "You will go with me, won't you? After all, you are my fiancé. It's about time you met my family."

Sean's genuine laugh put another bright star into the middle of all the blackness. "I can think of nothing more pleasurable."

That evening, Tara called her mother from Sean's apartment and told her they were coming. The following evening they were packing and baking pumpkin pies that Tara had promised to bring.

"Oh, shoot!" she called from inside the fridge.

"What?" he called back from the bedroom.

"I forgot to get more eggs. I've got to go back to the store."

"Do you want me to get them?" he offered.

"No," she grabbed her coat and the keys to the Blazer, "you keep packing. I'll just be a few minutes."

Tara hadn't been gone long when Sean went to answer a knock at the door. He was so stunned that it took him a moment to find his voice. "Melissa?" he finally said.

"Hello, Sean. I was in town and thought I'd stop by and see how you're doing."

"I'm great," he replied eagerly.

"May I come in? It's cold out here."

"Oh," he chuckled with embarrassment, "yes, please. I'm sorry. I was just so surprised." He closed the door and leaned against it while she took off her gloves and coat and glanced around. He was surprised to realize he hadn't thought about Melissa for several weeks. Their relationship had covered years in a roundabout way. Then, little more than a year ago she had taken a job over his marriage proposal and took off for California. At the time he'd been devastated. Now, he was grateful. As much as he had cared for Melissa, he'd had no way of knowing that what they'd shared was trite compared to that once-in-a-lifetime love he'd found with Tara.

"Baking?" she asked skeptically, sitting on the edge of the couch.

"Actually, it's a long story, but . . ." The timer on the stove rang and he hurried to turn it off and check the first batch of pies. "Do you know how to tell if these things are done?" he called.

"What is it?"

"Pumpkin pie. What else?"

"Stick a butter knife in the middle. If it comes out clean, it's done."

"Thank you," he said and did it. They looked done to him, so he set them out to cool and returned to the front room.

"So," he said, sitting across from her, "how are you doing? You look great."

"Thank you," she said with a smile, and he wondered what she was doing here. "I'm doing good, actually. But I have begun to wonder if I made some bad choices."

Oh, boy. Sean could feel it coming. But still, he didn't expect it to come so quickly.

"Sean," she cleared her throat and seemed nervous, "I know I hurt you very badly, and I want you to know I'm sorry about that. I've come to realize since then, that what we had together was something special and—"

"Melissa," he interrupted, "before you go any further, you should know that . . ." He hesitated when her eyes widened almost fearfully. Before he could think how to finish, Tara came through the door.

"It's freezing out there. I should have sent you out to . . ." Tara stopped with her coat half off when she saw the woman sitting on the couch. The first thing she noticed was the leather boots, the designer purse, the wool suit. The next was her obvious distress, as if seeing another woman come through the door was as much of a shock to her, as it was for Tara to walk in and find another woman sitting on Sean's couch.

"Well," Sean stood and helped Tara with her coat, "as I was saying, you should meet Tara."

If Melissa felt uncomfortable, she covered it quickly. She gave a genuine smile as she came slowly to her feet and held out a hand. "It's a pleasure to meet you, Tara," she said.

"Tara, this is Melissa James. She and I go way back."

"Hello, Melissa," Tara said kindly.

"Please, sit down and—"

"No, no. I can't stay," Melissa insisted. "As I was telling you, I was in town. My sister just had a baby, and I came to spend Thanksgiving with her and help out a little."

"Oh, that's nice. How is Ilene?"

"Doing good. This is their fifth now."

"That's nice," Sean repeated, and then there was an embarrassing silence. He put his arm around Tara and felt compelled to announce, "Tara and I are getting married."

"Oh, that's wonderful," Melissa said. In every tangible way she seemed genuinely pleased. But Sean saw something subtle in her eyes that made him wonder what was going on in her life to bring her back here now. "So, when's the big day?"

"Uh," Sean stammered, then he chuckled. Tara looked almost panicked. "Actually, we haven't set a date yet. I just convinced her yesterday. I guess that makes you the first to know."

"Well, I feel privileged."

"If you give me your address, we'll be sure to send you an announcement."

"It's still the same," she said.

"Then I have it. And what about Bryse and Ilene?"

"They're still in the same house in Salt Lake City. They'll grow old there, I'm sure." Following another silence she added, "So, how are Michael and Emily doing?"

"Good. We keep in touch."

"And the new baby?"

"She's more than a year now. The last pictures were adorable."

"That's nice," Melissa said. "Tell them hello for me."

"I will," Sean said easily.

Melissa gave her congratulations and made a graceful exit. Sean stepped outside with her and put a hand on her arm. "Are you all right?" he asked quietly.

"I'll be fine," she said, but he sensed she was fighting emotion. "She seems very sweet. I assume, then, that it *was* right for us to go our separate ways."

"She's incredible, Lissa. And one day you'll find someone who will make you feel more than I ever could have."

"I don't know about that." She looked at the sidewalk and cleared her throat. "But I wish you all the best. You deserve it."

"And you," he replied. "I'm glad you stopped by."

Melissa nodded and walked to her car—a BMW, he noticed. Sean was tempted to feel regret, but he only had to walk inside and take one look at Tara to know it was right.

"Another woman from your past?" The lightness in Tara's voice put him at ease.

"Actually, yes. But she's a *good* girl." He leaned against the counter and told her everything he knew she was wondering. "She waited for me when I went on my mission. Then I waited for her while she went on hers. I asked her to marry me, but she told me no and went to California for a high-paying job. At the time I was devastated. But I've hardly thought about her since I saw you."

Tara smiled while she stirred a huge bowl of pumpkin pie filling.

"She's very beautiful."

"So are you."

"She's obviously well off."

"She's not the woman for me." Sean pulled her into his arms and kissed her so long and hard she had to gasp for breath. "I love you, Taralee," he whispered against her face.

"For that I am truly grateful," she said, and he kissed her again. It was legal to kiss her while standing up in the kitchen.

Early Wednesday morning, Sean picked Tara up and loaded her bags into the back of the Blazer, next to the cooler full of freshly baked pies. They drove through Hardee's for breakfast and headed toward Colorado, while Tara's stomach churned with dread.

"Hey," Sean said lightly and took her hand, "it's not as bad as all that. They love you."

"I know," she admitted sadly.

"And I love you."

"I know," she smiled.

"And the Lord loves you," he added gently.

Tears pooled into her eyes as she said serenely, "I know."

CHAPTER EIGHT

"Tara," Sean said, when miles had passed and she was still staring out the window in apparent despair, "the shock will be hard for your parents. But they'll soon realize how well you're handling it."

"Am I?" She chuckled grimly.

"Actually, yes, if you must know. I think you're handling it very well. The emotion you feel at times is understandable. But you're willing to talk about it. You're not in denial. And you're making it through everyday life."

"I feel like I'm on the verge of a nervous breakdown."

"It may feel that way at times, but I really don't think it's that bad."

"I guess you'd know." She squeezed his hand. "I'd have gone over the edge if not for you."

"That works both ways, if you must know."

Tara had to smile. He really did love her.

They stopped at a Maverik store in Vernal to get gas, sandwiches, and frozen yogurt. Well-stocked on snacks to ease Tara's nausea, they continued east into Colorado.

"Tara," he said after a lengthy silence, "are you sure you want to tell them the truth?" She looked over in surprise. "I mean, maybe what they don't know won't hurt them. We'll just tell them we're getting married soon and leave it at that."

"I'm not going to even try to keep my pregnancy a secret, Sean. My mother and sister are very perceptive, and I feel too lousy to be putting on pretenses."

"Okay, so tell them you're pregnant. Tell them you fell in love with a scoundrel who couldn't keep his hands off you."

Tara blushed slightly and turned to look out the window. "That's hardly fair to you. You've been nothing but a perfect gentleman to me."

"Tara, you're their daughter. Let them blame me."

"Sean," she stated firmly, "you are about to become their son. They will likely be the only family you will ever have."

Sean kept his eyes glued to the road, but Tara didn't miss the tense twitch in his cheek.

"I won't have them thinking for the rest of their lives that you have wronged me when you didn't."

Nothing more was said for the next forty miles.

"You okay?" Sean asked when she put a hand absently to her belly. She nodded. "When do you want to get married? We should tell them our plans, don't you think?"

"I don't know. I'm ashamed to say I haven't really thought about that. You got any ideas?" She hoped he did. He was proving to be the brains for both of them these days.

"I've thought about it."

"And?" she prodded.

"Well, by a process of simple deduction, I figured that unless we are going to elope, which I think we'd rather not, we need a little time to plan a wedding. I'm sure your family would prefer it that way."

Tara nodded, grateful for his insight.

"And I would assume you'd want to get married at home, and maybe we could have a little open house in Provo."

She smiled warmly, feeling a glimpse of the reality.

"And logically, working around our school schedule, the best time would be during Christmas vacation."

Tara's eyes widened. To think of marriage in general, it seemed so soon. But to think of her condition, it seemed so far away. Still, he was right. "That sounds perfect."

"How about December 28th? Halfway between Christmas and New Year's Day."

"And every year for the rest of our lives, we'll have one extra holiday during the season."

"Yeah," he grinned, "we sure will."

"I'll agree to it on one condition."

"And what is that?"

"In a year, I expect you to take me to the temple and marry me again."

He squeezed her hand. "I would have it no other way."

Several miles later, Tara brought up something else she felt needed to be discussed. "Sean, if we are putting on the appearance that this is your baby, how are we going to explain coming home from the hospital with no baby?"

"I don't know," he said gravely. "I guess we'll have to think about that one."

"And speaking of hospitals," she continued, "how are we going to pay for this? Neither of us has any insurance that will cover maternity, especially under the circumstances. You've told me you'll support me financially, but I wonder if it's occurred to you that I could rack up some heavy medical bills in the coming year."

"It's occurred to me," he said as if it were nothing. "My job will cover our regular expenses with no problem. And I still have what I inherited from my grandfather put away that we can fall back on if—"

"That's for your education," she protested.

"Tara, when I came here from Chicago, I had practically nothing. The Lord has given me one miracle after another to provide for my needs. I am not worried about our financial situation. I'm certain we'll manage somehow. I have a few resources I can draw on. But chances are, by adopting, some financial aid will come from that direction."

"That's likely true," she said. "I hadn't thought of that."

"And just so you don't have to wonder, once we are married, I will make certain you have your tuition as well. I want you to get your degree, and I'll do whatever I have to, to make certain you do."

Tara glanced down humbly. "My parents will be glad to hear that, if nothing else. They've done a lot of scrimping to see that I got an education. My grandmother's helped some, but it's still been a challenge for them."

"Will anyone else be there tonight?" he asked, starting to feel nervous himself as the miles flew behind them.

"I don't think so. Mom said that my sister Debbie and her family are coming in the morning, and my brother Larry won't be able to come; which is just as well under the circumstances."

Sean gripped the steering wheel tighter when he knew they were getting close. Tara felt almost queasy as familiar landmarks began to appear.

"It's only another five miles," she said quietly, and a minute later Sean pulled over to the side of the road.

Tara looked at him in question as he took her hands into his. "A prayer perhaps?" he said and she nodded gratefully.

Tara's tears fell over their clasped hands as Sean uttered a carefully thought-out prayer, mostly on Tara's behalf. He asked that her parents' hearts would be softened, and that the words of explanation would come without difficulty or strain. He asked God's blessing to be upon their forthcoming marriage, and that they might be able to achieve their life's goals in spite of this setback. When it was done, he kissed Tara quickly and helped wipe away her tears.

"You'd better dry those eyes," he smiled. "We don't want to look like we've been fighting or something."

Tara chuckled and dug in her purse for a tissue and some makeup. While she touched up her face in the visor mirror, Sean followed her directions to the big, blue farmhouse sitting in the middle of endless acres of sheep-grazing land.

"How do I look?" she asked as he stopped the Blazer in front of the house.

"Beautiful," he said and touched her face. "Do you think they'll like me?"

"They'll love you!"

They were barely out of the Blazer when a middle-aged woman, as vibrant and slim as Tara, came running out the door, wiping her hands on the apron around her waist. Tara embraced her and they laughed together, making the time since she'd left home in August seem to disappear. While Sean unloaded their luggage, he observed the reunion from the corner of his eye. His heart pounded relentlessly.

"Mother," Tara said more loudly and turned toward him, "this is

Sean O'Hara. Sean, my mother, Mary Parr."

"It's a pleasure to meet you, Mrs. Parr." He extended an eager hand.

Mary took it into both of hers and squeezed. "I must say I was surprised when Tara called and said she was bringing you home with her. She's never brought anyone home for a holiday before. We're certainly glad to have you."

"It's a real pleasure to be here," he smiled, proud of his calm exterior.

Mary laughed softly. "Come in the house, Sean, and make yourself at home." He picked up their bags and followed her up the porch steps. Tara winked at him. "George is out checking some fence lines," Mary continued, holding the door open for them. "But he'll be back shortly for dinner."

She led the way up a narrow staircase in the center of the house, into a bright bedroom with sloped ceilings. It looked like something out of a movie with its perfect quaintness, right down to a homemade quilt spread over the bed.

"Now you just settle in, Sean," Mary said. "If you need something you can't find, just ask and we'll do what we can."

"Thank you," he said. "I'm certain I'll be fine. Tara takes good care of me."

He caught a subtly conspiratorial smile pass between mother and daughter, and he wondered what Mary was thinking. Tara had said she was perceptive, and it was apparent she knew they were serious.

He and Tara hardly had a moment alone before George Parr came in for dinner, and they were all seated around the kitchen table. Mary apologized for dinner not being much, since she was working on the Thanksgiving feast, then she served the best meatloaf he'd ever tasted, baked potatoes with real butter and sour cream, home-grown carrots and peas from the freezer, and a jello salad with home-grown berries floating in it. For dessert she produced a chocolate cake, and Sean swore he'd never been so full in his life.

The conversation hovered around the happenings on the farm, and Sean felt a genuine interest in something he'd never been a part of before. They talked a little about the classes Sean and Tara were taking, but the table was cleared with nothing personal being said.

Sean insisted on helping Tara wash the dishes while Mary put the leftovers away and mixed up a whole wheat pudding that had been a Thanksgiving tradition in her family for generations. While that was steaming and the kitchen was declared clean, the four of them went to the front room to visit.

Sean had sensed Tara's nervousness through the evening, though she did well in concealing it. As they sat close together on the couch, she took his hand. Her palm was cold with sweat. She squeezed so hard it almost hurt, but when he looked at her, she just smiled almost carelessly.

"So, where is your family for Thanksgiving, Sean?" Mary asked kindly.

He glanced toward Tara as she apparently realized she'd made an oversight in not mentioning his circumstances to her mother. But Sean was determined not to let such a thing make this evening any worse. And he had to admit that being in this home, with the prospect of finding family among these people, had already helped ease the ache a little.

"I'm afraid I can't tell you," he stated. "I haven't spoken to any of them for over five years."

George and Mary looked astonished, and perhaps concerned that he might be at fault, until he added, "My family comes from a strict Irish-Catholic origin. When I joined the Church, they made it clear they would never see me again."

Their faces filled with compassion, and for a moment Sean feared that Mary might cry.

Tara eased the silence by jumping into the subject that neither of them felt prepared to face. "But Sean's found a new family," Tara said proudly.

"Really?" Mary smiled while George just observed.

"I've taken the liberty of accepting him into ours."

Sean gave her a warm glance and saw the fear becoming evident in her eyes. He felt her grip tighten on his hand and returned it with reassurance. They both knew this would be their only opportunity to discuss their circumstances without the distraction of the holiday and Debbie's family flitting about.

"Is this an announcement?" George asked, seeming amused.

Tara looked nervous so Sean took over. "Yes, it is," he said proudly. "I've asked Tara to marry me, and she told me yes."

Mary put her hands to her face with a breathy laugh. "Why, that's wonderful. Did you hear that, George? Our baby's getting married."

"I've got ears, Mary," he teased, then to Tara, "That's fine, sweetheart. We're real happy for you."

"Well, when?" Mary laughed again. "Have you set a date yet, or—"

"Yes, we have," Tara interrupted and Sean could almost feel her insides trembling.

He finished the announcement. "December 28th."

Brows furrowed in question. "So soon?" Mary asked. "Why, we can't possibly prepare a big wedding in such a short time, with the holidays and all."

"Under the circumstances," Sean said, and Tara wished she could tell him how grateful she was that he could come up with words she couldn't find, "we felt it would be better to marry during Christmas vacation, rather than waiting for the next school break."

Mary's perception became evident. "What circumstances?"

Tara caught Sean's glance. How she wished she could just say that they were so much in love they didn't want to wait. Though it was true, it wasn't the reason they needed to hear. She saw Sean open his mouth to speak, but she held up a hand to stop him, knowing she had to tell them herself.

"I'm pregnant," she said stoically, blurting it out before she had a chance to think about it.

An angry hardness clouded George's expression. Mary's face reddened and tears came into her eyes. Unbearable silence hung in the room until George finally said, "I would have expected better than that of you, girl."

Sean put his arm protectively around her shoulders and felt them quivering. He was about to say something on her behalf when Mary finally found her voice. "Tara Parr. What kind of madness has gotten into you? Of all my children, you were the one I never worried about. I always thought you had the strength to—"

"Wait a minute." Sean held up a hand and moved to the edge of his seat, keeping a hand on Tara's shoulder. "Tara is not at fault here. I—"

"We'll get to you in a minute, young man," Mary interrupted crisply. "Right now, we are talking to our daughter."

Tara bit into her knuckles to keep from crying out. Sean continued to protest. "If I told you I was the father of this baby, and its conception was wholly my responsibility, would it make any difference?"

"It takes two people to create a child, Mr. O'Hara," Mary scolded. "My daughter is an adult, capable of making her own decisions, and paying the consequences for them. Perhaps you should leave us alone and let us discuss this."

"No, I will not," Sean insisted, wondering if it was really necessary for so much anger to be thrown about. "I am a part of this, and I will not leave Tara to face it alone."

"I can't believe this," George spoke up. "Of all the—"

"Wait a minute." Tara sat forward and held up her hands. "Stop it. All of you. There is a lot of misunderstanding flying around here, and I will not allow this to go any further without the facts being laid out." She met Sean's gaze and found the strength to go on. "First of all," she stated calmly despite her visible trembling, "Sean is just trying to be noble. And it only makes me love him all the more." He looked away and sighed. "But the truth is that Sean's only part in all of this is that he is the man I love and he is going to marry me. This is not his baby." Mary's eyes widened. George's brow furrowed. "Sean has been nothing but a perfect gentleman to me, and I will not have you thinking otherwise."

Tara took a deep breath. Sean turned to see her chin quivering as she squeezed her eyes shut.

"I assume there is a logical explanation for all of this," Mary said when no one else spoke.

Tara felt a knot gather in her throat so tightly she could hardly breathe. With a raspy voice she said to Sean, "I can't say it. Please tell them. They have to know."

Sean sighed, then nodded. He slowly crossed his ankle on his knee and took Tara's hand into his.

"Tell us what?" Mary's voice betrayed that she was beginning to fear this would not be something she wanted to hear.

"Uh . . ." Sean began carefully, "several weeks ago, right after Tara and I met, she . . ." He met her eyes. She nodded and bit her lip. "Tara was raped."

"Good heavens!" Mary gasped, then clamped a hand over her mouth and another to her middle as if she suddenly felt sick. George seemed to meld into his overstuffed chair. The sobs rose into Tara's throat and she turned her face to Sean's shoulder. While he held her and let her cry, the revelation was absorbed by her parents and Sean felt tears threatening in his own eyes. It was downright pitiful to see how one crime of passion hurt so many lives.

"Who did this to you?" George finally came to his feet. "I want to know."

Tara showed no response but a shake of her head.

"I've already tried that," Sean informed him quietly. "She . . ." He hesitated when he felt Mary's eyes on him as well, waiting for an explanation. He glanced again to George. "Maybe you'd better sit down. This could take a few minutes."

George backed into his chair again, and Mary sat forward in hers, keeping a hand over her mouth, tears brimming in her eyes.

"It happened in a dating situation," Sean explained. "Tara had gone out with him several times, but considered it merely a friendship. She's told me he occasionally showed signs of being obnoxious or disrespectful, but they were actually friends."

Sean pulled Tara closer. "After she and I had gone out three days in a row over a weekend, we both felt strongly about our relationship. When she told this guy about it, he just . . . went crazy. The rest is not worth repeating."

"Well, where is he?" George demanded. "The man should be behind bars."

"And I agree with you on that, Mr. Parr," Sean said firmly, "but Tara insists this is to remain a private matter. She tells me he laughed at her and told her it was her word against his, and she could count on him testifying that she had led him on and . . ." He stopped when Tara became more upset. "Well," he finished, "you know what I'm saying. Personally, I'd like to get my hands around the guy's throat, but she's determined to keep it private, and I must say I understand why."

A moment later, Mary came across the room and sat on the other side of Tara. Gingerly Mary touched her arm. Tara turned and fell into her mother's arms, where they cried together. Sean was surprised when Mary looked up at him over Tara's shoulder. Her eyes filled with genuine warmth and she pressed a hand to his face. Sean put his hand over hers and silently thanked God for having the worst behind them.

George soon joined the circle and put his arms around his daughter. Then he offered Sean a firm handshake, declaring soundly, "Forgive us for jumping to conclusions, son. We're glad to know Tara's had you to help her through this."

"She's easy to love," he replied softly, and Tara managed a meek smile.

When emotions had quieted and everyone returned to their original seats, Tara said shakily, "It was Sean's idea to marry now, rather than waiting as we had originally discussed."

"But won't people believe that . . ." Mary didn't seem to want to finish.

"I figure whether I marry Tara or not, people will assume the baby is mine. Let them believe what they want. At least I can make it right. We've made the decision to tell no one except our bishops and Debbie. Tara wants her sister to know. Beyond that, this is my baby, and my responsibility."

Mary made a noise that was a combination of joy and anguish. "Tara told me over the phone you were too good to be true, but I never dreamed . . ."

Sean felt embarrassed and decided now was a good time to set the record straight. "I'd like to say something, if I may. I am not doing some great, heroic thing here. I fell in love with Tara the moment I saw her, and it's purely selfish for me to want to be with her. If Tara had told me she had cancer, or even AIDS, I would have loved her just the same, and I would have married her and been grateful for whatever time we were allowed together. I admit these are difficult circumstances to begin our life together with, but in the eternal perspective, it will only be a temporary setback. We plan to be sealed a year after we're married, and we will carry on with that as our primary goal." He leaned back. "That's all I wanted to say, except that I believe Tara would have done the same for me if tragedy had struck my life, and she would not have called it a sacrifice."

After a moment of silence while Tara admired Sean openly, George announced, "We're proud to have you a part of the family, young man."

"Amen to that," Mary added, then she sighed and clapped her hands together. "Well, I guess we have a wedding to plan."

"We don't want to go to too much trouble," Tara said, her expression betraying the relief she felt to have this over with. "But we do want it to be memorable. Neither of us ever intends to get married again." Sean smiled at this. "We'll try to keep it simple and keep costs down as much as possible. Sean and I can help some, and if we can't afford something, we'll manage without it."

George announced that he had some money put away with Tara's wedding in mind, then Mary began spouting off ideas. Sean leaned back and put his hands behind his head, stretching his legs out and crossing them at the ankles while he listened with pleasure to his wedding being planned. He and George gave little input, but were included nonetheless, and Sean felt better about everything to see Tara's obvious display of happiness and relief. He knew there was much ahead that would be difficult, but they were making considerable progress.

They decided at Sean's suggestion to decorate in reds and greens, using typical Christmas decor to save money and create a unique atmosphere. Mary had acquaintances who could do the cake and flowers and help her prepare simple refreshments. And Sean had a friend who was fast becoming a professional photographer and would certainly be willing to do pictures for much less than normal.

They talked late into the evening while Mary jotted everything down in a notebook, knowing they would need to have much of this planned and decide who was going to do what before the weekend was through, in order to save time and long-distance calls. When it seemed to be planned as much as it could be without consulting others, the reality hit them again.

"Tara," Mary asked softly, "are you all right?"

"I'm better now." She smiled weakly. "Knowing I have your love and support makes everything much easier, and the wedding will not only ease the shame, it gives me a distraction and something to look forward to." She touched Sean's face. "I think we'll have a good Christmas."

"I know I will," Sean grinned. "I'm glad I won't be spending Christmas alone."

"Oh, how dreadful that must have been for you," Mary said. "Have you been alone all these years?"

"I was alone my first year in Utah, which I admit was one of the hardest times in my life. But then a family took me in and made me feel right at home. However, they've gone back to Australia now, and I was a bit worried about what to do with myself through the holidays."

"I assume you'll both be coming here as soon as classes end," Mary said with enthusiasm. "We'll have such fun."

"Mother," Tara felt the need to make another point while they had the chance, "I'm going to tell Debbie, and I know I can trust her, but beyond that, I don't want anything said. Since we'll be living in Provo, I doubt anyone around here will figure out that I'm pregnant, and it's better that way. Let them come to their own conclusions. In a few years when we've been through the temple and all of this is in the past, it will be forgotten."

Mary's brow furrowed as a thought apparently occurred to her. "But of course, there will be the baby."

Tara exchanged a supportive glance with Sean. "I've made the decision to place the baby for adoption."

George and Mary exchanged an anxious glance. "I can understand why that might be better in many respects," Mary said, "but it could also be very difficult. Might I ask why?"

"All I can say is that I prayed about it, and I know that this baby is not for me." Her emotion returned, choking her up again. "It's difficult to explain, but something inside me knows there is someone out there who desperately wants a baby and can't have one of their own. This is their baby."

"You're quite a girl, Tara," George said.

"You can say that again," Sean agreed.

"I have to say," Mary interjected, "I can't believe the coincidence. When I named my baby Tara, I never expected her to marry a man named O'Hara."

"I think I'll start going by Taralee," she said with a chuckle. "Tara O'Hara sounds pretty silly."

"I like it," Sean grinned.

Mary started to laugh and said, "It's a good thing I didn't name you Scarlett."

CHAPTER NINE

Far past bedtime, Sean and Tara sat together at the top of the stairs.

"Feeling better?" he asked.

"Oh," she laughed softly, "you can't imagine."

"I think I can." He smiled and brushed a light kiss over her cheek. "They're good people, Tara. I can see why you're such an incredible woman. I love them already."

"And I believe they love you, too." She laid her head against his shoulder. "I can't thank you enough for what you did down there."

"It was purely selfish." He chuckled. "Purely selfish."

"I don't believe that for a minute."

"Tara," he said in a hushed voice, "it's difficult for me to explain the things you have done for me; things that somehow make up for parts of my life that have been less than favorable."

"Like what?"

"Uh . . . I don't think this is the right time."

"But you told me you didn't want any secrets between us."

He smiled. "Yes, I did. And I don't believe there are any *secrets*. There are simply things that aren't easy to talk about. But one day I will; I promise."

"Okay," she agreed reluctantly. "I suppose we should get some sleep. Debbie only lives an hour away. The house will be crawling with children early, I'm sure."

"How many did you say she has?"

"Four, ranging from one to ten."

"And Larry's still single, eh?"

"Forever, I believe."

"Do you think he'll come for the wedding?"

"I assume. He usually comes home for Christmas, so that makes it easy."

"We were clever about that, weren't we." He chuckled and hugged her tightly.

Tara slept better than she had in weeks, and woke feeling a deep sense of contentment. She could smell roasting turkey, and she knew Sean was sleeping in the next room. Anticipation hurried her out of bed, and in no time she was showered and dressed. She made her bed and straightened her room, feeling well prepared for a much-needed holiday. Even the prospect of telling Debbie didn't seem too ominous.

Tara went to Sean's room and found it empty, then she realized she could hear the shower. She made his bed, too, and pondered what it might be like to be married to him. Feeling a flutter of anticipation, she decided she could nearly forget about her pregnancy if not for the smoldering nausea. Not wanting it to worsen, she hurried downstairs in search of something to hold her over until breakfast.

"Good morning, dear," Mary beamed. "It's so good to have you home."

"It's good to be home."

"How are you today?"

"Just a little . . . nauseous," she admitted, but her mother only smiled. "Got any crackers?"

"Should be in the usual place."

Tara found them and began to nibble on one. Mary rinsed stuffing from her hands and put an arm around her daughter. "It's just you and me, dear," she said softly. "Are you all right?"

Tara hugged her mother tightly. "It's been really hard," she admitted, "and there are moments when it hits me and . . . well, I know there is much ahead that won't be easy, but I can honestly say that I'm doing okay. Sean has been so good to me. He treats me like a queen." She chuckled at the thought of their first date. "I have a lot to be thankful for," she concluded. "Most especially for such good parents. You can't know what your acceptance means to me."

"Oh, my baby." Mary hugged Tara and got teary. "You have

been so precious since the minute you were born. We would love and accept you no matter what. As awful as it is, I was relieved to know that you hadn't lowered your standards. I think that would have hurt us more, in some respects. But I want you to know that even then, we would have dealt with it, Tara. We would love you no matter what."

They embraced once more. "Thanks again," Tara said, grateful she'd told them the truth.

"And thank you," Mary replied, "for not letting us down."

"Well, it *is* Thanksgiving," George said from the doorway where he kicked off his boots, coming in from morning feedings.

Tara laughed and hugged her father. "Good morning, Dad. It's good to be home."

"It's good to have you home, sweetheart. And that's quite a man you've found there. God must have had that one set aside for somebody as special as you."

Tara beamed and headed for the stairs with a handful of crackers. "I'd better see if he needs anything."

She found him in front of his bedroom mirror, combing through his wet hair. He smiled when he saw her leaning in the door frame. "Good morning, the future Mrs. O'Hara."

"Good morning, my love."

He nodded toward the crackers. "You're going to get addicted to those."

"No, I think I'm going to get sick to death of them."

"How you doing?"

"Fine, and you?"

"I'm perfect," he grinned, setting down the comb. "I've got just about everything a man could hope for."

Tara held out a hand and he took it. "Let's go eat breakfast."

"I think this house has pixies," he whispered on their way downstairs. She looked up in question. "One of them made my bed."

"Good morning, Sean," Mary beamed. "Did you sleep well?"

"Never better," he told her. "I don't think I've ever been in such a comfortable bed."

"It's an old one," George said. "They don't make them like they used to."

"Sorry, it's just toast and cold cereal for breakfast," Mary apologized. "But we'll make up for it at dinner."

"This kind of breakfast will make me feel right at home," Sean said, and they gathered around the table to bless it.

They had barely finished eating when Debbie's family arrived and the house became a delightful frenzy. Introductions were made, then Tara left Sean with Debbie's husband, Derrick, while she and Debbie went upstairs to talk.

Sean enjoyed watching the children, especially the one-year-old, toddling around and getting into things. He thought of the baby Tara was carrying and realized that letting it go would not be easy. But he reminded himself that they would have their own children in time.

Sean and Derrick shared some casual conversation, then Derrick turned on the television to find the Macy's parade for the children. While Derrick became absorbed in the newspaper, Sean's mind was with the conversation taking place upstairs. He picked up a *Reader's Digest* and read the jokes while he intermittently watched the parade. He played a quick game of checkers with eight-year-old Brad, then tickled the baby a little and sent him giggling to his father for refuge. He went to the kitchen and asked if he could help; Mary insisted it was all under control, but she assured him he could help when it was time to set everything out. He promised to be back when he was needed and wandered through the house a little. When he could stand it no longer, he went upstairs but found Tara's bedroom door closed. He sat in his room a few minutes and had nearly decided to go outside when he heard a door opening and Tara's voice in the hallway. He moved to the doorway of his room and leaned there, trying to appear casual. Tara and Debbie turned to see him, and they both smiled. That was a good sign, especially considering the evidence that they'd both been crying.

"Everything okay?" he asked and Tara nodded. Debbie moved toward him and reached her arms around his neck with a firm embrace. Sean could do little but return it. "What was that for?" he asked when she stepped back and said nothing.

"For falling in love with my sister," Debbie said and hurried down the stairs.

"I think she likes me," Sean chuckled, then accepted a hug from Tara.

"I like you, too," she said. He laughed and kissed her.

Sean couldn't remember Thanksgiving ever being so complete. He'd never realized, until he found this opportunity to compare, that his memories of Thanksgiving with his family were always marred by the rigidity in his home. Of course, spending holidays with the Hamiltons had always been a treat, and they had been much like family to him. But this was different. He truly felt a part of this family, and the gratitude part of the holiday was taken very seriously. The blessing George Parr gave prior to the meal brought the Spirit into the room with such strength that all adult eyes were teary when heads came up after the amen. The food was perfect, the company incomparable. Much of the conversation centered around wedding plans, and Sean appreciated the attitude of happiness toward the marriage, without letting it be marred by the circumstances.

If Thanksgiving was a nearly perfect day, the following day was even better. Sean rose early and went out with George to help with the sheep. He found that he actually enjoyed the work. It felt good to be active with a purpose beyond keeping himself in shape. Sean truly liked George, and respected him a great deal. This was the kind of man he would want for a father-in-law, and he said as much on their way into the house. George just slapped him on the shoulder and said, "The feeling is mutual, son."

Following a hearty breakfast, the entire family went out to go sledding down the hill behind the barn. Then they made snow sculptures in front of the house. Mary herded her freezing family into the house for hot chocolate and turkey sandwiches before the little ones were put down for naps.

Before Debbie left in late afternoon, some phone calls were made, and the wedding plans began to take structure. Debbie was to be the only bridesmaid, and they went into town to choose fabric for dresses for Mary and Debbie, and Debbie's only daughter, five-year-old Megan. They politely took into consideration that Sean's family would not be there, and opted for a casual atmosphere, rather than a formal receiving line that would make the absence of the groom's parents too obvious. Tara tried on her mother's wedding gown and found it would fit with some minor adjustments. Mary pinned and tucked and declared she'd be able to adjust it. And the full skirt and high waist would easily disguise any weight she might gain in the coming weeks.

With lists made in detail, Debbie and Tara said their good-byes until Christmas. Hugs were shared, then the house became almost eerily quiet after they waved Debbie's family off.

When Sean commented on the lack of noise, George put on some old big-band records. He laughed when Sean got Tara dancing in the crowded front room. When Mary came to investigate, George took her hand and joined them. They spent more than an hour exchanging dance steps from their different generations, and occasionally exchanging partners.

After mutually collapsing from exhaustion, they all went to the kitchen to heat up leftovers. Sean declared it almost tasted better the second time.

"Let's see what you say when you have turkey for breakfast," Mary said, and he laughed.

On Saturday, Sean went with George to move the sheep, for reasons he didn't understand. Mary and Tara went to arrange for use of the church cultural hall, and to discuss flowers, cake, and refreshments with ward members and acquaintances who were willing to help. Tara reported later that no one seemed ill at ease over the hurried wedding. It seemed Christmas vacation was a logical time for students to get married, and as far as they knew it had been planned for months. If anyone had doubts over it not being a temple marriage, they were not voiced.

After Saturday evening's turkey pot pie, Sean declared that with Mary's cooking, he would probably enjoy turkey for breakfast after all. "What can you do with turkey and oatmeal?" he inquired with feigned innocence, and she gave him a friendly slug in the shoulder.

On Sunday Sean was introduced to an endless throng of ward members, who declared they would see him at the wedding next month. Congratulations were given genuinely and with enthusiasm, and he noticed that Tara looked brighter and more lively than she had in most of the time they'd been dating.

Following meetings, they spoke with the bishop to formally

request that he perform the ceremony. Neither of them intended to tell him the circumstances, but he seemed to sense that something wasn't right. When he came right out and asked, Tara told him the situation without getting terribly upset. The bishop showed full acceptance, and he took time to find a few scriptural references to assure Tara that she would not be held accountable for what had happened. He complimented them on the way they were handling the whole thing, and said he would look forward to the wedding.

Mary fed them lamb roast and potatoes that had been cooking through church, then they gathered at the front door to say their good-byes.

"Don't you worry, sweetheart," George said as he hugged Tara tightly. "Everything will be all right. And don't you let what anybody thinks or says bother you. Just do what feels right in your heart."

"Thank you, Dad," she said with tears in her eyes, then she hugged him again.

"I'll call you Saturday," Mary said, taking both of Tara's hands, "and let you know how the plans are coming. If you could pick up those gifts for Debbie's kids, it will help. I think we'll manage just fine."

"Thanks for everything, Mom." They embraced, then the attention turned to Sean. George shook his hand and Mary hugged him mercilessly.

"You watch out for her now," George said as they were walking toward the Blazer, and Sean realized there was a lot of concern and pain that George and Mary were dealing with that wasn't showing outwardly. He could almost imagine them crying together in the privacy of their bedroom, as they discussed the tragedy of what had happened to their youngest daughter.

"I'll take good care of her," Sean promised. "And thank you," he said with sincerity, "for one of the best holidays I've ever had."

"There will be many more," Mary assured him, and they got in the Blazer and drove away.

They hadn't gone far when Tara let out a whoop of pure joy, and Sean laughed. Everything was going to be all right.

It was late when they emerged from Provo Canyon and drove into the city. Sean had intended to go straight to Tara's apartment,

but he could see Christmas lights in the distance on University
Avenue and had an urge to go see them. He nudged Tara awake and
drew her attention to the scenery. A light snow was beginning to fall,
and the center of Provo appeared almost magical. The tabernacle was
framed in tiny white lights, as were the historical buildings on the
other two corners. The county courthouse was lit up as well, and red
and green lights were strung across the streets. Dozens of trees lining
Center Street were filled with lights. Sean had become accustomed to
living here, but he couldn't help thinking what a beautiful city it was,
in many ways. He would never forget the peace he'd felt when he
finally arrived here from Chicago, alone and scared.

"It's incredible, isn't it?" Sean said after making a U-turn so they
could see the highlights again. The snow was thickening a little, and
he was glad they weren't still in the canyon. But the effect at the
moment was beautiful.

"Yes, it is," Tara agreed.

The anticipation of Christmas and the forthcoming wedding
consumed him. And if that weren't enchanting enough, a popular
version of "Winter Wonderland" began on the radio.

In the meadow we can build a snowman,
Then pretend that he is Parson Brown.
He'll say, "Are you married?" We'll say, "No, man.
But you can do the job while you're in town."

Later on we'll conspire, as we dream by the fire,
To face unafraid the plans that we made
Walking in a winter wonderland.

Tara smiled and squeezed his hand. He knew she could feel it,
too, and he couldn't help laughing.

* * * * *

The remaining weeks of the term flew by with horrible weather
and a frenzy to get everything done. Amidst the classes and studying,

Sean and Tara spent hours searching for rings, a cake top, white shoes for Tara, and a number of other odd things required for a wedding. They found a veil that would go perfectly with the dress, and bought a number of items from BYU food services to assist the refreshment situation. Tara decided a tuxedo was a waste of money when Sean looked so fine in his double-breasted suit. And Sean decided he'd do without a best man. He had many casual friends, but there was not any one more special than another.

In a rare quiet moment, Sean called Michael and Emily. They were thrilled that he was getting married, and almost as disappointed as Sean that they would not be able to come. But they would try to arrange a visit soon after the wedding. Sean sent announcements to his family. He knew they wouldn't come, or even acknowledge it, but he felt they should know he was getting married.

Along with wedding preparations, they went shopping several times, trying to find just the right gifts for everyone in the family, as well as the things Mary had wanted them to pick up. One evening they went to the mall and split up to choose combination wedding-Christmas gifts for each other, with the agreement to spend only a specified amount.

Three nights before they were to leave for Colorado, Sean and Tara sat in his apartment to sort and wrap gifts while they listened to Christmas music on the stereo. Sean wrote everything down and checked all the wedding lists while he quipped, "I guess this is making a list and checking it twice."

"What else would it be?" she laughed and stretched after putting a tag on the last gift. She rubbed an ache in her lower back as she attempted to come to her feet, but only made it to her knees.

"You okay?" Sean asked.

"Just sitting too long," she said, but Sean suspected she was already beginning to feel the strain of pregnancy. Everything was going as well as could be expected, but still, Sean was concerned.

"I should call Mom and see if there's anything else she wants us to pick up, but I'm not sure I can get up."

"I'll call her," he said with mischief in his eyes, then he punched out the number. "Mother," he said when she answered, and Tara smiled. "You knew it was me? How did you know?" He paused. "Yes, she's fine. She's sitting right here, looking rather elfish in the middle of this mess of Christmas paper and bows. Yes, I think we're ready. We're just stacking everything in the front room here that goes. Tara's moved in all but the bare necessities, and we've checked our lists twice. I was wondering, do we get turkey for Christmas? Ham!" He feigned disappointment. "Well, what can you do with ham and oatmeal?" He chuckled, then he laughed harder. "You wouldn't dare," he said, then he laughed again. "Here, I'll let you talk to her."

Sean handed the phone to Tara, then took his turn listening while he folded the extra Christmas paper and stacked it up.

"I'm not feeling too bad. I still get nauseated, but I'm learning to control it. Yes, we went to the doctor yesterday. We told him the situation and he was wonderful. He said everything looks fine."

She told her mother about the shower her roommates had given her and all the wonderful gifts she'd received, most of which were stacked in the corner of Sean's kitchen; except for the personal things that were stashed in a drawer back at her apartment. Tara listened quietly for a few minutes, then said, "Yes, we love you, too. We'll see you in a few days."

Sean waved frantically to remind her of the reason they'd called. "Oh," Tara said, "do you need us to get anything else?" Tara tipped her head back and forth to indicate she was waiting for Mary to think about it. "Candy canes," Tara said and Sean wrote it down, "and icicles."

"Icicles?" Sean questioned. She shrugged and he wrote it down.

"Okay, Mom, we'll call the night before we leave and do a last-minute check. Tell Dad hi. We'll see you soon."

"Icicles?" he asked again when she hung up the phone.

"You know, those thin silvery plastic things, to hang on the Christmas tree."

"Oh," his eyes widened with enlightenment, "icicles."

The following evening, Sean and Tara had an interview with his bishop. Since they were going to be living in this ward, they felt it was appropriate to let him know they were getting married. And they both agreed that he should know the truth.

Before Sean had a chance to explain, Bishop Jensen said outright, "I can't help wondering why this is not going to be a temple marriage."

Sean glanced at Tara, relieved that she didn't seem upset or offended. He quickly explained the circumstances while Tara fidgeted with her hands. When he was finished, Bishop Jensen remained silent for a long moment, then cleared his throat and said, "Do you think it's wise to get married at this time?"

Sean was briefly caught off guard, but he answered with firm conviction, "We have prayed carefully about this, Bishop, and we both believe we're doing the right thing. As I said, we will be going to the temple together as soon as possible. It's not that we aren't worthy, we simply feel it's more appropriate to do it this way."

"I understand what you're saying, Brother O'Hara," the bishop replied stiffly, "but I wonder if you realize the difficult situation you're dealing with here."

Sean glanced at Tara and tried not to let her rising tears add to his frustration. He reminded himself that this man was his bishop, and calmly said, "We have weighed the options, Bishop, and we have carefully discussed every aspect of the situation as much as possible at this point. I can honestly say we have no doubts about what we are approaching. Of course, this is not an ideal situation to be married in, and we don't expect to get through the coming year without some difficulties. But better that we face them together."

The bishop cleared his throat again. "Forgive me, Brother O'Hara, but it's my opinion that you should wait to be married until this child is born and—"

"Excuse me, Bishop," Sean interrupted, keenly aware of Tara's quiet sniffling and her constant effort to keep the tears wiped off her face, "but I get the impression I'm not being heard. Tara and I are getting married next week because we love each other and we are meant to be together. We have prayed about it and we know it's the right thing to do. It has always been my understanding that the purpose of marriage is to commit yourself to a spouse for the rest of eternity, to bond together for the purpose of helping each other through the trials that will lead us back to our Father in Heaven.

"What Tara is going through right now is likely the most difficult thing she will ever face. I will not step back to allow her to face it alone for the sake of some abstract propriety, or the fear of gossip, or because it might be a strain. She needs me, Bishop. She needs someone to rub her feet when they swell, and rub her back when it aches. She needs someone with her in the middle of the night when she's having nightmares, or can't sleep because she's uncomfortable. She needs someone to be there when she gives birth to that baby, and when she has to give it away. I can't do that and adhere to my standards without putting a ring on her finger. We have made our decision through the proper methods outlined in the gospel, and I can tell you with all my heart and soul that we are doing the right thing. We would appreciate your blessing in that, and we hope to be involved in the ward and have opportunities to serve."

As Sean finished his little speech, Tara felt her heart swell with love for him. He thought of things that had never occurred to her. His commitment to her was heart-stopping. She wondered why she should be so blessed, to have a man so willing to give his all for her. In that moment, she realized that his ability to love so completely had not come easy for him. She knew the last several years had purged and refined him, and she could only be grateful to have come into his life now.

While Tara was caught up in her admiration for Sean, she almost forgot about the things Bishop Jensen had said. The bishop cleared his throat again and almost startled her. "It's apparent that the two of you are determined to see this through," he said as if they had told him they were joining the circus or something. "You are both free agents and have the right to do as you wish. I only hope that the consequences of your decision will not be too difficult."

Sean was so shocked that it took him a minute to consciously realize he was angry. While he was attempting to come up with something to say, he felt Tara's soothing hand on his arm. He turned to look at her and she subtly shook her head. It was obvious what she was trying to tell him, and he took a deep breath, knowing she was right.

He was wondering how to get out of here without making a scene, when Tara came to her feet and said graciously, "We apologize for taking so much of your time, Bishop. We will certainly consider everything you've said."

They were in the Blazer before Sean let his anger loose. "How could he be so insensitive and—"

"Sean," Tara put a gentle hand to his face, "bishops are human beings, just like the rest of us. He said what he felt he had to, and we have the confidence of knowing that we're doing the right thing. I'm certain he's a good man. If nothing else, it's helped remind us that we *are* doing this for the right reasons."

Sean sighed and pressed his face to her shoulder. "You're right," he admitted. "I'm glad you were there to keep me calm."

She laughed softly. "I'm beginning to recognize that Irish streak in you." He looked up in surprise. "You can be awfully stubborn and hot-headed when you think you have a right to be."

Sean was tempted to feel insulted, but she said it so genuinely, he had to admit she was right. And it was no fault of hers that he related the thought to a sore point.

"Is something wrong?" she asked.

"Maybe," he admitted. "You just described my father. Perhaps we were never able to come to terms, because we're too much alike."

"Perhaps," she said, then she touched his chin and kissed him softly. "I'm sorry it has to be this way, Sean."

He shook his head slowly. "I'm not sorry to be marrying you now—for any reason." He smiled and lifted his brows almost comically. "You know what else the Irish are known for?"

"What?"

Sean put his lips close to her ear and whispered breathily, "We're passionate."

Tara drew back and her eyes went wide. Sean wasn't certain if she was just surprised, or somehow alarmed.

"I'll have to take your word on that for the time being," she said straightly, and changed the subject.

The morning they were to leave dawned with cloudless skies. With the Blazer loaded to its full capacity, they began the drive to Colorado, admiring the scenery, snow-covered and glittering.

Sean laughed out of nowhere, then explained when Tara looked at him in question. "Do you realize we are getting married in less than a week?"

"Yes," she smiled. "Though it's gone so quickly, I can hardly believe it."

"You still want to, don't you?" he asked, not totally serious.

"You'd better believe it," she said and he took her hand to kiss it.

Christmas came and went, much like Thanksgiving—only far better, in Sean's eyes. He did things he'd never done before in his life, like going into the mountains to cut a tree down with a hatchet. He made a mess of himself, helping bake little cookies that they later frosted. They trimmed the tree and watched old Christmas movies. They went caroling and spent an evening poring over the Christmas story in the Bible. The house was constantly filled with music and laughter and pleasant aromas. Debbie's family arrived Christmas Eve, adding to the festivities.

Sean was surprised when all of the adults hung stockings as well, and he laughed when Mary presented him with one. She'd made it from leftover fabric, since she'd remade all of the stockings just a couple of years before. After the children went to bed, he helped set out Santa's offerings, then he was initiated into the family by taking the first bite out of the cookies left for Santa.

Christmas day was a glorious frenzy of activity and love shared, and it was difficult to say good night and put the day behind. Except that he knew he would be married in three days.

The following morning, the entire household was hurled into a whole new frenzy. Everyone helped where possible with last-minute preparations of cooking and sewing, phone calls and errands. Each time Sean looked at Tara, he was struck freshly with the reality of his upcoming marriage, and he could hardly believe it. He could honestly say he'd never been happier in his life, and there was only one cloud that hovered in the back of his mind. But his new family was so good to him, they made it easier to not dwell on the absence of his own.

On the twenty-seventh, the reality settled in with a nervous excitement and a thousand little things to do. By ten in the evening, Tara was exhausted and finally found time to relax, sitting alone with Sean in the front room. All the lights were out except those on the Christmas tree.

"It's going to be wonderful, Sean," she whispered, and he kissed her brow.

"Yes, I know," he replied.

It was difficult to find words to express the strength of their feelings and the anticipation of what tomorrow would bring. They sat in peaceable silence until Tara fell asleep against his shoulder and Sean helped her up to her room. He kissed her good night, then went to sleep elsewhere for the last time in his life.

Their wedding day dawned with blue skies and sunshine. Soon after breakfast they loaded two cars, a truck, and the Blazer with everything they needed and drove into town to start decorating the church cultural hall.

Mary had talked everyone she could think of into donating their Christmas trees, and the effect was like a forest. A cluster of ever-greens made the backdrop, adorned with red bows and thousands of shimmering icicles. Clusters of trees decorated the same way were scattered through the room and behind a long table adorned with tinsel and more red bows, where an endless supply of home-baked cookies, fruit breads, and sparkling red punch would be set out. The cake was decorated with red roses and green bows, and the flowers were mostly poinsettias, white and red, mixed with roses of the same colors.

When everything was ready except for the wedding participants, they dispersed from the cultural hall to change. In the mother's lounge, Mary and Debbie helped Tara into her gown. As she slipped her arms into the sleeves, she realized she was almost trembling from the anticipation.

"You're happy, aren't you, dear," Mary stated as she helped set the veil into place with hidden combs.

"I am," Tara admitted, but sad tears welled into her eyes as if to contradict her words.

"What is it?" Mary insisted. Debbie put her arms around Tara.

"I love him so much," Tara cried, "and I know he loves me. I only wish that . . . it didn't have to be this way."

Mary took Tara's face gently into her hands and looked deep into her eyes. "Now you listen to me, my darling. You are a good girl and you always have been. There's no good to be had in regretting what's done, but I know in my heart that you will be blessed. You and Sean are going to be very happy together, and one day you will be able to put all of this behind you and your joy with him will be complete. I'm absolutely certain of it."

Tara put her arms around her mother. "I love you, Mom." She sniffed and pulled back. "I don't know what I'd do without you."

Debbie handed her a tissue and squeezed her hand.

"Sean is an incredible man," Tara admitted, attempting to repair her makeup. "I have much to be grateful for."

"We all do," Mary said. "We all do."

CHAPTER TEN

The ceremony was simple, but rich with feeling. Sean and Tara's eyes never parted through the length of it. Rings and a kiss were exchanged, and they were declared husband and wife. It seemed so easy that it was difficult to comprehend the sacred nature of marriage and the commitments they were making.

"I'm so happy," Tara whispered in Sean's ear as he hugged her vibrantly when it was done. He laughed and lifted her momentarily off the ground, then they went hand in hand to mingle with their guests as a light buffet meal was served in the multi-purpose room.

Sean felt certain this day could be no better, until his eye caught a lone woman, standing across the room, watching him closely. He wondered for a moment if his eyes were deceiving him, but she smiled and he knew it was real by the way his heart began to pound.

"What is it?" Tara set a concerned hand over his sleeve, noticing the apparent distress in his expression.

"I can't believe it," he muttered.

Tara turned to follow his gaze. A tall woman with dark hair, dressed in a cream-colored suit, stared back at him. She looked as if she had just stepped out of *Vogue* magazine, and Tara suddenly felt intimidated, wondering if this was the woman from Sean's past he had spoken of.

"Excuse me," Sean said absently. "I'll be right back." He walked toward the woman as if he were mesmerized, and Tara looked on, wondering how she should feel.

Sean's own movements felt somehow dreamlike as he stepped across the room and his sister moved forward to meet him. He blinked away the mist in his eyes and finally found his voice, though it came with strain. "Is it all right if I talk to you?" he asked.

"I was hoping you would," she replied softly.

Sean hesitated only a moment before he pulled Maureen into his arms with something near to desperation, as if just holding her close could bring back everything he had lost. He kissed her cheek and pressed his face to hers, almost ashamed of his tears until he realized she was crying, too.

Tara watched Sean's interaction with this woman and felt suddenly alone. She knew him well enough to know that he would not have such feelings now for another woman. Didn't she? Tara was just trying to gather her wits enough to escape to the ladies' room, when Sean relaxed his embrace, turned, and motioned for her to join him. There was no shame or guilt in his expression, and she felt better as she walked toward him and slipped her hand into his. Her relief was intense when he said, "Tara, this is my sister, Maureen."

Tara's discomfort melted into joy on his behalf, so intense she could hardly think how to respond. He put his arm around Tara's shoulders and added, "Maureen, my wife, Tara."

"So I see," Maureen said kindly, taking Tara's hand into hers. "I did manage to slip in just before the ceremony started. It was beautiful." She added more to Sean, "You look great." She took his hand. She squeezed it, then she looked at it as if something wasn't right. "Your hands are healed," she said. "You mentioned it in a letter, but I couldn't believe it."

"I was never sure if you got my letters," he said quietly.

"I'm sorry." Fresh tears welled up in Maureen's eyes. "I just couldn't . . . I mean, I see Mom and Dad at least once a week, and I . . . I just couldn't spend so much time there . . . without a clear conscience. And he was so . . . so adamant, Sean."

"I understand." Sean bowed his head and cleared his throat tensely. "I really do. You don't have to apologize." He looked up and smiled. "I'm just so glad you came now. How did you . . ." He didn't know how to ask.

"When the announcement came, Mother and I cried. I don't think Dad saw it at all. It was just as well. I told Dad you were getting married, but he . . ." Maureen looked down and Sean knew she didn't want to repeat it. "That's not important." She shrugged.

"Please," he pressed. "What did he say?"

Maureen's eyes filled with compassion. "He said that he had no interest in it; that you were not his son."

Tara put a sustaining arm around Sean's waist and felt him lean into her slightly. He squeezed his eyes shut and nodded.

"Mother wanted to come," Maureen hurried on, "but she said to tell you that she just couldn't; not without setting off too much trouble. You understand. And then, she's not been well for quite some time."

"What's wrong?" Sean demanded.

"We don't know," Maureen replied. "They've done all kinds of tests, and so far they've found nothing to explain it. Her doctor wants her to go in for exploratory surgery, but she keeps putting it off. You know how she is."

Sean nodded.

"But anyway," Maureen brightened slightly, "we decided that I could come to the wedding and Dad would never know. Mother said she felt God would understand this once." Maureen hugged him again and Sean returned it with feeling. "I'm so glad I came," she murmured. "Oh, Sean. It's been so long . . . too long."

Tara's emotion finally got the better of her as she watched the way they held each other.

"So," Sean stepped back and took a deep breath to compose himself, "you flew out just for this?" The joy in his eyes was evident. She nodded and he grinned. "How long are you staying, then?"

"I have a flight out early tomorrow, but I was planning on hanging around here all evening, if it's all right with you."

"It's more than all right with me." Sean fairly beamed. "How about you?" he asked Tara.

"It almost makes our family complete," she said and gave Maureen a careful embrace.

"She's beautiful, Sean," Maureen said, looking at Tara.

"Yes, I know." Sean took both their arms. "Come along, you've got to meet everyone."

"Mother," Sean called and Mary turned from visiting with her brother, "look what I found. It's my big sister."

Mary first looked surprised, then she hugged Maureen as if they were long-lost relatives, which Sean decided in a way they were. While introductions were exchanged and Sean and Tara mingled with their guests, the reality of being married began to sink in. During a moment when everyone was occupied, Sean ushered Tara into the hall where he took her into his arms and kissed her like he'd never dared before. Her response made him long to be alone with her. He felt something subtly guarded in her manner, but her eyes had a dreamy quality when he pulled away.

"How are you feeling?" he asked.

"Wonderful," she smiled.

"No," he chuckled, putting a tender hand to her belly, "I mean, how are you feeling?"

"A little tired," she admitted, "but I think I'll hold up without too much trouble."

"You take it easy, all right?"

"I will," she promised, and he kissed her again.

"Are you happy?" he asked.

"Oh, yes. And you?"

"More than I can believe."

"I'm so glad your sister came."

He sighed as if he still couldn't believe it. "So am I. I must admit, it softens the blow a little."

The guests dispersed except for immediate family, and they moved to the cultural hall for pictures. Maureen was included in all the group pictures, while she and Sean exchanged an occasional glance of disbelief.

When the photographer declared they were finished with time to spare, Maureen asked Tara if she might talk to Sean alone for a few minutes.

"Just have him back before seven," she said. "I can't have a wedding reception without a groom."

"I promise," Maureen smiled. She ushered him to the parking lot, where she unlocked the trunk of a rented car and pulled out a package. "Is there somewhere we can go so you can open this privately?"

Sean found an unoccupied classroom where he closed the door

and they sat down.

"I don't know what you managed to get away with," she said. "You left in such a hurry. But Mom and I knew this was something you didn't have that would be appropriate for your wedding. You will want to show it to your children."

Sean opened the box with some hesitation, then he laughed to find it filled with keepsakes of his growing years. There were certificates and ribbons from his accomplishments, and odd souvenirs from family outings and vacations. From the bottom of the box, Maureen pulled out a leather-bound book that she set on his lap and opened. Sean caught his breath.

"You see," she said softly, "it starts with pictures of you when you were a baby." She turned the page. "Here's you and Dad after your first baseball game." She turned another page to show him pictures of his relatives, his home, his life. But it all disappeared behind the veil of mist that seeped into his eyes. He looked up at his sister and blinked, letting the tears spill over his face.

"It's not right, Maureen," he said. "Families should be together."

"I know," she said and cried, too.

Sean turned his attention back to the album in his lap, using every ounce of control he could muster to keep the emotion back. If he let it all come forward now, he would never make it through the evening.

"It's beautiful, Maureen. Tell Mother how much I appreciate it. It's priceless." He looked up. "And tell her that I love her. Tell her how grateful I am for the way she raised me, and tell her I'm trying hard to be a good Christian."

"I will," she agreed. "And what should I tell her when she asks me if you're happy?" Sean looked down and gave an ironic chuckle, thinking of the bittersweetness of his life. "Was it worth it, Sean?" she added.

Sean looked at his sister intently, saying with strength, "Becoming a Mormon was the rightest thing I have ever done. I love this church, and I love being a part of it. I know it's true, and I could never regret it. My only heartache has been my desire to be close to my family, Maureen. But I had to do it or I could not have lived with myself. And yes, I am happy. Tara is absolutely incredible, and I love her with all my heart and soul."

Maureen smiled. "I'll tell her."

"I don't suppose you can say anything to Dad at all," he mused.

Maureen shook her head slowly. "If he even knew I had spoken to you, he would never speak to me again. I'm certain of it. It's preposterous, I know. But he's our father, and we have no choice but to accept it. We must go on as we have been, and pretend that I was not here."

Sean swallowed hard and nodded, however reluctant he was to accept this reality. They watched each other through a poignant moment, then Sean forced himself back to the present, for fear he'd burst with emotion otherwise. He turned the last page of the album.

"And this," Maureen announced with a bright voice, "is my daughter."

"Really?" he laughed. "You had a baby?"

"She's nearly two now," Maureen said proudly, "and she's so precious. She's got her daddy wrapped around her little finger, but he loves it."

"How is David?" Sean asked.

"Fine. He's been a good husband, in spite of the struggles."

"That's great," Sean commented.

"And how is Peggy? Is she still determined to—"

"She's taken her vows," Maureen interrupted.

Sean shook his head in disbelief. "My sister, a nun. I never guessed she would really do it. And Margaret?"

"She's still living with old what's-his-name in Manhattan. She's had another of his babies, but he still won't marry her."

Sean made a noise of concern. "And Matthew?"

"Matthew is doing well," she stated more optimistically. "He's working with a law firm in Chicago. He's got three children now, and they seem quite happy." She pointed out a copy of Matthew's most recent family portrait in the album.

"Oh, that's nice," Sean said. "And dare I ask how Robert is doing?" he inquired hesitantly about his oldest sibling.

"The same," was all she said. "The evidence of his problems only deepens."

Sean sighed. "I guess that spreads our family across a pretty big spectrum of life."

"It certainly does."

They sat for a moment in contemplative silence, then Maureen carefully returned everything to the box and closed it up tight. "I'm certain you'll be rather occupied the rest of the evening, but I'm glad we had a little time together." She sighed and put a hand to his cheek. "Have a good life, Sean."

"And you," he replied, trying to swallow his emotion. "Thank you for coming. You can't know what it means to me."

Maureen smiled and glanced at her watch. "It's almost seven. You'd best hurry along."

Sean agreed and took a deep breath to compose himself before he went back to the cultural hall.

"Are you all right?" Tara said when Sean found her admiring the wedding cake.

"I'm fine," he said with sincerity. "How about you?"

"I'm Mrs. Sean O'Hara. I couldn't get much finer than that."

"Tara O'Hara," he chuckled. "I like it."

"I think I'll go by Taralee, for the record."

"That's probably a good idea." Sean laughed and kissed her.

The celebrating continued through the evening. During a quiet moment, Sean pulled Tara's mother aside and put his arm around her shoulders. "There's something I wanted to tell you . . . Mother," he added, and she smiled. "Just so you don't have to wonder, Tara and I are worthy to go to the temple."

Mary put a hand to Sean's face and tears pooled in her eyes. "Thank you," she said softly. "That means more to me than you know." Sean chuckled and hugged her tightly.

When the cake had been cut, Sean and Tara were escorted to the Blazer, which they could barely find amid all the balloons and toilet paper. In turn they embraced each family member, lingering an extra moment with Maureen. Sean wondered if he would ever see her again. Turning back to the present, they cleared away enough paraphernalia to make the Blazer drivable, then drove away with cans rattling behind.

A few blocks later, Sean stopped near a dumpster and removed everything from the Blazer except the *Just Married* sign across the back. Then he got in, kissed Tara and drove on, laughing genially.

The air became quiet around them as they drove the thirty miles to their wedding-night destination. Tara knew they were going to a bed and breakfast inn she had suggested, which was much more appealing than the narrow choice of motels. She had admired the huge old home for years, and going there now was like a dream come true. But her anticipation was tainted with other thoughts that she couldn't push away any longer. Any apprehension Tara had felt previously concerning this night had been disregarded with the rationalization that when the time came, she would not be afraid.

There was no room to question her trust in Sean. But no matter how she tried to look at it, Tara couldn't separate what had transpired between her and Danny from what would transpire this night. She often recalled the brief passionate moments she'd spent in Sean's arms. Nothing happened that shouldn't have, but it had frightened her for reasons she couldn't explain. The doctor had assured her that she'd healed well and there was no reason she should not be able to have a normal marriage relationship. But there were deeper wounds that had not healed, and she knew it. Sean was well aware of those, she felt certain, but physical intimacy was something they had not discussed beyond a certain level. Had they just been too busy, or was he as afraid to bring it up as she was?

As the miles passed and Sean held her hand, fingering the wedding band she wore, Tara kept telling herself she had to speak up now. She couldn't go to an inn with this man—her husband—and expect everything to go normally when there were panic buttons going off in her head. She convinced herself that she wasn't afraid to discuss this with Sean, and all she had to do was say it. But still, she had trouble finding the words to begin.

Tara nearly found the courage to speak when she realized they had stopped. Within minutes, Sean was carrying her over the threshold, her gown crinkling at his every move. He kicked the door shut with an endearing laugh, then set her feet on the floor without letting her go. He kissed her, and she couldn't help responding. But when their eyes met, he quickly became concerned.

"What?" he asked, and she knew he expected an answer. When she didn't speak right away, he added with conviction, "You're afraid, aren't you." It was not a question.

Tara glanced down until Sean lifted her chin. "I know I shouldn't be," she said tearfully, "but . . ." Her words faltered. "We should have talked about this before now." She turned her back to him and pulled the veil from her hair.

"But we didn't," he stated. "So we'll have to talk about it now."

"You make it sound so easy," she said almost angrily, hoping he knew her anger was not directed toward him.

"Perhaps you're making it too hard," he replied calmly.

"It *is* hard," she insisted, then said nothing more.

"Tara." He placed gentle hands on her shoulders. "Just talk to me. That's all I ask. If we can just talk, anything else can wait until you feel comfortable with it. If it bothers you for the time being, so be it. But don't push the feelings down inside. Don't shut me out."

Tara turned toward him, her skirts rustling. "Why must you be so endlessly good to me?" she asked softly.

"It's purely selfish," he smiled.

"No," she said firmly, "it is *not* purely selfish. A selfish man does not tell his wife on their wedding night that it's all right to wait until another time."

"I want you to be comfortable. I want you to be happy."

"See, there you go again. Why can't you just be frustrated with these circumstances, even for a minute? Why can't you *hate* what's happening here? Why can't you wish we could have a normal marriage and a normal wedding night?"

"There is no person on this earth who has a *normal* life, Tara. Everyone has their own trials and problems."

"Yes, I know. But we are talking about *my* problems."

"*Our* problems, you mean."

"See, there you go again. Stop being so blasted perfect."

Sean gave a dubious chuckle and stuffed his hands into his pockets. "I am far from perfect, Tara, and you know it. So, why don't you tell me what the real problem is here? What are you trying to get at?"

Tara pressed her fingers over her eyes and tried to maintain control. "I don't understand how all of this can be so easy for you to accept and deal with, when there are moments when I feel like I'm falling apart."

"I was under the impression that you had been doing quite well."

"Most of the time I feel all right, but I wonder if I'm just in denial or something."

"If you've been feeling that way, why didn't you tell me?"

"Because I didn't want to talk about it!"

"Just because you don't want to talk about it, doesn't mean there's something wrong with you. Truly, Tara, I believe you've been doing very well under the circumstances."

"Yes," she laughed cynically, "under the circumstances. Why does everything in our life have to be justified with *under the circumstances?*"

"You want to know why?" His voice picked up an edge. "I'll tell you why." He pointed a finger at her. "Because this is *life,* Tara; real life. This is what we bargained for when our spirits chose to come to this world. And if we are not here to bear one another's burdens, then what exactly do you figure we are here for? We exchanged vows today, Tara—vows that stated plainly your problems are mine, and my problems are yours. I did not come into this marriage ignorant of the circumstances, by any means. And if it appears that I'm not upset by any of this, you can credit it to one thing. Self-control. I learned a great deal of self-control when I had to survive without the use of my hands and I couldn't turn around without wanting to bawl like a baby because my father had kicked me out. You have no idea what's going on inside of me, because I didn't figure you needed to hear it. You have enough of a burden to bear without having to listen to me whine and complain. And I suppose I didn't want to talk about it, either. But just so you don't have to wonder, I'll tell you now. It hurts, Tara." He put a hand to his chest. "It hurts every time I think about it. I also wake up at night in a cold sweat sometimes because I have nightmares about what happened to you. And I have an urge to turn my back on Christianity just long enough to hunt him down and kill him with my bare hands. Every time you cry, I want to cry, too. I wish as much as you do that we could just walk into marriage with no problems, no past. But we didn't, and we have to live with it. The coming months are not going to be easy for either of us, but if I can be there to sustain you through this, then my life has some worthwhile purpose. You're the one going through the real pain here, and I am just trying to do my best to be patient and somehow help you through. I don't claim to always handle it right, but I'm here because I love you."

Sean took a deep breath and stuffed his hands into his pockets. "As far as I can see, the only way to make this work is to stay as close as we have managed to be so far. And that means that both of us have got to start talking more, about the real feelings. Maybe we've been apprehensive to bring up certain things, because it didn't seem appropriate. But we're married now, and there's no reason why we can't talk about anything. You have to let me help you carry these burdens, Tara. Physical intimacy we can work around, but a marriage cannot survive without emotional intimacy, and spiritual intimacy—and that takes communication."

Sean took her face into his hands and rubbed a thumb over one tear-stained cheek. "Tara," his voice softened, "I'm new at this husband stuff. Feel free to straighten me out. I'm just trying to be strong enough for both of us."

For the millionth time, Tara looked into his eyes and silently thanked God for Sean's presence in her life. How blessed she was! He kissed her quickly and pressed her face to his shoulder. She believed she could endure anything, as long as he held her hand. He truly was strong enough for both of them.

"Tara," he whispered, "it's been a long day. You're tired. Why don't you get out of that dress and we'll get some sleep. We'll talk in the morning."

Tara looked into his eyes. "Will you be disappointed?"

Sean sighed. "Yes," he admitted. "But as long as I have you in my life, I will always have something to look forward to."

Tara decided she felt better and turned to lift her hair, indicating that he unfasten the buttons down her back.

"That's all," he announced when it was done, and she rustled into the bathroom.

While Tara freshened up and changed, she thought hard about the situation in light of all he'd just said. She uttered a prayer for guidance and strength, then went out to face him with a fresh resolve. She draped her wedding gown over the back of a chair, then turned to see Sean sitting near the bed, his legs stretched out casually, wearing pajama pants and a white T-shirt. Her eyes went to the bed. It had been turned down. Then she quickly looked to Sean when he said, "You look pretty."

She felt his eyes absorbing her in the modest white nightgown of billowing tricot and elbow-length sleeves.

"Mom and Debbie gave it to me," she said, and he smiled slightly. She didn't add that they'd told her the color was to remind her of her purity.

"I think I'll brush my teeth," Sean said a bit tensely and moved past her into the bathroom.

Tara nearly climbed into the bed, but habitually she went to her knees to say her nightly prayer. She became so absorbed that it was a surprise to feel Sean's hand slip into hers. She glanced up but he was apparently praying beside her, so she closed her eyes and finished, then waited until he turned to look at her.

"I can't sleep," she said. "Can we talk now?"

Sean nodded, then held up a finger. He bowed his head again and she did the same as he began a fervent verbal prayer on behalf of their marriage, their relationship, and the child Tara carried. When the prayer was finished, he looked into her eyes, then kissed her. "Now that," he said, "will be a daily requirement from now on. A prayer and a kiss before bed."

"Agreed." She smiled and moved gingerly into the bed.

Sean slid between the covers beside her, but left the bedside lamp on. He put his arm around her and kissed her brow, saying gently, "All right, let's talk."

"It's difficult to know where to begin." She took his hand. "If you were my counselor, where would we begin?"

He chuckled. "I don't think I could be your counselor."

"I think you already are."

"I'm too involved to look at this objectively and give you advice on how to deal with your feelings."

"So, just tell me how they taught you to approach such things," she said as if they were discussing a recipe, while she nervously fingered the edge of the blanket.

"Well," he leaned back against the headboard and folded his

arms, "you have to try to find the root of the fear to be able to dissolve the secondary fears. Does that make any sense?"

"I think so."

"Then tell me, Mrs. O'Hara, what is the root of your fear?" She looked at him almost sharply. "We have established that you are afraid, haven't we?"

"Yes," she said, deciding she didn't necessarily like this approach. "But I already know the root of my fear. It's the secondary fears that are bothering me now."

"Such as?" he asked blandly.

"I don't know how to explain it," she said in exasperation.

"All right, I'll guess and you tell me if I'm right or wrong." She nodded in agreement and he continued. "You're afraid of me."

"No. Not in the slightest."

He smiled. "Okay. You're afraid it will be painful."

"Yes, but not enough to keep me away from you."

Sean took her hand and squeezed it. He wished he could see inside her head, but at least they were making some progress. An obvious possibility came into his mind and he voiced it. "You're afraid of memory association."

"Clarify that," she stated, narrowing her eyes.

"Well, in this case, I'd guess you're afraid of the bad memories crowding in to interfere with the present."

Tara said nothing. He gave her time to absorb it, and still she said nothing.

"Tara?" he prodded.

"In which case," she imitated his clinical tone, "the best thing would be to face the present and allow something good to replace the bad memories."

Sean lifted a brow. "Who is the counselor here?"

"Am I right?"

"That depends on the extent of your fear, and the inner strength you have to face it."

Tara touched his hair and smiled. "I believe you're strong enough for both of us."

"Tara," he whispered, "we can wait. It won't matter."

"To me, it will. One day, when our daughter is getting married, she may come to me and say, 'Mom, what was it like on your wedding night?' And I'm going to tell her it was beautiful, because her father is a gentle, patient man."

Sean felt touched by her courage. But still, he was hesitant. She had not expressed enough emotion to make him believe she was ready to face what he felt sure she feared. But words seemed trite. She reached across him to turn out the light, then she moved into his arms and settled her head against his shoulder.

It was easy now for Tara to hold him close and press her lips to his. Without a word spoken, Sean eased all her fears by his gentle patience and his boundless love for her. And when she was momentarily seized by fear, Sean drew back, wooing her gently, soothing her with tender words and a patient touch. Gradually she became so caught up in longing, all memories were forgotten in the face of his affection, and she knew with all her heart and soul there was nothing they could not conquer together.

CHAPTER ELEVEN

Tara awoke in Sean's arms, oblivious to anything in her life that could mar this happiness. She eased back slightly to get a better view of his face as he slept. Recalling their intimacy, she was caught by a rush of butterflies. Then she noticed something in the light of day that she'd been unaware of in the night. Certain he was sound asleep, Tara hesitantly touched his scars, one after the other, wondering what each one represented. Most of them were obviously surgical by their preciseness, but there were so many it was hard to tally them.

"Now you know the truth about me," he said facetiously, then he chuckled when she jumped.

"And what truth is that?" she asked when his eyes came open, squinting and sparkling at the same time.

"I'm actually a creation of someone named Dr. Frankenstein. As you can see, he put me together a piece at a time."

"Does that make me the bride of Frankenstein?" she giggled. Sean laughed again and kissed her.

"I assume," she said more seriously, "these are from your accident."

"Every one of them," he said almost proudly, then he went on to briefly explain the reason for surgery on most of his vital organs, and a number of different places where tubes had once been. Tara ate crackers and listened with interest, then she held up her finger.

"What is this?" he asked.

She showed him a tiny, white U-shaped line. "This is from trying to cut open a package of cheese. The knife slipped."

Sean hugged her and laughed.

"It's the only one I've got, honestly."

Sean chuckled as he showed her scars on his legs from surgeries to repair broken bones, and one on his upper left arm.

"Well, you're just a walking miracle," she said more seriously. "I think you survived just for me."

"Exactly," he agreed. "And to become a Mormon. But it took me a while to figure that out."

"I'm glad you're alive," she said and kissed him.

They took their time checking out and getting brunch, as Sean called it. He insisted they could not call it breakfast when it was eaten at 11:30. He told her the package of crackers she'd eaten in bed didn't count. "But don't make a habit of it," he added with a stern facade. "The only reason I let you eat them in bed today is because I don't have to sleep in that bed tonight."

They arrived at what Sean called *their* parents' home in the middle of the afternoon and proceeded with a gift-opening party that was almost as much fun as Christmas had been. Then Sean announced that Mary truly did love him when she served roast turkey for dinner.

Sean shared Tara's room that night, and early the next morning they were off to Provo, the Blazer loaded more tightly than it had been on the trip out. Once home, they began to unload and put things away. At ten-thirty they gave up and went to bed.

The morning of New Year's Eve, Tara's family arrived in Provo for the open house. After checking out the newlyweds' apartment, they all went out for a buffet lunch together, then made certain everything was ready for the big event.

There were few similarities to the open house and the reception. This time the cultural hall was decorated with colored serpentine and party horns, and the atmosphere was more casual. Friends filtered in and out through the evening, on their way to and from various parties. Many stayed through the evening and brought in the new year with the bride and groom. They toasted midnight with white grape juice in plastic champagne glasses, and it was past one before the custodian broke away from the fun to declare it was time to go home and they could clean up the building the following morning.

With family dispersed to their motel rooms, Sean carried his bride over the threshold of their apartment and announced they were going to have a wedding night like normal people do.

In the middle of breakfast, the phone rang. Sean went to answer it then came back to report, "We're going to have some company in about ten minutes."

Tara glanced around and frantically started straightening before she asked, "Who?"

Sean helped her while he explained. "Do you remember Melissa?"

Tara stopped a moment. "Your old girlfriend—the one who came by before Thanksgiving?"

"That's her," he stated, then went on quickly. "Her sister, Ilene, lives in Salt Lake. She and her husband are on their way to St. George to see Bryson's father. Bryson's her husband."

"I figured that much."

"She just called to say they hadn't been able to make it last night, but she was hoping they could stop by and meet you."

This brought panic to Tara. "I look awful," she declared, and left Sean to finish straightening the front room while she put on some makeup and brushed her hair. She had barely emerged from the bathroom when they came to the door. Tara held back while Sean shook hands with Bryson and they laughed briefly over something. Sean then embraced Ilene, an attractive dark-haired woman who looked very little like her sister. Four children of various ages hovered politely around their parents as Sean ushered them to the front room. Two of them held packages wrapped in wedding paper. The oldest girl was holding a baby. A baby that caught Tara's attention to a point that she didn't hear a word that was said until Sean gently nudged her. He made introductions and they all sat down.

"How old is your baby?" Tara asked, and Sean realized why she was distracted.

"Six weeks," Ilene reported. "And growing fast."

"She's beautiful," Tara said.

"Would you like to hold her?" Ilene asked sweetly.

Tara turned to Sean, as if seeking permission. He gave her an encouraging nod and Tara was handed the baby. She was aware of Ilene sitting close beside her, talking about all of the little things that babies do. Trying to distract herself from the sweet smell and tender noises, Tara thought how she liked these people. She also thought of the irony that Sean could have easily married into *their* family. She was glad he hadn't.

The baby yawned and Tara chuckled. She played with the tiny fingers and swallowed hard to keep her emotion under control. The reality was too difficult to comprehend. She really was pregnant, and she really intended to give her baby to someone else. Perhaps needing sustenance, she looked up at Sean and immediately found it. She knew by his eyes that he understood, and she reluctantly handed the baby back to Ilene.

"She really is beautiful," Tara commented again. She was grateful when they changed the subject and began talking about the wedding. They handed over the gifts, declaring that one was from Melissa.

"You know Melissa and I are very close," Ilene said, and Tara sensed Sean becoming slightly tense. "I want you to know that she is truly happy for you. And I know that one day she'll find the right man."

"Do you think I should warn the poor guy when she does?" Bryson chuckled.

Sean relaxed. "I suspect there's little to warn him about."

"Anyway," Ilene continued, giving her husband a sidelong glance, "we're all very happy for you, Sean. And you, Tara. You've got a good man there."

"Yes, I know," she agreed emphatically.

They didn't stay long, but Tara's mind lingered with that baby until she consciously forced it elsewhere. They opened the gift from Bryson and Ilene first, and Sean laughed. He'd just said this morning that he wished someone had given them a new toaster—one that didn't burn the toast every other time.

Tara opened the one from Melissa, intrigued by the set of dark blue glasses, with sun, moon, and stars scattered over them in gold. They looked expensive, and very pretty.

"I like them," she stated, then she noticed Sean's expression. "Is something wrong?"

"I was with her when she bought these," he stated, holding one up to examine it closely, nostalgia showing in his eyes. "She called them dream glasses. I'd forgotten all about them. She said that drinking together from them would make our dreams come true. We packed them away before my mission without using them. She was on her mission when I got home from mine, and we never used them."

"Well, it seems an appropriate gift."

"Yes," Sean smiled, albeit sadly, "I think it is."

They hurried to meet the custodian and George and Mary at the church, and quickly had everything in order. Since Debbie and her family had started home early so Derrick could be to work the next day, Sean and Tara gave their parents a tour of Utah Valley, then took them to the apartment and cooked Sean's specialty, lasagna.

It was a bit of a letdown to see George and Mary leave the following day. Classes would start again soon, and the reality of the struggles had to be faced. But the newness of married life put a brighter perspective on the world, and they quickly established a comfortable routine.

Bishop Jensen called and asked if they would speak in sacrament meeting. He was congenial and seemed completely accepting of their marriage, but still, Tara felt nervous. Sean assured her there were few people who didn't get nervous about speaking in sacrament meeting.

It all went well, and afterward, many ward members expressed warm congratulations on their marriage. Everything was fine until a single sister, who introduced herself as Elva Shard, casually said to Tara, "That's a pretty dress, Sister O'Hara, but if I didn't know you just got married, I'd swear you looked pregnant."

Sean was as amazed at Tara's composure as he was by this woman's brashness. He squeezed her hand unobtrusively and tried to figure out why this woman looked familiar. Of course, he must have seen her at church a number of times, though he was known for keeping to himself and most of these people just melded into a crowd. He felt proud of Tara when she said in a perfectly bland voice, "I shall have to be more careful what I wear."

"You wouldn't want to give someone the wrong impression," Elva said, something subtly smug showing in her eyes.

Sean tried to smile and ushered Tara away. When they'd been home for nearly an hour and she'd hardly said a word, he prodded, "I assume something's bothering you."

"I'm beginning to show, Sean."

"I know," he stated.

"We've been married two and a half weeks, and I'm starting to look pregnant. Do you really think people won't notice?"

Sean wanted to tell her it was silly, but he had to tell her the truth. "Most people *will* notice, Tara. And many of them are likely crass enough to be counting the weeks. You can choose to let it bother you, or you can just—"

"It's not that easy, Sean," she interrupted. "Why do people have to judge from appearances and jump to conclusions?"

"Because they're human."

Tara pressed a hand over her eyes to hide the tears, wondering if anyone cried as much as she did.

"Hey," he took her into his arms, "if you're concerned what people will think, you must remember that the Lord knows the truth and—"

"But it's not fair that they have to assume this is your baby and—"

"Tara, there is nothing we can do about this."

"Yes, there is," she insisted. "There is *always* some kind of option."

Sean was stunned for a moment, then finally said, "Okay. What are the options?"

"We could stop going to church," she said, and he was relieved when he realized she wasn't serious. "Okay," she added, "so that's not an option. But we could move."

Sean's eyes widened. "Do you really think that running away from it will—"

"Do you think that making an attempt to alleviate the stress in this situation is running away? Isn't it difficult enough without having to face the speculations of people who have no idea what they're talking about?"

"There is another option," he said soberly. "You could just admit the whole thing publicly and end the speculation."

"No," she snapped. "I've just realized how it feels to have someone speculating about my being immoral. I will not have people looking at me and wishing they could ask me how horrible it really was. People who don't know me well enough to get a personal explanation have no business knowing what I've been through. I'd feel violated all over again every time I went to church. I know most people mean no harm. They just don't stop to think. But I need to be able to go to church and be rejuvenated, not come away feeling torn down and reminded that I'm in a bad situation."

Sean tried very hard to think of a retort, but he couldn't. "Okay," he said, "we'll see if we can find another place, but it could be difficult now that classes are underway. We can't afford anything more than we're paying right now."

"I know, but I could go back to work, and—"

"No, you can't. We didn't make the decision for you to quit your job, just so you could turn around and get another one. We can live on my income if we're careful, and you need to take care of yourself."

Tara sighed in a way that was becoming familiar. Sean read it as a silent, *Why does it have to be this way?* He kissed her gently and urged her head to his shoulder. "We'll pray about it. Everything will be okay, one way or the other."

"Just keep telling me that," she replied and hugged him tightly, wondering what she would have ever done without him.

Tara diligently looked for another apartment, but the only thing she found available that was within their budget needed so many repairs she knew it would end up costing them more in the long run. It just didn't feel right, and Sean agreed. Still, going to church was a challenge for her. She felt prone to leave her coat on, and frustrated when most of her clothes no longer fit around her waist. Sean took some money out of savings and bought her some clothes. But the bottom line was simple. She was pregnant and she looked it.

The same day that Elva told Tara she looked positively glowing, Sean remembered where he had seen her. She worked at the supermarket, and she had checked him out a particular day last fall. He remembered it clearly now, since she had tried to make conversation with him, and at the time he hadn't realized she was in his ward. Now he recalled it: that was the day he had purchased a home pregnancy test.

Sean felt sick inside at the implication. This woman had put the pieces together, and was somehow gloating over what she believed she knew was going on. He told himself to not let it bother him, just like he'd told Tara a number of times. But it *did* bother him. He told himself they couldn't move and they couldn't stop going to church. As long as Tara chose to keep the truth quiet, which he understood completely, there were no other options. Since it was fast Sunday, Sean fasted with that particular problem in mind. He was surprised at how easily the answer came. During priesthood meeting, a neighbor shook his hand and said, "We were glad you decided to stay in the student ward, instead of attending a regular ward. After all, we do have a lot more fun here." He laughed, but Sean's mind was wandering.

By the time they went home, Sean had all the information he needed. Of course, he knew the way these wards were set up. But he'd always been single and a student, and he'd simply never thought of it before. The renovated house they lived in was surrounded by homes with families, who went to a regular ward. Student wards covered the same districts, and for a student, it was a choice. But now that he and Tara were married, the option was there. They simply had to have their records transferred, and they would be going to church with people who didn't know who they were, and didn't know how long they'd been married.

Tara was ecstatic over the news, but a subtle sensitivity to the situation hovered over her that he figured would not go away until the baby arrived.

They were barely into February when Sean got a call from Australia. The Hamiltons were coming to Utah, specifically to see them.

* * * * *

"You're going to love Michael and Emily," Sean said for the third time since they'd entered the airport. Then he glanced at the clock again.

"So you tell me." Tara fidgeted with her purse. "But will they love me?"

"Is that what you're nervous about?" he asked lightly then gave her a quick hug. "They will absolutely adore you," he insisted. "I can promise you that. They're wonderful people, Tara."

"I know," she smiled weakly, "but what if they find out that . . ." She couldn't finish.

"If you don't want them to know, fine. But even if they did, they would understand, Tara. You really don't look that pregnant, in spite of what old what's-her-name said. Just act normal, and they'll never suspect."

"How can I act normal? I act pregnant because I feel pregnant."

Sean took her hand and kissed it. "I love you, Tara."

"I know." She managed a smile. "And I love you, too."

"There it is," he said, glancing toward the huge windows where they could see a plane taxiing to the gate.

Tara took a deep breath and stood beside Sean, watching passengers file through the gate door. Sean's obvious happiness deepened the evidence that Michael and Emily *were* good people. He'd told her much about what they had done for him, how they had become his family when he lost his own. Perhaps that was part of her nervousness. She'd never been confronted with meeting her husband's parents, but this was close. She quietly observed as Sean exchanged jubilant embraces with these people. In a way, they were everything she should have expected. Hearing of their wealth and the story of how they had come together, Tara somehow expected them to be glamorous, or perhaps . . . sophisticated. In the moment she observed them before they turned to acknowledge her, Tara was struck by how ordinary they were. True, they were refined and dignified; attractive people who looked young and vibrant for their years. But still, there was nothing about them to make Tara feel intimidated or uncomfortable.

"This must be the beautiful bride," Michael Hamilton said with that distinct Australian accent she'd heard over the phone. He took both her hands into his and looked her over with a sparkle in his eyes.

"This is Tara," Sean said proudly as Michael gave her a firm, almost fatherly embrace.

"Oh, you sweet thing," Emily Hamilton said, squeezing past her husband to also embrace her. "We've heard such wonderful things about you."

"I could say the same about you," Tara said.

Emily held Tara's hands in hers and fairly beamed as she said to Sean, "Oh, she's precious. From what you've said, I've no doubt this was a match made in heaven."

Tara glanced down timidly. Sean said with warmth, "Amen to that."

"We really wish we could have been here for the wedding," Emily said as they walked toward the baggage claim area. "But as we told you, it just couldn't be helped."

"That's all right," Sean insisted. "With all of it behind us, we've got more time to visit anyway."

"Good point," Michael said.

Tara mostly observed as they collected the luggage and took it to the Blazer. She knew Michael and Emily's oldest daughter was on a mission, but they acted almost as if they were newlyweds. She recognized the warm glances that often passed between them. It was much the same way Sean looked at her.

"Nice Blazer," Michael said as they loaded luggage into the back of it.

"Well, don't think I'm giving it back," Sean said.

Michael laughed. "I wouldn't take it if you did."

They drove together to Mullboons, where Michael treated them to a fine meal. Though Tara participated little in the conversation, she found it easy to relax and be comfortable. The drive to Provo went quickly as she listened to them reminisce about their experiences in Utah, some that went way back. As they pulled into the front drive of the Park Hotel to let them off, Michael said he'd arranged to rent a car, and they would come by sometime the next afternoon to see the apartment and visit.

"We have some errands," Sean informed them. "If we're not home, the key is under a rock to the right of the porch. Just come in and make yourselves at home. We won't be long."

Michael nodded, then he took Tara's hand. "It was a pleasure meeting you, young lady. One of these days the two of you will have to come to *our* home, and we'll show you a *really* good time."

"It sounds delightful," Tara said. "Thank you—both of you—for a wonderful evening."

"It's our pleasure," Emily insisted.

As they drove home, Sean's happiness was apparent. Tara was glad for the Hamiltons' visit. Perhaps it made up for only having one sister at the wedding.

The following day they exchanged some duplicate wedding gifts and did grocery shopping. By the time they got through a long checkout line, Tara was so nauseated she thought she would pass out. As soon as they were paid for, she took the crackers to the Blazer and ate several while Sean loaded groceries in the back.

He seemed to be adjusting to her not wanting to talk during these bouts of nausea, but he smiled at her occasionally as they drove home. As always, his concern was evident.

"Are you okay now?" he asked as he helped her out of the Blazer.

"I think so," she scowled, "but I wonder why you never complain when you always end up doing all the work."

"What work?"

"Loading all the groceries and—"

"Oh, for heaven's sake," he said, handing her a light-weight bag, "it's not that big of a deal."

He picked up another two bags and followed her up the walk. "Still," she insisted as she turned the key and opened the door, "it wouldn't be this way if you hadn't married a pregnant woman and . . ."

Tara stopped in the doorway and felt Sean freeze beside her. Emily was sitting on the couch, looking sleepy as if she'd been resting there until she heard them at the door. For a long moment they just stared at each other. Tara wanted to slither into a hole somewhere and never have to face these people again.

"I'm sorry," Emily said lightly. "Michael went to pick up a few things while I lay down. I guess the jet lag got to me. I'm sorry if . . ."

She trailed off while Tara put together in her mind the reason they'd not seen a strange car and had no reason to think the conversation would be overheard.

"It's okay," Sean whispered behind her ear. But his words only made the reality set in. She hurriedly set the bag on the table and went to the bedroom, closing the door behind her.

Sean sighed and set his bags down. "Excuse me," he said, moving toward the hall, but Emily stopped him.

"Sean," she said in a near whisper, "give her a few minutes. Why don't you get the groceries? I'll find what goes in the fridge."

Sean nodded, appreciating a woman's perception. He brought in the rest of the bags, then began helping Emily sort through them and put things away. She said nothing as they worked, and he wondered what she was thinking. A part of him was relieved to have it out. He didn't want secrets between them. They were his family, and this was a difficult thing. They could use the support. But could he convince Tara of that?

Before they were finished, Michael returned. He walked in and apparently noticed the somber expressions. "Is everything all right?" he asked immediately.

"I . . ." Sean glanced toward Emily. "I think we need to talk."

"What's wrong?" Michael questioned.

Emily folded her hands and glanced down, making it clear that it was up to Sean whether or not anything was said to Michael.

"Excuse me a minute," Sean said, realizing he needed to think this through. He found Tara leaning against the headboard, staring at the wall with several overused tissues beside her on the bed.

"It's okay," Sean said, taking her hand, touching her face.

"No, it's not." Her voice was scornful.

"It's out, so let's talk about it. Come in the other room, and . . ."

She squeezed her eyes shut and shook her head. "You tell them. I can't listen to it. I can't."

"Your family knows, Tara, and they have been very supportive. There is no reason to think that Michael and Emily won't be the same."

"Fine," she almost snapped, "but you tell them."

Sean contemplated it a moment. "Okay. You let me know if you need anything."

She nodded, and he sensed her relief in letting him handle it. Perhaps it was better this way.

Sean closed the bedroom door and found Michael and Emily seated on the couch, looking concerned. He sat down across from them and leaned his forearms on his thighs. "Did Emily tell you?"

"She told me that she overheard something she probably shouldn't have, which is the reason Tara is upset. She didn't tell me what. If you don't want me to know, then—"

"It's not that," Sean interrupted. "Actually, I wanted to tell you a long time ago, but . . . Tara wanted to keep it quiet and . . . well . . ."

"I understand, Sean," Emily said. "But I think we should talk about it."

Sean nodded and took a deep breath. He met Michael's eyes and informed him of what Emily already knew. "Tara is pregnant."

Michael lifted an eyebrow in surprise. While Sean was wondering where to take the explanations from here, Michael asked, "How pregnant?"

"She found out in November," Sean said, and Michael blew out a long breath. Emily only watched Sean with a combination of empathy and concern showing in her eyes.

"Well," Michael said, "that certainly explains why you weren't married in the temple."

"I couldn't expect you not to wonder about that," Sean replied.

"Things like this happen, Sean, even to good people who try to do what's right." Emily's voice was gentle with understanding. "You mustn't let it hold you back from—"

"I know all of that," he interrupted, "but before we go any further, I need to clarify something." He pushed a hand through his hair. "It's not my baby."

He didn't miss the confusion that passed over their faces. "But I don't want you to be thinking less of Tara, because—"

"She's obviously a wonderful girl," Michael said adamantly. "It's good she has someone like you to help her through this, but I hope this marriage wasn't just for the sake of—"

"I understand what you're saying." Sean tried to buffer his frustration and get to the point. "I'm doing my best to help her through this, but you need to know that we made the decision to marry before we knew she was pregnant. The two have no connection, I can assure you."

"That's good," Emily said firmly.

"But the biggest reason I wanted you to know about this is because, well . . ." Sean wasn't prepared for the emotion he felt.

"We're not keeping the baby, because . . ." He saw Michael and Emily exchange a concerned glance, but they patiently allowed him to compose himself and go on.

"When Tara discovered she was pregnant, she had a strong impression that the baby was for someone else; someone who couldn't have children of their own. And even though it's going to be hard . . . and it's hard now . . . and . . ." He tried to laugh, but it erupted as a little moan. "Well . . . we know this is best, because we have to put it behind us, and . . . well, the thing is . . ." He looked down for a moment and took a deep breath, then he looked directly at them. "She was raped."

"Merciful heaven!" Michael muttered breathily. Emily leaned back and clamped a hand over her mouth.

Sean tried quickly to answer all their questions before they could ask them. Emily actually cried.

"I guess that's it," Sean concluded. "There's nothing more to tell, except that it's hard. While we were planning the wedding and settling in, she seemed to be doing better. But now, I guess she doesn't have as much to distract herself with. She doesn't feel good much of the time, and it's difficult not to think about it."

Emily shook her head in disbelief. "Well, that is certainly under-standable. What she must have been through!"

"She didn't want you to know," Sean said quietly. "I can't explain why, exactly. But it's hard for her. She knows how close we are, and I think she wanted you to be happy about our marriage."

"But we are, of course," Michael insisted.

"I know that, and you know that, but . . ."

"May I talk to her?" Emily asked.

"You're welcome to try. Sometimes I think she needs another woman around more."

Emily quickly composed herself and knocked lightly on the bedroom door.

"Come in," Tara called, quickly gathering the used tissues and tossing them in the wastebasket. She knew it wasn't Sean, because he wouldn't knock.

"Are you all right?" Emily asked, peering in as she slowly opened the door.

Tara nodded feebly, wondering what to expect.

"Sean told us everything. I hope you don't mind."

Tara said nothing. Emily sat on the edge of the bed.

"Were you afraid we would think less of you, Tara?" she asked gently.

Tara shrugged. "I don't know what to think. I don't believe I've been able to think for months, now."

"It's okay," Emily said. "You shouldn't be keeping such secrets from family. We should be helping you through this, instead of causing more stress."

With all the good that Sean had told her about Emily Hamilton, Tara shouldn't have been surprised to see how easily she accepted the problem. It took only a few minutes for Tara to feel completely at ease as Emily talked of struggles in her own life, subtly weaving in suggestions that gave Tara a new outlook and fresh courage. Tara delighted in hearing how Sean had come into their lives, and some of the experiences they had shared as Michael and Emily had supported his mission and helped him through the surgeries on his hands.

"He's changed, you know," Emily said, warmly taking Tara's hand. "When Sean first came into our home, it was obvious his testimony was deep and his spirit strong. But there was such a sadness about him. He went through a lot of ups and downs, but I've never seen him looking more vibrant." A new peace settled into Tara as Emily added, "It's obvious that you were the part of his life that he needed to be happy."

Instinctively Tara put her arms around Emily with a warm hug. "I'm so glad you came," she said. "For my sake as well as Sean's. You're like family to him."

"I guess that makes us *all* family," Emily said, and together they went to the front room where Sean and Michael were both looking glum and bored.

"Everything okay?" Michael asked.

"Everything would be perfect if we could get you to cook some dinner," Emily said to Michael.

"I thought you'd never ask," Michael said with exaggerated relief. Tara met Sean's eyes and saw him smile. She reminded herself that he had told her Michael and Emily would understand. She needed to learn to trust him more in the future.

After sharing a delicious meal, Michael announced that it was time to open the wedding gift.

"I thought the Blazer covered that," Sean said.

"Oh, no," Michael shook his finger at Sean, "that was payment for tending the kids all night. Remember?"

Sean chuckled and shook his head at the absurdity. "I remember, all right. But I think I owe you some change."

"Naw," Michael said, pushing his hand through the air abruptly. Then he motioned toward Emily. "Where's the gift, darlin'?"

"I gave it to you," she said.

"No, you didn't," he retorted, while he checked his pockets. With an embarrassed chuckle he sheepishly pulled out a folded piece of paper. "Okay, so maybe I'm going senile."

Emily smiled at her husband as he elaborately unfolded the piece of paper and cleared his throat histrionically. "Actually," Michael said, "this is a combination wedding-graduation gift. You can't use it until you have that master's degree. Understood?"

"You're making me nervous," Sean said lightly.

Michael set the little paper on the table and slid it toward Sean. Sean and Tara both looked down at it, but it was blank. "There's nothing on it," Sean insisted.

"Well, turn it over, boy," Michael said impatiently.

Sean picked it up with exaggerated caution and Emily chuckled. "They're always like this," she said to Tara.

Tara nodded and curiously looked over Sean's shoulder as his expression sobered. "You've got to be joking," Sean said.

Tara squinted to read what was written there but couldn't quite make it out, so she took it from Sean and read aloud, "This coupon is good for one all-expense-paid trip for two to Queensland, Australia." Tara gasped, then she laughed. "Are you serious?"

"Of course I'm serious." Michael feigned disgust. "Sean claims to be part of the family, but he's yet to even set foot in our *real* home. It's about time he did." He smiled and added more seriously, "So plan on it. We'll get the tickets for you when you get that degree and have some time. If you're coming, you might as well stay a few weeks and make the most of it."

Sean laughed and put his arm around Tara. "I know better than to argue with you when it comes to money," Sean laughed. He reached a hand across the table, and Michael shook it eagerly. "Thank you, Michael. And you, Emily." He reached over and kissed her. "You're the best family a disowned Mormon boy could ever ask for."

Michael tousled Sean's hair as if he were just a kid, and they laughed together.

The next day, Emily took Tara to the mall while Sean and Michael watched a game on T.V., though they mostly visited. During halftime, Michael said without preamble, "So, are you making it all right?"

It only took Sean a moment to figure what he meant. "Financially, you mean," he clarified.

"Yes, that's what I mean." Sean hesitated, and Michael looked him in the eye. "Don't get all proud on me, Sean. There's nothing wrong with admitting that it can be difficult to make ends meet. If I can help you out, then—"

"I can honestly say we're doing fine, Michael. But I'm not too proud to admit that it might change. My savings are getting low, and I don't know what will happen exactly with the medical expenses. I must admit I've felt some peace in knowing I could turn to you if I needed to."

"Would you do it?" Michael asked pointedly.

"If I got desperate, yes."

"Don't wait until you get desperate, Sean."

"Well," Sean chuckled, "it wouldn't be the first time God used you to answer my prayers."

"It's only money," Michael muttered and leaned back to watch the game.

An hour later, the women returned with enough packages to make it evident that Emily had been equally generous. She'd insisted on buying Tara some more maternity clothes, and a few things for the house. Emily casually justified it away with a simple, "We're family and we want to help you get started. No big deal."

A week later, Tara stood holding Sean's hand as Michael and Emily turned back for one last wave before boarding the plane.

"They truly are wonderful people," Tara said. "I can't help but love them."

Sean smiled down at her. "I knew you would," he said and kissed her quickly. "Come on. Let's go home."

By March, Tara was managing well with her classes and becoming accustomed to keeping the apartment under control. In spite of the ill effects of the pregnancy beginning to ease up, she was grateful she didn't have to be working. Sean had heavier studying, but he managed to keep up his job, find time to be with Tara, and even help a little in the kitchen.

As they attended their new ward regularly, Tara relaxed and the new associations made it easier to feel somewhat comfortable. Wearing maternity clothes now was a must, and she had little choice but to admit to it and sound happy about it. Outside of church association, they were occasionally affronted with remarks, and they suspected that words were being whispered concerning their hurried marriage. But together they managed to handle it positively and concentrate on the happiness they were sharing in their private lives.

At moments, it was difficult for Tara to comprehend the pure joy she found in her intimate relationship with Sean. She marveled at the beauty and pleasure of this God-given ability that accomplished more healing than she believed years of counseling ever would. The love she shared with Sean put her experience with Danny into its proper perspective. There were no similarities. And the time she spent alone with Sean, whether in passion or peace, lifted and rejuvenated her, making the struggles somehow easier to face.

Late one night while the wind howled outside, Tara became lost in Sean's love and thought it somehow symbolic. While struggles raged around them, the love they shared kept the world at bay. At moments like this, consumed with feelings she would have never dreamed possible, Tara believed she could face anything, as long as Sean was by her side.

She woke alone in the middle of the night and realized the front room light was on. The wind had settled some, but she could hear rain falling. Grabbing Sean's robe and tying it around her, she went to find him.

"Are you okay?" she asked, startling him.

"Yeah," he muttered and turned his attention back to the book on his lap. Tara recognized it as the album Maureen had given him for a wedding gift.

"Are you sure?" she asked, sitting close beside him.

Sean pushed an arm around her and pressed his lips into her hair. "No," he whispered, his voice cracking.

Tara attempted to distract him from his emotion by asking questions about the pictures. His mood lightened as he talked of his growing years with warmth. She was intrigued by the pictures of him during his "rebellious" years. It was difficult to comprehend the Sean O'Hara she loved as a disagreeable youth with long hair and a beer in his hand. Sean was amused by the contrast, and seemed to enjoy the reminiscing.

"There's my old truck," he said with delight, pointing to a picture of a blue Ford pickup. "It was a good old thing. I sold it just before I left on my mission."

"Then you must have driven it to Utah," she said.

"Yeah," Sean murmured, but his countenance sobered and his eyes grew distant.

"What?" she prodded when he remained silent.

"I just . . . remembered something I hadn't thought of for years."

Tara was relieved when he went on. "Well, the day after I was baptized, I loaded everything I had into the back of that truck and headed for Utah. I was terrified. I had very little money, and I had absolutely no idea where I was going. I only knew I was headed for Provo, Utah, because that's where the Mormon university was. I had no relatives anywhere that would go against my father's wishes. And the friends I'd had before the accident simply quit coming around. Some friends, eh?" He gave a toneless chuckle and leaned back as he continued.

"Anyway, I remember just driving until I couldn't keep my eyes open, then I'd pull over and sleep in the truck. I had a little cooler and bought cheap groceries that I could eat without cooking. What little money I had, I knew I would need to get me by until I got a job and a place to live. I think I was somewhere in Nebraska when the reality hit me. I started to wonder how I was ever going to survive. I remember watching my hands on the steering wheel, and all kinds of horrible images started flashing through my mind. I was alone, practically penniless, and disabled. It started to rain, and I started to cry. It was almost dark when the truck quit."

Sean shook his head and sighed. "I couldn't believe it. I had prayed with all my heart and soul that the truck would at least make it to Provo. In that moment, I felt like God had abandoned me. After I quit cursing, I got out and opened the hood, trying to find the problem. But it was pouring, and I didn't have a clue what was wrong. I couldn't see anything in any direction; no houses—nothing! I started to pray, but after sitting there in the rain for an hour, I remember just . . . giving up. I decided to go to sleep, thinking that in the morning I would have to hitchhike or something into the nearest town. I made up my mind to get the truck fixed and go back to Chicago. I thought it all through—everything I would say to my father, how I would apologize and start going to mass again, and . . ."

He stopped and rubbed a hand over his face as the inevitable emotion overcame him. Tara took his hand and squeezed it, silently encouraging him to go on.

"I was just settling in when this car pulled up behind me, and two men got out. They told me I wasn't likely to get the truck fixed that late, especially with the bad weather. But one of them insisted that I come home with him and get a hot meal and spend the night."

Sean paused again to gain his composure. "I was just beginning to think that maybe God hadn't abandoned me after all, when I walked into that house and the first thing I saw was a picture of the Salt Lake Temple." He met her eyes. "This guy was a bishop, Tara."

She smiled serenely and shook her head, as if it were too incredible to believe.

"He asked me where I was headed. When I told him where and why, he actually got tears in his eyes. The next morning he helped me fix the truck, bought me some groceries, and gave me the address and phone number of his sister, who lived with her family in Provo. He had already called her and made arrangements for me to stay with her until I could find a job and an apartment."

Tara shook her head again. "That's incredible."

"Yeah," Sean chuckled intensely, "it is. I was ready to turn my back on it all, totally unaware that God had it completely worked out. The repair on the truck was minor; but if it hadn't quit, I would have arrived in Provo with nowhere to go. This family was terrific and treated me well, but I actually only stayed there less than a week. Things just seemed to fall into place."

He chuckled again, more lightly this time. "Selling that truck was hard, mostly because of that trip, I think." He looked again at the picture and drew a deep breath. Then he turned the page and continued to reminisce. Eventually the emotion overtook him. Tara could almost feel the pain seep into his countenance, and he cried himself into exhaustion. It was the first time she had seen him exhibit *real* emotion in regard to his circumstances. Tara urged him back to bed, and he slept soundly until she nudged him awake.

"Hey, handsome. Breakfast is ready. You're going to be late."

Sean stretched and grinned. "You mean you've already buttered my toast?" he chuckled.

"No, silly, I *cooked* breakfast."

"Ooh," he teased, "what's the special occasion?"

"Just . . . hungry," she said with a subtle glow of mischief in her eyes.

Sean dressed quickly and sat down at the table just as she set pancakes and scrambled eggs in front of him. She poured milk into his glass, then sat down across from him.

"What?" she asked, perfectly innocent when he gave her a dubious glare.

"Everything's . . . *green.*"

Tara gasped as if he'd insulted her. "Why, Sean O'Hara, I'm ashamed of you. Is it, or is it not, St. Patrick's Day?" Sean threw his head back and laughed. Tara made a huffy little noise and added, "You told me you celebrated this holiday religiously, and now you—"

Sean reached over the table and kissed her. "You're an angel, you know that?"

"I'm just trying to be a good Irish wife," she smiled.

"Well, I've been Irish a long time, but I've never had a green breakfast before." He picked up his glass of green milk, looked at it skeptically, then raised it high. "To the luck of the Irish," he said and they both drank. "It still tastes the same," he added as if he were disappointed.

Several times through the day, Sean thought about his breakfast and chuckled to himself. It was a little thing, but it let him know how much Tara loved him. Somehow, it helped buffer the loss of his family in a way he couldn't explain. She made up for so much that he wondered what he'd ever done without her.

Sean wasn't expecting to come home and find green candles on the table, green Kool-Aid in a pitcher, and green napkins set out with the dishes. Tara emerged from the bedroom to greet him, dressed in green from head to toe. He laughed and kissed her, then she served baked chicken coated with something crispy and green. Green rolls. Green mashed potatoes with green gravy, peas, and green jello. For dessert she provided a green cake with green frosting.

When the meal was finished, Sean leaned back in his chair and said in an accent that imitated his father's, "I've never felt s' Irish in m' whole life."

Tara laughed and started the dishes. Sean came behind her and kissed her neck. "Thank you," he said gently. The true depth of his feelings seemed momentarily inexpressible, so he kissed her again and said, "You have the most beautiful neck."

"I'm tryin' t' wash dishes, Mr. O'Hara." She attempted the Irish accent, then laughed at her poor effort.

Sean chuckled and lifted her into his arms. "Th' dishes 'll wait, Mrs. O'Hara." With that he carried her to the bedroom and kicked the door shut.

* * * * *

As Tara began to feel better and accomplish more, it was almost easy to forget that she was pregnant. But a day came when she had to face it.

Sean was just coming awake when he heard her gasp. "What's wrong?" He sat up immediately and found her lying beside him on her back, her hands against her belly.

She looked up with tears in her eyes and said sadly, "I can feel it moving."

Sean knew why it made her sad, but she still had months to go in this, and he was determined to keep this as light as possible. "Is it dancing or playing hockey?"

Tara laughed. "Where do you suppose it would find a hockey puck?"

"Oh, it's just practicing moves."

"Sean," she said soberly, "I'm scared."

"So am I," he admitted.

"But we have to face this. We can't keep putting it off."

He knew what she was talking about, and later that week they were sitting in an office at LDS Social Services, explaining to a kind woman why they wanted to give this baby away. Tara held up well until they got back to the Blazer, then she cried all the way home.

"I don't know how I can do it," she said over and over. "How can I feel it growing and moving inside of me every day, and go through labor and delivery, just to have it taken away?"

When they were home and Sean could sit down to face her, he said carefully, "Tara, this is your baby. It is your decision. No one is going to make you give it away. If you're having trouble with it, maybe you need to pray about it and reevaluate. If you decide to pursue this course, I will be there for you every minute."

"And if I decided to keep it?"

"I will be there for you every minute," he repeated with the same conviction. "I would gladly raise this child as my own, and I wouldn't begrudge it. It's for you to decide, but I think you'd better decide soon. Either way, you're going to need the coming weeks to be prepared."

Tara knew he was right, and she spent the following days seeking the guidance of the Spirit. The answer was more difficult to come by this time, as if God were saying, *I already told you once, but if you must know, I'll tell you again.* Tara went to Sean and interrupted his studying to announce, "This baby is not for me."

"I know," he said and held her while she cried.

The following week Tara returned to Social Services while Sean was in classes, and talked through several aspects of the situation. The whole thing felt awkward and difficult, but she reminded herself it would take time to adjust. She couldn't deny that they treated her well, and their reassurances helped. Still, she knew there was much ahead that she feared facing.

When she felt lowest, Tara turned her mind to the dream that had helped her make this decision. She reminded herself that this would all be worth it. There was someone out there who needed this baby.

Chapter Twelve

Veronica Raine pulled the handful of mail out of the box and shuffled through it as she walked back to the house. She was almost to the door when the letter from their lawyer in Provo appeared. Momentarily frozen, Veronica contemplated the possibilities. Jane was a good lawyer, who had been recommended to her by a friend of a friend a few years back. Since Provo was the nearest major city to their ranch in central Utah, the arrangement worked nicely. Except that the results they'd been hoping for still evaded them.

Veronica told herself not to get her hopes up. She'd had too many disappointments to imagine opening the envelope to find good news. But a part of her couldn't help wishing this was it as she hurried in the house to toss aside the rest of the mail. With trembling hands she tore open the envelope and scanned the letter quickly. The inevitable tears rose in her eyes, blurring her vision before she could finish reading all the details. They didn't matter anyway, she told herself as she flung the letter to the table and turned away. The bottom line was always the same. She and Matthew had been married eight years, and the opportunity for children continued to elude them.

Veronica attempted to choke back the emotion and distract herself. She was sick to death of crying over this, tired of feeling this way. It hadn't been so long since she'd felt some real hope, and she had believed with all her heart that this time it would happen. But she cursed those feelings as she hurried to the kitchen and threw open the refrigerator.

With vehemence she pulled out an assortment of raw vegetables to prepare them for chicken stir-fry. While she washed and sliced mushrooms, Veronica thought about the joy she'd felt when she and Matthew were married. The circumstances that brought them together were unique, but the intensity of their love was undeniable. She recalled the happiness they'd shared, speculating over the family they would raise. And how could she forget her father's pleasure at the prospect of his youngest daughter finally being married and giving him grandchildren? To this day, for all his goodness, Joshua Leeds didn't let a week go by without letting her know in one way or another how it broke his heart that there were no children.

Veronica sliced celery and thought about the years it took to finally be willing to admit there was a problem they couldn't solve at home. She peeled and sliced carrots, recalling how difficult the doctor's appointments had been. How much she'd hated the tests and exams, and the strain she'd felt between herself and Matthew as they waited to determine which one of them was responsible for this terrible circumstance.

Part of Veronica was relieved to find out it was her. Matthew was a good man who did so much for her, and she knew it would be difficult for him to deal with such a thing. But a day hardly passed when she didn't remind herself that if Matthew had married any other woman, he could have had two or three children by now. Of course he was always sweet and reassuring. Never once had he said anything to make her feel like any less of a woman because of the problem. He loved and adored her, and she knew it. But she also knew that he ached for children as much as she did.

Veronica tore apart the stems of broccoli in heated spurts as she thought about the work they'd done to find a good adoption lawyer, and all the effort they'd put into every step of the process. Their first disappointment was handled well; the mother changed her mind at the last minute and decided to keep the baby. The next one was a little tougher to swallow. The mother had chosen her and Matthew as parents for her baby, but a few weeks before the birth something else opened up and she gave it to another couple. This same thing happened again, with immense waiting in between each episode. And now, once again, a potential birth mother had made a decision that left Veronica without a baby.

Veronica couldn't hold the tears back any longer as she rinsed the bean sprouts and her emptiness erupted into bitterness. If she heard one more newscast about abortion rights, or saw one more baby at the grocery store, or—

Veronica sucked in her emotion when she heard the door and knew it was Matthew. Quickly she grabbed a paper towel and wiped it over her face and blew her nose. She purposely turned on the garbage disposal and rinsed out the sink, giving her a minute to gain some composure. She was just wishing she'd thought to put the letter away when she turned to see him standing there, the letter hanging limply in his hand.

"I'm so sorry, Ronni," he said, and she knew he meant it. "We'll—"

"Don't you dare say it!" she interrupted, wishing it hadn't sounded so sharp.

"What?" he asked quietly.

"You were going to tell me there will be more opportunities. Well, I don't believe it any more. I don't want another opportunity." The tears returned all too easily. "I don't even *want* a baby anymore. I don't want to—"

"You don't mean that and you know it," Matthew retorted, tossing the letter onto the counter.

"Yes, I do," she cried, scornfully throwing the dishrag into the sink. "I can't do this again, Matthew. I can't! If I have to feel this way one more time, I think I'll die." Her emotion surfaced fully and she pressed her face into her hands. "I'll just die."

Matthew's arms came around her and she leaned into him, wondering why he never seemed to get tired of holding her while she cried. He was always there, always kind. And though he tried to hide it, she knew he was crying, too.

Later that evening they sat together on the couch. Beyond the soft music playing on the stereo, the house was perfectly still. The silence was something they'd both grown to hate. They'd talked many times about the desire to hear a child playing in bed because he didn't want to go to sleep, or perhaps interrupting them every few minutes for another drink of water. But the only noise they had was the music and each other. Everything on television was either depressing or senseless most of the time. They'd watched every good movie they could get their hands on at least once. They read every good book they could find, and often reread them aloud to each other.

But tonight, there was nothing to interest them, nothing to distract them from the reality. There was simply nothing to say that hadn't already been said many times before. Veronica knew Matthew loved her, and she loved him. But there were times when that just wasn't enough. Oh, how she ached to hold a child in her arms and know that it depended on her for its every need. How she longed to sit here and watch Matthew playing with a baby on the floor, or perhaps rocking it against his shoulder.

But what could they do that they hadn't already done? As soon as she asked herself, she knew the answer. They had to try again. She was mustering the courage to say it aloud when Matthew said firmly, "I know it's hard for you, Ronni, but we have to try again."

Veronica turned to him with tears in her eyes. "I know," she said quietly, and he pulled her into his arms.

The next morning at breakfast, Veronica attempted to share with her husband the thoughts that had churned through her head in the night. But they were so complex, she didn't know where to begin. "Do you think that God really answers prayers?" she asked.

Matthew looked as surprised by the question as she expected. They both believed in a supreme being, and basically accepted the Christian beliefs of the Bible. But neither of them had any religion in their backgrounds whatsoever. It simply wasn't a part of their lives.

"I suppose he does," Matthew answered noncommittally. "Why?"

"Well," she admitted, feeling somehow reluctant, "I must confess I've been praying for a baby, and I've believed that God would help us. But I've begun to wonder if . . ."

"If what?" he asked, his brow furrowing.

"Well, maybe he only answers the prayers of people who go to church and stuff like that."

"I couldn't tell you." Matthew seemed somehow concerned. When Veronica said nothing more, he added, "I get the impression you're trying to get to a point. Why don't you just get to it?"

Veronica chuckled tensely. "I'm not sure, really. I was just lying in bed last night, praying that I could go on, that we could somehow get a baby; that if we were on the wrong track, we would know how to get on the right one. And it just occurred to me that maybe God expects something in return. Like maybe we should go to church or something."

"Forgive me, Ronni, but I don't see how the ritual of going to church makes that much difference in whether or not a person lives a good life. We're good, honest people who try to do the right thing. I don't think we need to go to church to prove anything to God or anybody else."

"I suppose you're right," she said, wondering why she felt like she was lying.

"Besides," he added, "if we did go to church, where would we go?"

"There are several to choose from around here."

"That's just my point," he stated. "How do you know which one is *God's* church, if such a thing even exists? Personally, I have my doubts."

Long after Matthew went out to feed the animals and get to his work, Veronica contemplated the things he'd said and tried to make sense of it. But she just couldn't shake the feeling that God expected something of her. If only she knew what it was.

Convincing herself that she was getting carried away with her frustration, Veronica put it out of her mind and wrote a quick letter to their lawyer, asking her to keep their file current. She couldn't give up. She just couldn't!

Drawing courage, Veronica did something that she rarely did anymore. Cautiously she turned the knob an a seldom-used door and pushed it slowly open. The expected tears fell as she moved her fingers with longing over the edge of the crib. She wiped thick dust particles off the top of the dresser where a music box and baby paraphernalia were set out. Gingerly she picked up the stuffed animals, then toyed with the mobile hanging above the crib.

When she and Matthew were first contacted with the possibility of getting a baby, they had rushed out and bought everything they needed. Veronica recalled the excitement she'd felt wallpapering this room with little pastel bunnies, and the curtains she'd made for the window. But after their third disappointment, she'd found it practically unbearable to even come in here. Even now, the pain was undeniable, but she tried to replace it with a glimmer of hope as she closed the door again and searched for a distraction.

* * * * *

Tara got into her car and slammed the door. She tried to find the motivation to put the key in the ignition and drive home, but she was so confused and upset, all she could do was stare out the window, trying to pinpoint the cause for her concern.

She'd started the day with her usual doctor's appointment. Everything went well. In a way the time seemed to drag, while in other respects it was running out quickly. She'd gone straight from there to LDS Social Services, where she looked over files on potential parents for her baby. She had been praying for weeks for the necessary guidance and inspiration so that she could find the right home for this baby. But nothing felt right. She knew the baby was to be put up for adoption. There was no question about that. So why did she feel so confused and distraught every time she talked to these people about it? It simply made no sense.

Realizing she was hungry and feeling a little queasy, Tara started the engine and drove toward home. Her mind wandered through the situation until the inevitable tears appeared right on schedule.

"I don't understand what you want me to do, Lord," she said aloud. "You've got to help me. If I'm on the wrong track, help me get on the right one."

Tara became so caught up in her emotion that she didn't realize she'd passed a stop sign until she felt the impact. It only took a moment to know she wasn't hurt, but with the realization that she had just caused an accident, she practically became hysterical. Her first thought was to make certain the other driver was all right. But she jumped out of the car so quickly that the blood rushed from her head, and she woke up in a moving ambulance.

"Where are we going?" she demanded. But her attempt to sit up was halted by a gentle hand on her shoulder.

"It's all right." The paramedic soothed her with a kind smile.

"You passed out. It looks like you're all right, but with you being pregnant and all, we thought it best to take you in and make sure everything's okay."

"The other driver?" she asked.

"Oh, she wasn't hurt at all. The accident was pretty minor, actually."

Tara was grateful for that, at least. She looked at her hands and realized she was trembling.

"You are a little shaky," the paramedic said, "but you'll be fine, Mrs. O'Hara."

"How did you know my name?" she asked, trying to remain calm.

"It was on the car registration," he stated. "They've contacted your husband."

Tara felt a fresh rush of panic. Sean would be frantic. She wanted to ask how they had found him so quickly, but the ambulance pulled up behind the hospital and she was wheeled inside. She was only there a few minutes before Sean was ushered into the room. He sighed visibly when he saw her, then rushed to her side and pulled her into his arms.

"Oh, you're all right," he muttered. "Thank God. You're all right."

"How did they find you?" she asked.

"I stopped home for lunch, hoping you'd be back. I was wondering how it went this morning." He touched her face and hair, so grateful to see her alive after all the worst possible scenarios had flashed through his mind on his way over.

"The accident was my fault, Sean," she admitted tearfully. "I didn't even see the stop sign. I'm so sorry. I—"

"It's all right," he insisted, almost chuckling. "It doesn't matter. The insurance will take care of it."

"Oh," she cried and hugged him tightly, "you're so good to me."

"I'm just glad you're all right," he said again and kissed her.

Tara's doctor was called and he ordered some tests to make certain the baby was all right. Everything appeared to be fine, but he made the decision to keep her at the hospital overnight, since she had a nasty bump on the head—not from the accident, but from passing out afterward. Sean sat by her bed through the evening while she told him the turmoil she'd been feeling when the accident occurred. She was just expounding on the confusion she felt when a woman peered through the partially open door.

"Excuse me," she said, "are you Mrs. O'Hara?"

"Yes," Tara said warily.

The woman stepped into the room, wearing a kind smile and a conservative skirt and blouse. She was in her middle thirties, Tara guessed, slender, and pretty in a plain way.

"My name is Diane Hayne," she said holding out a hand to Tara. Tara shook it and she turned to Sean. "You must be Mr. O'Hara."

"That's right." Sean stood and shook her hand as well.

"Well, you probably don't remember much," Diane said, "but I was driving the other car in that accident you had earlier."

Tara leaned forward, apologizing eagerly. "I am so sorry. I don't know what was wrong with me. I just—"

"It's all right, Mrs. O'Hara," Diane assured her kindly. "I just came to see how you were doing. They told me you're pregnant and they were concerned."

"Everything's fine," Sean said. "We appreciate your stopping by."

"I wanted to stick around earlier, but I was on my way back to work and . . . well, I work for a lawyer and she had appointments I had to be there for, and . . ."

"You aren't going to sue me, are you?" Tara asked so innocently that Sean chuckled.

"Of course not," Diane smiled. "I've already talked to your insurance company, and they assure me that everything will be taken care of."

"If you have any problems," Sean insisted, "don't hesitate to let us know. We'll make it right."

"I know you will," Diane smiled. "I can see that you're good people. And just so you don't have to wonder," she nodded toward Tara, "the woman I work for wouldn't even touch a legal suit. She believes it's better left alone for the most part."

"I could agree with that," Sean said, and Tara realized she liked this woman.

"What exactly do you do?" Tara asked, if only for the sake of having a conversation that wasn't based on the problems in her life.

"Me or the lawyer?" Diane asked.

"Both," Tara replied.

"Me, I'm just kind of a secretary. I do whatever she needs me to. Jane handles a number of things, but her main focus is adoption."

Tara and Sean exchanged a glance of disbelief, then turned to look at Diane Hayne, eyes wide.

"Did I say something wrong?" she asked in apparent distress.

Tara clamped a hand over her mouth for fear of crying out loud. Hadn't she been praying to be put on the right track at the moment the accident occurred? Was it ridiculous to think that the Lord had intended for this to happen?

Following a length of awkward silence, Sean finally said, "No, actually, you said something I think we need to hear."

"I don't understand," Diane stated.

Sean glanced at Tara for approval and read it in her eyes. "You see," he began, "we are in need of someone to help us with an adoption situation."

Diane's eyes widened, but she said nothing. Sean didn't know if this woman was LDS or not, but he suspected she was. Mormons just seemed to have a certain quality about them. Still, he readily admitted, "I think this little accident might not have been an accident. Does that make any sense?"

"I think so," Diane said. "But if Mrs. O'Hara is pregnant, then why would you . . ." She stopped when it became obvious that she had begun to perceive the implication.

Sean explained. "The baby is the result of a rape. We feel that under the circumstances, it should be placed for adoption."

"Oh, I see," Diane said slowly, her eyes filling with compassion. She smiled before Tara had a chance to feel uncomfortable, then said almost triumphantly, "Well then, I guess you ran into the right person."

The next morning, Sean picked Tara up at the hospital and they drove straight to Jane Richardson's office. Diane was there, and the four of them sat down together to discuss the situation. Both women were open and congenial, and Tara felt completely at ease. They quickly learned that both Jane and Diane were LDS. Jane had chosen to go into adoption because she had been unable to have children of her own. She had been married for seventeen years, had adopted two sons, and was currently a counselor in her ward Relief Society presidency.

Diane's husband had walked out on her soon after her fifteen-year-old daughter was born. She lived with her daughter in Oak Hills, and she taught a Primary class.

After learning some personal things about both of these women, it was easy for Tara to feel comfortable enough to get into the real feelings of her situation. She cried a little but didn't feel embarrassed. Diane jotted down notes, and Jane agreed to get back to them soon with some files they could look over.

On the way home, Tara felt a degree of peace settle upon her. It was much the way she'd felt when she had originally realized this baby was not meant for her. She knew now that the reason she didn't feel right about going through LDS Social Services was simple. This baby was meant for someone in particular, and that someone could only be accessed through Jane Richardson.

The following week, Tara was a bit disappointed when she looked over the files Jane provided. Nothing stood out strongly as she'd hoped it would. But she talked with Jane and Diane about it, and concluded that she had several weeks left and she would pray about it.

Feeling confident that she was going in the right direction, Tara relaxed and concentrated on her studies. Her family kept in close touch, which helped considerably, and she was relieved when the term ended and she came through with satisfactory grades. Sean declared they were going out to celebrate.

"How are you feeling?" he asked, reaching a hand across the table to take hers.

"Good, actually," she smiled.

They ate and talked over their plans to fill in the small break they had before Sean started another term, which would be finished before the baby came. Then he planned to take the summer off and be with Tara continually if she needed him. He spoke to her, as he often did, of the honeymoon they would take in August. He didn't care where they went or what they did. It was only for the sake of making a fresh start.

Tara felt good as she talked of goals beyond the birth of this child, imagining a bright future. In the midst of their conversation, she happened to look beyond Sean's shoulder at a couple being seated nearby. Suddenly she felt nauseated, and the room began to spin. Unwillingly she pressed a hand over her mouth and closed her eyes.

"What's wrong?" Sean leaned forward with concern.

Tara said nothing, but almost against her will, her eyes went back to where Danny was seated, as if to convince herself he was really there.

Sean glanced discreetly behind him to see what she was looking at. A sick knot formed in his stomach. "Is that him?" he asked, wanting to be certain. He'd only gotten a brief glimpse of Danny once in a dim restaurant. Tara hesitated, her eyes showing fear. Sean glared at her and she nodded.

"Will you take me home?" she managed.

"I'd rather beat the hell out of him, if you want to know the truth."

Tara shook her head firmly, then came to her feet and hurried toward the door, grateful that Danny didn't notice her. Sean paid the check and followed. But he became steadily more angry as Tara vented her feelings through heaving sobs. He hadn't seen her this upset since she'd told him she was pregnant.

"I . . . I can't believe it. There he is . . . oblivious . . . going on with his life . . . as though . . . it were *nothing!*"

"Did you think he'd just disappear off the face of the earth?" Sean asked cynically, wishing he'd made the effort to find Danny again before now.

"I didn't even think about him!" she cried. "I . . . I don't know. I guess I just . . . shut it out. I didn't . . . want to face it." She turned to look at him fearfully. "He was with a woman, Sean. Do you suppose he's done it before? Has he done it since? Am I one of many, or just a select victim?"

"I don't know," he said in a sad voice, tainted with anger.

"I should have . . . pressed charges." She hit her fist on her thigh. "I should have done it . . . while I . . . had the evidence . . . of what he . . . did to me."

"That's easy to say now," he consoled. "But you know as well as I do that you weren't up to it. Besides, should-have-beens don't count."

"You're just saying that . . . to ease my conscience."

"No, I'm not," he lied, not wanting her to regret what couldn't be changed now. At this point, her testimony on its own would likely do little good. He turned to look at her. "Let it go, Tara."

"I'm not sure I can," she said, and he didn't try to argue. He could hardly advise her when the bitterness he felt in that moment could eat him alive.

Sean took Tara inside and suggested she lie down. When she was comfortable and somewhat calmed, he said, "I'll be back in a few minutes."

"Where are you going?" she demanded.

"When I get back, I'll tell you where I've been."

"Sean, no!" She followed him to the door, but he ignored her. "It won't change anything. It won't make any difference."

He turned with his hand on the knob and pointed a finger at her. "While I'm gone I want you to tell yourself that a thousand times, and then we're going to let it go."

Tara was so stunned that she had no choice but to let him go, praying he wouldn't get himself into trouble and make things worse.

Sean returned to the restaurant to find the parking lot dark. He stepped casually inside and glanced around just enough to be sure Danny was still there, then he returned to the Blazer and waited. Ten minutes later, Danny walked out with a pretty girl on his arm, laughing carelessly. Sean waited until this girl was in the car, then he got out and walked over, putting a hand on the driver's door just as Danny reached out to open it.

"I beg your pardon," Danny said haughtily. "Do I know you?"

"No, but I know you," Sean said coolly. "And begging my pardon has nothing to do with it."

Danny laughed and pushed Sean aside like some grade-school bully. "Get out of my way."

Sean grabbed the collar of Danny's jacket and slammed him up against the car. This sent the girl scrambling out to investigate, but Sean ignored her.

"I don't know who you think you are," Danny said as he struggled, "but—"

Sean slammed him again. "You're not so tough when your opponent's bigger than you are. Let's see you try to wrestle me to the ground and knock me around a little."

Something flashed into Danny's eyes that bordered on true fear.

"Now that you know what we're talking about, let me introduce myself. Do you remember Tara Parr?" Danny's eyes widened. "You'd better remember," he added through clenched teeth.

"What's he talking about?" a feminine voice inquired.

"Go ahead and tell her," Sean sneered. "Was Tara the only one, or do you make a habit of forcing yourself upon women? Does this one know what you're really like?"

"I don't know what you're talking about." Danny laughed flippantly until Sean shook him.

"You *do* know what I'm talking about, and we both know it."

"I haven't seen Tara for months," he said lightly.

"Yes, I know," Sean hissed. "Five months and three weeks. That's how pregnant she is."

"What's he talking about?" the girl persisted, this time with an edge to her voice.

"I don't have any idea," Danny said. "He's crazy."

"Tell her about Tara," Sean challenged, still holding him against the car by his collar. Danny made no effort to struggle or challenge him, and Sean knew he was a coward.

"Come on," Sean said louder, "tell her how you took her out all those times and treated her like a friend, and how you turned on her and—"

"She led me on," Danny interrupted, and Sean slammed him hard enough to make him groan. "I didn't force myself on her. We just got carried away."

That did it. "God forgive me," Sean muttered just before his fist connected with Danny's jaw, then Sean sent the other into Danny's belly as he dropped to his knees.

Sean leaned over and spoke from low in his throat. "Getting carried away doesn't account for a black eye, bruised throat and wrists, and a number of abrasions, Danny boy. She could barely walk for a week."

"You're a liar." Danny spat blood and gingerly touched his

bleeding lip.

"You can say what you want, and you can think what you want. But it will never change the fact that you are sick. Very sick. If I were you, I'd get some help before you ruin any more lives and end up where you belong."

"Nobody's got enough proof to put me behind bars," Danny snapped defensively, and it took great self-restraint for Sean to not hit him again.

"Maybe not," Sean stated coolly, "but one day, God will be your judge, and justice will be met."

Danny's eyes flickered, but his countenance remained set. "Who are you, anyway?" Danny asked, lumbering to his feet.

"I'm Tara's husband," he said and Danny's eyes narrowed, as if he were somehow disappointed that he hadn't ruined Tara enough to keep her from marrying.

"What's your name?" Danny demanded, and Sean knew why.

"Wouldn't you like to know."

Danny proved Sean's suspicions when he looked at the blood on his fingers and said proudly, "I'll get you for this, if I have to hunt you down and—"

Sean leaned forward again and actually grinned. "It's your word against mine."

Their eyes turned at the same time toward Danny's date, who stood looking dazed.

"I've got a witness," Danny said smugly. Sean wondered if she believed anything that had been said, or if she was blind enough to think this guy was worth the time of day.

"I didn't see anything," she said innocently, and Sean smiled.

"Neither did I," Sean added. He glanced at the distraught and befuddled Danny, then back to the girl. Knowing Tara would understand, he asked quietly, "Is there someone I can call to come and get you, or—"

"Oh, I can call my roommate. I think I've got a quarter and—" While she dug into her purse, Danny got into his car and sped away.

"Here, I've got it." Sean started toward a pay phone on the outside of the restaurant and she followed. He stuck a quarter in and handed her the receiver.

"Thank you," she said and made her call. When she hung up, she cleared her throat tensely and informed him, "She'll be here soon. I'm sure that—"

"If it's all right with you, I'll just wait and make sure he doesn't come back before you get a ride."

She smiled, seeming relieved. "Thank you," she said again. A minute later she asked timidly, "Is it really true?"

"Yes," Sean said gravely, "but for my wife's sake, no one else knows. We'd like to keep it that way."

"I understand." She nodded and a car pulled up in front of them.

"Take care, now," Sean said as he held the door for her. She smiled and they drove away. Sean arrived home to find Tara frantic. She practically jumped into his arms. "Oh, you're safe," she cried. "I was so worried."

"No need for that." He smiled at her, realizing he felt better. "The guy's a wimp if he's not fighting a woman."

She smiled. "What happened?"

Sean held up his hand and put hers over it. She looked puzzled and he said, "I just thought you'd want to touch it before I wash it off. It's kind of a souvenir." He added almost mischievously, "Danny's blood."

"Sean!" She followed him into the bathroom.

"Yes, I know," he scolded himself before she could, while he washed his hands, "it wasn't Christian, but I think he'll recover from a fat lip faster than you'll recover from *his* lack of Christianity." Sean smiled. "And it sure made me feel better."

"What happened?"

Sean repeated the encounter in detail, which spurred mixed emotions in Tara. Through the following days it was difficult to not be reminded of the things Danny had done to her, but Tara stayed close to the scriptures and found peace there. In spite of it all, she knew in her heart she had much to be grateful for.

Chapter Thirteen

May was unusually cold and wet, and Sean became absorbed with intense study. He often wondered if they would survive the stress. Tara had been sweet and patient, but he knew he'd been absorbed and irritable. He told her every day he'd make it up to her. She just smiled and did everything she could to help.

"Sean," she interrupted his study with a gentle hand on his shoulder, "the mail just came and . . ." He looked up when she hesitated. ". . . there's a letter from Chicago."

"You're kidding," he said as she held it out for him. Sean stared at it a long moment, certain it was bad news. His hand almost trembled as he took it. Tara sat close beside him as he tore the seal, pulled out a single page, and unfolded it. He glanced first to the bottom. "It's from Maureen."

Tara watched him closely as his eyes scanned the letter. "No," he muttered breathily. "Please, no."

"What is it?" she asked when he had apparently finished. He absently handed her the letter, then he planted his elbows on the table and pushed his head into his hands.

Silently Tara read:

My Dearest Sean,

I'm sorry to be writing under these circumstances, but I felt you had to know. Mother went into the hospital last week to have some tests done. I told you that she's been ill off and on for quite some time now, without any explanation. They found cancer. She is so full of it, there is nothing they can do. The doctors say she could go at any time;

they estimate that she could live no longer than three to four weeks at the most. She has returned home now, with a nurse there to care for her. She said that she refused to die in a hospital. I can't tell you what to do, Sean. Mother told me she only wished she could see you once more, but when she suggested it to Dad, he exploded. If you decide not to come, we would understand, but I felt you should know. If there is anything I can do without making the situation worse, please let me know. God bless and much love,

Maureen

Tara set the letter aside and wrapped her arms around Sean. "I'm so sorry," she whispered close to his face. With that he almost crumbled into her arms.

"It's not right," he cried. "She's my mother, Tara. I ought to be able to see my own mother without provoking a war."

Tara held him close to her while he cried, and for a long while after in thoughtful silence.

"Sean," she finally said, "maybe I'm wrong, but if you did go see her, what could your father do worse than he already has? You've been concerned about making things more difficult for your mother, but if she's dying, don't you think that for her to see you again would be worth the price? If it were my son, I think it would."

Sean looked up at her, wondering how a woman could be so discerning and beautiful at the same time. "What did I ever do without you?" he asked.

"You managed for more than a quarter of a century."

"Not very well," he admitted. "Do you think you could make the trip?"

"I could probably manage, but I would likely slow your travel. Maybe you should just—"

"Oh, no." He shook his head with determination. "If I've ever needed you, it's now. If I can't take you with me, I'm not going."

"Does that mean we're going to Chicago?"

Sean actually smiled. "We could probably get away the day after tomorrow. I only hope we can make it in time."

Though Sean seemed distracted, Tara was amazed at the efficient way he pulled together his obligations and made arrangements for them to be gone. He took some money out of savings and had it put into traveler's checks. Tara contacted Maureen and let her know their plans. They left before dawn.

The trip actually went well. As long as Tara rested and didn't let her stomach get empty, she felt pretty good. She often drilled Sean from his textbooks to keep him distracted and awake, and occasionally she drove to give him time to study. They ate and drove, and stayed in cheap motels along the way, only long enough to get the minimum sleep.

Sean said very little through the entire journey. Tara was amazed at just how far they were going, and how different the country looked from what she was accustomed to. She had never been further from her home than Provo. It was a whole new experience for her.

When they finally got to Illinois, Sean started talking and hardly stopped. He told her details of the rigidity in his home that she'd never heard him speak of before, and she could well understand how stifling it would have been to a high-spirited child. He told her of the events that had led up to his conversion, and he repeated in detail the encounters with his father that had preceded his being disowned.

"The day I left home," he said sadly, "my father would not even speak to me. He was so cold. My mother tried to give me some money, but he saw her and became furious. Maureen managed to slip me some that I knew Mother would cover. It was only a few hundred dollars, but it was all I had. I hadn't been out of the hospital very long, so I hadn't been working. I had nothing."

Tara waited for him to swallow his emotion. Though his eyes remained sharply fixed on the road, there was no mistaking how difficult it was for him to talk about this.

"I can't deny the miracles that got me to Utah," he stated. "I felt the Lord with me, Tara." He turned to look at her, and she saw the pain rise into his eyes as he finally touched the real heart of the problem. "But I could not understand, Tara; I *still* do not understand, how my father could have done something like that. I had *nothing.*" Anger crept into his voice to mask the pain. "How could he do that? How could he turn his own son out into the street, crippled and penniless? I just . . . *don't* understand!"

Tara allowed him to vent his emotion, then she took his hand

and said quietly, "It wasn't right, Sean, and you have every reason to feel hurt. But look at the things in your life that you never would have had if your father *hadn't* turned you out. You would have never met Michael and Emily, or appreciated all they brought into your life. You've told me so many stories of the little miracles in your life, and the way they have strengthened your testimony. You can't begrudge those things, Sean. You told me you would go through the accident again, if only to have the things in your life that resulted. Surely this thing with your father has the same spiritual meaning."

Tara saw his eyes soften as he admitted quietly, "I'm sure you're right, but . . ." His words faded into emotion, but Tara understood. It would take time to heal wounds so deep. She prayed that this trip to Chicago might spur the process along.

Several miles later, Sean said, "Part of me wants to see him, Tara. But I have so many things I want to say to him that have been mulling around in my head for years. I'm afraid if I *did* see him, he wouldn't be the only one erupting. I pray that I can just see my mother and get out of there before he even knows I came."

"You're a good man, Sean," Tara assured him. "I'm certain that whatever is best will work out."

Sean took her hand and squeezed it. "I don't know what I'd do without you."

"That's what I'm supposed to say to you." She smiled and squeezed back.

When they arrived in Chicago, Tara was stunned. Salt Lake was the biggest city she'd ever seen. She knew now that it was small in comparison. It seemed the city went on forever. They stopped to eat and freshen up just a few miles from the house. The wind was fierce, and even the cold felt different. At moments Sean was quietly somber, at others he was full of nostalgia. Before they backed out of their parking place at the restaurant, he took Tara's hands into his and prayed that all would go well and that his desires could be accomplished. A few minutes later, he pulled the Blazer into a circular drive in front of one of the most beautiful homes Tara had ever seen.

"This is it?" she asked in surprise.

He turned off the Blazer and just stared up at the house. "This is it. When my parents had saved enough to buy a home, this was old and run down, practically falling apart. Over the years, while they were having children, they were fixing it up a little at a time. As you can see, it's been completely restored."

"No wonder you've missed it."

"It is a beautiful house," he said, "but that's not what I've missed."

"I know."

Sean looked at her and took a deep breath.

"Are you ready?" she asked.

"No." He chuckled in an attempt to subdue his emotion. "I'm terrified."

Tara silently allowed him the time he needed. Finally he took a deep breath and got out of the Blazer. He held her hand tightly as they approached the door. He hesitated, took another deep breath, and rang the bell.

"I hope my father doesn't answer," he said in a light tone that didn't begin to cover his anxiety.

"I'm sure Maureen will be here," Tara assured him. A moment later, Maureen opened the door. Their eyes met for a long moment, then with no words spoken, they embraced.

"How is she?" Sean asked as they parted. "I've been praying she'd hang on until I saw her."

"Today, she's doing quite well," Maureen said quietly. "But she is showing signs of kidney and liver failure. They don't think it will be long. Right now, however, she's fairly alert. Your timing's good. Yesterday she was awful. I won't bore you with the details."

Sean nodded stoically, trying not to think of what those details might be. "You remember Tara," he said, putting his arm around her as Maureen closed the door.

"Of course." Maureen smiled and squeezed her hand. "That was clever of you, Tara, to call and talk to me yourself, so I could honestly say I hadn't spoken to Sean."

"Oh, she's clever." Sean managed a smile, then he cleared his throat and his palms began to sweat.

"I believe she's awake," Maureen said, motioning toward the staircase that ascended from the entry hall where they stood. "Why don't you go on up. I've got to make a call."

"Thank you, Maureen," he said.

"It's my pleasure." Her eyes filled with emotion. "I hope it goes well. Dad left the house a while ago, but I have no idea when he'll be back."

Sean glanced toward the stairs. "We'll just have to take it on the best we can, eh?"

Maureen nodded. "Oh, you should know . . . sometimes the medication does strange things. At moments she's clear and coherent, at others, she kind of drifts off into left field."

"I understand," Sean said. He took Tara's hand into his and started up the stairs.

"Are you okay?" she asked when they paused at the top.

"I'll let you know after my heart starts beating again."

Memories rushed over Sean as they walked down a hall of polished hardwood floors. The door to his parents' bedroom was open. He squeezed Tara's hand tightly as he peered in, not knowing what to expect. The afternoon sun shone brightly through a west window, illuminating the same old room. The only difference was the hospital bed that stood where the old four-poster bed had once been. The head of the bed was elevated, giving him a perfect view of his mother's face where she lay against the pillows, apparently asleep. He leaned into Tara and was grateful to have her there, especially when he pressed his lips to her brow to keep himself from crying out. His combination of joy and anguish was acute. He took a step closer, with Tara's arms around him. A floorboard creaked, and his mother opened her eyes.

Sean froze. Helen O'Hara stared, then blinked. She lifted a hand toward him and muttered weakly, "Sean?" She leaned forward slightly and squinted. "Is it you, Sean?" She spoke slowly, her speech almost slurred. He assumed it was a result of the drugs. But the quaint trace of Irish in her voice was still evident. "Please do not tell me I'm hallucinatin'."

Sean remained frozen until Tara gave him a little nudge. As if he only needed a push, he hurried to his mother, taking her hand into his. "You're not hallucinating, Mother. I'm here, and I'm real." He kissed her hand and pressed it to his face. "And we're together."

"I can't believe it," she muttered and urged him close to her.

Tara fumbled in her pocket for a tissue as she watched Sean bury his face in the pillow next to his mother's. They cried and kissed each other over and over. They touched each other's faces and their tears turned to laughter.

"How did ye know?" she asked slowly.

"Maureen wrote to me. I didn't want to cause any trouble, but when she told me . . . I *had* to come. I had to see you again."

Helen smiled. "M' prayers have been answered. I only wanted t' see ye once more; t' know that ye are well an' happy." As if a thought had just occurred to her, she took his hands into hers and looked at them closely. "Yer hands. They've healed." She met his eyes. "How?"

"It's only one of many miracles in my life, Mother. There's so much I want to tell you, but . . . I don't want to tire you, or . . ."

He stopped when her eye caught something behind him. Sean turned and reached an arm toward Tara, and she stepped closer.

"Is this one o' those miracles?" she asked, smiling at Tara.

"Well put," he chuckled and put his arm around her. "Tara, meet my mother, Helen O'Hara. Mother, this is my wife, Tara."

"It's such a pleasure to meet you," Tara said warmly. She bent to give Helen a careful embrace. "I wondered if I ever would."

"I'm so glad ye've come," Helen said, more to Tara. "I wanted s' much t' see ye. Maureen told me how lovely ye are." Then more to Sean, "She *is* lovely. I assume she is also a Mormon."

"Yes," Sean said with conviction. "She is one of many reasons I am grateful that I made the decision I did."

"You do not regret it, then?" Her tone was almost as severe as her eyes.

"I have only one regret, Mother. I have missed my family very much." The tears came again to his eyes. "It was the hardest thing I ever did," he admitted, "but I've not once had to wonder if I did the right thing. God has blessed me, Mother, in so many ways."

"That's good then. And he has blessed me, t' send ye back now." Helen turned again to Tara. "And t' allow me t' meet yer sweet wife." She asked Sean, "Were ye married in th' Mormon temple?"

Tara glanced down, trying not to wish it could be different. Sean wondered if his mother's memory was disjointed. Surely Maureen would have told her about the ceremony. "No," Sean said without regret, "but we will be. And do you know what that means?" Helen shook her head. "It means we will be together forever, Mother. After Tara and I die, we will still be married." His mother narrowed her eyes with skeptical interest. Sean leaned closer to her and added with conviction, "And when you get to the other side, Mother, and you can see this life in a different perspective, I want you to know that I will do everything necessary to make certain that we are *all* together forever."

Helen said nothing for so long that Sean began to wonder if this was one of those moments when the medication had taken hold of her. She looked toward the window. "It's a beautiful day, isn't it? I do love th' sunshine." Sean exchanged a glance with Tara, then his mother turned to him again and said, "Tell me about those miracles, Sean. Just talk t' me."

"I think I'll leave the two of you alone for a while," Tara said and graciously slipped out the door, certain she could find a bathroom and then somewhere to sit down for a while.

"She's lovely, Sean," Helen smiled serenely. "I can tell that she loves ye."

"And I love her, very much."

"Tell me all that's happened," she said, relaxing against the pillow.

"Well, first of all, there's something I've wanted so badly to tell you. I went to Ireland, Mother." Her eyes widened pleasantly. "I lived there for nearly two years. And I actually met some relatives."

"Tell me about it," she insisted, her eyes glowing with excitement.

Sean went on and on, talking and laughing with his mother, trying to ignore the evidence that she was not well at all and this was likely the last time he would ever see her. Instead he just held her hand and smiled, enjoying every moment.

The bathroom wasn't too hard for Tara to find, but she felt a little uncomfortable wandering around as if she belonged here. She couldn't find Maureen, so she sat down in a parlor-type room at the front of the house where there was a stack of magazines on an end table. She glanced through a *Time* magazine, but her thoughts were upstairs with Sean. She smiled to recall his tenderness in seeing his mother again, and the warmth they had exchanged. At this point it was difficult to know how this would affect Sean's father, but she felt certain Sean would feel that this time with his mother was worth the risk.

Her thoughts were jolted by the front door closing. She looked up to see a man regarding her curiously. His presence took her breath away before she consciously realized why. He looked so much like Sean that she almost felt chilled. If not for the completely gray hair and deep wrinkles around his eyes, Tara would have guessed him to be much younger than his years. He wore a thick gray mustache, a tasteful tweed jacket, and dark slacks.

"Well," he said, tossing his hat onto a nearby chair, "it's not every day I come in t' find a lovely young lady sittin' in m' house." His Irish accent was more intense than Helen's. "To what do we owe th' pleasure?"

Tara smiled warmly, almost mesmerized by this mature image of her husband. "Uh . . . well." She wondered what to say without bringing the feared eruption upon herself. "You see . . . my husband is upstairs visiting with your wife."

He made a contemplative noise and sat down across the room. "And how does yer husband know m' wife?" he asked. She sensed nothing in his purpose but simple curiosity for the sake of conversation. He was congenial and refined—everything Tara would have expected from Sean's father.

"Oh," Tara managed a calm smile, "they go way back, from what I understand."

He smiled at her again, and for a moment Tara felt extremely self-conscious. She felt sure if he knew who she was, he would kick her right out; yet she had trouble comprehending this kind man exhibiting the anger and stubbornness that Sean had spoken of.

"Oh," he chuckled, "I'm Brian O'Hara, and ye are . . ."

"Tara," she stated, realizing they weren't going to get very far without getting to the truth.

"Just Tara?" he asked with a raise of his eyebrow that was so much like Sean she almost giggled.

"Uh . . . Tara . . ." While she was wondering what to say, she glanced up to see Sean in the doorway. He glanced quickly from her to his father, and back to her. The anxiety in his eyes was apparent.

She could see no reason for holding back now. "O'Hara," she finished firmly and turned her eyes back to Sean's father. "My name is Tara O'Hara, and it's a pleasure to meet you." Her eyes were naturally drawn back to Sean, and Brian O'Hara's eyes followed.

When Sean felt his father's gaze come upon him, his heart pounded into his throat. He'd had fantasies and nightmares about this moment. And he had to wonder which this would turn out to be. His father had aged a great deal in five years. But far worse, Sean saw the fury fill Brian O'Hara's countenance as he came slowly to his feet. The hints of gray had overtaken his dark hair, and the lines in his face had deepened enough for ten years.

When the silence became too long, Sean wondered if it would be better to just turn around and walk away. There was so much he wanted to say, even felt he *should* say. But the rage surrounding those words frightened him. He held out a hand toward Tara and simply said, "We should be going." Tara stood and slipped her hand into Sean's.

"Oh, I see," Brian said with disdain. "Ye brought this pretty young lady here t' try an' finagle yer way back in."

Tara was amazed at the change in Brian O'Hara since Sean had come into the room. It was almost frightening. Carefully she put a soothing hand on Sean's arm, hoping he would remain calm.

Sean glanced down at Tara, then back to his father. He swallowed hard and told himself there was no good to be had in venting his anger. "This pretty young lady is my wife," Sean stated. "And I brought her because I needed someone to hold my hand."

"Perhaps we should be going, and—" Tara was interrupted by Brian's booming voice.

"Forgive m' brashness, young lady. Ye must understand this has nothin' t' do with ye."

While Tara was trying to think of a response, Sean quickly said, "It has everything to do with her. Would you turn *her* out on the street right along with me?" Sean was aware of Tara's attempt to soothe him, but he chose to ignore it. "Do you never want to see the children we'll have, or—"

"Ye've no business bein' here," Brian stated coldly.

"I came to see my mother. She's dying. I should be entitled to at least that."

"Ye're entitled t' nothin'."

"I am her son." Sean's voice became husky with emotion. "I am *your* son!"

"Ye are not my son." Brian's voice hissed with venom. "Th' son I had, willfully turned his back on everything he was raised t' be. He made his choice."

"Choice?" Sean echoed hoarsely. "You gave me no choice. *You're* the one who taught me to have integrity; to do what God wanted me to do at all costs. I *did* what I knew in my heart God wanted me to do, and *you* turned me out—with *nothing!*"

"Ye're deceivin' yerself if ye think this . . . *heathenism,*" he spat, "that ye've become a part of, is what God wanted ye t' do. Ye turned yer back on *everythin'* I gave ye."

"Do you honestly believe in your heart that I would give up so much for something I didn't know was true? I left here on faith, Father, and I've had too many miracles to ever doubt that it's true." He held up his hands. "Do you see this? They function. I am whole, and I am making it, in spite of your attempts to manipulate me into going against what I believed in."

"There is no point even discussin' this," Brian stated firmly. But now that the wounds were opened, Sean was determined to clean them out—hopefully, once and for all.

Sean forced himself to take a deep breath and calm down. But he felt he had to say, "And what about Robert? Is *he* the fine, upstanding man you always wanted in a son?"

Tara didn't know what Sean was talking about, but she didn't miss the soaring rage in Brian's eyes. Sean had hit a sore point, and she knew it.

"Do you condone Robert's lifestyle, and turn me out for trying to be a good Christian man and do what I believe is right?"

"There is no proof that Robert has ever—"

"Oh, there's proof enough," Sean countered, "but you choose to ignore it. You choose to accept him because he doesn't have the guts to tell you to your face what he's become."

"This has nothin' t' do with Robert or anyone else. This is between ye an' me, Sean, an' I will not have ye—"

"Well, at least you remember my name. That's something. But if it has nothing to do with anyone else, then why do you forbid me to see my brothers and sisters—my own mother, for heaven's sake?"

Silence hung a long moment while Sean actually wondered if his father would strike him and call him a blasphemous hellion, as he'd done once before. But with a quiet rage, Brian finally said, "Ye've seen her. Now get out o' m' house. And don't ever come back."

Tara gripped Sean's arm tightly as her eyes filled with mist. She had never doubted the things Sean had told her, but to witness it, she was stunned.

"I am your son," Sean stated, his voice cracked.

"No." Brian shook his head, the stubborn pride almost streaming from his countenance. "Ye're not m' son. That is all I have t' say." He stepped toward them, and Tara momentarily feared he would try to bodily force Sean out. But he only moved abruptly past them, into the hall.

Sean turned and called after him. "Is that what you'll tell God on your day of judgment?" Brian stopped walking but kept his back turned. "Will you be able to face God with a clear conscience, knowing you turned one of your children away, penniless and crippled?"

Brian turned to look over his shoulder. "God would not approve o' m' condoning this barbarian religion."

Sean took a deep breath as his father turned away again. "If you truly believed that, would you have to fight so hard to convince me?" Brian said nothing. "Do you cling to your belief because you *know* in your heart that it's right, or because you're stubborn, Irish-blooded, and you can't tolerate the possibility that you were wrong?" Brian started to walk away, but Sean called after him, "Families are supposed to be together, Brian O'Hara. Can you live with your accountability in keeping this one apart?" Brian continued to walk away. Sean choked back a sob, then cried out with fervency, "I love you, Father."

Brian stopped walking, but Sean's hope that he would turn around and acknowledge his son was dashed a moment later when he walked into the den and closed the door. Sean stood frozen until the depth of his hurt sank in and he had to remind himself to breathe.

He didn't realize he was leaning on Tara until she shifted her weight to steady him.

"We should go," she said firmly. He nodded, knowing he couldn't think for himself.

Tara found a whole new kind of fear as she guided Sean to the Blazer and opened the passenger door for him. The dazed shock that consumed him left her feeling helpless and frightened. Not knowing what to say, she just got into the driver's seat and put the key into the ignition.

"Where to?" she asked.

"Just get me out of here," he muttered.

Tara pulled carefully onto the street and around the corner. She was conscious of his shock wearing off by the way he began to breathe sharply. He pushed his hands into his hair and tugged at it almost brutally. She began to tremble when he groaned from deep in his chest and wrapped his arms around his middle as if he were experiencing physical pain. She spotted a park up ahead and pulled over near a big tree, fearing she'd only get them lost, or worse, if she didn't.

"Sean?" She touched his hand tentatively. He immediately responded by grabbing her hand, as if she were a lifeline. He buried his face in her lap and clung to her as if he might stop breathing without her. He groaned again. Then he sobbed and held her tighter.

"Why?" he cried, his voice muffled in the fabric of her skirt. "Dear God, why does it have to be this way?"

Tara only stroked his hair and held him, crying silent tears as she witnessed his pain. She thought how grateful she was to have been born into a wonderful family with good parents, and the gospel in her home. Then she tried to comprehend the depth of what he must be feeling. He had just seen his home and parents for the first time in over five years. His mother was dying, and his father had completely rejected and shunned him. Wishing she could do more, Tara whispered words of assurance and told him over and over that she loved him, and so did the Lord. He finally quieted down and just lay with his head in her lap, staring at nothing.

"Are you going to be all right?" she asked gently.

"I don't know." His voice was hoarse and dry.

"Do you think you could give me directions to a motel? I think we both need some rest."

Sean took a deep breath and sat up. He wiped a self-conscious hand over his face and pointed. "Turn left up ahead, then go a mile or so. There should be something that direction."

When they were settled into the room, Sean sat on the edge of the bed and just stared at his hands. Tara called Maureen's house and left a message on her machine regarding where they could be reached and when they were leaving. She left Sean alone for nearly an hour, then she sat beside him and spoke softly. "How did it go with your mother?"

"Good," he said easily. "She got sleepy, but I told her everything that really mattered. I . . . " His voice broke with emotion. "I told her I loved her, and . . . she said she would always love . . . me." Tears pressed out and he quickly wiped them away. "Then she closed her eyes and went to sleep."

"Was it worth it?" she asked.

He hesitated, then nodded firmly. "Oh, yes. It was well worth it, if only for the time I had with her."

"Then I'm glad we came." Tara attempted to put a positive spin on a difficult and painful situation. "And I'm glad I was able to meet her, and . . ." Tara hesitated saying it, but she felt it needed to be brought up. "And I was glad I got to meet your father as well . . . in spite of the circumstances."

Sean looked up, surprised by her sincerity.

"You look so much like him," she added, and he chuckled tensely.

"Ironic, isn't it?"

When he said nothing more, she went on. "I think it's good you said the things to him that you did."

He looked even more surprised. "You do?"

"Yes," she said firmly. "I think he needed to hear it; all of it. If it's as bad as it seems, it may not make any difference. But it might . . . even if it takes years for it to sink in, I think he'll remember what you said to him today."

Sean shook his head in disbelief. She was always telling him how good he was to her. Did she have any comprehension what it meant to have her here now? He put his arms around her and held her with a desperation that almost scared him. "Do you know how badly I needed to hear that?" he muttered against her ear. "Do you have any idea how much I love you; how I need you?"

Sean held her face in his hands and kissed her, long and hard. He almost literally felt his pain move into her and back again, as if she could somehow soften it and make it bearable for him. She was like a filter in his life. Just her being with him made everything easier to face. She made life worth living.

Sean was not prepared for the passion that rose up to push the pain aside, but he welcomed it and grasped for it. The more he kissed her, the tighter he held her, the less he felt the reality of his father's words pounding through his head.

Long after the passion had subsided, Sean held Tara close to him, silently thanking God for all he had been blessed with, and praying in his heart that, one day, his father's heart would be softened.

Later that evening, they went out for dinner. Sean drove past the house again and pulled over, just watching it for a few minutes before he drove on.

"Are you going to be all right?" Tara asked as he drove aimlessly through the streets of his neighborhood, his eyes filled with a dazed nostalgia.

"I think I will be," he said quietly. "I don't expect it to ever stop hurting," he added. "But I've done all I can do, and I am grateful for the life I have." He looked over at her and squeezed her hand. "If I had to do it over again, I would make the same choices. The Lord has kept his promises to me, in more ways than I would have ever comprehended. As long as I have the gospel, and as long as I have you, I'll be all right."

Tara reached over to kiss his cheek, then she listened as he told her stories from his childhood, and drove her past the schools he'd attended.

"Tell me about Robert," Tara said during a quiet lull, hoping she wouldn't offend him.

Sean gave a humorless chuckle. "There's not much to tell, really. He's several years older than I am. He went into the military when I was still a child. It was apparent several years ago that he had some . . .

struggles. The friends he'd bring home, his behavior. It was pretty obvious, but my father chose to ignore it."

"I don't understand," she said, almost embarrassed.

Sean smiled, warmed by her innocence.

"Let's just say that his lifestyle explains the reason he's never married." Tara made a noise of enlightenment as he went on. "He's done everything but come right out and admit it, but my father will not acknowledge that the problem exists."

"Under the circumstances, I can see why that would bother you."

"It certainly does bother me," he said, trying not to think too hard about it. "You must understand. I love Robert as a brother. Even though I don't condone what he's doing, he is a free agent. It's my father's hypocrisy about the whole thing that gets to me." His voice lightened a bit. "But my sister Peggy has made up for it somewhat."

"How is that?"

"She's a nun."

"You're kidding."

He shook his head and chuckled. "No, I'm not kidding. Maureen told me at the wedding. Funny, isn't it? I'm a Mormon returned missionary, my brother is gay, and my sister is a nun."

Tara laughed softly and enjoyed listening to him talk about his family in a way he never had before. She could already tell that the events of this day had been healing to a degree. He was talking about his brothers and sisters openly and freely, and even about his parents.

They returned to the motel and he continued to talk. Occasionally he became emotional, but there was a degree of peace, even in that. Again they made love, then fell asleep holding each other.

The phone ringing startled them awake, and Sean groped for it in the darkness. "What?" he demanded, already knowing it was bad news. Tara turned on the light and sat up to watch him, wondering what had happened. He said very little before he hung up the phone. Her fears were confirmed when he stated, "That was Maureen. My mother died about twenty minutes ago."

Tara said nothing. She just put her arms around him and let him cry until exhaustion finally put him back to sleep before dawn. He didn't wake up until the phone rang again, mid-morning. Tara answered it then handed it to Sean, announcing quietly, "It's Maureen." She sat close by and listened, concerned and curious.

"No," he said almost indignantly, "I don't see any reason for me to stick around here and go to the funeral when my presence will do nothing but cause a scene. I have a thesis to work on, and—" He stopped and listened, sighing as if he were frustrated, and Tara wished she could hear what Maureen was saying. She was surprised when his eyes widened, as if he were alarmed. The next thing he said was a firm, "All right. I'll be there." He hung up the phone and looked at Tara, almost dazed.

"I take it we're staying." He nodded but said nothing. "It's a good thing we brought nice clothes," she added. He nodded again. "Sean, are you all right?"

"Just a little . . . shocked, I suppose."

"What did she say?"

"She put my father on the phone."

Now Tara's eyes widened. "What did he say?"

"Not much. He just said my mother had requested that I be one of the pallbearers. And she apparently insisted he be the one to ask me. He said that he would tolerate my presence there for her sake, but not to expect anything more of it."

"That's good . . . isn't it?" she asked hesitantly.

Sean nodded slightly. "Yes, I think that's good."

Through the following days, Sean tried to study and not think too much about the rest of his family, involved in things surrounding his mother's death that he was not asked to be a part of. The funeral came and went without incident. Brian O'Hara never made eye contact with Sean or Tara. He simply ignored them and stayed far out of reach. Sean's siblings did the same, obviously out of respect for their father. But Sean was grateful to be there, and he could not deny that it was a gift, aided by the hand of the Lord to ease this burden.

Since Sean had joined the Church, he had been to a couple of funerals. But it wasn't until now that he thought to really compare. Tara did well at not appearing conspicuous by her naivete regarding old Catholic traditions, but he knew it was all very foreign to her. The rituals, the somber aura, the faces veiled in black lace, the anguish of death and separation with no hope of ever being together again. Sean observed it all, trying to balance himself in a way that would not offend his family, and at the same time not compromise the beliefs he had embraced. His most prominent emotion was the sorrow of knowing his mother was dead. But he couldn't deny the underlying peace he felt in knowing they would be together again. He silently contemplated plans to do her temple work as soon as possible, and he felt sure she would accept it. He felt an added sorrow to look around at his family members—cousins, uncles and aunts, all caught up in the pain of loss, ignorant of truths that could bring them so much peace if they would only be willing to change. But the last thing Sean could do was even attempt to share his beliefs with anyone in his family. As long as Brian O'Hara was alive, Sean knew he would have to be content to live his life as he was.

During the drive back to Utah, they encountered some bad rain that made them grateful to have a Blazer with four-wheel drive, and the faith that God would guide them home safely. Once back in Provo, as they tried to merge back into a routine, an emotional and physical exhaustion settled over them. They tried to find time every day to talk, and as the weather warmed into early summer, they walked together nearly every day, following the doctor's advice for Tara's exercise. As the child inside her seemed to blossom, Tara knew there were many things she had yet to face. And time was running out.

CHAPTER FOURTEEN

Tara slid the file across Jane's desk and said with confidence, "This is the one."

Jane put her hand on it without taking her eyes off Tara. "Are you absolutely certain?"

Tara didn't even hesitate. "I have no doubt. I can't explain how I know. I just know."

Jane glanced at the papers and smiled. "They're wonderful people, Tara. They've waited a long time, and had a lot of disappointments." Jane folded her hands on the desk and looked at Tara intently. "But I wonder if there is something you've overlooked."

"I don't understand."

"They are not LDS."

Tara glanced at Sean, hoping he might have an answer. He looked as puzzled as she felt.

"I don't know if it makes that much difference to you," Jane said. "You feel confident about it being right, but you did say you wanted the baby in an LDS home."

"I . . . don't know what to say," Tara said. "I mean . . . it does matter, but I *know* this is the right couple for my baby."

Jane was thoughtful a moment. "Why don't you let me talk to them, and you keep an open mind. We still have a little time yet."

Tara nodded in agreement and left the office feeling unsettled, when she'd expected to feel such relief.

"Does it really matter?" Sean asked as they drove toward home. "As long as they're good people, won't it all work out somehow?"

"You tell me," she stated firmly. "How different would your life be if you had been brought up in a Mormon home?"

The question hit Sean with such impact that he lost his breath momentarily. "Boy," he sighed, "you got me on that one."

"I don't know, Sean. Maybe I shouldn't worry about it so much. If the Lord has let me know this is the family for my baby, shouldn't I have the faith to know he'll work out the rest?"

"That makes sense to me," he stated.

Tara smiled and guided Sean's hand to her belly where the baby was kicking. He grinned when he felt it, and Tara tried not to think about the reality that this baby would not be hers much longer.

* * * * *

Veronica walked out the door ahead of Matthew and waited for him to make sure he had his keys before he locked it. She was anticipating a night out, away from the echoing silence of the house.

Matthew rolled his eyes when the phone rang. "Let's just go," he said. "It'll—"

"No," she insisted, "we better get it."

He sighed and stepped back inside while Veronica glanced quickly in every direction at the endless acres surrounding them. This ranch was a beautiful place to live—a perfect place to raise children, she thought sadly.

"Ronni," he called from the doorway, "it's Jane Richardson." Her eyes widened. "She wants to talk to both of us."

"Oh, help," she whimpered under her breath and hurried inside. Matthew handed her the phone and went to get the cordless extension so they could sit close together.

"Okay," Matthew said, "we're both here."

"Hello, Veronica," Jane said in her usual sweet manner.

"Hello, Jane."

"How are you doing?"

"The same. And you?"

"We're all good here," Jane said, and Veronica wished they could get to the point. "I was glad I caught both of you home," she continued. "I want to talk to you about something."

"Go on," Matthew urged.

"I don't want to tell you I have a baby for you," Jane said with compassion, "because I know you've had more than your fair share of disappointments." Veronica listened quietly, appreciating her approach at least. "But I do want to tell you about this situation— just so you can be aware of it."

"Okay," Veronica said in a calm voice that belied the way her heart was pounding.

"There is a mother who is not the typical unwed teenager. She's a rape victim."

Veronica felt a pang of compassion. Matthew squeezed her hand and she knew he felt it, too.

"She's married now," Jane went on, "but when she found out she was pregnant, she prayed and asked God to help her know what to do. She had a dream, and knew that her baby was meant for someone else."

Veronica felt suddenly overcome with emotion. The look in Matthew's eyes only enhanced it and she laid her head on his shoulder.

"Veronica," Jane said carefully, "this woman told me that her baby was meant to be yours. She said she had no doubt that God intended for this baby to come to your home." Following a long silence, Jane said, "Are you with me, Veronica? Matthew?"

"Yes," they both managed to say. There was no disguising their emotion.

"I wanted to talk to you in person, but three hours is a long drive. I hope you'll hear me out."

"We're with you," Matthew stated.

"There's only one problem, and—"

"If you think she'll change her mind at the last minute," Veronica began, "I don't know if—"

"Hear me out," Jane interrupted gently. "I have no doubt that she will follow through with this. Her conviction about this runs deep. As I said, there's only one problem, and she is flexible on it, but we felt you should at least know."

"We're listening," Matthew said firmly. Veronica was grateful for his strength in this, when she knew this was as hard for him as it was for her.

"The mother is LDS, and she wants the baby raised in an LDS home."

"What's that?" Matthew asked.

"It's The Church of Jesus Christ of Latter-day Saints," Jane stated. "You know, the Mormons."

"I see," Matthew stated. Veronica didn't know what to say.

"Utah is the Mormon capital of the world, you know," Jane said lightly.

"Yes, we know." Matthew sounded subtly irritated. "Are you telling us, then, that this woman knows we're supposed to have her baby, but because we're not Mormons, she won't let us—"

"That's not what I'm saying, Matthew." Jane's voice was calm and soothing. "She would prefer it that way, but I don't believe she's so set on it that it would overrule her feelings about your being the right ones. I simply want you to be aware of the situation, and I want to ask one thing of you—something that I feel would soften the circumstances."

"And what is that?" Matthew asked warily.

"I'm going to send you some Mormon literature. All I ask is that you read it with an open mind. If nothing else, I believe if she knows you're familiar with the concepts and doctrines of the Church, it will be sufficient."

Veronica held her breath, almost expecting Matthew to tell Jane to forget it; he could be stubborn and proud at moments. But she was filled with surprise and relief when he said strongly, "We can do that. We'll read it. I can't promise anything beyond that."

"Thank you," Jane said with a breathy sigh. "I can honestly say you've been some of my favorite clients. You're good people, and sooner or later I'm going to make certain you get a family."

"Thank you," Veronica said. "We'll be watching the mail."

Long after they hung up the phone, Veronica and Matthew sat in silence, trying to absorb this new turn of events.

"So," he finally said, "what do you think?"

"I don't know *what* to think."

Matthew touched her chin and almost smiled. "You're the one

who said that maybe God wanted us to go to church."

"I did say that, didn't I," Veronica recalled. She'd forgotten all about it.

Nothing more was said about Jane's phone call until the package arrived in the mail. It was as if they didn't dare speculate any more, for fear it would only increase their disappointment when bad news came. The material came by priority mail. What Jane had spent on postage alone made Veronica feel that she was serious about this.

After dinner was cleaned up, she and Matthew sat on the couch together with soft music playing. Veronica opened the package. A book and several pamphlets spilled over her lap. She picked up a handful, shuffling through them curiously, while Matthew picked up the book and thumbed through it. Veronica was drawn to a pair of pamphlets, one directed to mothers, the other to fathers. She handed one to Matthew and said, "You read first."

Matthew cleared his throat and took a deep breath before he began to read aloud. They took turns until late into the night, reading and discussing at great length. Veronica didn't know what she'd expected, but this wasn't it. While something inside tempted her to embrace these new ideas, she wondered if it was only her desire for a child that made her interested. She hardly dared voice her opinion to Matthew, sensing something skeptical in him.

Past eleven, Veronica drifted off to sleep, listening to Matthew read something about a fourteen-year-old boy who went into the woods to pray and received a vision. Some time later she woke up and tried to focus on the clock. 3:37 a.m. She lifted her head and found Matthew sitting at the other end of the couch, intently reading the Book of Mormon.

"What are you doing?" she asked. "You've got work waiting for you at sunrise."

"I know," he said, barely glancing toward her to acknowledge that she was awake.

"I'm going to bed," she said, and left him where he was. "I've got work coming through on the computer at seven."

At six the alarm went off, and Veronica returned to the front room to find Matthew sitting in the same spot, the book in his hand, staring into the distance.

"Matthew," she said and he turned, startled. "Are you all right?"

"I'm fine." He reached a hand toward her and she stepped forward to take it.

"It's time for you to go out and—"

"I know," he interrupted.

"But you must be exhausted."

"Actually," he chuckled, "I'm not. I feel pretty good . . . considering."

Veronica took the book from his hands. "How far did you get?" she asked.

"I skipped around. I must admit, it's amazing. I always thought Mormons were eccentric descendants of polygamists; some kind of cult or something. But this is basic Christianity, as far as I can see." He rummaged a hand through the pamphlets scattered over the couch. "They strongly promote good family values and righteous living. There is much I don't understand, but as far as I can tell, there is little about Mormonism that doesn't coincide with the way we already live."

Matthew stood and stretched while Veronica wondered what exactly had erased his cynicism. She was about to ask when he headed toward the bedroom to change, pausing only to say, "But I will not join a church just so I can adopt a baby."

Once Veronica had completed her work and sent it back through the computer system to the company that employed her, she spent the day perusing Mormonism, intrigued with the things Matthew had said. She kept expecting him to come in, exhausted, but he only grabbed a sandwich for lunch and worked on through the day. By the time he came in for dinner, Veronica was beginning to understand his interest. She felt somehow grateful that the opportunity to adopt had evaded them until now. Instinctively, she almost feared what the rest of her life would have been like if her mind had not been opened to spiritual concepts she'd never considered before.

On Sunday, they attended a local Mormon meeting. They went again the next Sunday. On the following Monday they drove to Provo to see Jane Richardson. Diane greeted them warmly and showed them into Jane's office. Matthew sternly walked across the room and planted his hands flat on the desk. He looked Jane in the eye and said sternly, "I will not join a church just so I can adopt a baby."

Jane looked alarmed, but her voice was calm. "I would not expect you to. I'm certain that—"

"But," he interrupted, and Veronica nearly laughed, "I will join it because it's true."

After Jane closed her mouth and dabbed at the tears in her eyes, she flew out of her chair and embraced Matthew, then Veronica, then Matthew again. They talked for nearly an hour, not realizing until then that Jane was LDS. They embraced again before they left for Salt Lake City, their destination Temple Square. It was nearly sundown when they walked up the circular ramp in the North Visitors' Center and stood a long while before the Christus statue, staring up at the likeness of Christ, the nail prints evident in his hands and feet. Veronica didn't realize she was crying until Matthew wiped a tear from her cheek and smiled.

"It's okay," he said, putting his arm around her shoulders, "I feel it, too."

* * * * *

Tara lay awake far into the night, wishing she could sleep. She was amazed at the consuming ache in her body that never seemed to relent. The few weeks left seemed like forever. They had successfully completed a childbirth course, and Sean had practiced breathing exercises with her regularly. She felt as prepared as she was going to get. More than anything, she just wanted to have it over with and put it behind her, while a part of her feared having to let go of this life within her. As always, such thoughts brought out her emotions, and she cried quietly into her pillow, grateful that Sean was asleep. He listened to her cry far too much as it was.

She got up around three to use the bathroom and blow her nose. Determined not to dwell on it, she returned to bed with a fresh resolve to get some much-needed rest. But over an hour later she was crying again, wondering how she would ever make it through this.

She couldn't deny that she had much to be grateful for. She had been blessed a great deal. But at moments, it just seemed unbearable. How could she not wonder what it would be like if this was Sean's baby? They would likely have a little bed in the corner of the bedroom, and perhaps a drawer in the big dresser would be filled with tiny undershirts and nightgowns. She would be comparing the prices of diapers and strollers, and perusing books of baby names. As it was, all she did was cry. Sean encouraged her to find something to occupy herself, but she had no concentration, and she simply didn't feel good enough to do much of anything beyond keeping up the apartment and cooking a meal once in a while.

Tara tried to imagine the couple in her dream, this man and woman without faces, and the happiness they would feel in finally getting a baby. Jane had said they'd waited a long time and had experienced much disappointment. Tara found some gratification in her thoughts, but they were so abstract that it was difficult to conjure up a clear image. Though she tried not to think about it, she still felt a little uncomfortable knowing they were not LDS. But Jane had told her she'd sent them some Mormon literature, and they had agreed to study it. At least they would be aware of her desire. And what more could she do? It was in the Lord's hands.

The tears rose again, but this time Sean's arms came around her, easing her close to him. "I didn't mean to wake you," she sniffled.

"You didn't wake me. I think I was dreaming you needed to be kissed."

"Oh?" She chuckled softly and nuzzled her face against his throat.

"That's what's wrong with you, Scarlett." Sean lowered his voice to imitate Rhett Butler in *Gone With the Wind.* "You need kissing badly, and by someone who knows how."

Tara countered with Scarlett's response, in a perfect southern accent, "And I suppose you think you're the proper person."

"But of course," Sean said in his own voice. Then he kissed her. And kissed her and kissed her. Tara clung to him and relished his love. She was amazed that even in her condition, he managed to give her such pleasure, make her feel so loved and adored.

In the most peaceful part of the night, Sean held her close, his hand against her belly, marveling at the activity of the child within her. "Why were you crying?" he asked softly.

"Same old thing," she said, not wanting to talk about it.

"Tell me," he urged.

"Honestly, Sean, there is nothing we haven't talked about many times over. It's just depressing. I hate to admit it, but there are moments when I almost wish I'd have had an abortion and gotten it over with. At least I'd—"

Sean sat upright so quickly it startled her. "You wouldn't and you know it!" He sounded angry.

Tara put a soothing hand on his shoulder. "No, I wouldn't," she assured him. "In my heart I know I'm doing the right thing. I simply said there are moments when it's hard, and I—"

"I know what you said," he stated and swung his legs over the edge of the bed, pressing his head into his hands.

"Sean?" Tara snuggled up against his back and rubbed his shoulders gently. "Something's bothering you," she said gently, feeling suddenly unnerved. Beyond the situation with his family, Sean had always been so strong and predictable that Tara didn't know what to think. She had sensed there were things from his past that troubled him to a degree, but this made no sense.

"Yes," he admitted more softly, "something's bothering me." Sean wanted to say more, but the words wouldn't come. With all the pain and struggles he'd had in his life, there was one sore point that towered above the rest. Far worse than his recovery from that accident, and being disowned by his family, that one incident made his stomach churn. He tried to recall how many years it had been, and still the pain was there. Logically he knew that talking about it would help. He'd never told *anyone*. But facing the reality on an emotional level seemed unbearable.

"Sean?" Tara repeated when he remained silent.

"This has nothing to do with you, Tara. I'm sorry if I sounded angry. It's just that I . . ."

"You what?" she urged.

"I can't talk about it, Tara. I just can't."

Tara swallowed hard and uttered a quick silent prayer that she could say the right thing. She reached over and turned on the lamp. She wrapped the sheet around her and sat beside him, taking his hand into hers. "Sean, you're getting close to achieving your goal of becoming a counselor. Can you be an effective one if you have your own unresolved baggage?"

Sean turned to look at her sharply as the question pierced deep. Then he had to turn away. The truth in her words made him feel somehow like a hypocrite. She was right and he knew it.

"Okay," he said reluctantly, "but give me a minute." *Help me, Father,* he prayed inwardly. *Help me be free of this, once and for all.*

Tara silently waited for him to gather his courage. He cleared his throat and gazed at the knobs on the dresser drawers. "I told you that before the accident, I had a relationship with a woman."

"Liza," she stated, and he was surprised that she'd remember.

"Yes," he cleared his throat again, "Liza." The name came through his lips with a bad taste. "Well," he took a deep breath and just blurted it out, "she got pregnant."

Tara held her breath momentarily.

Sean chuckled tensely. "After I recovered from the shock that birth control didn't always work, I told her I would marry her. I didn't want to. I knew I didn't love her; at least not enough to spend my life with her. But that baby was my responsibility, and I told her I would take care of her and the child. Well, marriage wasn't in her plans either, and she would have nothing to do with it. Her motto was *free agency.*" He said the last words with spite. "That was what drew me to her initially. After growing up with all that pious rigidity, I wanted *free agency.*" He sighed deeply and continued. "Anyway, I told her I would find a way to support her through the pregnancy, and then she could put the baby up for adoption."

Sean turned to meet Tara's eyes. She knew her emotion was evident. Was that why he was so patient and kind about all of this? Had he been through it before?

Sean turned away and said nothing for a full minute. "She said she'd think about it, but the next day . . ." Sean put his head into his hands and sighed. He finally choked the words out on the wave of a breathy sob. "She told me she'd had an abortion."

Tara caught her breath and sat up a little straighter. It made sense now. Compassion filled her as all the pieces of Sean's character came together in her mind. She put her arms around him and he turned his face against her, crying as he finished. "I . . . I couldn't believe it! We argued and fought for hours, until I realized that nothing I could say or do would ever bring that baby back." He looked into Tara's eyes and clenched his hand into a fist. "It was my baby, Tara, and she just . . . killed it. Then she turned around and went on with her life as if she'd thrown out an old pair of shoes."

Sean's anger melted into sadness. "My clearest memory of Liza is the way she looked in that moment when I knew I had to get out of there. She was sitting on the couch, painting her toenails bright pink. She told me she wasn't going to let some baby take away a year of *her* life. She reminded me that she had her *free agency.* 'What about *my* free-agency?' I asked her. She said nothing. 'What about that baby's free agency?' I asked. She told me to lighten up." Sean looked at Tara and wiped a thumb over her tear-streaked face. "I was packed before she finished painting her nails, and I never saw her again." He glanced down and fidgeted with the edge of the sheet. "That was when I started drinking. I thought I could somehow forget about it and it would go away. Drinking didn't do it, so I started into drugs. You know the rest."

"I'm so sorry, Sean," she said. "I shouldn't have said what I did. Truly, I didn't mean it. I—"

"I know," he said gently. "It's all right." Cleansing tears trickled down Sean's face as he took Tara's shoulders into his hands. "Do you have any idea what it means to me, Tara, to be with you through this, to see what you are willing to go through to give a child *life?* Do you know how much you have renewed me, and made me feel that I am somehow making up for the worst thing that ever happened to me? I know what you've been through is unspeakable, Tara, and I would never have wished for it to happen. But I know that the people who will have this baby will be incomprehensibly grateful for what you are doing. And beyond that, Tara, I consider it a blessing in my life. This experience has renewed me in ways you could not possibly imagine."

The full extent of that renewal surged through Sean at the realization that he had just freed himself from the shackles of his past. In his heart he knew that the Lord had taken the burden from him many years ago, when he'd entered the waters of baptism. But only now had he chosen to come to terms with it. Not knowing what to say, he took Tara's face into his hands and kissed her over and over. "I love you," he murmured. "I love you more than life."

They held each other close and talked it through until they drifted to sleep together. Sean got up with the alarm and left Tara sleeping. Through the day he felt the reality settle in further. He felt so much better about himself and his life. If only he'd had the sense to just talk about it a long time ago.

Tara finally hauled herself out of bed by mid morning. She dragged through her usual routine then sat down to rest, wishing there was something on T.V. besides soap operas, depressing talk shows, and Sesame Street. The knock at the door startled her, but she was not disappointed to open it and see Diane Hayne.

"Come in," she said eagerly.

"I hope I'm not intruding or anything. I—"

"Of course not," Tara assured her. "The days get so long with Sean gone. He's finished the term, but he's working extra hours to get ahead before the baby comes. It's nice to have some company."

Diane seemed to relax some, and they sat together on the couch. "Well, Jane had some news for you, but she's got a busy day and I wanted to talk to you anyway, so I volunteered to come by."

"Oh, that's nice," Tara admitted.

"Well, it's news that should likely be given in person."

"Okay, I'm ready," Tara said, wondering what on earth it could be.

"Well, first of all, the couple you've chosen for your baby have not only agreed to the arrangement, they are insisting that they pay 100 percent of your expenses, and even reimburse you for any expenses relating to the pregnancy that you've spent up to this point."

Tara absently put a hand to her heart. "That's wonderful." She thought how tight the budget had been since they'd had to make regular payments to the doctor.

"But that's not the best part," Diane beamed. "Jane told you she sent them some Mormon literature."

"Yes."

"Well, it seems they were quite taken with what they read. They've started going to church, and they have arranged for the missionary discussions." Tara gasped and Diane went on, "They told Jane adamantly that they would not join a church just so they could adopt a baby, but it seems they were genuinely intrigued with what they learned of Mormonism. So, my dear," Diane took Tara's hand, "it looks as though your feelings were on the mark. You're not only giving these wonderful people a baby, you've led them to the gospel."

Tara felt the inevitable emotion, and the next thing she knew she was crying on Diane's shoulder. She chuckled with embarrassment and dried her eyes, then they talked for over an hour of all the mixed emotions Tara had dealt with during this process. But the joy of what Diane had just told her made the final stretch seem bearable.

"Oh, look how the time has flown," Tara said with a glance at the clock. "I didn't mean to keep you so long and—"

"It's all right," Diane assured her. "Jane told me to take the afternoon. I had everything under control. She knew there was something else I wanted to talk to you about."

Tara was caught off guard by the intensity in Diane's expression. She listened patiently.

"Well, maybe I should talk to Sean, but I wanted to discuss it with you first. Perhaps it's easier to talk to another woman."

"Go on," Tara encouraged.

"Well, you see, it's my daughter, JannaLyn. She's fifteen, and my only child." Diane seemed suddenly nervous or upset as she continued. "It's just that something's not right with her. I can't explain it, and I don't understand it. I've prayed and prayed, and it just occurred to me the other day, that with Sean's education, perhaps he could help JannaLyn. Of course, I don't want to be a burden, but the problem is that I simply can't afford what it costs for counseling. But I know in my heart if she doesn't get some help, she could end up with some serious problems. Do you think he'd be willing, Tara, I mean—"

"Don't you even wonder," Tara insisted. "I'm certain he'd be glad to do what he can." She laughed gently. "He's certainly helped me through some tough feelings. Of course, with such things, it's always unpredictable, but I'm sure he'll do all he can."

"Oh," Diane sighed deeply, "any time he would be willing to talk to her would help, I'm sure. You can't imagine how grateful I would be. I'll find a way to—"

She stopped when the door opened and Sean walked in.

"Hello," Tara said eagerly.

"Hello," he replied with a smile. Diane stood and greeted him with a friendly handshake, but Tara only made it to the edge of her seat before he kissed her and said, "Don't stand up, love. It's too much work."

"We were just talking about you," Tara said as Diane sat back down and Sean removed his tie.

"Really?" he chuckled. "I hope it was good."

"Of course," Diane said.

"Diane was just telling me her daughter, JannaLyn, has been having some struggles, and she was wondering if you'd be willing to talk to her. Maybe you could help. I told her I felt sure you would do all you could."

"Of course I will," he said eagerly. "I can't make any promises about the results, but—"

"Oh," Diane interrupted, "anything you could do would help, I'm sure. I mean, if she doesn't want to be helped, I know there's nothing anyone can do. But even if I could understand what's troubling her, perhaps I would know how to deal with it."

"I'll do what I can," Sean said, then he winked at Tara. "My first client."

"I'll pay you what I can," Diane said. "I can't afford what most counselors charge, but I hoped that you would work with me and—"

"Don't you even consider it," Sean said adamantly. "I will not take a penny. It will be good experience for me, and an honor to help someone who has been very good to us."

Diane almost looked like she was going to cry. "I can't thank you enough. When can I—"

"Why don't you bring her over this evening?" Sean asked, then he turned to Tara. "Is that all right?"

"I don't see why not."

"Okay, I will." Diane rose and moved toward the door. "I'm so grateful. If there's ever anything I can do for you, please don't hesitate to ask."

"You've already done so much," Tara said. "Thank you for the visit, and the good news."

"What good news?" Sean asked.

Tara volunteered it eagerly. "The couple who will be adopting the baby; they're interested in the Church, and they're going to take the missionary discussions."

"Really?" Sean's eyes widened with pleasure. "Wow. That's incredible."

"That's what I thought," Diane agreed.

Once Diane had gone, Tara caught Sean up on all the details, nearly forgetting that the answer to their financial struggles would be solved.

Sean laughed and hugged her. "In that case," he said, "I think we can go out for a pizza."

Tara was only too eager to get out of the house and not have to cook. She felt better than she had for several days, and had to admit that her emotional state had a great effect on how she felt physically.

Diane arrived with her daughter right on time. JannaLyn was a beautiful young woman with long, curly brown hair and green eyes. But Sean quickly picked up on an obvious aura of insecurity that didn't seem to fit her character.

The four of them talked casually for a few minutes, then Diane said easily, "I've told JannaLyn that you were willing to talk to her."

"Are you okay with that, JannaLyn?" Sean asked. "I'm not as scary as I look."

JannaLyn gave a hint of a smile. "It's okay with me."

Tara graciously said, "I think I'll go hang out in the bedroom and read or something." Impulsively she added to Diane, "Do you have plans, or would you like to keep me company?"

"Sounds nice to me," Diane agreed.

Tara grabbed some snacks from the kitchen and flitted off to the bedroom with Diane close behind. "Good luck," Tara said and closed the door.

Tara had forgotten how fun it could be to just spend time with another female to talk and laugh. She hadn't felt this kind of friendship since high school, and enjoyed her visit so much that she was oblivious to what might be happening in the other room.

CHAPTER FIFTEEN

Sean felt his time with JannaLyn went well. He wouldn't have expected to get into anything heavy with a first visit, but he was certain he'd made headway in earning her trust and getting to know her. Three days later, on a Saturday morning, JannaLyn came again; and this time Diane and Tara went to the mall. Tara felt sure the exercise would do her good, if not the change of scenery.

Tara enjoyed the outing and called before they went back. She wanted to be certain they had the time they needed. Through the evening, Sean was quiet and seemed concerned. When she asked what was on his mind, Tara had a glimpse of what it would be like when he became a professional counselor. His response to her inquiry was a polite, "I'm afraid I can't talk about it, love."

"Is it JannaLyn?" she asked carefully.

"Yes."

"Then you found out what the problem is?"

"I'm afraid I did. That's all I can say for now."

Tara squeezed his hand. "I understand."

"But," he added, "I think there might come a time when *you* will be able to help her."

"Me?" Tara squeaked. But Sean said nothing more about it.

The following evening, at Sean's request, Diane came by without JannaLyn. Tara graciously went to the bedroom to read, knowing that Sean was getting somewhere with the problem and he needed uninterrupted time. Whatever it was, Tara knew it troubled Sean, but she reminded herself to get used to it and quickly became distracted by a good novel.

Sean motioned Diane to the couch and sat down across from her, leaning his forearms on his thighs. He was grateful for the years of education that had supposedly prepared him for moments like this; not to mention the practical experience he'd gained from working at the hospital. But he doubted he would ever become accustomed to the difficulty of cleaning out emotional wounds in order to help them heal. He knew that what he needed to tell Diane was going to sting, and he wasn't looking forward to it.

Diane met his eyes eagerly. "Are you making progress with her, then?"

"I believe I am," he nodded resolutely. "But I need to talk to you about something. JannaLyn agreed that I should. So nothing I tell you now is betraying my confidence with her." Diane nodded again, and he continued. "I'd like you to tell me a little about Janna's father."

Diane was obviously as surprised as he expected her to be. She talked briefly of their hurried marriage following a passionate escapade that left Diane pregnant. He didn't stick around long, and Diane eventually divorced him on grounds of abandonment.

"And did you ever see him again?" Sean asked.

"He came back once a couple of years ago. He hung around a lot, trying to manipulate me into taking him back. The first few days I enjoyed the attention, but it didn't take long to see that he hadn't changed. I told him I never wanted to see him again."

Sean swallowed hard. "Were you aware that he spent time alone with JannaLyn?"

"Well, he was there a couple of times when I came home from work, but . . ." Diane stopped, apparently sensing what he was getting at. She shook her head slowly. "Oh, Sean." Her chin quivered and she leaned back slowly. "Please . . . don't tell me that . . ."

"Diane," he said with compassion, "JannaLyn told me that on three different occasions, her father sexually abused her."

There was nothing surprising or unusual about Diane's reaction to one of the worst things a mother could be told. But Sean felt helpless as he tried to keep an objective focus on her emotion, knowing it was necessary. Following the initial shock, they talked for over an hour about the situation's emotional impact on JannaLyn, as well as on Diane. Though there was a long process of healing ahead, Sean could see that Diane was a strong woman and she had deep roots in the gospel. Her fortitude strengthened Sean's testimony of the difference the Atonement made in people's lives. Already she had something to hold onto that those without the gospel didn't have. She was immensely relieved when Sean told her that JannaLyn was actually handling it quite well. He believed that just having the secret out and giving her the assurance that she was not to blame, would go a long way in helping her get over this. Sean also shared with Diane his hope that perhaps some time in the future, Tara could help JannaLyn by offering some empathy, if nothing else.

By the time Diane left, Sean felt exhausted. He found Tara sitting on the bed, reading.

"Is she going to be all right?" Tara asked. "I heard her crying. I couldn't hear anything that was said," she added quickly to reassure him.

"I believe with time they'll both be fine," he said, if only to remind himself.

Over the following week he met with Diane and JannaLyn several times, both alone and together. Their progress was gratifying, and he was grateful to have it settle somewhat as Tara's due date approached and she became increasingly discouraged. He often reminded himself, as well as her, that it would soon be over. And one evening he came to the conclusion that just having her feel good enough to do something besides sit and read would do wonders for both of them.

The next day, Sean came home to find Tara scrubbing the kitchen floor on her hands and knees. "What on earth are you doing?" he demanded.

"I'm cleaning. What does it look like? It's about time I did. This floor was horrible."

"Why didn't you say something?" he asked gently. "I would have done it."

"I just felt like cleaning, that's all." She sat back on her feet and smiled. "There, now, doesn't that look better?"

"Yes," he drawled, "but I don't want you to overdo it."

"If I told you I cleaned the shower and washed windows, too, would that be overdoing it?"

Sean chuckled in disbelief. "You're joking."

"I'm afraid not." Tara struggled to her feet until Sean took hold of her and pulled her into his arms.

"You know," he said, "it will be nice to be able to hold you against me without this . . ." he glanced down and grinned, "in between us."

"Yes," she agreed, "it will."

Sean insisted that Tara do nothing more the remainder of the evening. She fell asleep much quicker than usual and slept well until somewhere in the night, when she awoke with a start. She gasped at the realization that she was wet. Wondering if her water had broken, she slipped quietly out of bed, expecting gravity to bring on a sudden gush. But nothing happened. With the aid of the hall light she changed into dry clothes and climbed back into bed. The moment she lay down, water whooshed beneath her again.

Heart pounding, Tara tried to remain still. It would do little good to change again at the moment. She was tempted to wake Sean, but when nothing else was apparently happening, she decided to let him rest. Staring into the darkness above her, she tried to prepare herself for what she knew was coming. She wondered what it would feel like to be expecting to bring the baby home. Would she and Sean have a bassinet and little clothes and diapers sitting about? Would she feel even a degree of excitement instead of this unspeakable dread? And then there was the fear. She suspected every mother felt afraid at this point. How could one anticipate inevitable pain that was described to often be unbearable, and not feel fear?

As if Tara's body reacted to the thought, a tightening came from her lower back and pressed forward until her entire midsection was hard as granite. She held her breath, and a moment later it was gone. She wished she could see a clock, but instead she counted seconds in her head. Four minutes and twelve seconds later it happened again, slightly stronger. Then three minutes and fifty-eight seconds. Then three minutes and forty-three seconds.

"Sean," she said, numb to the panic until she heard it in her own voice.

"What? What?" He groped for her hand in the darkness. "Is

something wrong?"

"This is it," she whispered.

"It?" he questioned, still half asleep.

"I'm in labor, Sean."

"Labor?" he squeaked, and the light came on.

His brief frenzy made her smile, then she motioned for him to sit beside her. "My water broke a while ago. I'm lying in a puddle. I'm having contractions, less than four minutes apart."

"But it's not due for ten days."

"Eleven. Yes, I know. But apparently it's anxious to get here."

"Does it hurt much?" he asked as she drew his hand to her belly to feel the hardness.

"Not yet," she said, then added, "Sean, I'm scared."

"Would I sound like a wimp if I said that I am too?"

"No," she smiled. "I'll be the wimp." She sobered and asked, "Will you give me a blessing? And then I think we'd better go to the hospital."

Sean did his best to free his mind of panic and concentrate on calling upon the Spirit to help him say the right words. At first he went slowly, speaking mostly from his own thoughts, but gradually the words came more easily. He heard himself promising Tara that the Lord was mindful of the difficulties she had suffered, but there was nothing so righteous as her selfless gift of motherhood to those who were anxiously awaiting the arrival of this child. He told her that although the pain of childbearing was inevitable, she would come through safely and the baby would be healthy and strong. And he promised her that when the grief of this loss was behind her, she would find joy like unto her pain.

After the *amen* was spoken, Sean kissed her warmly and whispered, "I love you, Tara. And I'm proud of you."

"I love you, too," Tara replied. "I could never have done this without you." He kissed her again, then she voiced the thought that had come to her during the blessing. "Call Jane."

"Right now?" He glanced at the clock. "Do you think—"

"I want this baby to be in its mother's arms the minute it's born. Please call her."

Sean made the call while Tara changed clothes once more and

threw a couple of things into the bag she'd already packed. She grabbed a towel to sit on in the Blazer, and they arrived at the hospital in a matter of minutes.

* * * * *

A sharp ringing pierced the darkness, and Matthew haphazardly reached toward the bedside table for the phone.

"Hello?" he muttered, barely coherent.

"Sorry to wake you," Jane said.

At the realization of who it was—and the cheery tone in her voice—Matthew sat up abruptly, suddenly wide awake. He reached for the lamp with his other hand while he nudged Veronica with his foot.

"I assume there's a good reason," Matthew finally found the voice to say.

"Your baby is on its way, Matthew. As soon as you get here, I'll drive you to the hospital myself. The birth mother wants that baby in Veronica's arms the minute it's born."

"We're on our way," Matthew managed to say before he slammed the phone down so quickly it fell to the floor. By the time he picked it up and got it where it belonged, Veronica was practically hysterical from her ignorance.

"What?" she demanded.

Matthew took her by the shoulders and grinned close to her face. "That was Jane. The mother is in labor. She wants us at the hospital."

For a long moment Veronica just stared at him in disbelief. The numbness finally wore off and she fell into his arms, laughing and crying at the same time. They finally managed to get dressed. Veronica grabbed a hairbrush and some makeup to put on in the car. Then she hurried into the nursery and opened the closet, laughing out loud as she picked up the little bag she'd packed with everything she needed to bring a baby home from the hospital. By the time she got to the car, Matthew had buckled the baby car seat in, and he was turning the key in the ignition.

The first several miles passed in silence, while Veronica sorted her thoughts through. She finally came to the conclusion that she didn't have to be afraid anymore. She didn't have to wait and wonder and fret. Instead, she would be waking up for night feedings and changing diapers and washing bottles. As all the fears slowly dissipated and the long-subdued hopes came forward, Veronica started to talk. They talked and talked of things they'd stopped talking about years ago. They speculated over this child's future and all they would do together. They argued about what to name it, then laughed until they cried.

The sun came up as they drove, and Veronica could almost literally feel God's love in the first morning rays. How grateful she was for the blessings that had come into her life. She thought about this woman who was giving so much to provide them with a child, and her heart filled with silent prayer on her behalf. Veronica could not comprehend what she might be going through right now, but she felt peace in knowing that God would surely bless her for this great sacrifice.

* * * *

Tara insisted on walking from the parking lot into the hospital, hoping it would hurry this birth along. In the elevator she leaned against Sean and groaned as it suddenly became more painful than uncomfortable. It only took a few steps onto the third floor before a wheelchair was beneath her and she was checked in quickly.

In labor room seven, Tara lay quietly while monitors scratched out her contractions and beeped the baby's heartbeat. The nurses were kind as they went in and out, keeping close track of mother and child. But the progress was slow. At five o'clock she had dilated to four centimeters. By seven it was four and a half. By noon she had reached seven, and the doctor ordered an I.V. While the nurse was taking care of that, Sean hurried downstairs to choke down a sandwich at the snack bar. He would have never believed a man could feel so sick with worry. He thought of the promises in the blessing and felt some peace. But the process was proving to be extremely difficult. Tara looked so exhausted that he wondered how she could possibly have the strength to push that baby into the world. And he wondered if having the incentive to take a baby home would have made it easier to exert the needed energy.

And though Sean had done his best to avoid thinking about the baby, he had to admit now that he'd become attached to it. A part of him ached at the thought of letting it go. He couldn't comprehend the dread of separation Tara must be feeling now.

Just out of the elevator on the third floor, Sean practically ran into Jane, who was getting on.

"Everything's going fine, they tell me," she said warmly.

Sean nodded. "I believe so, but . . ." He couldn't find words to express his concern without blubbering.

"It's hard, I know," she said with a compassionate squeeze of her hand over his arm. "But it will soon be over. And remember, there are two people experiencing a miracle in getting that baby."

Sean smiled and couldn't resist giving Jane a big hug.

"I have to get back to the office, but everything's under control. You call me when it's over."

He nodded again, and she stepped into the waiting elevator. It wasn't until she'd gone that Sean realized those two people she'd just mentioned had to be here in the hospital. He knew it was likely best that he didn't meet them, but he couldn't help being curious. Reminding himself that Tara was in labor and anything else was not his concern, Sean took a deep breath and headed down the hall. He passed a waiting area that he'd barely noticed earlier, and from the corner of his eye he saw a couple sitting close together, the man's arm around her shoulders. It only took an instant to surmise that they were tired and concerned. And another instant to know, by his feelings if nothing else, that this was the couple waiting for Tara's baby. They barely made eye contact as he passed by, but the warmth that lingered with him made it easier to return to Tara's room with hope and courage.

Sean entered the room to find her writhing in pain and clawing at the sheets. "It's getting closer," the nurse reported.

Sean nodded and took Tara's hand, but the words of comfort he whispered were not received. The nurse looked concerned and took Tara's other hand. "Tara," she said with calm expertise. "Look at me, Tara." Tara only gasped for breath and looked disoriented. "Look at me," she insisted, and Tara did. "Now, slow down and breathe with me, or you're going to hyperventilate."

As the nurse took her through the breathing several times, Tara calmed somewhat. The practicing they'd done in their classes came back to Sean, and he found it easier now to coach her and feel like he knew what he was doing. They gave her something to take the edge off the pain, and she relaxed a bit. Sean took advantage of the moment to tell her what Jane had said, and that he thought he'd seen the parents of her baby. This made her smile, if only briefly.

Tara was quickly absorbed with trying to breathe properly in order to withstand the pain. The nurse checked her often, but progress remained slow while the pain only seemed to intensify.

"Sean," Tara gasped when they were left alone for a moment, "I don't want to see the baby. I'm going to close my eyes, and when it comes, make them take it away. I've prayed about it, and I know it will be easier this way. Promise me."

"I promise," he said, and beyond that she became incapable of speaking, as the pain seemed endless and contractions seemed to have no beginning or end. When she began insisting that she needed to push, the nurse instructed Sean to coach her with panting so she couldn't bear down. The next time she was checked, the room flew into a flurry. Tara was moved onto another bed and wheeled to the delivery room. Sean was helped into hospital garb and ushered into a room that made him wonder how women had ever done this on the prairie.

While she was being moved onto the delivery table and draped, the doctor arrived and Tara seemed to relax a little at the sound of his soothing words. "All right, Tara." He sat on a stool and pulled sterile gloves onto his hands. "If you give me a few good pushes, we'll have this baby out and it will be over."

Tara listened carefully to the instructions and did as she was told, just wanting to have this finished. She bore down with everything she had while Sean held her hands, feeling like a cheerleader. Sean's heart nearly quit beating when the monitor on the baby's heart slowed dramatically. Tara groaned, then screamed. The doctor ordered an emergency C-section, and suddenly everything was orderly chaos. Medical personnel swarmed into the room and Sean was ushered into the hall. Tara was moved to another room to be put under general anesthetic.

Sean stood dazed for several minutes, praying with everything he had that Tara would be all right. He had just talked himself into relaxing when a nurse appeared with a bawling bundle in her arms. She paused and glanced toward Sean in question. He decided he couldn't resist just a peek. She opened the blanket to reveal the tiny, wrinkled baby.

"He's perfect," she said with a warm smile, "and a big one. I'm sure he's going to make somebody very happy."

"Yes," Sean barely managed to say as he bravely touched the little hand. "Thank you," he said, and she hurried toward the nursery.

Sean was grateful to be alone in the hall when the emotion struck him. He was grateful to know that Tara was presently unconscious, and wondered if the brief trauma was God's way of sparing her from that final moment she'd dreaded so much. He thought of the joy that baby was bringing about, then he turned his mind to Tara.

* * * * *

Veronica finally convinced herself to relax, and nearly drifted off to sleep against Matthew's shoulder. Her head came up with a start at the sound of a crying baby. She focused on the nurse standing above her, just as she said, "Mrs. Raine?"

"Yes." Veronica shot to her feet, grateful to feel Matthew close beside her when she teetered slightly.

"It's a boy." The nurse smiled and handed over the wiggling bundle. Veronica trembled slightly as she pulled the baby into her arms. It took several moments for the mist to clear out of her eyes so she could see him. "Oh, he's beautiful," she cried, meeting Matthew's eyes long enough to know that he was crying, too.

The baby calmed a little when Matthew took him, then they

followed the nurse to watch as the baby was weighed and measured. Veronica didn't feel tired in the least as she stood at the nursery window and watched her baby. Matthew stayed close to her, talking and laughing softly, cooing over the baby so sweetly that Veronica was moved to tears. It was a miracle, plain and simple.

"Thank you, Lord," Veronica breathed and leaned her head against Matthew's shoulder. Her prayers had finally been answered.

* * * * *

Sean walked casually toward the infant nursery, telling himself he just wanted to know that everything was all right with the baby. *A boy,* Sean thought; then he quickly stopped himself from imagining how it might be if it were *his* son. He paused several feet away from the huge glass window of the nursery. The couple he'd noticed earlier were standing close together, admiring Tara's baby as it was being bathed. *Not Tara's baby,* he reminded himself. It was *their* baby. But the sad little tug at his heart was quickly replaced by joy as he observed these people. Their emotion was evident, and he silently thanked God for this tangible evidence of Tara's incredible gift.

Sean sat close to Tara and held her hand as she emerged into consciousness. He stood and leaned over her to press a warm kiss to her lips. "Welcome back, Sleeping Beauty," he whispered, smiling when her eyes focused on him.

"What happened?" she asked raspily.

"The cord was wrapped around the baby's neck, but they worked fast and he's fine."

Tears came into her eyes, but Sean had expected them. "Did you see him?" she asked. Sean hesitated, then nodded. "Tell me," she insisted.

"He was big," Sean smiled, trying to keep the conversation light. "Or at least they said he was big. He looked awfully tiny to me. Eight pounds, nine ounces. He had just a little bit of dark hair." Sean wanted to tell her there was an uncanny resemblance to the baby's father, but he figured he'd save that information for another time.

"Tara," he added, "I saw them." Her eyes widened and he clarified with a broad smile. "They were at the nursery, watching the baby."

"Did they look happy?" she asked groggily.

"Oh, yes," Sean assured her. "There was no question about that."

Tara squeezed her eyes shut and cried silent tears. She squeezed Sean's hand and announced, "I want to go home."

"Just as soon as the doctor says you're able. In the meantime, I'll stay with you every minute I can." He kissed her again. "It's over, love," he whispered. "Just as soon as you're able, we'll take that little vacation—a second honeymoon. Just think, by the time you reach your due date, you'll be feeling like new."

"I love you, Sean," she replied softly.

"I love you, too," he said, and stayed with her as the pain medication lulled her into a peaceful sleep.

Tara had been home from the hospital a few days when circumstances made it evident that they should move. An apartment opened up closer to campus, and the rent was better. Sean handled the majority of the work and they were quickly settled. It wasn't until they went to church in their new ward that Tara realized what a blessing it was. No one here knew she'd just had a baby, so there was no need to explain its absence. She couldn't deny that it was an answer to her prayers, and it was one more thing that made the transition easier.

The months following the birth of Tara's baby passed quickly in spite of the struggles. As promised, Sean took her on a long and relaxing honeymoon in August, and he could honestly say he'd never been so happy in his life. As the trauma surrounding the baby eased into the past, Sean could see a new vibrancy coming out in Tara; a part of her he had only seen glimpses of since that first weekend they had gone out.

They both started classes in the fall, and Tara went back to work part time, certain that staying busy would aid in the healing process. She thoroughly enjoyed their celebration of the anniversary of their first date, but a few days later she couldn't help but recall that one year ago she had been raped. She talked with Sean about her feelings, and he assured her it was all part of the process and she was doing well. But her biggest regret was that Danny had never faced the consequences of what he had done. Tara knew if she had to do it over again, she would have followed Sean's advice and gone straight to a doctor, so that a police report could have been filed and charges pressed. She knew she couldn't change the past, but still it bothered her as she wondered if Danny had hurt other women.

As the regret refused to go away, Tara began praying that she would find a way to be free of it. Weeks passed and nothing seemed to change. She started to wonder if she was doing something wrong. At Sean's suggestion, she began attending a support group for victims of rape and abuse. It was comforting to realize that she had handled it better than some, and she found it therapeutic to offer empathy and compassion to women who were struggling with feelings she had endured. However, she found her most healing encounter with JannaLyn.

Tara wondered why Sean had made such a big deal of suggesting she take JannaLyn to the mall for the evening. They had a good time and stopped for a malt on the way home. JannaLyn talked freely of her growing relationship with a fine young man named Colin Trevor. He was the son of a stake president, who treated her well and made her life full. Then, with no warning, JannaLyn said, "Colin is so good to me that I can almost forget what my father did to me." Tara's bewilderment apparently showed in her face as JannaLyn added, "I thought you knew."

"Why would I?"

"Well, because Sean . . ."

"Sean keeps such things completely confidential, I can assure you."

JannaLyn smiled, almost serenely. "I should have guessed. Though I wouldn't have minded if he told *you*. I knew you would understand."

With little prompting, Tara was pouring out her own experience to this girl who seemed so much older than her years. They talked and cried all the way home, then sat in the car for over an hour. Tara told Sean what had happened, and how she felt one giant step closer to putting it behind her. But time still left that little nagging doubt as she wondered about Danny. Where was he? Was he bringing pain into other women's lives?

Early in November, Tara was cleaning the apartment and came across a rolled-up newspaper by the door. It was left free on the porch twice a week. Sean often read them, but Tara was rarely interested. She had tossed it into the recycling box when something told her to open it and read. Impulsively she picked it up, then told herself she didn't have the time or interest. Again she tossed it into the box. She walked into the bedroom to gather laundry, then walked right back and took the newspaper out of the box. Sitting at the kitchen table, she unfolded it and began turning pages, wondering why she was doing this. She didn't wonder long before she saw Danny's picture, plain as day. Momentarily stunned, it took her a minute to realize it was in the crime report section. Frantically she read the minimal information that stated he had been arrested for charges of rape and assault. Tears welled into her eyes as she wondered about the poor woman who'd had the courage to press charges against Danny. She was still crying when Sean came home.

"Whatever's wrong?" he asked immediately, sitting close beside her.

Tara showed him the newspaper. He read the report and let out a long sigh.

"I could have stopped it, Sean," she cried. "If I'd had the courage, I could have prevented this from happening to someone else."

Sean pulled Tara to his shoulder where she cried without restraint. "There's no good in regretting what you can't change, Tara." He took her face in his hand and wiped at her tears. "But maybe you could make a difference to this woman now."

Tara felt an excited hope in the prospect that already eased her guilt somewhat. Together they talked about it, and prayed. The following day, Sean helped her track down the lawyer handling this woman's case. It was so easy that Tara didn't have to wonder if God's hand was involved.

A week later, Tara's testimony put the finishing touch on a case that had previously been weak. Danny was sentenced to prison time and counseling. And Tara made a new friend in this woman who had suffered much the same as she had.

By Christmas, Tara hardly thought of her ordeal. Her mind was centered on enjoying the holidays with Sean and her family. For their wedding anniversary, Sean took her to the same bed and breakfast inn where they'd spent their wedding night. And the first week of January, he took her to the Salt Lake Temple, where they were sealed for time and all eternity. Tara felt such joy that she could hardly believe she had been through the horror of all that had occurred through their dating and early marriage. Her joy was added upon in February when she suspected she was pregnant. Nothing gave her more pleasure than the prospect of having a baby—Sean's baby—to fill the void left by having to give up the last one.

Tara occasionally wondered about the child she'd given birth to the previous summer. But there was so much peace in knowing she'd done the right thing, that the little twinges of sadness were quickly outweighed. In early March she received a letter, delivered through Jane. Sean cried with Tara as they read it together.

Dear friends,

I do not know who you are, or even your names, and I can only introduce myself as the adoptive mother of your son. I know very little about you, but Jane told us a little concerning your circumstances. I must take the time to express to you the gratitude that fills our hearts completely. Little Joshua is the most wonderful thing that has ever come into our lives, and we are eternally indebted to you for the pain and sacrifice you went through when it would have been easy and acceptable to do away with his young life before it had hardly begun. We realize the difficulties you must have faced for his sake, and for ours, and no words can express our gratitude.

We also want to thank you for bringing our attention to the LDS Church. We have found much peace in the gospel, and we were both baptized not long before Joshua came into our home. We admire your conviction in wanting Joshua raised in an LDS home, and we thank you for that as well. It has changed our lives.

We want you to know that Joshua is healthy and growing fast, and my father swears that he looks like me. Somehow I know that he was meant to come to us, and I thank you for being the instrument in God's hands to bring this miracle about.

Affectionately,
Your son's other mother

The letter gave Tara the strength she needed when she realized she wasn't pregnant after all. Counting the months, she began to wonder if something had gone wrong and she would be unable to conceive again. Knowing that it would do no good to worry, Tara put her efforts into finishing the term and supporting Sean through his final weeks. He was close to finally getting his degree, and they planned to go to Australia in May. With that foremost in her mind, Tara resigned herself to enjoying the life she shared with Sean and to allowing time and nature to take their course.

* * * * *

The day prior to Sean's graduation ceremony, he came home feeling a nervous excitement. He had to remind himself that it was all behind him, and that this was a big turning point in his life. There was only one little gray cloud hanging over it. He wondered if his father had even seen the announcement he'd sent. Would he be pleased to know Sean had achieved his goal, or simply disconcerted because he had achieved it by means of a *Mormon* university?

Sean forced the thoughts away, knowing from years of experience that it would change nothing. He was contemplating a number of possibilities for celebrating with Tara when he came through the door to find the apartment dark. But the door hadn't been locked.

"Tara?" he called, flipping on the light.

"I'm here," she answered from the bedroom.

He found her lying down and sat carefully on the edge of the bed. "Are you all right?" he asked, pushing a stray curl back from her forehead.

Tara looked up, and the hall light illuminated the tears in her eyes. "I'm not pregnant . . . again."

"Hey," he managed a smile and pulled her close, "we've got our whole lives, Tara. Just give it some time. There's no hurry."

"I know," she muttered. "It's just that . . ."

"I understand," he assured her when she didn't finish. "But . . ." Sean hesitated admitting something that had been on his mind far too much for comfort. "Tara . . . maybe it's me."

Tara met his eyes, surprised. "How could that be when . . . I mean . . ."

"You don't have to remind me that I've fathered a child," he said in a tone of self-punishment. "But have you also considered the fact that I . . ." He pushed a hand through his hair. "I got into drugs pretty heavy for a while, Tara." Tears gathered in the corners of his eyes. "What if—"

Tara pressed a finger over his lips. "Don't say it, Sean. I don't believe it. You said we just needed time. I'm sure you're right."

Sean nodded, telling himself there was no need to assume the worst. But he couldn't deny the very personal fear that his past would come back to haunt them.

"Hey," Tara said, finding some comfort in the need to distract *him* from obvious distress, "didn't you say we were celebrating tonight?"

"Are you up to it?" he smiled.

"I'm rarely not up to dinner out," she said, and was ready to go in less than ten minutes.

CHAPTER SIXTEEN

Tara enjoyed their evening out and returned home feeling good. It didn't take much effort to look at her life and see all that she had to be grateful for. The love she shared with Sean in itself made anything and everything else bearable.

She was on her way into the bathroom when the phone rang. Sean answered it in the bedroom.

"Sean," Emily Hamilton said from the other end, "are you ready for the big day?"

"I think so," he chuckled. "After all these years, it's hard to believe I've finally got my master's."

"You've worked hard," Emily said. "I wish we could be there."

"Well, so do I, but it's just a silly graduation ceremony. It'll probably be boring."

"It will be nice for you, and you know it."

"Yes," Sean had to admit, "I'm sure it will be nice."

Tara walked out of the bathroom and Sean put his hand over the mouthpiece to tell her it was Emily. She nodded and went to the kitchen for a glass of milk before she changed for bed. A knock at the door interrupted her. She glanced at the clock. 9:58 p.m. She couldn't imagine who might be here at this hour as she pulled the door open.

For a long moment Tara stood in disbelief. In spite of what she saw, logic told her it was impossible. This made the reality difficult to swallow until Maureen said, "Hello, Tara. You remember my father?"

Tara nodded toward Brian O'Hara, feeling as uncertain as he appeared. Forcing herself to the hope that this truly was the miracle it appeared to be, she motioned them inside.

"Please . . . come in. Forgive me. I was just . . . surprised."

"I can't blame ye for that," Brian said lightly, though the tension in his voice was evident.

"Have a seat," Tara said eagerly, but Brian's eyes were glued to the wall decor. She was so used to it she hardly thought about it, but Brian seemed somehow touched by the Irish flag and plaid, and the O'Hara family crest.

Not knowing what to say, Tara quickly backed into the hall. "Make yourselves at home. I'll get Sean. He's on the phone, but I'm sure he's nearly finished, and . . . well, have a seat."

Tara hurried into the bedroom and grabbed the phone from Sean. "What are you—" he began but she interrupted.

"Hello, Emily," Tara said, "forgive me, but Sean has to go. It's kind of an emergency. We'll call you back later and let you know what's going on. Nothing to worry about. Bye."

Tara nearly slammed the phone down and realized her hands were shaking.

"What was that all about?" Sean asked, a hint of exasperation in his voice.

"There is someone here to see you," she said quietly, "and it can't wait."

Tara took Sean's hand into hers and led him to the front room. They stopped walking just as Brian turned to meet Sean's eyes. Tara had to adjust her footing to keep Sean from falling over when he leaned into her. Nothing was said for an excruciating length of time. Brian finally broke the silence with a tense, "I heard ye were graduatin' tomorrow. I stopped by t' offer m' congratulations."

Sean tried to think of an appropriate response, but his voice was lost somewhere between his heart and his stomach. He was relieved when Tara said kindly, "We're glad you came. Won't you sit down? Are you hungry? Would you like to—"

"No, no," Maureen said. "We've eaten, and we apologize for coming so late. But we just drove in and we were afraid we might miss you in the morning, so . . . ." Her eyes went to her father, then to Sean. Expectancy hung thick in the air.

"Please," Tara repeated, "sit down."

Maureen guided her father to the couch and they sat close together. Tara urged Sean to the chair across from them and he sat cautiously, keeping his eyes acutely focused on his father. While every fiber of his being wanted to believe this was a gesture of acceptance, Sean couldn't help feeling skeptical. He couldn't recall the last time he'd been in a room with his father, without enduring contention. He looked to Maureen as if she could answer the obvious questions. But she only turned to her father, making it apparent that this was between father and son.

Unable to bear the suspense, Sean finally cleared his throat and forced his voice. "It's nice to have you here. But Utah is a long way from Chicago. You could have sent a card, or—"

"I don't blame ye for bein' skeptical, son," Brian said gently, and Sean had to blink several times. "But I felt I should tell ye to yer face . . . that I'm proud o' ye for achievin' this." Brian glanced down, apparently uncomfortable. "And ye did it on yer own. Ye should be proud."

"I didn't do it on my own." The crack in Sean's voice apparently got his father's attention and he looked up. "I had God's help."

Brian O'Hara nodded a subtle acknowledgment that intensified Sean's emotion. Was it his imagination that his father was showing acceptance of the life Sean had chosen? Following another poignant silence, Sean asked, "Might I ask what . . . prompted you to come here? I mean . . ." He held his breath, not quite daring to put words to his thoughts. He didn't want their past estrangements to be acknowledged. But this was too drastic a measure on his father's part to make Sean believe it was merely an incidental change of heart.

Brian cleared his throat, indicating that he intended to speak, but it was a full minute before he did. "Yer brother died, Sean."

Tara glanced quickly at Sean to gauge his reaction. He squeezed her hand so hard it hurt. Sean met her eyes, hoping for sustenance and not surprised to find it. He turned back to his father, needing an explanation, but not knowing how to ask. He had two brothers, neither of whom he'd ever been close to. But they were his brothers nonetheless, and his heart ached, wondering what was coming.

"Robert . . ." Brian began. There was no questioning the catch in his voice. "We didn't hear about it . . . until it was all over . . . but . . . he . . ."

Brian looked at Maureen in a silent plea. She coughed gently then looked at Sean. "He died of AIDS, Sean."

Sean squeezed his eyes shut, trying to comprehend the reality. Unpleasant images assaulted his mind. His father's voice brought him back to the moment.

"I couldn't help thinkin' about what ye said, Sean . . . about Robert, I mean. Ye were right, son. I'd blinded myself because I didn't want t' know. I don't understand why ye did what ye did, but it's not for me t' question."

When only silence followed, Sean knew he'd said all he was going to say. Brian O'Hara was a proud man, and Sean had just heard the closest he would probably ever get to an apology. But it was enough. He wanted to just run to his father's arms and bawl like a baby, but something held him back. Perhaps he knew this was difficult for his father, and too much emotion would only embarrass him. He was relieved when his father's attention turned back to the wall decor.

"Maureen had told me ye went t' Ireland. I didn't know it meant s' much t' ye."

"My Irish heritage is something I've always been proud of," Sean admitted, hoping his father knew it was true. In a lighter tone he added, "I lived there for about two years. It was an incredible experience."

Cautious explanations gradually filtered into a semi-relaxed conversation as they exchanged experiences of common ground. While Sean felt mostly numb at the realization of what was taking place, his heart silently leapt for joy. He couldn't believe it. With all the miracles he'd had since his conversion, this seemed the ultimate. His father had finally come around.

A little past eleven, Brian and Maureen left for their motel room. Sean said nothing as he prepared for bed. Tara called Emily back and quietly explained, then she slipped between the covers and pulled Sean close. His emotion finally erupted, and he cried helplessly, tears of bitter-sweetness and irony; joy mixed with poignancy.

Sean's father and sister attended the graduation service and sat with Tara. She was grateful for their company, however tense at moments, since her father had come down with the flu and her parents were unable to come. Afterward they took pictures outside, then Brian took them all out for lunch at a nice restaurant. Gradually the conversation became more relaxed, and Sean had to keep reminding himself this wasn't a dream. Brian warmed to Tara with little trouble. He asked her many questions about her upbringing and her interests, and Sean could see a bond growing between them.

When they were nearly finished eating, Sean asked, "So, what now? Are you going back to Chicago soon, or—"

"We have a flight out t'morrow, but we don't have any plans."

Sean smiled. It was the perfect opportunity to say, "Maybe you'd like to see some sights while you're here."

"That would be fine," Brian agreed easily.

"I'd like to take you to Salt Lake City and—"

"Ye're not going t' take us t' that Mormon Temple Square, are ye?" Brian asked, but there was a subtle sparkle of humor in his eyes that put Sean at ease.

"Not if you don't want me to," Sean replied. "But there is one thing there I'd like to show you. You'd be far from the first non-Mormon to visit there just for the sake of sight-seeing."

"I suppose I could manage," Brian said with just a hint of caution in his voice. Sean accepted his willingness for what it was. Brian O'Hara would *never* embrace anything but the Catholicism he'd been born into. But he was being open-minded enough to accept his son's life. Sean's gratitude was beyond words.

The excursion to Temple Square had little of the tension Sean might have expected. Maureen helped buffer it by her interest and easy conversation. Sean and Tara took turns explaining the historical significance of the Tabernacle and Temple, and Sean mentioned that there were many Catholic cathedrals through the world that were big tourist attractions.

"So," Brian said while they ambled slowly around the flower gardens in the center of the square, "what is this *one* thing ye wanted us t' see?"

Sean motioned with his arm and took Tara's hand. "Follow me," he said and walked toward the North Visitors' Center. Sean ignored the attractions on the main floor and led the way up the circular walkway to the Christus statue. He said nothing to his father except, "I wanted you to see this, Father. *This* represents the central focus of our religion."

Brian O'Hara stood silently beside Sean and absorbed the likeness of Christ, his arms outstretched. Sean became vaguely aware of his father's emotion, but he was unprepared for his humble admission. "Ye must forgive me, son . . . for th' way I turned ye out like that. It was wrong o' me, and I can see that now." Sean turned and met his eyes, unable to hold back the tears. "Ye must forgive me," Brian repeated.

"It's forgotten," Sean spoke firmly, and didn't hesitate to put his arms around his father with an embrace that had ached inside of him since his childhood. Brian returned it with feeling, and Sean uttered a silent prayer of gratitude for this miracle in his life.

Brian insisted on taking them out to dinner, and gradually the numbness of all that had happened began to wear off. Tara could almost literally see the glow in Sean's eyes as he absorbed his father's love. She suspected that Brian O'Hara was not a warm man by nature, but his attitude spoke clearly of acceptance. She wondered what kind of anguish he'd gone through in losing his wife and son that had driven him to enough humility to face this reckoning. She briefly pondered that process of refinement and the effect it had on people's lives. She had certainly been through it herself, and so had Sean. Now it was evident that his father had also. She thought of that moment observing Sean embracing his father at the foot of the Christus, and a warm peace settled into her that suddenly brought the full spectrum of the gospel into her mind with a new understanding. How grateful she was to be a part of it, and to know that the Lord was a part of their lives.

The spiritual high Tara was feeling helped buffer the difficulty of Brian's kind inquiry over dessert. "Perhaps I shouldn't ask, but I can't help wonderin' . . . what happened t' th' baby?"

"Baby?" Sean echoed with a high pitch in his voice.

Brian's eyes narrowed slightly. "It was evident that yer sweet wife was pregnant when ye came t' Chicago for th' funeral."

Tara looked down and fidgeted with her napkin, hoping to get control of the tears before they surfaced. Sean took her hand under the table and thought quickly for an explanation that would satisfy his father without embarrassing Tara.

"That baby is no longer with us," he finally managed.

Brian's eyes betrayed that he didn't understand, but he seemed content with the answer. Maureen looked as if she was going to cry.

"I'm sorry," Brian said. "It must have been hard for th' both o' ye."

"It was," Sean stated, and Tara's emotion suddenly became impossible to ignore.

"I didn't mean t' make ye cry, dearie," Brian apologized as Tara wiped her face with her napkin.

"It's all right," she said kindly. "I'm certain we will be blessed with a family soon enough." Her words soothed the uncomfortable mood at the table, but they didn't comfort Tara's troubled heart. Inside she ached for a baby, knowing it would be the ultimate healing. She thought of the good people who had adopted her baby, and she felt a new empathy as she wondered how long they had waited. The irony was presently unbearable, and Tara had to force her mind elsewhere. She was relieved when Brian changed the subject.

"Before we leave, I wanted t' speak with ye about somethin'." He paused and added, "I would like ye t' come t' Chicago." He glanced at Maureen, who smiled and nodded with encouragement. "I want t' see m' family together, and I thought Memorial Day would be appropriate. We could have a barbecue in the yard like we used t' do, and we could go t'gether t' visit yer mother's grave . . . and Robert's."

It took every ounce of self-control Sean could muster to keep his voice steady as he replied, "That sounds great, Dad. We'll be there."

* * * * *

In light of recent events, Sean and Tara decided to wait until June to go to Australia. Sean's father paid for their flight to Chicago, and they stayed more than a week. The healing that took place was so consuming for Sean that he talked of little else all the way home. He continued to be obsessed with it while they prepared to leave for Australia, but Tara was so enthralled by his happiness that she could have listened to him talk about it forever.

Finally en route to Australia, flying somewhere above a seemingly endless ocean, Sean held Tara's hand while she randomly perused the scriptures that lay open on her lap. Contemplating something that she'd been wanting to tell Sean, she thought back over the experiences that had come into her life since she'd first met him. She was amazed at the enormity of the changes, the suffering, the pain, and the healing. It all came together as the book in her hand seemed to fall open to Second Corinthians, chapter twelve. Tara began to read, and just past verse nine her heart quickened. She went back to read it again, wondering what might have caused such a feeling. Everything made perfect sense as the words somehow touched her deeply: *And he said unto me, My grace is sufficient for thee; for my strength is made perfect in weakness. Most gladly therefore will I rather glory in my infirmities, that the power of Christ may rest upon me.*

That word *grace* caught Tara, and she looked it up in the Bible dictionary, feeling it was somehow significant. Warmth enveloped her as she read: *A divine means of help or strength, given through the bounteous mercy and love of Jesus Christ. It is through the grace of the Lord that individuals receive strength and assistance to do good works that they otherwise would not be able to maintain if left to their own means.*

Instantly Tara understood. The full spectrum of her experience came together in one heart-stopping realization that she knew had to be voiced.

"Sean," she whispered, nudging him. He looked over, surprised at the tears in her eyes. "If I had to do it all again, I would." His eyes narrowed in question and she clarified, "I never thought I could feel this way, but I am so grateful for everything I've learned since it happened. I wouldn't trade the strength, the humility, and the realization that the Lord loves me. He trusted me enough to allow me to have that baby, because it needed to come. And his grace makes up for everything else, Sean. I would; I'd do it over again if I had to."

Sean was too moved to speak. He just pulled her close and pressed his lips to her tear-stained cheek, tasting the salty moisture of her skin. After a long silence he finally said, "I know exactly how you feel, my love. It's hard to put into words, but I know the feeling well."

A few minutes later, Tara laughed for no apparent reason and

Sean looked at her in question. "I'm just glad you came along when you did, Sean. You're the best thing that ever happened to me."

Sean grinned and kissed her. "It's the other way around, Tara, I can assure you."

"Then I suppose you won't care if your baby looks like me," she stated flatly, belying the bubbling excitement she felt inside. Now that she was absolutely certain, she'd been waiting for the perfect moment to tell him.

Sean leaned forward in his seat, but kept his eyes acutely fixed on Tara. "My baby?" he asked gingerly.

"That's right, Sean O'Hara," she said, doing a fair job of imitating his father's accent. "I'm goin' t' have yer baby."